# Adrian Mole: The Cappuccino Years

*Also by Sue Townsend*

# Adrian Mole:
# The Cappuccino Years

Sue Townsend

First published in Great Britain by Michael Joseph
an imprint of Penguin UK

Published in the United States by

Soho Press, Inc.
853 Broadway
New York, NY 10003

Library of Congress Cataloging-in-Publication Data

Townsend, Sue.
Adrian Mole : the Cappuccino years / Sue Townsend.
p.    cm.
ISBN 1-56947-247-5 (alk. paper)
1. Mole, Adrian (Fictitious character)—Fiction.    2. Single
fathers—England—Fiction.    3. Young men—England—
Fiction.    I. Title.

PR6070.O897    A68 2000
823'.914—dc21
99-087241

10   9   8   7   6   5   4   3   2   1

To Louise

The great baby you see there is not yet out of his swaddling-clouts.

Shakespeare, *Hamlet*

True, we might never have arrived, but the fact is we did. If only people thought a little more about it, they would see that life is not worth worrying about so much.

Lermontov, *A Hero of Our Time*

# List of Principal Characters

ABBO and ALAN: Representatives of the Ashby-de-la-Zouch branch of the Terrence Higgins Trust, selected to walk in the procession behind Diana's coffin.

ANDREW: Archie Tait's cat.

ANNETTE: *Standard* vendor on the Strand, enjoying carnal relations with Malcolm, the washer-upper at Hoi Polloi, the restaurant where Adrian works.

ASHBY: Rosie Mole's plastic role-play baby.

ATKINS, JEFFREY: Adrian's second-opinion dentist. A gentle man with ginger eyebrows.

AZIZ: Assistant cook at Hoi Polloi.

BANKS, LES: Unlucky builder engaged by Adrian to do work to Archie Tait's house.

BAXTER, BERT: Deceased acquaintance of Adrian, Communist pensioner and Leicester's oldest and most objectionable man. Died one day short of his 106th birthday.

BELINDA: Zippo Montefiori's PA.

BOTT, GLENN: Son of Sharon Bott. Could have been fathered by either Barry Kent or Adrian Mole.

According to Rosie Mole, he is a psycho, but has Adrian's nose.

BOTT, SHARON: Old flame of Adrian's. Mother of Glenn Bott. Also mother of Kent, Bradford and Caister.

BRAITHWAITE, IVAN: Father of Pandora. Supposedly a freelance dairy management consultant and freethinker.

BRAITHWAITE, DR PANDORA: Prospective Labour MP for Ashby-de-la-Zouch. Self-appointed 'Brightest Star in Blair's Firmament' and 'The People's Pan'. First love of Adrian Mole, who was the first person to insert his hand (left) into her white cotton training bra, in 1981.

BRAITHWAITE, TANIA: Mother of Pandora. Teaches Women's Studies at De Montfort University.

BROADWAY, BILL: Les Banks's subcontractor.

CAINE, ALFIE: Fake Cockney and presenter of *The Fry-Up*, a Pie Crust Production.

CATH: Production assistant on *Offally Good!*, another Pie Crust production.

CAVENDISH, JACK: Pandora's older live-in lover. Alcoholic and Professor of Languages at Oxford.

CHANG, MR: Dentist who no longer caters for the poor because 'they bring tooth decay on themselves'.

CLEVER CLIVE: Criminal acquaintance of Adrian's, can supply parking permits for central London.

CLOUGH, MS: Labour supporter and single mother of three.

DALE, LILLIAN: Green Party candidate for Ashby-de-la-Zouch.

D'ARCY, MABEL: OAP supporter of Sir Arnold Tufton. Great-great-grandfather was a surviving officer on the *Titanic*.

DOUGGIE: Sharon Bott's live-in lover.

DOVECOTE, CHARLIE: Pauline Mole's lawyer.

EAGLEBURGER, BRICK: Barry Kent's literary agent.

EDDIE STOBART: A lorry firm. Some of their drivers wave, some don't.

ELF, MISS: Adrian and Pandora's timid but ethical drama teacher at Neil Armstrong Comprehensive.

FLOOD, ELEANOR: Remedial reading teacher at Neil Armstrong Comprehensive, with fragile wrists.

FONG, DR: Doctor at Leicester Royal Infirmary who examines William Mole.

FOX, LEN: Criminal. Mobile-phone magnate and friend of Sir Arnold Tufton.

GIPTON, FRED: Actor with inside knowledge of general-election results.

GOLDMAN, later GOLDPERSON, BOSTON: Personal assistant to Brick Eagleburger.

GRIMBOLD, MARCIA: Bring Back the Rates Party candidate.

HETHERINGTON, GLORIA: Godfrey's wife. Ideal casting: Pauline Quirke.

HETHERINGTON, GODFREY: Hero of *The White Van*, Adrian's hilarious serial-killer comedy. Accountant by day, serial killer by night. Ideally would be played by Harry Enfield.

HUMFRI: Cat adopted by Malcolm. Looks remarkably like Humphrey, the Downing Street cat.

JIMMY THE GREEK: Owner of Greek taverna next door to Hoi Polloi.

JUSTINE: Lap-dancer at Secrets club.

KENNETH: Waiter at Hoi Polloi.

KENT, BARRY: Ex-skinhead and local thug, now prize-winning poet and novelist. Author of poem 'Naked' and the modern classic *Dork's Diary*.

KENT, EDNA: Barry Kent's mum. Toilet cleaner, later double degree-taker and Pandora's secretary at the House of Commons.

KEVIN: Unhelpful sales personage at Hamleys.

LARGE ALAN: Owner of Secrets, as well as The 165, a fashionable new drinking den.

LEAF, SANDRA: Square-jawed security guard with Citadel Security Ltd, who invokes Pauline Mole's wrath and threats of legal action by giving her a random body search on election night.

*Lo! The Flat Hills of My Homeland*: Adrian's novel, later rechristened *Birdwatching*, for which he is still, incredibly, searching for a publisher.

LUCY: Staff nurse at Leicester Royal Infirmary and single parent.

LUIGI: Maître d' of Hoi Polloi. An Italian Communist who votes Lib Dem and lives in Croydon.

LUPIN, SKY: Adrian's stress counsellor.

MALCOLM: Washer-upper at Hoi Polloi. Voting position undecided.

MARILYN: A kamikaze bank official.

MICHELWAITE, AARON: Well-spoken but hideous youth whose company Rosie Mole enjoys.

MOLE, GEORGE: Adrian's father. Unemployed and suffering from erectile dysfunction.

MOLE, JO JO: Adrian's wife, from whom he is separated. Has moved back to Nigeria. Mother of William. Has beauty, brains, money and talent, and frankly was out of Adrian's league, as well as being four inches taller than him.

MOLE, PAULINE: Adrian's mother. Unsatisfied, unfulfilled Germaine Greer fan.

MOLE, ROSIE: Adrian's sister. Foul-mouthed fifteen-year-old vamp.

MOLE, SUSAN: Adrian's aunt and Prison Officer of the Year 1997. 'Married' to Amanda.

MOLE, WILLIAM: Adrian's small son. Fascinated by Teletubbies and Jeremy Clarkson videos.

MONTEFIORI, ZIPPO: Managing director of Pie Crust Productions, makers of *Offally Good!* and *The Fry-Up*.

MUTTON, KEITH: Monster Raving Loony Party candidate.

NEIL ARMSTRONG COMPREHENSIVE: *Alma mater* of Adrian, Pandora, Nigel and Barry Kent.

NG, DR: Adrian's doctor. Prescribed Prozac for him.

NIGEL: Adrian's best friend from school. Now a gay Buddhist van-driver for Next clothing store.

NOBBY: Labourer for Les Banks.

NORBERT: Nigel's boyfriend.

O'CASEY, LIAM: Student. Archie Tait's neighbour.

PANKHURST, MIRANDA: Sharon Bott's solicitor.

PARVEZ, MRS: Liberal councillor; owner of Kidsplay Ltd, William Mole's private nursery school.

PATIENCE, ROGER: New headmaster of Neil Armstrong Comprehensive.

PEACOCK, IDA: OAP Liberal Democrat supporter. Believes Tony Blair is going to give her new hips.

PERKINS, BOB: Owner of eponymous garden centre.

PURBRIGHT, LENNIE: Pandora's election agent. Cockney, formerly a whelk-stall owner.

RAJIT: BP service-station worker.

ROD: Owner of the Hot Rods shop in Soho, opposite Hoi Polloi.

SASHA: Assistant cook at Hoi Polloi.

SAVAGE, PETER: Foul-mouthed, aristocratic owner of Hoi Polloi. Believes in a 'Traditional English, No Choice' menu. Suffers from stress incontinence. Hates Tony Blair and New Labour.

SAVAGE, KIM: Savage's ex-wife and ex-society florist.

SEAN: Waiter at Hoi Polloi.

SCRUTON, MR: a.k.a Pop-Eye Scruton. Former headmaster of Neil Armstrong Comprehensive and rabid Mrs Thatcher devotee.

SINGH, DEV: *Double-entendre*-loving co-presenter of *Offally Good!*.

SPICER-WOODS, CHRISTINE: Socialist Lesbians Against Globalization Party candidate.

**STOAT, ARTHUR:** Editor and managing director of Stoat Books Ltd, wants to produce *Offally Good! – The Book.*

**SURINDER, DR:** Doctor at Leicester Royal Infirmary who examines William.

**SWAYWARD, JUSTIN:** Shoe Mania! employee and court representative.

**TAIT, ARCHIE:** OAP Socialist Labour Party voter.

**TRELLIS, MISS:** Glenn Bott's maths teacher.

**TUFTON, SIR ARNOLD:** Conservative MP for Ashby-de-la-Zouch and Pandora's rival in the general election.

**TWYSTLETON-FIFE, JULIAN:** Pandora's gay ex-husband.

**VALENTINE DUFF, RON:** Repatriate Foreigners Party candidate.

**VLJKJKJV, JAJKJ:** Belgrade translator interested in *Birdwatching.*

**WELLINGBOROUGH, MRS:** Mr Chang's receptionist.

**WONKY, DAVE:** Zouch FM DJ.

**WORTHINGTON, HARRY:** OAP Labour supporter.

**ZO:** Hair- and make-up artist for Pie Crust Productions.

# Dean Street, Soho

## Wednesday April 30th 1997

I take up my pen once again to record a momentous time in the affairs of men (and, thank God, because this is intended to be a secret diary, I am not required to add 'and women').

The day after tomorrow on May 2nd, as dawn breaks, I predict that the Labour Party will just scrape in, and will form the next government. Talk of a landslide victory is hysterical rubbish whipped up by the media.

My own prediction is based on 'insider' knowledge. The insider is an actor called Fred Gipton who was in *An Inspector Calls* with Tony Booth, the father-in-law of our future Prime Minister. Gipton spilled the beans in Hoi Polloi, the restaurant where I work, after two bottles of Jacob's Creek, a Pernod and a vodka sorbet. After begging me to keep 'shtum' he told me that he had heard, via a tortuous grapevine, that Mr Blair expected to win with a tiny majority. Three was mentioned. He also told me that Mr Blair wears a wig, but I have freeze-framed a *News At Ten*

3

video of him alighting from a helicopter on to a school playing-field and I am satisfied that no wig could stand up to the air turbulence caused by the chopper blades. Tony wears his own hair, it is *certainement*.

So, every vote counts, which is why I will drive up to Ashby-de-la-Zouch tonight after I finish my shift in the restaurant. When I told Savage that I would need to take a day off in order to vote, he went into a tirade about the foolishness of giving 'hoi polloi' the vote. 'If I ruled the f------ country,' he said (I cannot bring myself to write f------), 'I'd restrict the vote to men over forty-five years of age, and I'd narrow it down to those who earned over seventy K a year.'

'You wouldn't allow women to vote?' I checked.

'No, I f------ well wouldn't,' he raged. 'They're all f------ mad. If they've not got PMT they've got HRT or VPL.'

I pointed out to him that VPL stands for visible panty line, but he was, as usual, beyond reason. When he began to recount the crimes and misdemeanours of his estranged wife, Kim, I went into the kitchen and made onion gravy for the toad-in-the-hole.

After he calmed down a bit I approached him again. 'Mr Savage,' I said, 'I have not had a day off for six weeks.'

'How do you intend to vote?' he asked, challengingly.

I resented him asking, but I replied, 'Labour.'

'Then no f------ way, Jose,' he shouted, pushing a highball glass under the rum optic, and keeping it there until the glass was half full (or half empty, depending on your personality type). He drank deeply from it, as though the contents were Ribena.

'Why should I lose a valuable member of staff on one of the busiest days of the year and help that shirtlifter Blair get elected?' He coughed, lighting one of his filthy French cigarettes. I pointed out to him that Mr Blair is far from being a poofter, and has, in fact, fathered a trio of children. Savage gave a horrible phlegmy laugh, during which he crossed his legs (he suffers from stress incontinence). He took me to the front door of the restaurant, pointed at the Hot Rods shop opposite. Rod himself was in the shop window, arranging some studded leather underpants on a collection of tiered display plinths. 'Now that's a shop for poofters, am I right, Mole?' he said, breathing rum fumes in my face.

'The shop specializes in clothes and equipment for gay men,' I conceded.

'And are *none* of Rod's customers *happily married*?' he asked, dropping his voice theatrically.

I said, with heavy irony, 'So, Mr Blair's marriage is a sham and his children are nothing but ciphers conceived in the bed of cynicism, so that one day he will deceive the British people into voting for him, thinking him to be a heterosexual socialist, whereas . . .'

5

'Mark my words, Mole, Blair is a "friend of Rod's" if ever I f------ saw one, and he's no f------ socialist either.'

I began to cook the cabbages for dinner. Savage liked them to boil for at least half an hour. My work as a chef has been a doddle since Savage instituted his Traditional English, No Choice menu. Tonight's repast is:

*Heinz tomato soup*
*(with white bread floaters)*

❧

*Grey lamb chops*
*Boiled cabbage avec Dan Quayle potatoes*
*Dark brown onion gravy*

❧

*Spotted Dick à la Clinton*
*Bird's custard (skin £6.00 extra)*

❧

*Cheddar Cheese, Cream Crackers*
*Nescafé*
*After Eight Mint*

❧

*There are two types of wine – white £46, red £46*

❧

*Service charge not included. You are expected to smoke between courses. Pipes and cigars are particularly welcome.*

The restaurant is fully booked six weeks ahead. Savage turned Princess Michael of Kent away from the door last night. She was distraught.

The restaurant critic A. A. Gill said in his review in the *Sunday Times* that Hoi Polloi served execrable nursery food. 'The sausage on my plate could have been a turd: it looked like a turd, it tasted like a turd, it smelled like a turd, it had the texture of a turd. In fact, thinking about it, it probably *was* a turd.'

Savage has had Gill's review blown up at the Copy Shop and stuck it up in the window, where it draws admiring crowds.

Around about midnight I asked my fellow workers, those who could understand English, if they intended to vote today. Luigi, the maître d', is a Communist in Italy, but he will be voting Liberal Democrat in Croydon, where he lives. Malcolm, the washer-upper, said he was thinking of voting Conservative, 'because they help the self-employed'. I pointed out to Malcolm that he was only self-employed because Savage refused to pay for a National Insurance stamp and tax, but Malcolm then went on to say that he liked John Major because he (Malcolm) had been fostered by a couple who lived in Huntingdon, Major's constituency. As Malcolm grappled with the Spotted Dick tin in the sink, I asked him about the Conservatives' election pledges.

'They've said they won't put the taxes up,' he said, in his reedy voice.

I said, 'Malcolm, you don't *pay* tax, remember?

You get paid *cash in hand*. You're off the books, which enables you to draw *benefits* from the DSS. You get free teeth, free travel to hospital, free *everything*.'

Malcolm said, 'On the other hand, I might vote Labour.'

## Thursday May 1st

Dean Street, Soho, London, to Wisteria Walk, Ashby-de-la-Zouch, Leicestershire, in three hours. Not bad considering I kept under the speed limit all the way. On the way down I heard the Labour Party candidate for Ashby, Dr Pandora Braithwaite, talking about the importance of family values on Talk Radio. I was so outraged I almost choked on an Opal Fruit and steered into the fast lane. Talk about hypocrisy!

Pandora has shown open contempt for family life. Her first husband, Julian, was openly, in fact boastfully, gay. And her live-in lover, Jack Cavendish, has been married three times and has ten acknowledged children, three of whom have been in drug rehabilitation units up and down the country. The eldest is still languishing in jail in Turkey. Most of the others seem to be attracted to strange religious sects. Tom, the youngest, is a vicar in Hull.

How Pandora ever got past a Labour Party selection committee is a mystery to me. She smokes at least forty cigarettes a day. The radio interviewer asked her about her partner.

'He's a professor of languages at Oxford,' she replied, in her husky voice. 'And he's enormously supportive. But then,' she added, 'I support him too.'

'How very true,' I shouted at the car radio. 'He needs your support because he's a chronic alcoholic and can't stand up unaided after eight o'clock at night.'

At junction eighteen I ran out of Opal Fruits, so I pulled into the services and bought three packets. Are the manufacturers putting something extra in them? Something addictive? I seem to have been getting through rather a lot of them lately. The other night I woke at 3 a.m. and was distraught to discover that there wasn't a single Opal Fruit in the flat. I tramped the streets of Soho looking for them. Within two minutes of leaving home I was offered lesbian sex, heroin and a Rolex watch, but an innocent packet of Opal Fruits took over half an hour to track down. What does it tell us about the world we live in?

A Labour government will change all that. Mr Blair is a committed Christian, and I forecast that a religious revival will sweep the land. I long for the day that I wake up in the morning and realize that, Hallelujah! I too believe in God!

As I was tearing open the Opal Fruits on the way back to the car, a tall man in a lorry-driver's overalls approached me. I could tell that he was annoyed about something by the manner in which he barred my way with his thick arm.

'Are you the dick'ead in the Montego?' he said. 'The one who's been hogging the middle lane at sixty-five miles an hour?' I didn't like his aggressive tone. I pointed out to him that the motorway was quite damp, and that in my opinion sixty-five miles per hour was quite fast enough.

'You've had a bleeding truck behind you since Watford,' he said. 'Didn't you see me flashing my bleeding lights?'

I replied, 'Yes, I thought you were being friendly.'

'Why would I wanna be friendly to a dick'ead like you?' he said.

I sat in the car and watched him jump into the cab of his lorry. I was relieved to see that he wasn't driving for Eddie Stobart, whose drivers wear a shirt and tie under their overalls, and whose lorries are kept in immaculate condition. This oaf was driving a truck full of mineral water from Cornwall to Derbyshire. Why? Derbyshire *consists* of mineral water. You can't move without falling into a beck, tarn or raging river.

I sat in the car park for a few minutes to allow the lorry-rager to put a few miles between us, then I rejoined the motorway and, mindful of my recent contretemps, put my foot down and got up to sixty-nine m.p.h.

Immediately after I had turned off the motorway I was confronted by Pandora's lovely face staring down at me from an election poster nailed to the trunk of a chestnut tree at the side of the road. I stopped the car and got out to take a closer look. It was a glamour shot, reminiscent of 1940s Hollywood. Pandora's highlighted dark blonde hair fell to her shoulders in rippling waves. Her glossy lips were open, showing Harpic-white teeth. Her eyes said *bedroom*! She was wearing a dark jacket thing; there was a hint of white lace underneath, and beneath that more than a hint of voluptuous cleavage. I knew that every man in Ashby-de-la-Zouch would walk on his *knees* to vote for her.

And to think that I, Adrian Mole, was the first to kiss those divine lips, and the first to insert my hand (left) beneath her white cotton training bra. Also, on June 10th, 1981, Pandora declared her love for me.

The fact that she has been married once is of no consequence. I *know* that I am her only true love, and that she is mine. We are Arthur and Guinevere, Romeo and Juliet, Charles and Camilla.

When I married Jo Jo, Pandora came to my wedding and I saw her wipe the tears from her eyes before saying to my new wife, 'Commiserations.' She quickly apologized for her faux pas and said, 'I meant, of course, *congratulations*.' But I knew that her slip of the tongue betrayed her deep hurt that it was not *she* who was Mrs Adrian Albert Mole.

I said, 'I love you, my darling,' to the Pandora on the tree, then I got back into my car and continued my journey into Ashby-de-la-Zouch. Pandora's face smiled down at me from windows and signposts along the route. VOTE BRAITHWAITE – LABOUR, the poster said.

Occasionally, the grotesque porcine features of her Conservative rival, Sir Arnold Tufton, were to be seen on posters in the windows of the larger houses. Were he to enter for the Best Pig Class in the Leicester Agricultural Show he would stand a good chance of winning a rosette. Against the youth and radiance and intellectual brilliance of Dr Pandora Braithwaite he stands no chance at all – besides, Tufton has been embroiled in a row about his close friendship with Len Fox, the mobile-phone magnate (something about a Jiffy-bag in Marbella), decreasing his chances even further.

The people of Ashby-de-la-Zouch are not known for their tempestuous natures, so it was difficult to tell whether or not they were in the mood for revolution. Even the dogs and cats looked quiescent in the early-morning sunshine.

There was a Labour Party poster in the living room of my parents' house on Wisteria Walk, and a Spice Girls poster in my sister Rosie's window. Behind all the posters the curtains were closed. It took five minutes of banging on the door before it was opened. My mother stood before me in a grubby white towel-ling bathrobe and a pair of men's grey wool socks. A Silk Cut Ultra Low burned between her fingers. Her purple nail varnish was chipped. Last night's mascara was smudged around her eyes. Somebody, possibly in a hairdressing salon, had done something terrible to her hair. Two pairs of spectacles were slung around her neck on gold chains. She lifted one pair and put them on. 'Oh, it's you,' she said. 'I was hoping it was the postman. I've ordered a red trouser-suit from Next and it was supposed to come today.' She took off the first pair of spectacles and replaced them with the second. She peered up and down the avenue, sighed, then kissed me and led the way down the hall and into the kitchen.

My son, William, was sitting at the kitchen table eating Coco Pops with a serving spoon. When he saw me he jumped from his chair and hurled himself towards my genitals. I saved myself from considerable pain by snatching him up and throwing him into the air.

It's been three weeks since I last saw my son, but his verbal dexterity has improved considerably (I must stop using the word *considerably* – it's John Major's fault). He is only two and three-quarters, but is already, to my considerable alarm, besotted with that television motoring oaf, Jeremy Clarkson. My mother indulges the child horribly by videoing Clarkson's testosterone-driven programmes and allowing William to watch them continuously. I don't know where he gets this obsessive interest in cars from. Not from our side of the family, that's for sure. His Nigerian grandmother was once the managing director of a lorry-tyre importer in Ibadan. It may be a tenuous connection, but genes are funny things.

Nobody has ever been able to explain where I get my talent for creative writing and cookery from. My mother's family (Norfolk) were practically illiterate, and seemed to live on boiled potatoes with HP sauce, and my father's family (Leicester) viewed books with deep suspicion, unless they had pictures which 'broke up the pages'. My paternal grandmother, May Mole, was a plain cook, who regarded eating as a gross indulgence. Thank God she died before I became a professional chef. It was her proud boast that she had never eaten in a proper restaurant in her life. She spoke of restaurants as others speak of crack dens.

I must record that my son is a handsome boy. His skin is clear, and the colour of dark cappuccino. His eyes are the exact shade of 'dark oak' in the Cuprinol wood-stain range. Physically, his Nigerian blood predominates, but I think I can see a certain English something about him. He is very clumsy, for instance, and when he is watching Clarkson (for example) on the TV, his mouth falls open and he looks a tiny bit gormless.

'Have you heard from Jo Jo?' asked my mother, as she kicked out at the New Dog to stop it licking its prominent testicles.

'No,' I said. 'Have you?'

She opened a drawer and took out an airmail letter, which was plastered with Nigerian stamps.

'Read it while I take him upstairs and get him ready,' she said.

It gave me a jolt when I saw Jo Jo's extraordinarily beautiful handwriting. The slopes and curves of the black letters reminded me of her body, and her voice. My penis stirred slightly as if expressing interest in what my wife had to say.

My dearest Pauline,

I am sorry to have to tell you that Adrian and I are getting a divorce.

I know that you won't be surprised by this news, especially after my last visit when he lost the way to Alton Towers, blamed me and tore the map in half.

I was sorry that you and George (and especially William) had to witness such a scene.

The truth is, Pauline, that there have been many such unhappy incidents, and I feel that it is better to end our marriage now. I am sick with longing when I think of William. Does he speak of me? Please send an up-to-date photograph of him.

I thank you, Pauline, for caring for William in the absence of his parents. One day, when the political situation here has improved, I will send for him.

Love to you and the family, from Jo Jo.

'You should've told me you were getting a divorce,' said my mother. 'Why didn't you?'

I said, truthfully, 'I thought she might change her mind.'

15

'Fancy letting a beautiful wife like Jo Jo slip through your fingers,' she said. 'You must be bloody mad. You'll never get another woman in the same league as her. She had everything, beauty, brains, money, talent –'

'She couldn't cook,' I interrupted.

'She cooked Nigerian food superbly,' said my mother, Jo Jo's biggest fan.

'Yes!' I said. 'But I'm an Englishman.'

'A little Englander,' scoffed my mother, who rarely crossed the boundary of Leicestershire. 'D'you want to know why I think your marriage failed?' she asked.

I looked out at the back garden: the lawn was littered with garish plastic clothes pegs which had fallen off the washing-line.

'Go on,' I said.

'One,' she said, 'you resented the fact that she had a degree. Two, you postponed your trip to Nigeria five times. Three,' she continued, 'you never came to terms with the fact that she was four inches taller than you.'

I washed my hands in the sink in silence.

'There's a PS,' said my mother. She read the post-script with relish. 'PS. Did you see the A. A. Gill review of Hoi Polloi in the *Sunday Times*? I have to hide it from my family.'

So even in Lagos, Nigeria, they are sneering at my culinary skills! I should never have allowed Savage to persuade me to put bangers and mash on the menu.

And why, oh, why, did Gill and his blonde companion have to choose *that* night when we ran out of the traditional hand-made sausages I buy from the butcher's in Brewer Street? I should have looked Gill in the eye and admitted to the fact rather than send out to the supermarket.

There was the throb of a diesel engine outside, then an urgent knocking on the front door. I answered it to find a handsome blond man carrying a parcel. It was Nigel. He used to be my best friend at Neil Armstrong Comprehensive.

'Nigel!' I said. Then, 'What are you doing driving a van? I thought you were gay.'

Nigel snapped, 'Being gay isn't a *career*, Moley, it's a sexual orientation.'

'But,' I stammered, 'I expected you to be doing something *artistic*.'

'You mean like *cooking*?' he asked, laughing.

'But I thought you were a Buddhist,' I continued, digging another conversational grave.

He sighed, then said, 'Buddhists are allowed to drive vans.'

'But you've dropped the yellow robes,' I said, unnecessarily, as he was wearing denim from head to toe.

'I now realize that the outer manifestations of spirituality mask the inner,' he said.

I asked about his parents: his father had been in hospital to have a new steel plate in his head, and his mother was still asking her son when he was going to settle down with a nice girl.

17

'You haven't told your parents you're gay?'

'No,' he admitted, looking at the van throbbing at the kerb.

'Look, this is a longer conversation, why don't we meet up sometime?' he said. We swapped our mobile numbers and he drove off.

When my mother came down with William she ripped open the parcel eagerly, saying, 'It's my Labour victory outfit. I'm wearing it at the count tonight.' Her face sagged past its normal levels when she saw the navy-blue trouser-suit nestling between the sheets of tissue paper. 'I ordered *red*,' she shouted. She ranted on about the impossibility of wearing navy blue at Pandora's victory party tonight. She threatened to sue Next for the psychological trauma she was suffering. I extracted the order form from the wrapping paper and spotted that my mother had ticked Navy Blue in the colour column. There could be no doubting her own distinctive mark. Eventually she conceded that Next was not at fault. Had he known, her lawyer, Charlie Dovecote, would have wept for his lost fees. She is waiting to appear in court against Shoe Mania! because a stiletto heel fell off on the summit of Snowdon. Privately I hope that she loses her case. If she were to win, the law would be made to look even more of an ass. Charlie Dovecote is clearly taking advantage of a half-crazed menopausal woman who can't find an HRT treatment to suit her.

I offered to ring Next and arrange an emergency delivery of a red suit. She said scornfully, 'As if.' But

I called Nigel on his mobile and he promised to do what he could, though he warned that 'anything red' was sprinting out of the warehouse and prophesied that there was to be a Labour landslide. I tried to tell him about my informer, Fred Gipton, but my phone signal broke up. I was annoyed to see that some of William's spilled milk had seeped into the holes in the microphone.

I was even more annoyed when William, distracted by the New Dog, upset his second bowl of cereal and a vile mixture of brown milk and sugar dripped off the edge of the table and on to the crotch of my stone-coloured chinos. I leaped to the sink, grabbed a dishcloth and wiped myself down, but the cloth had obviously been harbouring another, worse stain among its folds – orange juice, possibly – and this stain transferred itself to the Coco Pops stain. The two transmogrified into yet another stain – one speaking of long-term incontinence. I looked around for the washing-machine, only to be informed that it was the subject of a dispute, and was residing back with the manufacturer. More work for Charlie Dovecote.

'You'll have to borrow a pair of your father's,' said my mother.

I laughed out loud at the notion that I would be seen *decomposing in a ditch* in my father's trousers. 'Where is he, by the way?' I asked.

'Upstairs in bed. He's got clinical depression,' my mother said, unsympathetically.

'What brought it on?' I asked, as we climbed the

stairs (which were dangerously littered with a myriad toy cars).

She lowered her voice on the landing. '*One*, he knows he won't work again, not in a proper full-time job. *Two*, he's got piles, but he's scared of the operation. *Three*, he's been impotent for three months.'

My father shouted from the bedroom.

'*Four*, he's sick of his bleeding wife blabbing his sexual secrets to all and bleeding sundry.' My mother threw the bedroom door open. 'Adrian is *not* all and sundry,' she shouted, through the cigarette haze.

'No, but the bloke in the bleddy video shop is,' he roared.

William threw himself on to my father's recumbent form and kissed him passionately. My father murmured, 'This little lad is the only reason I haven't topped myself.'

'What's "topped myself", Grandad?' asked William, who had begun to unfasten the buttons on my father's pyjama jacket. (His physical dexterity is amazing.)

I leaped in quickly – my parents are perfectly capable of attempting to explain the notion of suicide to a two-and-three-quarter-year-old child. 'Topped myself, means . . . er . . . it means . . . getting better at something,' I lied. 'Wouldn't you feel better if you opened the curtains and the window and got some air and light in here?' I asked.

'No,' whined my father. Then, sounding like Blanche Du Bois, 'I don't like the light.'

I looked around the room and realized that my mother's mad clutter of books, magazines, cosmetics and beauty aids was missing. Apart from my father's bottles of tranquillizers, the room was devoid of those personal touches that make a house a home. They were obviously sleeping apart.

'Are you going to get out of bed and let me drive you to the polling station?' I asked him kindly.

My father groaned and turned his face to the wall. I noticed that his bald spot, the size of a fifty-pence piece on Wednesday April 2nd, 1997, the last time I saw him, was now the size of a digestive biscuit (McVitie's).

I decided to attempt a breakthrough in our relationship: i.e. I would try to talk to my father *as if he were a real person*. I started by pushing William aside and lying next to my father on the bed. I patted his bony shoulder and said something I'd heard an expert in family therapy suggest on the *Oprah* show. 'I'm sorry you're not happy, Dad,' I said. 'How may I help you?'

My father turned to face me. 'You sound like a bleeding shop assistant,' he replied. 'And I'm sorry I'm not happy, Adrian, but do you know what Freud said about happiness?'

'No,' I admitted, 'I'm a follower of Jung.'

My father raised himself on one elbow. 'Freud wrote, in the *Reader's Digest*, "To be happy a man needs two things: Love and Work," and I haven't got either any more.' His mouth crumpled and he turned his face back to the wall.

'Oh, thank you *very* much, George,' said my mother, with heavy sarcasm. '*My* love doesn't count.' Tears were gathering in her eyes, threatening to spill down her cheeks and bring brushfuls of mascara with them. She addressed my father's back. 'Tony Blair will give you a job, George,' she said, 'and we can sort the love thing out.' She turned to me and lowered her voice. 'When he says *love* he *means* sex.' She leaned over and kissed my father's bald spot. 'We'll go back to that sex therapist, shall we?' I got up and inched towards the door, wishing now that I had not instigated this *Oprah*-like family confessional. William put his hand in mine, and we left the room together, but unfortunately not before I had heard my father say, 'But I'm not having those injections in my dick, Pauline.'

'Who's Dick?' said William, as we walked down the stairs.

One of the Spice Girls, Emma, was ironing a skirt the size of an African postage stamp in the kitchen. It was Rosie, my sister.

'How's your revision going?' I asked.

'What effing revision?' She sniggered. I felt it was my duty to remind her of the importance of taking her GCSEs seriously. Her parents were obviously too busy trying to revive their clapped-out sex life to care about their daughter's education. I was only halfway through my little lecture when Rosie flew into a tantrum and slammed the iron down on to the board.

Steam hissed as she shouted, 'Chill out, man, I'm, like, cool about the effing exams, y'know?'

'Please,' I said, 'don't swear in front of William.'

'*Effing* is not swearing, you sad bastard,' she said.

In a deliberately calm voice I pointed out that the iron was burning her so-called skirt. She snatched up the iron and stood it on end. A cloud of vapour momentarily obscured her face, reminding me of a horror film I'd seen about a female killer running amok in a New York sauna.

As I watched my son chomp through his third bowl of Coco Pops, I tried to remember if I had been as obnoxious as Rosie when I was a young teenager. But quite honestly, dear Diary, I feel sure that I was a happy-go-lucky lad, polite, considerate and extremely well adjusted. And, bearing in mind that I had no parental encouragement (no encyclopedias, no Anglepoise) I did quite well in my GCSEs: five at C grade.

I rang the Next headquarters and ordered a pair of chinos from their catalogue. I then rang Nigel on his mobile again, and requested that he deliver the chinos to me, together with my mother's red trouser-suit.

He said, 'How about a duvet cover and a pair of pillowcases?' But I assured him that I was OK for bedlinen.

I said to him, 'Please check the size of the trousers, thirty-two-inch waist, thirty-one-inch inside leg.' I heard him crash the gears, then without him saying goodbye, his phone went dead.

To keep myself awake as William chewed each individual Coco Pop twenty times (the kid is a genius – how many almost-three-year-olds can count to twenty?), I read Pandora's election leaflet, which was fastened to the fridge with a Postman Pat magnet. It was a tawdry document. She'd been far too profligate with her exclamation marks.

Dear Voter [it started]

- Are you sick of hearing the same tired excuses about sleaze from the clearly morally bankrupt Tory candidate for Ashby-de-la-Zouch, Sir Arnold Tufton? *Yes! So am I!*

- Do you think that his record on civil liberties (petitioning Ashby-de-la-Zouch council to deter vandals by installing closed-circuit TV cameras in the cubicles of public lavatories) is disgraceful? *Yes! So do I!*

- Do you agree with Sir Arnold Tufton that TV licence dodgers should be jailed for a minimum of fifteen years? *No! Nor do I!*

- Do you demand an explanation as to why Sir Arnold Tufton was photographed in Marbella in the company of the notorious criminal Len Fox? Would you like to know what was inside the Jiffy-bag that was passed from Len Fox to Sir Arnold in the Bar Español? *Yes! So would I!*

- If you vote for me on May 1st, I pledge that I, Dr

Pandora Braithwaite, Oxford Don, Linguist of Leicester-shire Stock, will work conscientiously, honestly and fearlessly to represent the wishes of the people of Ashby-de-la-Zouch. In this cradle of democracy! The mother of parliaments! Send me to the House of Commons!
- IT CLEARLY MAKES SENSE!


At nine o'clock I took a cup of Nescafé up to my father. He lay where we had left him, his face to the wall, his hands clasped together as if in anguished prayer. He said he could hear Tony Blair's voice whispering from the corner of the room. For a split second I thought madness had set in and that he would leave the house in a straitjacket, but then I realized that the clock radio had turned itself on and Radio Four was transmitting Tony Blair's sound-bites. I crossed the room, turned it off and my father seemed to relax a little. But I couldn't persuade him to leave his bed and come with me and my mother to vote.

I went to his side of the wardrobe and riffled through his pathetic collection of trousers, a hymn to man-made fibres and Elvis-in-Las-Vegas styling, and discarded them all. However, in a drawer in his side of the chest of drawers I found a pair of 501s that he'd never worn, a Christmas present from my mother in 1989 apparently. As I tried them on and looked in the wardrobe mirror, a shaft of sunlight touched the top of my head, and I saw with horror

25

that my hair had thinned so much that light was able to penetrate to the very follicles. I went into the bathroom and examined my scalp in the devastating light of the magnifying mirror on the window-ledge. The evidence was unmistakable: I was losing my hair.

Even as I watched, a hair detached itself, floated from my head, and landed in the bottom of the washbasin. With great difficulty I picked it up, and put it into my shirt pocket with the Ralph Lauren logo. Don't ask me why I did this.

I took William and the New Dog for a walk around the block. The street was a riot of cherry blossom. Is it compulsory to have a cherry tree in your front garden in Ashby-de-la-Zouch? Did the council pass a by-law? There were drifts of fallen blossom on the pavements. William ran through it, grabbed handfuls and covered the New Dog. It looked like a grizzle-faced bride.

I've tried hard but I can't get used to the New Dog: it's got a miserable kind of face – the Old Dog was always smiling. Also, the New Dog displays no curiosity: it never tugs on its lead or gets excited. However, when a white van trailing blue balloons, blasting 'Land of Hope and Glory' from a crackling public-address system, went by, the New Dog turned its shaggy head and bared its teeth. So I warmed to it, very slightly.

While William was on the swings I phoned Nigel in his van and cancelled my order for the chinos. He was very short with me, said he'd been to the warehouse in person, and had been to enormous trouble, etc., etc. He said he was on his way to deliver them as we spoke. I explained about the 501s but he didn't want to know. I hate ending a conversation on an unpleasant note, so I asked him if he was going to vote for Pandora. He said he had already voted for the Green candidate, Lillian Dale, who had canvassed on a mountain bike until it was stolen. Nigel is a keen cyclist now, apparently. I pointed out to him that too much pressure from a saddle could affect sperm production (according to an American report). He said, sarcastically I thought, 'Oh dear, and I'd planned to have at least four children, with that nice girl my mother is always going on about.'

I asked him where we were going to meet up and have that drink, but he said he hadn't got his electronic organizer with him, so we said goodbye. I dragged William off the swings and we went home.

My mother and I left William in the care of his depressed grandad and his foul-mouthed aunt and walked the quarter of a mile to vote.

There was a gaggle of voters outside the Scout hut polling station. Some enterprising senior Scouts had set up a stall and were selling chilli-flavoured Doritos and little pots of salsa. There was a choice of Coke or Diet Coke to drink. 'Whatever happened to tea and home-made scones?' asked my mother of a Scout-master-type person, who appeared to be in charge.

'We've had to move with the times,' he said politely. 'This is what the public want.'

'Baden-Powell would turn in his grave,' she said.

The man blushed and turned away, and began fiddling with the salsa dip as though embarrassed. 'What did I say?' she asked of me, as we went into the smelly hut.

'Baden-Powell has been discredited by *World in Action*. He got a bit too *fond* of the boys,' I said.

'There are no heroes left any more,' she said. 'Apart from Tony Blair . . .'

A woman in urgent need of orthodontic treatment smiled and handed us our ballot papers. It gave me a thrill to see Pandora's name – I had forgotten that she had two middle names: Louise Elizabeth. I wondered if she ever used her initials. I went into the voting booth and took up the pencil on the string and paused, savouring the moment. I, Adrian Mole, was about to exercise my democratic right and vote for a government of my choice. My reverie was broken when a scrutinizer inquired, 'Are you all right in there, sir?' I drew a thick, pencilled cross next to Pandora Louise Elizabeth Braithwaite's name, and withdrew from the cubicle.

As I stood before the ballot box, folding my voting paper into a small square, I tried to fully realize the awesome significance of the moment. It may have been the tawdry surroundings of the Scout hut – the limp pennants hanging from the walls, the battered stacking chairs, the faded photographs of summer camps – that prevented me from registering any strong emotion, apart from a slight feeling of anti-climax. Surely our voting procedure should be accompanied by the sound of trumpets or massed choirs, or at the very least a singer singing freedom songs accompanied by a guitar. We should celebrate our democratic rights. Perhaps champagne or beer should be served (strictly one glass per voter) after we have dropped our papers into the ballot box. If I see Pandora tonight I may mention it to her.

My mother took my arm as we strolled home together. I didn't mind because she looked so old now (she is fifty-three) and I knew that nobody seeing us together could possibly mistake us for lovers. As we reached the top of Wisteria Walk, she dug her nails into my arm and said, 'I don't want to go home.' She sounded like a small child. When I asked her why, she said, 'Three reasons: George, Rosie and William.' Seeing my face, she said, 'They're all such *hard work*, Adrian.' She sat down on a low wall where some blue stuff was growing, and lit a cigarette. 'I'm constantly on the go,' she said. 'And the New Dog is nothing but a bloody nuisance. I've wasted my life.'

I rushed to contradict her, but after saying, 'No, no, you *haven't*,' I couldn't think of anything else to add. The highlight of her life seems to have been in 1982, when she ran away to Sheffield with rat-fink Lucas, our next-door neighbour.

'Look at all the initials Pandora's got before and after her name.' She took a crumpled election leaflet out of her pocket, and we both looked down at it. 'She's a Doctor, a BA, and MA, a PhD, and she'll be an MP by tomorrow. I've got *nothing* after my name and only Mrs before it,' she said bitterly. 'And,' she added, 'Pandora speaks *six* foreign languages, fluently. All I can say is "Two beers, please" in Spanish.'

Just then an old woman with a zimmer frame came round the corner of the house and shouted, 'You're squashing my aubrietia.' I had no idea what she was talking about, but I apologized to the wall owner, and we moved on.

I was waiting for a Sainsbury's lasagne to defrost in the microwave when the phone rang. It was Ivan Braithwaite, Pandora's father. He asked if my mother was there. I said, 'Hello, Ivan, it's Adrian.'

'Oh, hello,' he said, unenthusiastically. 'I thought you were in London. I read something about you in the *Sunday Times*, something about sausages – or was it sewage?'

Dear Diary, is that A. A. Gill piece going to dog my footsteps for the rest of my life? Perhaps I should get in touch with Charlie Dovecote and ask him to write to Gill threatening litigation unless Gill retracts his ridiculous statement.

I shouted my mother to the phone. She came into the kitchen with William clinging to her hip and passed him over to me, saying, 'Don't put him down on the floor, he's pretending it's the open sea.'

After saying, 'Ivan, how lovely to *hear* from you,' my mother fell silent, only nodding now and again (Ivan Braithwaite always did like the sound of his own voice). Eventually she broke in and said, 'Of *course* we'd love to help, we'll see you in half an hour.'

When she put the phone down, her tired eyes were shining with excitement. 'We're needed, Adrian,' she said. 'Pandora is short of cars and drivers to ferry old people to the polling stations.'

'Will they pay for the petrol?' I asked, not unreasonably, I thought. A dark look came over my mother's face. 'This is an opportunity to unseat that fat scumbag, Sir Arnold Tufton, and you're quibbling about the price of a few gallons of petrol,' she said, stretching for her make-up bag, always within reach. By the time she had disguised her face it was 2 p.m. I'd been on the go for eighteen hours.

The Labour Party had set up a temporary office in an abandoned sweet shop, which was in a dismal shopping parade on the outskirts of Ashby-de-la-Zouch. The headquarters were flanked by Jolie Madame, a hairdresser's in which could be seen several unJolie-looking Madames, sitting under metal drying hoods. On the other side of the campaign headquarters was a futon shop. A man with a droopy moustache was staring out of the window, there were no customers in the shop and, judging by the man's disconsolate expression, there never had been. The futon revolution has bypassed Ashby-de-la-Zouch.

Pandora was sitting with her back to me, her stockinged feet resting on the old sweet-shop counter. A pair of black suede court shoes was lying on the floor, where she'd kicked them off. She was wearing a tight-fitting scarlet suit, a large red rose was pinned over her left breast and a rosette was fastened over the right. She was talking in a husky voice into the smallest mobile phone I'd ever seen. Her other hand caught up her long golden hair and scrunched it into a topknot, before letting it fall to her shoulders.

A plain-faced woman in a gored skirt and a cardigan handed her a cup of tea. Pandora smiled her radiant smile, and said, 'Mavis, you're a sweetie.'

Mavis beamed as though Richard Gere had just declared his love for her and asked her to run away with him to Malibu.

I stood at Pandora's side and waited for her to finish her conversation with somebody called Boris from the *Daily Telegraph*. 'Boris, darling, if I'm elected tonight, I promise we'll have a celebratory dinner very, very soon, and if I lose we'll have dinner even sooner. Bye, you horrible Tory, you.'

She switched the smile off with the phone, stood up and put her shoes on. 'What are *you* doing here?' she said. 'I thought you'd be in London cooking turds for A. A. Gill.'

'I've come to help,' I said, ignoring her mocking laughter.

She lit a cigarette and one of the volunteers, a thin man with a beard, rushed forward with an ashtray. 'Chris, you're a sweetie,' she croaked. Chris stumbled away, as though he'd glimpsed paradise.

'You've got everybody eating out of your hand, as usual,' I said, looking around at the volunteers, who were doing busy things with paper, tea-bags and phones.

Pandora said, 'They're happy to be associated with my success. They know I'm going to win tonight.'

I replied, 'The last I heard you were slagging the Labour Party off, saying it had betrayed socialism.'

'Oh, grow up!' she snapped. 'Do you want the bloody Tories in or out?'

'Out, of course,' I replied.

'Then shut the fuck up,' she said. 'I live in the *real* world.'

I looked around the HQ. It was the real world all right. My mother was holding a clipboard, and having a red rosette pinned to her jacket by Ivan Braithwaite. The back of his hairy hand brushed her left breast, and he apologized. She stretched her lipsticked lips and dipped her head to one side, in a submissive gesture I'd last seen on an animal-behaviour documentary (gorillas) on television. I'd seen that head-tilt gesture before, and it usually spelled trouble.

Mavis rushed up and said, 'Pandora, the latest exit polls are awfully good.'

She handed Pandora a piece of paper, which Pandora glanced at briefly before crumpling it and throwing it into a wastepaper basket. 'I'm going to romp home,' she said. She laid a red-taloned hand on my shoulder. 'It's so good to see you, sweetie,' she said.

'Don't you *dare* call me *sweetie*, Pandora,' I said. 'I've known you since you were thirteen and three-quarters. I lived in your boxroom when you were in a *ménage à trois* with a gay husband and a dyslexic bodybuilder. I know your *secrets*.'

33

'Sorry,' she said. 'I've turned into a bit of a monster since this campaign started. I've been taken over by *ambition*,' she added sadly, as though ambition were a terminal illness. Her mobile phone trilled. She pressed a button. 'Mandy!' she said, and turned her back on me.

I prised my mother away from Ivan Braithwaite and his silly sculptured side-whiskers, and we drove to the first of our pick-ups: an old woman called Ida Peacock whose house smelled of dead cats. She walked with sticks. She told me that Tony Blair was going to give her two new hips. Our second pick-up was Mabel d'Arcy, whose great-great-grandad was a surviving officer on the *Titanic*; she bragged to my mother about the fact until Ida Peacock said, 'He shoulda gone down with his ship like a gent.' They didn't speak to each other again.

Our last pensioner was an old bloke called Harry Worthington. He said he hadn't been out of the house for a week. My mother said how sorry she was that he was so isolated. Worthington said he was far from isolated, he'd recently fallen in love and had spent most of the time in bed with his new girlfriend, Alice Pope. Ida and Mabel giggled like girls and gave Harry many admiring glances. He was seventy-nine, but the old git carried on as if he was Hugh Grant. He'd got a thick head of hair, and a bushy moustache. I asked him why Alice wasn't voting, and he said that she was an anarchist who didn't believe in any form of government. I asked him who, in the unlikely event of Alice Pope's anarchists coming to power, would maintain the drains. He said Alice didn't believe in drains. I pointed out that drains are absolutely pivotal to civilization. Worthington said that Alice didn't believe in civilization. No wonder he didn't get out of bed for a week. She sounds like an animal.

As I helped Mabel out of the car at the polling station at Rosie's school, it transpired that she was a supporter of Sir Arnold Tufton, and intended to vote Conservative. 'He was very good when I was burgled,' she said.

'Did he catch the burglar, or recover your stolen property?' I asked in a *faux-naïf* fashion.

'No, but he told me that if he was Home Secretary he'd chop the thieves' hands off,' she said, benignly.

'Dr Pandora Braithwaite is very strong on *Crime and Punishment*,' I said. This was no lie. I knew for a fact that Pandora had studied Dostoevsky's masterpiece for A level, and received the highest grade in the East Midlands.

As Mabel staggered down the drive of the comprehensive, I tried to brainwash her into changing her political affiliation. I told several lies: that Pandora was a blood relation of Winston Churchill, that Pandora hunted with the Quorn, that Pandora made her own bread. But who knows how the old bat voted in the end?

Harry was a Pandora devotee; the things he admired about her were 'her kissable lips, her delightful breasts' and her legs, 'like Cyd Charisse'.

Ida Peacock voted for Paddy Ashdown because 'He is a military man.' Didn't she mind his admitted adultery? I asked. Ida smiled, showing her eighty-one-year-old teeth. 'All the nice girls love a sailor,' she sang.

Harry Worthington joined in, then sang the hideous song 'I'll See You Again', complete with throbbing vibrato and ludicrous Noël Coward accent, all the way back to his pensioner's bungalow. I was glad to see the back of them all.

My life was once blighted by a pensioner called Bert Baxter, a Communist with an unstable Alsatian called Sabre who was addicted to beetroot (Bert, not the dog). Baxter bullied me into such unsavoury activities as cutting his horny toenails, and burying his decomposed dog in hard-baked earth with a coal scuttle. Sabre's interment was one of the worst days of my life. It still rankles with me now. Bert died two years ago. I was quite surprised at how much I cared, though I have to admit that my main emotion on hearing the news was relief that I wouldn't have to cut his toenails ever again. Bert was Leicester's oldest and most objectionable man. On his 105th birthday Pandora and I were present when he was interviewed in the lounge of the Alderman Cooper Sunshine Home, where he was surrounded by the Lord Mayor, Lady Mayoress, fellow residents, staff and friends. The interviewer, a young woman in a pink suit called Lisa Barrowfield, tried manfully to stop Bert from making references to her breasts, which were not particularly prominent, as I recall: slightly larger than Jaffa oranges, but not quite the size of Marks & Spencer's grapefruits.

Lisa asked, 'Bert, you're 105 years of age. To what do you attribute your long life?'

Poor Lisa asked this question fourteen times. None of Bert's replies could be broadcast before the watershed of nine o'clock. Eventually, after the mayor and his wife had dissociated themselves from the occasion, Lisa phoned her boss at Central TV and asked for guidance. She was told to record several interviews with him and they would do a 'heavy edit' job in the studio.

My disenchantment with television began the next night. Bert Baxter had been edited into a harmless, pleasant old man. Here, just for the record, is one of Baxter's real replies.

LISA: Bert, you are 105 years old. What's your secret?

BERT BAXTER: Well, I reckon that the sixty Woodbines a day I've smoked have sort of put a healthy lining on my lungs. I've never jogged or played games or been to bed sober, so I've slept well. I shagged my way around Europe during the war, and I live mainly on beetroot sandwiches, Spotted Dick and custard. But the secret of a healthy life, and I'd tell any youth this, is don't let your sperm collect up inside your balls, let it out! (*Laughs*) Let 'em all out! (*Coughs*) Light me a fag, Pandora, there's a good gel.

What was transmitted was this manifestation of the TV editor's black art.

BERT: Beetroot sandwiches have kept me healthy, I've slept well, and played a lot of ball games in my youth. I've never smoked and I've jogged my way around Europe.

Bert was horrified when he saw *Midlands Today*, which had been trailed by teasers all day, e.g. an unseen announcer would say between programmes, 'And in *Midlands Today* at six-thirty, the Leicester *pensioner* who says that jogging around Europe *has* kept him alive for 105 years.' Why the stress on 'has' was there, I don't know. Was there a dispute about this? I don't think so.

I was glad that Bert died in a stair-lift accident the day *before* his 106th birthday. I couldn't have gone through another grisly birthday party. And I know for a fact that the Mayor and Mayoress of Leicester had booked a holiday in Tenerife to encompass that very day, May 9th. Still, I think Bert would have been pleased with the size of the headline in the *Leicester Mercury*, if not the content.

STAIR-LIFT TRAGEDY: OLDEST JOGGER DIES.
Bertram Baxter, the oldest man in Leicester, died early

today in a tragic accident involving a dressing-gown cord and the mechanism of a stair-lift at the Alderman Cooper Sunshine Home, in Brook Lane, where he had resided for many years. Mr Baxter, whose wife Queenie died in 1982, was described by the senior nursing officer, Mrs Loretta Harvey, today, as 'quite a character, who didn't suffer fools gladly'.

Mrs Harvey recalled the time that Mr Baxter had sued the Alderman Cooper Sunshine Home for damages – claiming that he was not being provided with his dietary needs. Mr Baxter ate only beetroot sandwiches, Spotted Dick and custard. The case became a *cause célèbre* when Mr Baxter went on hunger strike and for a while he enjoyed considerable national notoriety, becoming known as 'Beetroot Bertie'. His victory was widely applauded as a triumph for common sense – though Mrs Harvey claimed that the kitchen staff were 'greatly inconvenienced'.


I shouldn't be sorry if I never saw another old-age pensioner again. I have decided that I cannot bear their slowness, their ill-fitting teeth and their mania for pickled vegetables. My mother soon got bored with assisting the pensioners: she said she'd rather be 'at the hub of things', so I dropped her off at Labour Party HQ. I continued alone.

The next person I picked up was another old man called Archie Tait. He was infuriatingly slow in getting into the car. He hawked and coughed into a large white handkerchief, and when I asked him sarcastically if he was all right he said no, he wasn't, he had pneumonia. He spoke very nicely for somebody who lived in a terraced house.

'Shouldn't you be in bed, or in hospital?' I said.

'No,' he said, 'I must vote, I'm a socialist.'

'Mr Blair wouldn't want you passing out at the polling station,' I said.

'Mr Blair?' he said, disdainfully. 'I've just said I'm a *socialist*, I'm voting Socialist Labour, for Arthur's party.'

'Arthur?' I checked.

'Arthur *Scargill*,' he said, as if talking to an idiot.

I tried to persuade him to change his mind and vote for Pandora. I told him that she had supported Mr Scargill during the miners' strike by holding a raffle at school and sending the proceeds (£19.76, I recall) to the Strike Fund, but he would not be deterred.

'I left my left lung and my right leg at Arnhem,' he informed me, as he lurched out of the back of the car. 'And I didn't do that so that English men and women would turn into Europeans, drinking luke-warm cappuccino.'

To try to counter his fanaticism I said, 'Cappuccino is a perfectly harmless pleasant-tasting beverage. I drink six cups a day.'

'It's a little bit of coffee and a bloody lot of froth,' he said.

He shook my hand and thanked me for the lift. I told him that I would wait and take him back home.

Morally I would have been perfectly entitled to leave him, with his right lung and left leg, stranded at Carts Lane Primary School.

I felt a bit aggrieved that he had accepted a lift under false pretences, claiming to be a Labour voter when he was, in fact, a socialist all along.

When we were driving back towards his house, he apologized for swearing earlier. I said I no longer noticed profane language. I explained that I worked in a Soho restaurant where derivations of the F-word were used as nouns and adjectives and verbs – they were the building blocks of most Soho sentences.

When we stopped outside his terraced house, he had a violent coughing fit that made his face go red and his eyes run. It took a long time for him to catch his breath, so I helped him out of the front passenger seat and supported him to his front door. He took a bunch of keys out of his trouser pocket and handed them to me while he leaned against the wall, gasping.

As the front door swung open, I saw a bookcase stuffed with books. Facing me were *Das Kapital*, *Ulysses* and Harold Nicolson's *Diaries*. Under the window that faced the street there was a single day bed. A low table stood next to it, covered with a clutter of medicines and jars. A coal fire glimmered in the hearth. A fat cat sat on the mat. Tait lay down on the bed and closed his eyes. He was a tall man, his feet (foot) hung over the end board. As I went into the tiny back kitchen to put the kettle on, I cursed God and socialism for sending this pensioner to me. Am I never to be free of them? Are pensioners my albatross? Am I destined to voyage through life with their liver-spotted hands circling my neck?

I made him as comfortable as a one-legged, one-lunged old man with pneumonia can be and took his phone number. I ascertained from him that he had no relations (of course), and no friends (*naturellement*), he had quarrelled with his neighbours (*mais oui*) and guess what? *Quelle surprise! He is alone in the world.* Apart from the huge ginger cat, which is called Andrew. I complimented Tait on the creature, saying it was the biggest cat I'd ever seen.

Then I wrote out my mobile number, stuck it under a jar of sweet piccalilli on the low table, and told him to ring me if he needed help tonight. He assured me that he was perfectly all right, and asked me to go away and leave him in peace. I knew he wouldn't drink the tea I'd made him in the big china cup with the rose design and the gold rim. He didn't look as if he had the strength to raise his head from the pillow.

As I drove back to the committee rooms, I wished that everybody over fifty years of age would commit mass suicide and give the rest of us a break.

I understand that certain 'grey' industries would collapse; garden-trellis and thermal-underwear manufacturers spring to mind. But the benefits are obvious: no pensions to pay out, no residential homes for the elderly to maintain, and at least half of the disabled parking spaces outside Marks & Spencer's would be reclaimed by the young and the able-bodied.

Once again I thank Pepys, the god of diarists, that my own journal will never be read in my lifetime. I would not like to be thought an uncaring ageist. I know that when I reach fifty, I will happily sacrifice my life so that the young are not saddled with the old.

On reflection, perhaps fifty is *too* young. Fifty-five would be a more reasonable cut-off point (if in good health or a non-smoker), but sixty would be my *absolute* limit. What's the point of anybody living after then? *Sans* teeth, *sans* muscle tone *et sans* sex?

My last job before the polling station closed at ten o'clock was to pick up a Ms Clough of Bevan Close, Beveridge Estate. To my horror she had three little kids with her. 'I've got to bring 'em with me,' she said. 'I 'aven't gotta babysitter.'

Ms Clough was excited by the prospect of a Labour victory. She thought that Tony Blair would 'support single mothers'. She had heard him say so on the Jimmy Young programme, so she knew it must be true. I assured Ms Clough that Mr Blair was a trust-worthy, caring man who had dedicated his life to righting the wrongs of our inequitable society.

'Do you know Mr Blair?' she asked, looking impressed.

I watched in the driving mirror as my expression changed from confident to enigmatic. 'Does anybody *really* know Tony?' I said. 'I think even Cherie would say she doesn't *really* know Tony.'

Ms Clough disciplined her children, who were fiddling with the pine-tree air-freshener, and, with a touch of irritation in her voice, said, 'But have you met him and spoken to him? Does he know your name?'

I was forced to admit that, no, I had never met him; that, no, I had never spoken to him; and that, no, Tony Blair did not know my name. We passed the rest of the journey in silence. Ms Clough should join the Leicestershire Constabulary – she would be very effective in the Criminal Investigation Department.

Nigel's Next van was parked outside the house when I got home. He was in the kitchen drinking tea with my mother and Ivan Braithwaite. My mother was parading between the worktops in a new scarlet trouser-suit, which (I thought) clashed horribly with her red hair. However, Ivan Braithwaite (fifty-five, so ripe for the cull) was saying, 'It's immensely elegant, Pauline, but it needs high heels.'

How dare Braithwaite advise my mother on suitable footwear! The man is a sartorial disaster area. He is the *Pompeii of menswear* in his hideous Rohan outdoor trousers and his Birkenstock sandals/white socks combo.

I remarked to him that I was surprised he had the time for tea-drinking – wasn't he meant to be Pandora's local media co-ordinator? He said he had already written the local press releases. One if Pandora wins, and one if she loses. He said there was a lot of national press interest in Pandora because she was exceptionally beautiful and had long hair. Most of the other women Labour candidates had short hair, and couldn't fill a thirty-six AA-cup bra. Also, despite grooming lessons, they applied their make-up as though they were toddlers who had run amok at Boots' No. 7 make-up counter.

I was shocked at Braithwaite's shallow attitude to the democratic process. At no time did I hear him talk about his daughter's beliefs, principles or policies. I said as much, and reminded him that he had once resigned from his local Labour Party branch on a point of principle (somebody had been fiddling the tea money).

No doubt to fill the conversational void that ensued, Nigel said he was sorry to hear that my marriage was over. I shot one of my venomous glances at my mother, who had the good grace to blush and look away (another hideous clash of reds). I said to Nigel that, on the contrary, I was better off out of it. My mother said, 'On the contrary, it's Jo Jo who's better off out of it.'

I said I could not understand why she had divorced me on the grounds of unreasonable behaviour. My mother replied, 'Come *on*! What about the Cotswolds sneezing row? *That* went on for three days.'

She was referring to the time when I accused Jo Jo of sneezing in an exhibitionist manner, by putting unnecessary emphasis on the *shoo!* of Ah-tish-shoo! And also of extending the *shoo* for longer than is functionally necessary. I accused her of wanting to draw attention to herself. Jo Jo pointed out that she was a five-foot-eleven, heavily pregnant black woman with braided and beaded hair walking down a Cotswold street, which was entirely populated by white people who were staring openly at her. 'I lack many things, Adrian, but what I do not lack is *attention!*' She sneezed again, extending the *shoo!* to ridiculous lengths. Men have murdered for less. I said so. My mother and father, whom I had foolishly invited to stay in our rented cottage, took Jo Jo's side totally. I was virtually sent to Coventry.

Meanwhile Jo Jo's exhibitionism worsened. She began to put even *more* stress, an *inordinate* amount of stress, I thought, on the *Ah!* before the *tish!* I was in torment. Dr Ng, my personal GP, put me on Prozac when we got back home to Soho.

Shortly after the Cotswold disaster, William was born into a paddling pool at the Royal Infirmary Maternity Hospital, Leicester – at my specific request – thus joining a dynasty of Moles who had drawn their first breath there (the Infirmary, not the birthing pool). It was my wish that William should enter the world via warm water, candlelight and Bach, as described in a leaflet issued by the Society of Radical Midwives. Jo Jo, however, was curiously resistant at first, saying that she would prefer to be unconscious throughout the labour. When I expressed surprise, saying, 'I'm sorry to hear you say that, Jo Jo. I'd have thought that you, as an African woman, would have had a more *natural* attitude towards childbirth,' to my utter *amazement* she became tearful and angry, and raised her voice to me, saying, 'When my waters break, why don't you find me a *field* that I can *work* in throughout my labour? And there must be a *tree* in this field, because, as an *African* woman, I will *naturally* want to give birth under its branches. And, of course, as soon as I have done so I will strap the child on to my back and return to my work in the fields.'

As it happened, the birthing pool was a grave disappointment. The midwife put me in charge of catching Jo Jo's afterbirth in a child's fishing net. The last time I used such a net I was eight years old, and my catch was tadpoles, which I put into a jam jar. Tragically I missed the actual moment of my son's birth because my mother chose that very same time to telephone the maternity unit and ask for a progress report. I will never forgive her for that.

Ivan Braithwaite invited my mother and me, and Nigel and Nigel's boyfriend, Norbert, to the count at the Town Hall, and to the celebratory party afterwards, at the Red Lion Hotel. At no time was my father or Mrs Tania Braithwaite mentioned. They have already been airbrushed out of history, like Stalin or Anita Harris.

After a horrible meal cooked with haste and ill grace by my mother (lobster nuggets and Uncle Ben's Oriental Rice), I went upstairs and tried to persuade my father to leave his bed. I told him that Pandora's exit polls looked good.

'I don't *care*, Adrian,' he said. 'I don't care about *anything*. My life has been a total waste, I've done nothing and been nowhere. Nobody knows my name outside my own family, and the storage-heating industry. I haven't even had my fifteen minutes of fame as promised by Andy-bloody-Warhol.'

'It was Marshall McLuhan,' I corrected.

'You see?' he said, and turned his back to the wall.

I tried to rally him by reminding him that he *had* been famous – perhaps not for fifteen minutes but certainly for five. When we were on holiday at Wells-next-the-Sea, he had been blown out to sea on a lilo shaped like false teeth. He had drifted for two miles before being winched to safety by the RAF. It made the regional TV news – *Midlands Today* – and the front page of the *Leicester Mercury*. Even the *Daily Telegraph* picked it up.

MAN SAVED BY SKIN OF TEETH!

A Leicester man who was rescued drifting in the Wash on a lilo in the shape of a pair of false teeth was described by Captain Richard Brown of the RAF Helicopter Rescue Service as a 'damned fool'.

'There was a slow leak in a lower left molar,' said Captain Brown, 'he wouldn't have lasted long.'

Captain Brown called for legislation which would ban civilians from using the sea. 'The sea is not a toy,' he said today.

This was a mistake. It brought it all back to him. 'The waves were *feet* high,' he said, with horror in his eyes. 'And all I was wearing was a pair of Speedos. I was *dying* for a fag.'

I calmed him down by lighting and handing him a Rothman's king size.

William cried and hung on to my legs when my mother and I were about to leave. Rosie, who was meant to be babysitting, was goggling at *The Jerry Springer Show*, where a hugely fat black woman was berating her husband for his transvestism. I carried the boy upstairs to my father's bedroom and said, 'Grandad is poorly. Do you want to play doctors?' I went into the bathroom and got the first-aid box out of the bathroom cupboard. I removed the pathetic out-of-date pills and medicines (a tube of eye oint-ment bore the date February 1989) and gave the box to William. I said, 'You are a doctor, William, make Grandad better, there's a good boy.'

My father lay apathetically on his pillows as William began to wrap a bandage around his left arm. As I went back downstairs my father whined, 'Not so bloody *tight*! You're cutting my sodding circulation off!'

Just before I closed the front door I heard William shout, 'Don't say swear words, Grandad, or I'll send you to *prison*.' The boy is certainly right-wing when it comes to law and order.

As I turned on the car engine, Radio Four boomed out of the speakers – a panel of writers were talking about the implications for literature of a Labour victory. Some old female git blathered on in a strangulated voice about Harold Wilson, somebody called Jennie Lee and the Arts Council, and then Barry Kent, ex-skinhead and prize-winning poet and novelist, interrupted her and said in his exaggerated Leicester accent, 'Yeah, but 'oo gives a toss about all that bleeding Arts Council crap? A writer's gotta be a *revolutionary*. His true function is to subvert the [bleeping] establishment, whether it's the [bleeping] Tory scumbags, or the [bleeping] Labour toe-rags. And if a writer needs a [bleeping] pathetic *grant* before he can put a few poxy words down on paper . . .' He laughed scornfully. 'Let him spend a few days with me. I'll open his [bleeping] eyes, I'll show him poverty and degradation, I'll take him to where people are on the [bleeping] line.' Here Kent went into one of his ranting poems. The type of ludicrous thing that has won him six poetry prizes (three British, three French):


Kill the rich!
Burn their houses!
Be unpleasant to their spouses!


Etc., etc., etc.

When he received his honorary doctorate from De Montfort University he grabbed headlines through-out the English-speaking world by parting his academic robes, revealing that he was totally naked beneath them, and intoning 'Yo! I'm a Man', the poem famous for being chanted on football terraces all over the civilized world.

> *Yo! I'm a Man*
> Yo!
> I'm a man!
> Don't!
> Wash the pan.
> Won't change a nappy,
> This makes me happy.
> I'm at the match
> This is my patch.
> Yo!
> I'm a man!
> Beer's in the can,
> Fags in the packet,
> Go on, boy, wack it!
> Swear at the ref,
> Threaten him with death!
> Yo! I'm a man!
> Yo! I'm a man!
> Yo! I'm a man!
> Yo!

The 500 students who had been sweating in an overheated marquee for three hours went berserk and gave Kent a standing ovation. Then Kent called his mother, Edna, up to the stage and said, 'And this is Edna, my mum. She's a toilet cleaner, and why should she be ashamed of it, eh?'

Mrs Kent, who had never to my knowledge shown any signs of shame in her job prior to this moment, fidgeted uncomfortably and looked as though, when she got Barry backstage, she would give him a good hiding for showing her up. I know all this because my mother told me about it as we drove towards the count.

There was strict security outside the Town Hall, courtesy of Citadel Security Ltd. We had to queue to have our names checked off against a list. My mother quickly grew impatient and began to complain in a loud voice. It was no surprise to me when she was pulled, supposedly at random, from out of the queue and taken away by a grim-faced, square-jawed female security guard called Sandra Leaf for a body search. When my mother returned she was muttering dark threats against Sandra Leaf and Citadel Security Ltd. She said she would ring Charlie Dovecote in the morning and see if she could 'do them' for sexual harassment.

As soon as we got inside the hall, Ivan Braithwaite rushed up to my mother and said, 'Yes, Pauline, those shoes are *perfect*!' What *is* it with the man? Is he a shoe fetishist? My mother pointed the toe of her vulgar red stiletto and Ivan practically ejaculated on the spot. I was relieved to see Mrs Tania Braithwaite approach and place herself between my mother and her husband.

I wondered how long Mrs Braithwaite had lingered in front of her open wardrobe before deciding on a suitable outfit for election night. Had she considered that she would be photographed and possibly filmed as the candidate's mother? It was a warm night. Was a green mohair sweater covered in embroidered French poodles a good idea? Was a pleated skirt in Prince of Wales check the perfect accompaniment? Did navy-blue Clarks sandals bring the outfit together? No! No! No! What had happened to the woman I had always admired for her elegant, bohemian style?

I consulted my mother. Mrs Braithwaite had suffered a slight stroke in December; she had made a good recovery, apart from the total loss of her dress sense. It was an appalling tragedy. I had been twenty-six years old before realizing that there were, in fact, *six* senses: sight, hearing, touch, smell, taste and dress.

Television crews were queuing up to interview Pandora. Between takes she used a small black compact, embossed with the Chanel logo, to powder her gorgeous face.

Sir Arnold Tufton stood in a corner surrounded by worried-looking men in pinstriped suits.

Meanwhile, on the trestle tables that lined the hall, there grew more and more bundles of Labour votes. The word 'landslide' was whispered around the hall. Pandora's election agent, a former Cockney whelk-stall owner called Lennie Purbright, introduced himself to me, saying, 'I'd like to shake your hand. I had the *best* meal in your restaurant the other night. In my opinion you ought to get a Michelin star.' Naturally I was flattered and asked him what he had eaten at Hoi Polloi. 'The tripe, fat chips and baked beans,' he answered, smacking his lips at the memory. 'Mind you,' he said, 'you kept us waiting.'

I explained to him that Savage would not allow a microwave in the kitchen, believing them to release 'evil rays' whenever the doors are opened, so thawing the frozen tripe is necessarily a slow process. He said, 'Yeah, yeah, they was worth waiting for, I ain't complainin'.'

I asked him about his unusual transition from whelk-stall owner to full-time political animal. He said he was driving back from Billingsgate early one morning, with a van full of whelks, and had heard Roy Hattersley on the *Today* programme on Radio Four, saying of John Major, 'He couldn't run a whelk stall'. Lennie Purbright was inspired by Lord Hattersley's metaphor into changing the direction of his life. I told him that Lord Hattersley was a regular at Hoi Polloi. Bubble and squeak with Fray Bentos corned beef and HP sauce was a particular favourite of his. Buster, his dog, was given special dispensation and allowed into the restaurant, providing he sat at his master's feet and didn't harass the poultry or the other diners.

At 1.30 a.m. an announcement was made, asking the various candidates to gather on the stage in five minutes. I ran to the lavatories. My bladder tends to be overactive at times of excitement. The urinal was crowded, so I looked under the door of the first stall to see if it was occupied. It was – by a pair of red stilettos and two Birkenstock sandals. There are, of course, many explanations for this conjunction of shoes, but nothing came to mind apart from the obvious one: that my mother and Pandora's father were so desperate for privacy that they were prepared to stand in a lavatory stall which reeked of uric acid to obtain it.

I fled from the men's lavatories and went into the ladies', where I found an empty cubicle. I was in mid-flow when I heard two women come in. They went into cubicles either side of me and they continued their conversation:

1st WOMAN: I dread it, I do. Nine days!
2nd WOMAN: My clots look like continents. I had a *perfect* Africa last month.

I fled without washing my hands.

The candidates were lined up on the stage. I noticed that Sir Arnold Tufton had a fly-button undone. A cheerful-looking woman with a shaved head was helped on to the stage, wearing a T-shirt with the acronym SLAG emblazoned across her chest. I asked my mother what it stood for.

'Socialist Lesbians Against Globalization,' she said. 'She's Christine Spicer-Woods, ex-RAF, all-round good egg.'

'What makes a woman have a hairstyle like that?' I said.

'Chemotherapy,' said my mother, with a withering look.

Ms Spicer-Woods was an arresting sight. But it was Pandora who drew all the eyes towards her. Nigel and his 'friend', Norbert, pushed their way to the front of the crowd where I was standing. Nigel said, 'She's the most beautiful thing I've seen since Leonardo DiCaprio.' His friend, an over-muscular man wearing Gucci sunglasses, said, 'Yeah, she's a babe, Nigel – and that suit's a nice bit of shmutter an' all. It's Chanel, ain't it?'

Nigel explained that Norbert was in the rag trade, and could identify a designer label at a thousand paces.

The returning officer, a small man with a face like a beaver, glared towards us, and silence fell, apart from some feeble chanting of 'Keith, Keith, Keith!' from a group of Monster Raving Loony supporters at the back of the hall, in support of their candidate, a sad-looking man in a Groucho Marx mask, called Keith Mutton. Eventually, after intervention by Sandra Leaf and her Citadel colleagues, the Loonies fell silent, and the declaration began. I looked for my mother and Ivan Braithwaite, but they were nowhere to be seen. Just as the returning officer was saying, 'Marcia Grimbold, Bring Back the Rates, 758 votes,' there was a disturbance at the back of the hall, and I turned round to see Jack Cavendish, Pandora's elderly lover, being held in an arm-lock by Sandra Leaf. A uniformed policeman was moving towards them through the crowd. Cavendish was heard to shout, 'I'm Pandora Braithwaite's partner! I should be on the stage next to her, you bloody Fascists!' before he was bundled through the fire doors and out into the yard, to join the wheelie bins and broken office furniture.

I looked up at Pandora to see how she was reacting to her lover's brutal ejection. Never once did the smile leave her lips. She is ruthless in her ambition. She turned her ravishing gaze towards the lens of the TV camera. The lens winked back. It was obvious that Pandora and the TV camera were on the brink of a passionate affair.

Sir Arnold Tufton's wife – a marsupial-like woman in a silk two-piece, and what looked like Marks & Spencer's wide-fitting shoes, pointed angrily towards her husband's crotch. Tufton fumbled repeatedly at the empty buttonhole, giving the unfortunate impression that he was pleasuring himself. Dear Diary, I hold no brief for Tufton, I loathe his 'greed is gorgeous' philosophy, but I must admit that my heart went out to him on that stage, especially when the TV monitor showed his hugely magnified hand continuing to fumble with his hugely magnified and gaping fly.

Christine Spicer-Woods earned a huge cheer from her fellow SLAGS when she grinned and raised her arms at the news that she had earned 695 votes.

Sir Arnold and Lady Tufton examined the fluorescent light fittings above their heads as his results were read out: 18,902. It was time for Pandora's result. 'Pandora Louise Elizabeth Braithwaite . . .' began the receiving officer. He got as far as saying, 'Twenty-two thousand, four hundred and fifty-seven,' before the room erupted in a sustained cheer, which brought down dust from the rafters.

Pandora licked her lips; whether it was at the prospect of her new enticing career or to add gloss to her television smile I couldn't say. She stood with her eyes cast down, and her hands clasped together, as though praying.

She is a skilful actress. Few who were there will ever forget her harrowing performance as Mary in *Manger!*, the Neil Armstrong Comprehensive School nativity play. Miss Elf, the director, said at the end, 'It was Pandora's decision to give Jesus a forceps delivery.'

Pandora appeared to 'recover' herself, and strode up to the microphone. Her voice cracked with 'emotion' as she thanked the police, Citadel Security, the volunteers who manned and *womanned* the campaign headquarters. She pretended to break down and fight back the tears while making a passionate speech about justice and freedom. She ended with 'Ashby-de-la-Zouch has thrown off its yoke of Tory rule. For the first time in over forty-five years, *you*, the people of Ashby, have a Labour MP. I hope I will prove worthy of the trust you have clearly placed in me.'

I took my mobile phone from its hip-holder, and phoned my father to tell him about Pandora's triumph.

William answered the phone. 'Hello,' he said. 'Who is it talkin'?'

'Daddy,' I said, alarmed. Why was he awake at 2 a.m.?

'Where's Grandad?' I said, trying to keep the panic I felt out of my voice. There was no reply, but I could hear William breathing heavily down the phone and making the odd Teletubby-like sound. I raised my voice, hoping to cut through the boy's introspective episode. 'WILLIAM, WHERE IS GRANDAD?' Terrifying images flashed across my mind:


- William fiddling with the gas taps next to the pseudo-log fire in the lounge.
- William finding the lighters and matches, which are kept in a Toby jug on the mantelpiece.
- William moving into the kitchen and messing about with the Sabatier knives I bought my mother last Christmas.
- William switching the electric kettle on and attempting to make tea.
- William easily unscrewing the childproof lid and throwing paracetamol down his throat.

- William letting himself out of the house and wandering the streets of Ashby-de-la-Zouch in his pyjamas.
- Police divers jumping into the municipal lake, watched by a regional TV news crew.

The signal on my phone started to fade. I screamed, 'WILLIAM, WAKE GRANDAD UP!' The signal went and I cursed whichever satellite had passed overhead without doing its bloody job.

After wasting a whole thirty seconds in futile button-pressing activities, I saw that the red 'battery low' warning light had come on. I looked around frantically for a phone. My mother ran up to me in a lather of excitement. Ivan Braithwaite was not far behind her. He said, 'We're going to La Zouch's to celebrate, as soon as Pan's addressed the crowd outside.'

I said to my mother, 'You've got to go home, William's roaming the house and Dad's asleep or dead!'

'He's your kid, and it's your father,' said my mother, belligerently. '*You* go home. I'm staying for the celebrations.'

After ordering the pair of them to keep phoning the house, I ran from the hall and pushed my way through the crowds of excited Labour supporters who were gathering on the road and pavement outside. All eyes were turned towards the upstairs balcony, where Pandora was expected to show herself, Evita-like, to the peons of Ashby-de-la-Zouch.

I drove the car slowly through the crowd at five m.p.h., nudging people aside. There was another obstruction ahead. A ludicrous stretch limo stood at the kerb. A chauffeur, wearing a grey uniform and cap, walked around the grotesque silver-coloured vehicle and opened all six doors. Barry Kent, in a scarlet leather jacket and sunglasses, got out of the car. Edna, Kent's mother, and his two lumpen brothers and three lumpen sisters emerged and stood awkwardly on the pavement. Edna pulled her dress free from the crack of her large bum.

Two grinning policemen escorted Kent and his entourage through the crowd. He saw me shouting through the windscreen and stopped. I wound the window down.

Kent poked his head inside my car. He smelled expensive. 'Moley, ain't you stayin' to celebrate with your old squeeze?' he said.

'No, I've got a domestic crisis on,' I said. 'Ask him to move the car.'

Kent whistled with two fingers and shouted, 'Hey, Alfonso, lose the wheels, sharpish!

Once free of the car park, I drove like a madman through the deserted streets. I crossed traffic lights on amber. A vein throbbed dangerously in my neck. A sponge had attached itself to the roof of my mouth. I cursed the day that one of my spermatozoa had forced itself on to and into one of Jo Jo's eggs and made William. Why had no one told me that becoming a parent would expose me to such torment?

I blamed Neil Armstrong Comprehensive School. I received no parenting lessons whatsoever from that so-called educational establishment.

There were no emergency vehicles in Wisteria Avenue, and no flames licking the roof. In fact, the house was in darkness. I let myself in and called, 'William! William!' I heard faint noises coming from the living room. A Teletubbies video was running, and my father was asleep on the sofa. Somebody (it could only have been William) had scribbled in black felt-tip pen on his bald patch. I checked the house quickly. William was nowhere to be seen.

It was Rosie – arriving home disgracefully late from whatever debauch she'd been attending – who found my son. He was asleep, naked, in the dog's basket under the sink. He looked like a fund-raising poster for the NSPCC. He'd obviously been eating Winalot: there were crumbs of it around his mouth, and he still clutched some in his baby fist. If Social Services ever got to hear about this, the kid could end up in a children's home, and subsequently be nicknamed 'Wolf Boy' by the *Sun*.

As a punishment to my father I didn't tell him about the scribble on his head.

After I'd put William to bed I switched on the television and watched the election results. Gratifying as it was to see the arrogant and pompous Tory pins knocked over by the balls of the electorate in the skittle alley of history, the highlight of the coverage had to be Pandora's appearance on the balcony of Ashby-de-la-Zouch Town Hall.

Barry Kent stood next to her, leading the crowd in singing, 'Oh, Pandora, we adore ya', to the tune of Beethoven's 'Ode to Joy'.

Her resemblance to Eva Perón was startling and, I am convinced, quite deliberate.

I remember the project on South American dictators she did in the fifth form at school, and how furious she was when she only received a B minus instead of her usual A plus. Mr Fagg, her history teacher, had written, 'A well-researched and, as usual, brilliantly expressed piece of work, but marred by the protracted and bafflingly irrelevant essay on Eva Perón's fondness for Balenciaga.'

Rosie joined me for a moment as I watched members of the new Labour government at the victory celebrations at the Royal Festival Hall. As they waited for Tony 'n' Cherie to join them, they jiggled their hips and clicked their fingers to the tune of 'Things Can Only Get Better'.

I squirmed with embarrassment. I was reminded of watching my father dancing at Auntie Susan's wedding reception in the prison officers' social club. As soon as the DJ (a convict on parole), put on the Rolling Stones' 'Brown Sugar', my father leaped to his feet and began strutting around the hall, à la Mick Jagger.

Auntie Susan's new 'wife', Amanda, stood next to

me at the bar, supping a pint of Guinness. The only comment she made was 'Poor, sad bastard,' as my father wiggled past, one arm stabbing the air, the other perched provocatively on his sunken hip.

I felt much the same disgust at the sight of Robin Cook's attempts to keep to a rhythm. I dread to think what he's like at sexual intercourse, where rhythm is all. Though I expect he must have given sex up long ago. I read somewhere that it's racing horses that inflames his passion.

As we watched the dancing politicians, Rosie put her fingers down her throat and made loud retching noises. I felt obliged to defend the new government, and their innocent pleasure in taking office.

I said, 'Show some tolerance, Rosie.'

'Tolerance!' she sneered. 'Tolerance is for, like, your saddo generation, not mine.' She sneered on, 'If I were a dictator I'd ban anyone over eighteen years old from f------ dancing.'

There was a shot of Peter Mandelson clapping his hands in a loose, American kind of way. She said, 'Gross,' and went to bed.

## Friday May 2nd

At 6.14 a.m. I heard Ivan Braithwaite's faulty exhaust pipe turn into Wisteria Walk and stop outside our house. (Together with the rest of his car, obviously.

64

*I mean, obviously!*) I dragged myself off the sofa, peered through a chink in the curtains and saw my mother and Braithwaite in passionate conversation in the front seats of the car. My mother was drawing heavily on a cigarette. Braithwaite's eyes were half closed against the smoke. Suddenly my mother yanked the car door open. Braithwaite leaned across the gear stick with an anguished look on his unshaven chops. My mother ran round the back of the car, then up the path without looking back. I heard her keys scraping around the keyhole in the front door. She has never, ever managed to unlock a door in under three minutes, so I put her out of her misery and opened it for her. She looked shocked to see me.

I said, 'What was going on in that car?'

She took off her red jacket and hung it over the back of a kitchen chair. The tops of her arms looked pasty and saggy, as though they'd been injected with a lumpy white sauce. She said, 'I've just had an argument with Ivan . . . about, er . . . which Dimbleby gave the best election coverage!'

It was an obvious lie. I said, 'And which Dimbleby did you favour?' with some sarcasm.

'David!' she answered, but she couldn't look me in the eye. I heard the frame creak upstairs as she got into bed. Then there was silence.

I lay awake on the sofa and wondered if I should intervene before my mother brought yet another tragedy to our family. Trust her to spoil my enjoyment of Labour's victory. What should have been a glorious new dawn of optimism and a celebration of the transcendence of all that is best in humankind had been tainted by the potential threat to the Moles' and the Braithwaites' family units. And all because two late-middle-aged people have restless genitals.

*1 p.m.*

The household slept late. It was Tania Braithwaite who woke us by phoning and asking if Ivan was at our house. Apparently he hadn't been home and his mobile was switched off. My mother overheard my feigned concern and snatched the phone off me. While she cross-questioned Tania, I fed the New Dog and William, and took a cup of Nescafé up to my father. He was lying on his side, facing the wall. His bald patch was still decorated with black felt-tip scrawlings. As I put the mug down on the bedside table, he begged me to close the curtains against the sunlight, which was flooding into the room.

I said, 'You ought to feel happy today, Dad. Tony could transform your life.'

He gave a harsh laugh as he sat up in bed and reached for his Rothman's. 'Listen, son,' he said, 'under Mrs Thatcher I was a three-times-a-week man, and if the sun was shining I was a bloody sex machine.'

I said, 'I was referring to the socio-economic aspects of the new government.'

66

'Yeah, well,' he said, sucking on his cigarette, 'all I'm saying is that when Maggie was in power I had lead in my pencil.'

I left the room. As I saw it, there was no point in reasoning with a man who could see no further than the end of his pencil.

Before I left for London, I tried to get up the courage to talk to my mother about the disastrous consequences certain to ensue if she were to embark on an affair with her local MP's father. MI5 would follow her around Asda. Her phone would be tapped and, more importantly, was she really prepared to put my father through a divorce for a *second* time?

I went to tackle her and found her in the living room, deliriously happy, watching a video loop of the expression on Michael Portillo's face as the realization dawned that he had been kicked from office by his former constituents. She shouted at the screen, 'Yes, you arrogant bastard, how does it feel to be on the scrap-heap, like George Mole?' I didn't want to prick her balloon of happiness. And, anyway, I couldn't risk us having an argument that ended with her refusing to look after her grandson.

William had to be prised from my legs before I could get into the Montego. Eventually he was persuaded to let me go by the promise that he could watch a video of Jeremy Clarkson test-driving a Lamborghini. The kid waved until I turned the corner of the avenue. I was almost tempted to reverse and pick him up, take him back to London with me. But reason prevailed. What would I do with him all day when I was working?

It was a gloriously warm day, and I wound the window down and enjoyed the breeze on my face. Unfortunately just before I joined the motorway, an insect of some kind flew up my left nostril, causing my eyes to run all the way to London.

Saw eleven Eddie Stobart lorries. Only received nine salutes, though. Perhaps the other two drivers didn't see my greetings. Otherwise the journey was without incident.

I arrived at the Brent Cross shopping centre car park, where I habitually parked the Montego at 1700 hours, arriving in Soho, via the bus, at 1800 hours. Why is Brent Cross the nearest free parking I can find to Soho? I've got my name down for a resident's parking permit, but the waiting list is 2,000 names long. 'Clever Clive', a criminal acquaintance of mine, offered to supply me with an illegally obtained permit. 'The geezer's dead. He ain't gonna need short-term parking. He's in Long Stay, permanent.' But I turned him down. I cannot profit from the dead, and anyway Clever Clive was asking £500.

I didn't have to start work until seven-thirty so I bought a *Guardian* and sat outside the Bar Italia in Greek Street. I was hoping to read that Frank Bruno, Paul Daniels and Bruce Forsyth had been spotted at Heathrow, fleeing a Labour victory as promised, but there were no reported sightings of them. I suppose it is early days yet. They've got mock-Tudor mansions to sell, and financial advisers to consult.

My friend Justine, who lap-dances at Secrets, joined me for an espresso and said that business had been excellent last night. 'You couldn't have got another bloke in the place if you'd cut their dicks off,' she said, causing me to wince at her graphic account of the crush. She went on, in her Gateshead accent, 'And they was mostly Labour supporters.' She told me that her boss, Large Alan, had been 'worrying his bollocks off' about a possible change of government. He had forecast massive redundancies for Soho's sex-industry workers should Labour win. 'It's the Conservative MPs who kept the "discipline" side of the business going,' Justine explained. 'Large Alan always gives them a good discount – on production of a Commons pass.'

'So, what special services do *Labour* MPs request?' I asked.

'Well,' she said, bringing her sunbed-tanned face next to mine, 'I've got one old Labour MP from Preston who has a list of things he likes me to shout out when I'm pretending to come.'

'Such as what?' I pressed, urgently.

'Weird things,' she said, as she adjusted her breasts inside her Wonderbra to show them to better advantage. 'I have to shout, "October Revolution", "Clause Four" and end up with "Betty Boothroyd",' she said.

She was obviously in complete ignorance of the

history of the Labour Party. I, of course, understood the references, because I was founder and leader of a political organization called the Pink Brigade. We were a bunch of radical teenage hot-heads.

We demanded:

- Cycling lanes alongside motorways
- A moratorium on library fines for pensioners
- Zero-rated VAT on skateboards
- Cigarettes to cost at least £10 per pack
- Babysitting wages to be linked to the cost of living index
- peace not war.

Pandora was on the Pink Brigade's executive committee, but resigned after three months after a bitter row about the party's anti-smoking policy. At the age of sixteen she was already on fifteen Benson and Hedges a day, plus the occasional cigar after dinner.

Justine repeated, 'October Revolution, Clause Four, Betty Boothroyd,' as if trying to discover the erotic charge. 'It's the easiest money *I've* ever made,' she said. 'He's come and gone in half an hour, and left me with me Tesco's money for the week.'

After she'd hurried off to work I pondered on the nature of our Soho village conversation. I couldn't imagine speaking of such worldly things in any of the villages in Leicestershire, apart from Frisby-on-the-Wreake where, if the rumours are true, paganism is practised on a large scale.

## Saturday May 3rd – 2 a.m.

I have just finished work and, though the hour is late, I am far too overwrought to sleep. Savage behaved like a beast tonight. A beast with a drug, alcohol and personality-disorder problem. The nightmare began when I got to work and saw that he had Blu-Tacked a large notice in the window:

No socialists
No mobile phones
No silicone breasts
No sodomites
No face-lifts
No credit cards
No Welsh
No vegetarians
No non-smokers
No pensioners
No teetotallers
No Filofaxes
No Groucho members
No media workers
No working class

No comedians
No disabled
No lesbians
No blind dogs
No fat people
No Liverpudlians
No children
No yoghurt-eaters
No designer handbags
No Christians
No Belgians
No poncy wankers asking for risotto
No redheads
No ex-wives

An angry crowd had gathered outside the restaurant. A fat woman carrying a handbag with a
bamboo handle was saying in a lilting Welsh accent,
'I was born in Liverpool and my partner is a lesbian
comedian. It's disgraceful.'

Savage could be seen inside smoking a fag, toasting the crowd in champagne. I let myself in and
passed through the restaurant on my way to the
kitchen.

'The provincial returns,' he bellowed. 'How is dear
old Leicester?'

'My family live in Ashby-de-la-Zouch now,' I
replied, coldly.

'You're such a *f------ pedant*,' spat out Savage.

'Better a pedant than a bigot,' I replied. 'That notice disqualifies most of your regular customers. You'll be bankrupt in a month and we'll all be on the street.'

'That's the idea,' he slurred. 'If I'm bankrupt, I can't pay Kim her allowance, can I?'

I took advantage of his drunkenness to continue. 'It's your fault that Kim is financially dependent on you. You refused to let her work during your marriage, didn't you?'

'*Work!*' shouted Savage. 'You call arranging a few fucking twigs in a bucket *work*?'

'She was a society florist,' I reminded him, 'with three shops and a contract with Conran.'

Savage laughed his horrible, almost silent laugh, as I went upstairs to the 'flat' above the restaurant. I use ironic quote marks around 'flat' because it is actually a storeroom. I share my quarters with catering packs of gravy mix and huge tins of vegetables. Two gigantic freezers full of offal and cheap cuts of meat crowd my 'living room'. However, there is just room for a small MFI desk 'n' chair set (in black ash) and a two-seater sofa covered in a sunflower-print throw. (I feel an affinity with Van Gogh: both of us were rejected in our lifetimes by the metropolitan élite.) I changed into my chef's whites, fed my goldfish, then went down to the kitchen and began to prepare for the few customers who would pass Savage's exacting entrance stipulations. Saturday's menu is always:

*Prawn cocktail*

❧

*Ox liver, bacon, onions*
*Boiled potatoes*
*Ringed carrots*
*Peas – Birds Eye*
*Oxo gravy*

❧

*Co-op jam roly-poly*
*Lumpy Bird's custard (skin £10 extra,*
*due to weekend supplement)*

❧

*Nescafé*
*After Eight Mint*


I was annoyed to find that no one had remembered to defrost the ox liver, so I had to put the frozen lumps into the oven on a low heat. The vegetables had been prepared, so I made up five litres of gravy. While that was boiling, I mixed the Bird's custard powder, milk and sugar together in a large bowl, being careful not to blend the mixture too carefully as this destroys the lumps when the hot milk is added.

Luigi came in and took off his coat, hat, shoes and socks. 'I gotta wash my feet inna sink,' he said, climbing on to the draining-board. 'I gotta that bleddy whatchewmacallit?' he said, placing his feet under the running cold tap. 'Athlete's feet!' He plucked the phrase triumphantly from the air of the doctor's surgery where he'd first heard it spoken. 'It's itching me like crazy,' he said, scratching between his toes.

I glanced at the notice on the staff toilet door: 'Please wash your hands,' it said. There was no mention of feet. Savage lurched into the kitchen and staggered into the toilet. He didn't bother closing the door and a sound like the Zambezi in spate was clearly heard.

I rushed down the passageway, and slammed the door shut. I came back to see Malcolm, the washer-upper, unzipping his blouson jacket. He was visibly upset. I asked him what was wrong.

'Tha's out of order,' he said, nodding towards Luigi's feet in the sink. 'Tha's my territory, that sink, an' whadif the 'ealth inspect us, eh?'

Luigi screamed, 'I been working in restaurants for twenty-seven year. I served Princess Margaret and Tony, an' Cassius Clay an' Tommy Steele. These are personal friends of mine. Sophia Loren came to see me whenever she was in London, and once she said to me, "Luigi, I gotta word of advice for you. Always look after your feet." ' Luigi swung his feet out of the sink and dried them on a couple of clean tea towels.

Malcolm said, 'As if!' and wrapped himself in his grease-stained apron.

I busied myself with defrosting the ox liver. I don't involve myself with the constant kitchen rows. I am called Head Chef but this means nothing: I am low down in the pecking order at Hoi Polloi. I am

75

employed solely for my pure English genes, and my authentic working-class food background.

Savage emerged from the lavatory after ten minutes, looking bright-eyed and happy. I pointed out to him that he'd got talcum powder on the end of his nose. He laughed and said, 'Missed a bit, eh?' and went into the restaurant to unlock the front door. The waiters, Kenneth and Sean, were half an hour late, and where were my assistant cooks, Sasha and Aziz?

It was fifteen minutes to 'dishing-up time' when Jimmy the Greek came into the kitchen from the taverna next door. He said that the Greek community in Britain voted Labour because of a promise made by Neil Kinnock twelve years ago that the Elgin marbles would be returned to the Parthenon as soon as the Labour Party gained power. Jimmy had come round in the hope of seeing a famous Labour Party face . . . one that he could petition.

As I turned the spitting slices of ox liver in the roasting tin, I said, 'I didn't know you were interested in historical artefacts, Jimmy.'

'We was stitched up by Lord Elgin and the Turks,' said Jimmy, flicking cigarette ash into the sink. 'I want justice for my country. I would *die* for Greece!' he added, melodramatically.

'I wouldn't die for England,' said Malcolm. 'It's never done me no favours.'

'Well, thanks to Nato and the nuclear deterrent,

neither of you will be asked to lay down your lives,' I said. 'Now, if you don't mind, I've got sixty-two people waiting to be fed, and no staff!' I threw a fish-slice across the kitchen. I occasionally indulge in fits of bad temper. People expect it of a Head Chef, and it reduces my stress levels, according to my ex-stress counsellor, Sky Lupin.

Malcolm said, 'I'll help you out with the waitering, but I ain't doin' it for three quid an hour.'

I said, 'Malcolm, look at yourself. You are seriously unkempt. You were born to live behind the scenes.'

To my amazement his eyes filled with tears. 'Yeah, well, that's what you think, Moley. Tony Blair's gonna look after me from now on. I'm workin' class, an' Labour 'as always looked after the workin' class.'

'Yes,' I agreed, 'but they're not going to provide free grooming and elocution lessons for you, are they?'

'No, but I'll get an education, won' I?' he said. 'Tony promised, he said it three times.' He spoke of Mr Blair as though he were a personal friend.

'You'll have to learn to *read* before you get an education,' I said. I regretted these words the moment they were out of my mouth.

Malcolm said, 'That's the education I'm talkin' about. Tone's gonna teach me to read.'

I began to slop chilled prawn cocktail from a catering pack into sixty fruit sundae bowls (two of the diners were allergic to shellfish). Savage came into the kitchen shouting, 'Where's the f------ starter? I've

77

got Michael Jackson waiting for his f------ dinner out there, on table twelve.'

Luigi said, 'Why's crazy Michael come to Hoi Polloi? I heard he only eats mung beans and bean-sprouts in a oxygen tent with a trained nurse standing by an' a helicopter hovering.'

Malcolm said, 'As 'e got Bubbles, 'is monkey, with 'im?'

As soon as Savage had gone back into the dining room, there was a stampede to the swing door and we all jostled to get a look at the singer and plastic-surgery victim. However, table twelve was devoid of a man with a plastic nose or a monkey. Four men in Armani suits were deep in conversation.

Luigi looked in the reservations book. One of the men was Michael Jackson, the newly appointed head of Channel Four. I sent Malcolm upstairs to the flat to bring down the synopsis of my twelve-part comedy-drama series, *The White Van*, which is about a man, Godfrey Hetherington, who by day is a BBC accountant but by night is a serial killer. Godfrey drives around the Home Counties in a white Bedford van, murdering women.

The BBC turned it down in February.


THE WHITE VAN – A SYNOPSIS

The White Van *is a television comedy drama in twelve half-hours.*

The hero is Godfrey Hetherington (Harry Enfield), who

by day is a BBC accountant and by night is a serial killer who drives around the Home Counties in a white van, murdering women.

The comedy arises from the fact that Godfrey's wife Gloria (Pauline Quirke) knows nothing of her husband's nocturnal activities. She thinks he's on a charity soup-run for the homeless.

The laughs come thick and fast as a blundering police inspector (David Jason) comes close to catching Godfrey, only to see him make his escape yet again.

There will be twelve glamorous victims who perish by twelve ingenious methods. The British public enjoy a good laugh, and also (perversely some might say) are fascinated by serial killers. *The White Van* is an ingenious fusion of the two.

To be shot at BBC White City and various Home Counties locations.

*The White Van* is a parable of our times.

A. A. Mole

(Note: the above actors have yet to be approached.)

END

Kenneth and Sean turned up just in time to help garnish the prawn cocktails with sprigs of not-so-fresh parsley. They claimed they were late because they'd been stuck at Mornington Crescent on the Northern Line for an hour and a half in the dark. I asked the reason for the delay. Sean said, 'Rats had chewed

through the electrical cables and stopped the train.'
I asked him how he knew. He said, 'I looked out of
the carriage window and there was this rat, as big as
a *dog*, it was, staring back at me, and, I swear on my
mother's life, it had a piece of cable hanging there in
its fat chops.'

Kenneth said, 'You lying Irish toe-rag. I saw no
rat, no, it was a suicide. It always takes an hour and
a half to scrape the body off the line. You could set
your watch to it.'

'Probably somebody what voted Conservative,'
said Malcolm, attempting and failing to make a
joke.

We discussed possible reasons for the no-show of
Sasha and Aziz. The consensus was that they'd been
rounded up by the immigration authorities, which is
a constant hazard in the catering industry. It makes
long-term planning impossible, and certainly screws
up holiday rotas, etc.

Malcolm formally asked to be promoted to kitchen
assistant. I said I would talk to Savage when he was
sober (never). Malcolm then started banging on about
a minimum wage, and rights and conditions. I warned
him against such dangerous talk in the kitchen,
though I said it kindly, to show him that I was
sympathetic, in principle, to improving our terrible
working practices at Hoi Polloi.

Without Sasha and Aziz, Savage was forced to help
me out as I plated up the sixty-two ox-liver dinners.
Malcolm was given a wooden spoon and entrusted

with warming up the gravy in the cauldron on the stove.

At 10 p.m. Kenneth and Liam reported that the diners were becoming tired of waiting for their main course, and several had complained about the withered condition of the parsley garnish.

Savage roared, 'Tell the f----rs to go to one of the Conran joints if it's *freshness* they want.'

Eventually, when all the diners were chewing on their ox liver (it had emerged from the oven slightly tougher than I had intended), I stood at the interconnecting door and scanned the dining room for famous faces. Mr Mandelson had his usual table in the far corner: he likes to have his back to the wall. Harry Enfield was eating with Edward, his father, and also at the table was Richard Ingrams, who is the editor of the *Oldie*, the magazine for old people. I have been a subscriber for a year. My subscription was a thirtieth-birthday present to myself. Some people scoffed at the time. (My wife Jo Jo is convinced I am the reincarnation of an ancient African woman, and indeed my grandmother used frequently to say to me, 'Adrian, you were *born* old.' It's true that we used to share many of the same enthusiasms: Radio Four, Jif Lemon, Yorkshire pudding, correct punctuation, etc., etc.)

Savage was dining *à deux* with a slim blonde woman, who was pushing pieces of liver around her plate with a look of disgust.

Kim Savage entered via the kitchen entrance. She

joined me at the door to the restaurant; her perfume almost made me swoon. 'What's your scent called?' I asked.

'Poison,' she said, narrowing her eyes as she watched Savage clinking glasses with the blonde woman.

Kim tossed back her mane of black hair. In 1987 she was voted Miss Flower by readers of *Floristry Today*.

I examined Savage's companion. 'Who is she?' I asked.

'Bridget Jones,' spat out Kim. 'Her diaries have been in the bestseller list for months.'

'Her diaries?' I checked. 'But she's not famous, is she?'

'No,' said Kim, 'although she might be if Savage makes her his fifth wife.'

But, as I watched, Bridget Jones got up from the table and left the restaurant abruptly.

Savage shouted after her, 'Yes, your bum *does* look big in those bloody trousers.'

Kim said, 'Tell that fat bastard he owes me three months' maintenance.' And left.

Savage saw me at the door and shouted, 'Get back to the f------ kitchen, Mole.'

Mr Ingrams looked at me sympathetically before I turned back to my lowly duties.

I dished up the jam roly-poly, and was angered when I realized that Malcolm had puréed all the lumps in the custard *and thrown the skin away*! There it lay in the pig bin, like a large withered yellow balloon. Luigi scooped up the skin between two fish-slices and washed it under the hot tap, saying, 'Nobody ain't gonna know it's been in the bin.'

I watched in shocked silence as he divided the custard skin into four pieces and took them out to table twelve: a special request, apparently, to celebrate Mr Jackson's new, exalted position.

In the lull between the pudding and the Nescafé-and-After-Eight course, I phoned Wisteria Walk. My mother answered. 'Your dad's got something wrong with his scalp,' she said.

'He's always had chronic dandruff,' I reminded her.

'No, this is something else,' she quavered. 'He saw the back of his head in the bedroom mirror and went hysterical. I had to call the doctor out.'

'What's wrong with him, then?' I said. 'Apart from the fact that he's being cuckolded.'

She ignored my mumbled reference to her probable infidelity.

'His scalp's gone *black*,' she said. 'It's especially bad on his bald spot. Dr Chaudri's baffled. It *looks* like gangrene,' she added.

'Gangrene!' I shouted. Malcolm and Luigi looked up from distributing the After Eights on the coffee saucers. 'If it's gangrene he'll have to have his head amputated,' I said.

My mother didn't laugh, but Malcolm and Luigi did. They laughed themselves stupid. They were still laughing when Savage announced that the politically incorrect notice in the window had been torn down by a delegation of journalists from the *Daily Telegraph*. Another sign that the formerly right-wing paper is slowly but surely moving towards left of centre.

## Saturday May 3rd

My father's gangrenous bonce is better, according to the latest medical reports.

After a restless night, he was persuaded to lie in a warm bath that had been infused with an essential oil (marigold). He massaged his scalp with seaweed and conditioned the little hair left on his head with a purée manufactured from an Irish bog plant. When he emerged from the bathroom, his scalp, according to my mother, was 'it's usual nice pink'.

My mother sees this episode as a glorious victory for the powers of plant therapy. I hope she never finds out about the felt-tip pen. She has been disillusioned too many times in her life.

Kim came round this morning with two beefy blokes, and removed five crates of champagne from the cellar. 'Tell Savage it's part payment for the money he owes me,' she said.

I couldn't work out why she had aged so dramatically overnight. Then I realized: it was the first time I had seen her in the cruel light of a Soho day.

## Sunday May 4th

After cooking lunch –

*Scrag end of lamb*
*Roast potatoes*
*Turnip chunks*
*Boiled cauliflower*
*Damp Yorkshire pudding*
❧

*Plum Duff*
*Tinned Carnation milk*
❧

*Nescafé*
*After Eight Mint*


– I left Malcolm toiling over the tins in the sink, and went upstairs to the flat. I worked all afternoon on my television series, *The White Van*. I made good progress on Part Three. I really feel that I have found my 'voice'. What a joy it is to hone my craft, and lose myself in the world that my characters inhabit. I got up and looked moodily out of the window. I expect that from the street below I looked like a character (a writer perhaps) in a French film. I was dreading the next day. I always hated Mondays. Tripe day. I have begged Savage to take it off the menu, but to no avail.

## Monday May 5th
*Bank Holiday, UK and Republic of Ireland*

I saw Will Self today. Talk about street cred. The man has everything. Height, looks, dress sense and the biggest vocabulary in London, if not the country. Also, he has written a ground-breaking book where a tramp has sex with a dead dog, or a dog has sex with a dead tramp, I forget which.

## Tuesday May 6th

The staff toilet floor was sprinkled with talcum powder when I went in tonight. Savage was the last occupant before me. What does he do in there that necessitates the use of talcum powder? I shudder to think.

## Wednesday May 7th
*Muslim New Year*

Pandora and her fellow Blair's Babes were photographed with Tony outside Parliament. Pandora showed the most teeth, cleavage and leg, and managed to position herself next to Mr Blair. In one photograph she has an arm draped casually around his shoulder, as though they were equals.

After work tonight I went to the exclusive opening of Large Alan's new drinking-club venture, The 165, which is named after the remaining Tory MPs. It's in a basement in Brewer Street.

Justine was there in the role of Alan's hostess. She seemed to know most of the MPs by name.

If pinstripes were water, I would have died of drowning.

Nicki Hasnun, designer of The 165, was there. He was banging on about his influences – which apparently include Pugin and what he called dictator kitsch! He is a friend of somebody called Mobutu.

If forced to describe the décor, I would have to say, 'Gothic classicism with animal prints, or St Pancras station meets Whipsnade Zoo.' The effect was horribly unsettling. I asked Large Alan how he managed to get the builders in and out in only five days. He looked down at me from his great height and said what sounded like 'kneecaps'. Though I may have misheard him – there was a high level of decibels in the cramped space.

Some of the noise was caused by a loud argument being conducted by a knot of Tory MPs, about the appointment of their new leader. Half favoured Michael Howard (the Extra Virgin of Smarm) and the others fancied William Hague (whom privately I believe to be Margaret Thatcher's Love Child).

## Thursday May 8th
*World Red Cross Day – Ascension Day*

Let's examine the facts that inform my Thatcher
mother/Hague son theory.

1. Hague was christened William. Presumably after William Pitt, one of MT's heroes.
2. Hague's so-called 'parents' manufacture and deliver fizzy drinks and cordials.
3. Margaret Thatcher's father *sold* fizzy drinks and cordials in his shop.
4. During the last four months before William Hague's birth on March 26th 1961, Margaret Thatcher was mysteriously out of the country in Switzerland. An obstetric centre of excellence.
5. When William Hague addressed the Conservative Party conference, aged sixteen, Margaret Thatcher listened to him with rapt *maternal* pride. I know, I've checked the video. Hers was the face of an adoring mother.
6. They have the same hair colour.
7. The same colour eyes.
8. They are both going bald.
9. They both read Hansard for pleasure, in bed.
10. There was another important fact, but I've forgotten it.

## Friday May 9th

Zippo Montefiori, the managing director of Pie Crust Productions, was thirty years old today, and he chose to celebrate this landmark by taking over the whole of Hoi Polloi for a private party.

The good-luck fairy must have spent longer over his crib than she did over mine. He is what I heard one woman describe as 'devilishly good-looking', with black floppy hair and eyes like a Labrador. He is never seen without his black Armani overcoat – yet he never sweats. He speaks slowly with a voice as smooth as a conker, and he looks into your eyes as though searching for your soul.

There is reputed to be a waiting list of women wanting to go out with him.

He is a great fan of institutional food – he went to Harrow. The menu included some of his offal favourites. I also threw a few plastic caterpillars in the salad for public-school authenticity. At the end of the evening Zippo came into the kitchen to thank the staff. 'Fab scoff,' he said, 'and the caterpillars were a hoot.' After a bit of a chat about where I had 'sourced' the caterpillars (a joke shop in Leicester), he asked me if I'd ever thought about appearing on television!

'As what?' I asked.

'As a cook,' he said. 'You could do some of your offal specialities.'

I explained that I was something of an intellectual, and didn't watch or own a television. He said that he would send one round and have it installed free of charge so that I could watch the cookery programmes that Pie Crust Productions made!

I found it hard to sleep, partly because of a loud brawl downstairs involving Savage and Kim, but mainly due to the terror I felt at the thought of appearing on TV as a chef. The truth is, I can't cook.

## Saturday May 10th

The television arrived today. Also a video.
  Savage is in St Thomas's Hospital having his broken jaw wired together. His ex-wife has been arrested for GBH. It's Savage's fault. He confessed (boasted) to her that during their marriage he had faked most of his orgasms.

## Sunday May 11th
*Sunday after Ascension Day*

Zippo rang me at 8.30 a.m. and asked me to watch one of Pie Crust's programmes, *The Fry-Up*, which was on at 9 p.m. He is certainly enthusiastic. I have made up my mind not to appear on TV. However, I did manage to video *The Fry-Up*, after phoning Dixons for instructions.

I phoned home and spoke to my father; only he and William were in. Rosie hadn't come home from the night before, and my mother has started taking the New Dog for long walks early every morning. 'The dog's knackered by the time it gets back,' said my father.

I was immediately suspicious and asked him about the average duration and exact route of these 'walks'. As I suspected, she usually goes down the bridlepath that runs at the back of the Braithwaites' house, and then into the woods. I happen to know that there is a gate in the wall that connects the Braithwaites' garden to the bridlepath. I also happen to know that Mrs Braithwaite leaves the house at 8.30 a.m. to go to her job, teaching Women's Studies at De Montfort University. I also happen to know another fact: Ivan Braithwaite works from home – *in the garden*, in a centrally heated wooden chalet with a Tyrolean-style sun-deck. I have been inside this chalet. It is well equipped; there is a desk, a modem, a swivel chair, mains drainage, a kettle, a cafetière, *and a chaise longue*. I, sadly, rest my case.

I must get hold of Pandora's phone numbers and warn her of the calamitous situation that has united the House of Mole and the House of Braithwaite.

## Monday May 12th

Savage is out of hospital. He can't eat solid food yet, but he seems happy enough sucking his rum and black through a drinking straw. Lunch today was:

*Fried eggs (two)\**
*Fat chips – cooked in lard*
*Marrowfat peas*
*Two slices of sliced white buttered bread*
*HP sauce* or *Heinz ketchup*

&

*Kit-Kat* or *Wagon Wheel*

&

*Nescafé*
*After Eight Mint*

\* Please be assured: all our eggs are laid by battery hens.

I got a delivery of videos of *The Fry-Up*. They were presented by a man with side-whiskers and a Cockney accent. It was a farrago from start to finish. The bewhiskered Cockney is, he tells us, in his tiresome rhyming slang, the owner of a Sylvia Plath (a workman's caff!). This Cockney person's name is Alfie Caine. I watched all six of his half-hour shows.

- Sausages: Thick or Thin?
- Eggs: The Membrane Factor
- Bacon: How to Reduce Pan Curl
- Tomatoes: Fresh or Tinned?
- Fried Bread: Guaranteed Success
- Beans, Mushrooms, Black Pudding: Do They Belong?

I transcribed a few sentences of this man's hideous patter from the Fried Bread show: 'So, you good steeple out there, wanna snow how to book dyed head, do you? Smell, whatcha gotta November is to keep your hat snot in the man.'

I have met many Cockneys since I moved to London eight years ago, including a man who was born in the very nave of Bow Bells, and none of them have ever used 'snot' for not, or 'November' for remember. Alfie Caine is a total fraud.

When Zippo rang I gave him my honest opinion of *The Fry Up*, and said that I couldn't be associated with such a tawdry enterprise. Zippo laughed and said that *The Fry Up* was a heavily ironic post-modernist deconstruction of the cookery show as naff entertainment. 'Didn't you get the Sylvia Plath clue?' he asked.

'So, it was meant to be *funny*?' I said.

'Of course,' he said.

'But it didn't make me laugh,' I said.

Zippo sighed. 'Laughter is kind of not where it's *at* with Pie Crust Productions. Our target audience are students who have failed to do any revision or any essays, and expect to fail their exams. It's a show for losers.'

I was dumbfounded and asked how many viewers watched the Pie Crust shows. 'Seven hundred and fifty-three thousand people tuned in to Tomatoes: Fresh or Tinned?,' said Zippo. 'We're getting a lot of interest from the advertisers.'

'Which products do failed students buy?' I asked.

'Catfood mainly,' he said, 'followed by Cadbury's Creme Eggs, Strongbow Cider and Pot Noodles.'

'So how much does Alfie Caine get paid per show?' I asked.

'Alfie's got an agent, so that bumps it up a bit,' he said.

'So how much does he get?' I pressed.

'I couldn't possibly divulge that, it would be terribly unprofessional of me, but let's say it's in the region of the price of a package holiday to Tenerife.'

'High or low season?' I asked.

'Oh, high,' he said. 'We're talking *August* here.'

'A one- or two-week holiday?' I asked.

'Two,' he said, 'half-board, balcony with a sea view.'

I didn't like the way he was assuming I would *know* the price of a package holiday to Tenerife in August, but I let it pass. 'And this Tenerife package, that's per show, is it?' I checked.

'Of course it's per show,' he said.

I said I would ring him back in half an hour. I rang Thomas Cook on Regent Street, then rang Zippo back and said I would do it.

*4 a.m.* Can't sleep, can't cook.

*5 a.m.* Read the *Leicester Mercury*, which my mother posts to me because it isn't available in London.

I was shocked to see that my old school, Neil Armstrong Comprehensive, has been deemed one of the 297 failing schools. A hit squad is due to stage a coup within days. In my time, when it was ruled by the headmaster 'Pop-Eye' Scruton, it had a good reputation. Its football team did well, and it regularly won the Midlands Inter-County Schools Chess Club Trophy. It also had a renowned school magazine, *The Voice of Youth*, edited by me. Then Roger Patience took over as headmaster. I expect he's sorry now that he asked the pupils to call him Roger, and told them to throw away their school uniforms.

## Tuesday May 13th

I wrote a letter to Delia Smith.

Dear Ms Smith,

Forgive me for addressing you as 'Ms' if you are in fact a married woman. I am writing to you in the strictest confidence. I am absolutely certain that you will respect my wishes in this matter as I have read somewhere that you are a Christian woman. I, too, live by the tenets of

95

the Christian philosophy. Though I have not been blessed, as you have, in that God has not visited me yet and assured me that He, or indeed She, exists. However, this letter is not about our respective positions on whether God exists or not. It is about cooking.

Perhaps you have heard of me. I am currently the Head Chef of Hoi Polloi.

My problem, Ms Smith, is that my position at Hoi Polloi does not require that I have any culinary skills. I simply defrost, boil, fry or warm up pre-cooked food. I literally cannot, satisfactorily, boil an egg.

I have searched the bookshops in vain for an absolutely basic cookery book. But in vain. Please help me. I have been asked to go on Cable TV's Millennium Channel to demonstrate my art, but there *is* no art. Please save me from utter humiliation.

I remain, Madam, your most humble and obedient servant.

A. A. Mole

## Wednesday May 14th

I rang Pandora at the House of Commons this morning. A polite man on the switchboard said, 'Ah, Dr Braithwaite, the member for Ashby-de-la-Zouch. She hasn't been allocated an office yet, sir, but if you'd like to leave a message, I'll make sure her secretary gets back to you.'

I asked for the name of her 'secretary' and was mildly amused to be told that it was Edna Kent – the same name as Barry Kent's mother! A strange coincidence.

I have been reading Bridget Jones's diary in the *Independent*. The woman is obsessed with herself! She writes as though she were the only person in the world to have problems. I'm sure that it is quite brave to share your sad life with perfect strangers, even if they are *Independent* readers, and therefore composed largely of caring professionals.

I drafted a letter to Ms Jones.


Dear Bridget Jones,

I have been reading your entries in the *Independent*, and we also have another tenuous connection. I am Peter Savage's Head Chef at Hoi Polloi.

I will cut to the chase: I have kept a diary since I was 13 or thereabouts, and believe it may be of interest to the general reader, and also to Sociologists and future Historians.

How did you get your Diaries published?

I would be grateful if you would write back to me – or alternatively ring me at the Hoi Polloi and we can arrange to meet somewhere over a coffee (or a glass of white wine!).

Yours, A. A. Mole

PS. I am a non-smoker.

I've decided to record my own personal daily fluc-
tuations.


Opal Fruits – 2 pkts
Alcohol – nil
Cigarettes – nil
Weight – 10 stone, 8 pounds
Bowels – sluggish
Potential bald spot – stable
Pains – throbbing in big toe (left foot)
Spots – one, on chin
Penis function – 3/10
Drugs – Prozac, Nurofen


**Thursday May 15th**

Zippo lunched on braised brains at Hoi Polloi today.
He wants me to make a 'pilot' on this coming Sunday
afternoon. The working title is to be *Offally Good!*. He
thinks that offal is the coming thing in food fashion.
'Offal is the new black,' he said.

I didn't know what he was talking about, but I
nodded politely. I haven't told anybody (apart from
Delia Smith) about the making of the pilot.

I promised to go to Leicester this Sunday to see
William, but I'll have to find an excuse. My mother
must not find out. I could not bear her disappoint-

ment if Pie Crust Productions decide not to go ahead with a series. Also, she will only tell Tout Le Monde of Ashby-de-la-Zouch. Listened to a discussion about the Queen's Speech in the kitchen. Malcolm was happy about the proposed Minimum Wage Bill, though Savage said if it becomes law he will sack us all and employ illegal immigrants from Somalia.

## Friday May 16th

Opal Fruits – 3 pkts
Alcohol – six double vodkas, 2 tonics
Cigarettes – nil
Drugs – 4 Nurofen, 1 Jazz Fag (shared with Malcolm)
Bowels – no movement
Weight – 10 stone 7 pounds
Thinning patch – stable
Spots – 1 on chin (growing)
Penis function – listless

Edna Kent rang me at lunchtime today. Savage is still answering the telephone, though his jaw is wired together (no wonder bookings are down), so there was an initial confusion about who she was, and to whom she wanted to speak. It took a couple of minutes before I could fully take in the astonishing fact that *Edna Kent*, council tenant, widow of a milkman, eleven-plus failure, secondary-school drop-out, aged *fifty-five*, is indeed working in the House of Commons as the secretary of the cleverest woman in Britain.

I asked how she had made the dramatic change from lavatory cleaner to her present prestigious position. She laughed. 'Education, education, education,' she said, sounding like Malcolm. 'I used to clean lavvies at the university, and to be quite honest with you, Aidy, I've never heard such bleddy rubbish what them professors and lecturers talked in there. So I enrolled on one of them Access courses.' (I longed to interrupt her and say, 'Not *them* Access courses, Edna, it's *those* Access courses,' but, of course, I couldn't, I couldn't. I was talking to a *graduate* for Christ's sake. *A double graduate.*)

'My first degree's in Family Law,' she said. She had a head start on this one: the amount of times her children have been up before the courts. 'And my second is in Business Studies. Our Barry reckoned I ought to be up to date with the new technology, e-mail, and the web and suchlike.'

I could hardly speak. I felt a paroxysm of jealous rage. I managed to croak out, 'Well, congratulations, Mrs Kent. I had no idea you'd changed careers.'

'I kept it quiet,' she said. 'You know how jealous folk get round our way if you try to better yourself. Our Barry found that out when he had all that success.'

'Well-deserved success,' I said, hypocritically.

I think Barry Kent is a talentless fraud who has

forged a career out of pandering to his fellow yobs. It kills me. *Kills* me to know that his *Dork's Diary* has been described as a modern classic, and that eight years on it is still to be found in a prominent position in most good bookshops. Whenever I see its gaudy cover (a cat wearing a football shirt and football boots), I take great delight in hiding all copies behind the books of Charles Dickens, who is at least a competent writer of the English language.

Mrs Kent said, 'Anyroad up, Aidy, what was it you wanted? Only I've got a lot to do. Pan's working on her maiden speech and I'm trying to get to grips with me new laptop.'

Through gritted teeth I said, 'It's a personal matter, Mrs Kent. Ask her to phone me on my mobile, will you?'

I gave her the number and she said, 'You must come and see us at the House, Aidy. We can have tea on the terrace.'

After I'd put the phone down I thought of the last time I'd had tea with Mrs Kent. We'd been surrounded by the unruly Kent children, the teapot was cracked, the kitchen stank because of an overflowing cat-litter tray, and Mrs Kent was dressed in a wraparound pinafore, her lank hair tied back in an elastic band. At no time did she *ever* display the intelligence needed to study for *two* degrees. Whereas I, with my knowledge of world literature and extensive vocabulary, struggled mightily to get two A levels (each on the third attempt). Why? Why? Why?

## Saturday May 17th

I rang my mother this morning and told her the lie that I had gone down with gastroenteritis, was dehydrated, never off the toilet, etc. While on the phone I asked her why she hadn't told me about Edna Kent's educational achievements. She went very quiet for a long time, and then said, 'Because I didn't know.'

## Sunday May 18th
*Pentecost*

A truly terrible day. I arrived at the Brent Cross shopping-centre car park, to find that my car had been towed away five days ago and was in a police compound. A £25 cab ride took me to somewhere in Archway, whereupon I found that I was required to stump up £239. I did not have enough cash on me, and I had left my credit cards in my second-best jacket. I took another cab ride back to Dean Street (£8.50), where I found my mother, father and William ensconced in my flat/storeroom. Savage had let them in, having managed to convey, through wired jaws, that I had lied to them about the gastroenteritis.

I found my Access card and persuaded my father to drive me to Purley, whereupon I managed to retrieve my car. Though it probably took a year off my life, so *enraged* was I. In fact, I could feel a stroke coming on as I signed the receipt and the credit slip. It didn't help when William decided to have one of his Vesuvius-like tantrums because I wouldn't stop the car and buy him a kid's meal at McDonald's. My mother insisted on coming to Pie Crust's production offices in Shoreditch, saying, 'This is something I have to see.' Her face fell when she saw that she would have to climb up six flights of fire escape.

Zippo and the others in the production team were very laid back about the fact that I had brought my family along, but I could tell that they were 'terribly amused'.

Zippo kissed my mother's hand, and complimented her on the shirt she was wearing. 'Is it Vivienne Westwood?' he murmured.

'No,' she murmured back. 'It's Bhs.'

'You clever *thing*,' he crooned.

He charmed my father by telling him an obscene joke about Prince Edward, and won William over by telling him that he drove a Ferrari in town, and a Cadillac pick-up truck in the country.

Because we were late there was no proper rehearsal time. After I'd changed into my chef's whites, a plump, middle-aged production assistant called Cath showed me quickly around the sink and stove. She opened the fridge and nodded towards a tray of assorted offal and several bowls of chopped-up vegetables. She pointed to the stock cubes, tapped on the saucepans, indicated the knife rack and pushed a jug full of wooden spoons towards me, all without speaking a word.

'Cath, who's the salt of the earth, will be helping out in the background,' said Zippo. 'Don't speak to her in front of the camera, whatever you do.'

'Is she a deaf mute?' I inquired.

'No,' said Zippo. 'We have to pay her Equity rates if she speaks.'

Somebody powdered my face and dabbed something on my lips. My mother spat on her forefinger and smoothed my eyebrows flat. The lights came on. Somebody else clipped a tiny microphone to my jacket.

Zippo shouted, 'OK, let's do it, people.' He pointed what he called a Steadicam towards me, the autocue started to roll, then his mobile went and he answered it, saying, 'Harvey, you old bugger! Yeah, it's called *Young Love*. We've got Goldie and Burt on board. It's 80 per cent financed. You will! You will! That's *magnifique*! Listen, Harvey, I'm in the middle of something *très, très ordinaire*, but can I call you back? Where are you? New York. Great! Great! Great! Great! Absolutely!'

My mother listened to this conversation with her lips parted and her tired eyes shining.

Zippo shouted to his PA, Belinda, 'We've got the green light for *Young Love*.' He turned back to me and said, 'Sorry about that, Adrian, but it's my first feature. OK, let's go through this as quickly as possible. Eh?'

It's not easy to read from an autocue while chopping offal at the same time, but here's what I said:

'Hi there, offal lovers or lovers of offal. It has to be said that offal has had a bad press. Jack the Ripper did this delicacy immeasurable harm and offal's image has never quite recovered. However, I hope to persuade you, our friends and viewers at home, that offal is the new black. So, if you've fed the cat, chomped on your Creme Egg and poured boiling water on to your Pot Noodles, all that remains is for you to grab a can of cider from the fridge. Push that essay to one side – you know you're never going to finish it. So, settle down and watch. I'm going to teach you how to make that pathetic student grant stretch. You can feed yourself really well for the price of a sheep's head and a few vegetables.'

William screamed when I produced a sheep's head from underneath the worktop, and he had to be taken out by my father when I cleavered the sheep's head in half. Unfortunately, 'Baa Baa Black Sheep' is his favourite nursery rhyme.

I looked into the camera lens and imagined 700,000 students watching. Some of them were bound to be studying French or French literature, so I threw in a few *bons mots*. As I scooped out the brains from the sheep's head I said, 'These are brains. Eating them won't necessarily make you clever, but who wants to be clever? As Flaubert said, "If you want to be happy, it is necessary not to be too intelligent."' I put the pieces of sheep's head in a stockpot full of water, with two lamb Oxo cubes and a sprinkling of dried rosemary. As it came to the boil, I lifted the scum off the top and said, 'This is scum. You'll be familiar with it if you frequent student-union bars.'

Zippo shouted, 'OK, that's it, it's a wrap.' There was applause, led by my mother. 'You're a natural, Aid,' he said. 'You pitched it perfectly. Liked the Flaubert, nice touch.' I didn't tell him that I'd been inspired by the Sylvia Plath rhyming slang.

Zippo had to rush off to Heathrow. He was going to LA to try and persuade Kim Basinger to make a trailer for his shows. For saying, 'Yum, if it's Pie Crust, it's gotta be good!' he's offering £50,000. Belinda (small, white face, red, red, full lips, Titian ringlets, DKNY sportswear and trainers) said that they'd be in touch to 'finalize a deal'.

As my mother and I trooped down the fire escape, she said, 'They'll stitch you up good and proper unless you get somebody who knows what's what.'

When we got to the car, she repeated this witch's warning in front of my father. He concurred with her, saying, 'Yeah, they're all sharks, these public-school boys,' and then he offered himself as my manager! A man whose only jobs have been in potato wholesale, storage-heater sales, spice-rack construction and canal-bank renovation. I politely turned down his offer. The atmosphere in the car was tense. Even William kept his mouth shut for once.

When we got back to the flat my mother took me aside and hissed, 'Thank you *very* much for destroying your father's confidence. It took a full hour to persuade him to get out of bed and drive me down here because of your *severe gastroenteritis*, which was so bad yesterday morning that you said you might have to go into hospital, *on a drip*.'

William gave me a get-well card that he'd made out of painted eggshells. I wish now that I had not told such a black lie: a grey one would have done perfectly well, and ensured that they'd all have stayed in Leicester. They left at 7 p.m.

My mother said she had to get back in time to walk the dog. She tried to kiss me, but I turned my cheek away from her adulterous lips.

## Monday May 19th

Pandora finally phoned me back at eight-thirty this morning. She said she'd already been to the gym and was now at her temporary desk in her temporary rooms in the Commons. I told her my suspicions about her father and my mother. She said, 'I know. They're in love – pathetic, isn't it?'

I asked her how she knew for sure, and she told

me that she'd found a fax from my mother addressed to her father. It was a verse of a John Betjeman poem. I was amazed on two counts:

(a) I didn't know that my mother had access to and knew how to use a fax machine.

(b) I didn't know that my mother liked the poetry of Sir John Betjeman, though I suppose he is still England's favourite modern poet. Just in front of Barry Kent (whom I *wish* were dead), Pam Ayres and Ted Hughes.

I asked her to fax the verse to me. She said she'd get Edna to do it. I asked her if our parents' affair could damage her politically. She said, 'I'm already under attack for wearing Chanel on election night. Some dreary little Labour Party Millbank *apparatchik* clad in a burgundy trouser suit from Principles said I must be seen to support the British fashion industry.'

I said, 'You're the Princess Di of the Commons, Pandora. You *should* set an example as *she* does.'

I heard the click of her lighter.

'Listen,' she said tersely, 'Princess Di may have been forced into wearing Catherine-bloody-Walker, but her handbags are still Hermès.'

I had no idea what she was talking about (I feel increasingly as though people are speaking in a sort of code, one to which I have been denied the key). I asked her what we ought to do about our parents. She laughed and said, 'We could encourage the other two, my mother and your father, to fall in love. They've both had mental health problems.'

'And they both dress badly.' I laughed. I asked Pandora if I could visit her in the House of Commons.

She said, 'I'm busy writing my maiden speech.'

I asked her what she proposed speaking about.

She said, 'You wouldn't be interested, Adrian.'

I said, 'Try me.'

She said, 'The recapitalization of defunct manufacturing industries.'

She was right. I wasn't interested.


## Wednesday May 21st

Kim Savage turned up at the restaurant just as lunch was about to be served to a full dining room. She overturned the bubble-and-squeak trolley and threw several bottles of HP sauce at the bar (only narrowly missing Nigel Dempster's head). The police were called, but she'd gone by the time they arrived, shrieking, 'That's what I think to your f------ injunction!' Savage went around the tables growling, 'See what you get when you marry into the lower classes.' He seemed uncaring of the fact that several members of the government and a high-ranking union official were in the room.

## Thursday May 22nd

Hoi Polloi was thronging with reporters from the tabloids and one from the Peterborough column in the *Telegraph* today. They were hoping, no doubt, for a report of yesterday's Kim Savage attack, which made most of the gossip columns in this morning's papers:

### SAVAGE ATTACK

Kim Savage, estranged fourth wife of Peter Savage (restaurateur and second son of the Earl of Boswell), astonished lunchers in Savage's fashionable Soho eatery, Hoi Polloi, yesterday, when she ran somewhat amok in the dining room, breaking a court injunction to stay away from the upmarket caff. Mrs Savage shouted at her cowering husband, 'And I know all about you and Ivana Trump, you dirty little s---.'

Mrs Savage, formerly society florist Kim Didcott, left the restaurant sobbing, comforted by a member of staff who commented, 'As Tolstoy said, each family is unhappy in its own way.'

Savage lined us all up tonight and demanded to know the name of the member of staff who comforted 'that mad bitch'.

Nobody said a word, but everyone in the kitchen

knows that I am a quarter of the way through *War and Peace*.

No word from Belinda of Pie Crust
No reply from Ms Smith
Alcohol – nil
Cigarettes – nil
Opal Fruits – 4 pkts
Drugs – 1 paracetamol
Bowels – large release of gas
Thin patch – no change
Penis activity – 5/10

## Friday May 23rd

Another snippet from the *Daily Mail* gossip column.

Yesterday's erudite spokesman on the sad business of the Savage marriage break-up has been revealed as Adrian 'Turd' Mole, Head Chef at Hoi Polloi. An insider said, 'He's been seen reading the Russian classics in lulls between courses.'

However, a little bird chirrups in my ear that Adrian may not be working at Hoi Polloi for much longer. He has been approached by Zippo Montefiori's company, Pie

Crust Productions, and is set to join the ever-growing ranks of TV cooks.

## Saturday May 24th

I came down this morning to find Savage slumped on a stool at the preparation table. He told me he'd been there since we closed at 3 a.m. and that he still loved his Kim. I asked him what had initially caused the marriage to break down, and he brushed away a tear. 'I paid for a ten-week course of elocution lessons for her,' he said. 'I couldn't bear that Essex accent on my pillow every morning.' He shuddered at the memory, as though his wife's accent was a physical thing: a loathsome insect crawling on his bedlinen. 'She ripped me off, Adrian,' he said. 'She didn't go to a single elocution lesson. She got her mate Joanna Lumley to give her a few pointers.'

'What did she spend the money on?' I asked.

He broke down completely, and sobbed like a small child. I patted his heaving shoulders. 'I gave her a thousand quid for those lessons,' he gulped, 'a thousand f------ quid. And d'you know what she blew it on?'

'Shoes?' I ventured.

He shook his head.

'A lover?'

'No, no.'

'Cocaine?'

'No!' he roared. 'Worse than that!' He lowered his head and his voice and whispered, 'She donated it to the f------ Labour Party!'

Was ever a man deceived?

It explains why Joanna Lumley is barred from Hoi Polloi for life.

## Sunday May 25th
*Trinity Sunday*

I took advantage of Savage's deep unhappiness to ask for a day off today. He said, 'Yeah. Going to see your son, the half-caste kid?'

I said, 'No, I'm just going to see *my son.*'

'I didn't know you had two,' he said.

I was determined to press the point home to him. 'I don't call him "my son the half-caste kid",' I said. 'His name is William.'

Savage could benefit from going on a racial-awareness course. I might suggest it to him. I find his prejudices most offensive. He is like *all* aristocratic people. They are *all* inbred, deranged sexual deviants who should be put up against the drystone walls of their country estates and, if not actually shot, then at least . . . made to feel very uncomfortable indeed.

I rang last night to tell my mother that I would be coming to Wisteria Walk and bringing a piece of illegal beef on the bone with me. Rosie answered the phone in her usual ungracious manner, which entails using the least possible vocal power without resorting to complete silence.

'Is Dad there?'

'Yuh.'

There was a long pause, though I could hear snotty breathing. 'Rosie?' I said.

'Yuh.'

'Can I *speak* to Dad?' I shouted.

'He's in bed,' she shouted back, and then she actually volunteered the information that he'd been in bed for a week with severe depression, brought about by the stress of his driving in London last Sunday. I asked where William was and she told me that he was sitting in an empty Kellogg's cornflakes box in front of the television, watching a Jeremy Clarkson video. This bleak image brought a lump to my throat, and I couldn't wait to get to Ashby-de-la-Zouch and hold the boy in my arms.

*Later*

Apart from seeing William my visit was a waste of valuable time. Nobody would eat the beef on the bone. My mother was out most of the afternoon, 'walking the dog', my father was in bed with the curtains drawn, and Rosie left the house with a hideous-looking youth called Aaron Michelwaite, whose face is deformed with lip, eyebrow, nose, eyelid, ear and tongue rings. Rosie saw me gawping and said, 'You should see his Prince Albert.' Once again I didn't get the reference.

I could barely be civil to the youth. He is extremely well spoken, but he is far too old for Rosie (he is nineteen), and I hinted to him that my sister is a virgin and I would prefer it if she stayed in that condition for as long as possible. I said, 'Rosie may look like Baby Spice, but she's an *innocent*, do you understand, Aaron?'

'Innocent.' He snorted. 'I've had more than *cider* with Rosie, mate.' At the time I took his punning remark to mean that they shared a taste for strong alcohol – vodka, perhaps. But as I drove back to London I pondered on his oblique reference to Laurie Lee's classic, and I am now convinced that they are in fact having a full-blown sexual relationship.

Saw thirteen Eddie Stobarts. Nine waved, four didn't.


Bowels – blocked
Penis – unresponsive to stimuli

## Monday May 26th

Belinda from Pie Crust Productions rang, but I was in the middle of a tricky stage with some lambs' testicles, so I couldn't take the call.

Luigi tells me that a Prince Albert is a ring-chain device worn on the penis. I have written to Rosie. I feel that I am *in loco parentis*.

'My dear Rosie . . . that' is as far as I got. I was so outraged by the thought of Aaron Michelwaite's Prince Albert that I threw down my pen in disgust.

## Friday May 30th

Malcolm took a message from Belinda at Pie Crust, begging me to ring her back. Malcolm said, 'She sounded as if she was gagging for it.' I led him to believe that Belinda's interest in me was sexual.

Edna rang, cancelling my appointment with Pandora. She has to wait in – she's having a futon delivered. I pointed out to Edna that I could go round to Pandora's flat, which I've never seen, and wait in with her, but apparently she wants to wait for her futon alone.

## Saturday May 31st

Belinda strode into the restaurant kitchen today and said, 'OK, I'm not proud. I've come to you to beg you to do it.'

Malcolm, Luigi and the temporary kitchen assistants, Sven and Boris, goggled at her Lycra-clad breasts and bum in her cycling shorts-vest combo. I steered her outside into the yard where all the fire extinguishers are kept until the fire officer rings to tell us he's coming round to do an inspection.

'I've changed my mind,' I said. 'I can't cook,' I admitted.

Ever since Savage spilled his guts to me (if only he had literally spilled them, I would have gladly cooked them up with a bit of garlic salt and enjoyed eating them) – about his undying love for Kim, he has totally ignored me. I asked him this morning if he had ordered the tinned carrots, saying, 'We are dangerously low.' But he looked straight through me. I am always aware when we are low on carrots because I use the stacked tins as my bedside tables.

## Sunday June 1st

I spent the day alone, with the *Observer*. There was a cat in the kitchen yard today that looked amazingly like Humphrey, the cat who once resided at No. 10 Downing Street before Cherie Blair begged her husband to dispose of it, 'by foul means or fair' – this is according to a high-ranking member of the RSPCA, who told Luigi, who told Malcolm, who told *me*.

The cat I saw this morning was undoubtedly Humphrey: thinner, scraggier, flea-ridden and lacking any formal identification, but it was *he*, of that I have no doubt. Stories of him 'going to a good home, somewhere in Streatham' are false. No doubt the truth will come out one day when Cabinet papers are released under the thirty-year rule. I will be sixty-plus by then, but I will have the quiet satisfaction of knowing that I fed several cod's heads to the Prime Minister's spurned cat, thus helping it to survive in the mean streets of Soho.

### Monday June 2nd

Humphrey was at the kitchen door mewing pathetically this morning. Malcolm wanted to take him home, but I pointed out that a dormitory in a hostel was a home in name only. I think he saw my point. But he went out after his duties at lunchtime and bought Humphrey an engraved cat collar. Unfortunately Malcolm was 'taught' by the phonetic method of spelling, so the cat is now called 'Humfri'.

## Tuesday June 3rd

Humfri now has two bowls, a bed, a basket, a scratching post, a puffer bottle of flea powder, worm tablets, a ball/bell combination, a grooming brush, and is registered at a veterinary surgeon's in Beauchamp Place.

Malcolm has showered the animal with his savings and his love. Yet the cat does not show the least sign of gratitude.

Zippo came into the restaurant tonight and said, 'OK, Adrian, you win. You held out for nine-fifty a show, and that's what we're offering. And we'll throw in a limo there and back, plus a set of pans.'

To test him I drawled, 'A thousand *five hundred*, plus residuals.' *Plus residuals* is a term I have heard many times in Hoi Polloi. I'm not exactly sure what it means, but television people have the phrase continually on their negotiating lips. But at that moment his mobile trilled.

He shouted into it, 'OK, five hundred thou' for Burt's hairpiece, but that's my final offer.' He snapped the mobile shut, turned to me and said, 'We'll go for six shows in two days, terribly knackering, I'll supply the bennies.' More code speak – I feel alone in a parallel universe.

## Wednesday June 4th

I rang Edna Kent this morning and asked her for the
name and phone number of Barry's agent. She gave
me his name, but said his phone number was ex-
directory. Then she divulged it anyway. There is a
solidarity among us Ashby-de-la-Zouchians.

His agent is an American called Brick Eagleburger.
I rang Mr Eagleburger and was immediately put
on hold after a harsh-voiced American woman (a
recording) said, 'Hi, I'm Brick's assistant, Boston.
Neither of us is available right now, but if you'll hold
a moment we'll be right with you.' I was then played
an excerpt from *Porgy and Bess*. I was singing along
to 'Bess, You Is My Woman Now', when the same
harsh-voiced woman broke in, 'Hi, Boston Goldman
here, how may I help you?'

I managed to stammer out that I was one of Barry
Kent's oldest friends, and that I required advice as I
was possibly about to embark on a TV career. Boston
said, 'Sounds kinda *exciting* but Brick's had closure
on his client list since January 1st.'

I wasn't sure what she meant and asked her to
rephrase her words.

'Since January 1st,' she said, slowly, as though
speaking to an idiot, or a foreigner, 'Brick has had
closure on his client list.'

'So, he's not taking on any more clients?' I checked.

Boston sounded less friendly. 'Congratulations! As

your own talented Sir Cliff Richard would say,' she joked, though with little humour, I thought.

## Thursday June 5th

I rang Edna again and reported yesterday's conversation. She told me that Boston was a failed stand-up comedienne. It explains a lot. Edna told me to persist until I got to speak to Brick himself. Savage has found out about Humfri's tenure in the kitchen, and has ordered us to get rid of him. Large Alan has tipped him off that the health inspectors are planning midnight raids in the Soho area. Malcolm is distraught, he said tonight. 'No 'uman ever wants to get near to me, an' I never get to touch another 'uman. But Humfri, 'e can't wait to sit on my knee.' Humfri is only interested in him because of the food Malcolm feeds him, on an hourly basis. I almost pointed this out to him, but I drew back from the brink.

## Friday June 6th

Humfri now has another possession: a litter tray. In my flat.

## Saturday June 7th

Phoned Brick, got Boston. To try to get into her good books I asked her if she had been christened Boston. She flew into a rage. 'You're assuming I'm a *Christian*, are you? British boy! That my mom and pop stood at the font in some f------ Midwest tight-assed Protestant church and *christened* me into the *Christian* community, eh? Is that kosher with you?'

I said that I was sorry if I had offended her. Though to be honest, dear Diary, I didn't know what I was apologizing for.

I asked, once again, to speak to Brick; she once again put me on hold. I now know all the words to most of the songs from *Porgy and Bess*. I could give a recital.


## Sunday June 8th

William rang me today. He wanted to know when I was coming up to see him. I said I wasn't sure (which is true: I need to be in London for the Pie Crust negotiations). The kid droned on about somebody or something called Barney, then put the phone down abruptly before I could say a proper goodbye. I felt guilty for at least half an hour after his call.

Apparently Savage and Kim are reconciled. I only

know this from reading the Taki column in the *Sunday Times* today. I'm personally very pleased: Kim is the only person who understands the stock-control data on the computer. Perhaps I'll get those carrots I asked for days ago.

## Wednesday June 11th

A bad day. At 2300 hours we were raided by the public health. It couldn't have come at a worse time. Malcolm had brought the cat down from the flat and was cradling him in his arms, next to the dried goods store. Luigi, *curse him*, was on the draining board, sitting cooling his feet in the sink.

Savage and Kim were totally drunk and seemed to be under the impression that the public health inspectors, a Mr Voss (thin, pale) and a Ms Sykes (thin, tanned), were a showbiz double act.

A fine-tooth comb would have been a blunt instrument compared to the meticulous scrutiny that kitchen underwent during Voss and Sykes' inspection. They left, eventually, at 2.30 a.m. after finding one hundred and twenty violations of the Public Health Act. Including traces of foot fungus in the sink.

The restaurant was closed down until all the work stipulated in the order had been completed.

Thank God I have another string to my bow with Pie Crust Productions.

## Thursday June 12th

There is a new notice in the window of Hoi Polloi.

Closed by MI5 on the orders of Commissar Blair – due to the fact that Hoi Polloi is a libertarian stronghold.
    Signed – Hon. P. Savage

## Friday June 13th

Large Alan has offered Malcolm a job sweeping up sequins and feathers from the dressing room at the lap-dancing club. Free meals, £5 an hour, minicab home. Malcolm said he is going to think about it. Why?
    Luigi is riddled with guilt as well he may be. His feet alone accounted for seventeen public-health violations.
    I record the first three shows on Monday.

## Saturday June 14th

My auntie Susan has been honoured with the prestigious Prison Officer of the Year award. It was presented to her by Jack Straw. She told my mother that Mr Straw said he intends to conduct an inquiry into lesbianism in prisons. 'Among the staff or the prisoners?' asked my aunt. She reported that Mr Straw blushed at the question, and turned the conversation to a safer subject: the menace of garden slugs.

Nigel called and asked if he could sleep on my settee over the weekend. He says that he is coming to London to be counselled by a group called Outings. They specialize in advising gay men and women on how to tell their parents they are gay. (Not that the *parents* are gay, of course. Presumably if the parents were gay they would know already. Though I suppose it is possible to be gay and not know. In that case, am I gay? I've been an admirer of Judy Garland for years.) I said I would allow him to sleep on the sofa (or settee, as he calls it) and I warned him about the storeroom decorative motif. He said he didn't care so long as there was a spare shelf for his exfoliation skincare products.

### Sunday June 15th

Nigel will be out all day, being advised by Outings. I told him that my aunt Susan, see above, told my grandma and grandad she was gay by saying, 'I'm a lesbian, like it or lump it.' 'It was all over in five seconds, bar the shouting,' I said.

Nigel shuddered and said, 'Without an anaesthetic, how brave,' as though Aunt Susan were an amputee.

I am surrounded night and day by the sex industry of Soho and by people whose lives are ruled by sex. Yet I am myself as chaste as a sea-horse. I think Justine has made a few 'moves' in my direction. I bumped into her at the Café Italia yesterday, and she spoon-fed me the froth off her cappuccino. She said she has heard a rumour that Savage and Kim are selling Hoi Polloi and setting up an oxygen bar, which sells fresh air to health freaks. Savage will blow the place up within days. He leaves burning cigarettes on every surface.

Nigel cut my hair, ready for the camera tomorrow. He said, 'I won't allow you to hit the screens looking like Princess Diana on testosterone.'

A moment after he'd started, I heard him take a sharp intake of breath and knew he'd spotted my thin/bald patch. I asked him to measure it, using the device on my Swiss Army knife.

He told me that the bald patch has a circumference of one inch. However, we worked out that if I use a strong hairspray and comb my hair in a south-westerly direction, my secret will remain safe.

Nigel has gone back to Leicester to tell his parents and Next about his lover, Norbert. Savage has given me notice to quit the flat. I will take him to the highest court in the land before I do so. Though I have to admit that a move back to Leicester seems more and more attractive.

## Monday June 16th

Up at five, fed fish, changed cat litter, shaved, dressed, caught the tube to Shoreditch. An hour early, Pie Crust closed. Nowhere to buy a cup of tea. Streets full of mad men and women. Walked about. Felt conspicuous in three-piece and overcoat. Hoped wouldn't be knocked over as had pig's head in Next nylon tote-bag.

Belinda, Zippo and a hair-and-make-up artist called Zo, arrived together at 7 a.m. in black cab. Looked surprised to see me. 'Have sent limo to pick you up,' said Belinda. She very annoyed. She rings driver of limo on mobile. 'Yeah, I know, the dick-head's *here*,' I heard her say.

*Later*

Zo looks at hair. 'Who did hair last?' she asks. 'Club-fingered friend with blunt scissors?' Say yes. Ask how did she know. She rolls eyes and restyles hair so I look '1940s, like Hitler'. Say I don't like Hitler hairstyle. Zo says, 'Zippo, how 1940s d'you want him?' Zippo and

Belinda and Zo confer over my head. Apparently hairstyle has to reflect offal theme. War years, etc.

*I'm sick of writing in Bridget Jones telegramese, so will revert to my natural free-flowing prose style.*

'Which is why I went for the Hitler,' says Zo, who, it transpires, knows very little about twentieth-century political history. I pointed out to her that Hitler was a monster, responsible for starting the Second World War. 'I didn't *do* the history module,' she says, defensively. 'I dropped it for environmental studies.'

To Zo, and many of her generation, Hitler is merely the Old Brown.

We settled on a Dambusters concept for my TV hairstyle, 'a sort of short back and sides with attitude', as Zo called it. She warned me that I was going thin on top and recommended an American spray called Falshair, which settles on the scalp and gives the appearance of real hair. It is available on Cable TV's shopping channel. She said it comes in seven colours, 'including your colour – mouse with a hint of grey'. I remarked (quite coolly, given that my heart had almost stopped), 'Going grey already, hey?' Which made me sound like Jerry Seinfeld.

Zo said, 'It's only at a 2½ per cent ratio, but if you want to cover it up, there's a product called . . .'

I didn't take it in, dear Diary. It was one of those moments. I felt acutely aware of my own mortality. The swift slide towards the death of follicles, the breakdown of tissue, the hardening of some arteries, the narrowing of others. The piping voicebox of adolescence would return.

I have reached my prime without noticing it or enjoying it. I am only a few short decades away from being unable to cut my own toenails. Can I trust Mr Blair? Will the future National Health Service provide adult Pampers on prescription, should I need them? These thoughts flashed through my mind in a nano-second. I was brought back to the present world by Zo asking me to close my mouth while she applied a heavy-duty foundation to my 'acne-scarred' face. Meanwhile, the lights and camera were being adjusted in the mock kitchen in a corner of the studio. I was introduced to my on-air 'co-presenter', an Indian man called Dev Singh. He had thick glossy hair, large brown eyes, eyelashes like black palm trees. The teeth! The lips! He said, 'I haven't closed my eyes for two nights. I'm so, so scared.'

I admitted that I was also a little apprehensive. 'Oh, thank you, thank you for sharing that with me,' he said. He then confessed to me that he was a strict vegetarian and that even the thought of handling offal made him retch. Belinda broke in and said, 'Dev, you're only here to look pretty. We don't expect you to touch the filthy stuff.'

I asked Belinda what Dev's exact role was to be, and pointed out that no mention had been made about me needing a co-presenter. 'Yeah, well, we looked at your pilot tape again, and thought we needed to sex it up a bit,' she said.

Thankfully I still had Cath. She had already prepared the ingredients and placed them in little bowls. She'd even cleaved halfway through the pig's head for me. I changed into my whites, and Dev changed into a red silk shirt, and a pair of tight white Levi's, and we staggered through a rehearsal, miming the cooking as we went. At the end Zippo said, 'Cath, find us some raunchy-looking vegetables and fruit, there's a love.' She came back five minutes later with a bag full of carrots, cucumbers and melons, and dumped it on the worktop. 'See what you can do with those, Dev,' said Zippo. 'Five minutes' rehearsal, then we go.'

Dev moved among the suggestive fruit and veg like a magician practising a trick, then he looked up from his work and said, 'Well, I'm ready, as you can see from the state of my trousers.'

Everyone in the studio laughed, apart from me, Cath, and Zippo, who was on the phone to LA arguing about the cost of Burt Reynolds' just-woken-up wig.

I've had worse moments in my life – sitting in Casualty aged fifteen with a model aeroplane Super-glued to my nose was unforgettably awful – but being upstaged by Dev and his *double entendres* came quite near. As I was limo'd home, I was visited by a feeling of self-disgust. I have not written a single creative or poetic word for weeks. I have sold my soul for a mess of pottage.

## Thursday June 19th

Justine asked me this evening if I was gay! I blame Pandora. I have been passionately in love with her since I was thirteen and three-quarters, and I am unable to give myself emotionally (or sexually) to any other woman.

## Friday June 20th

Zippo rang me to say that they have edited the first three shows. Dev Singh's contribution has been kept to an absolute minimum. That grotesque business with the cucumber and the pig's ears has been edited out totally.

Zippo confided in me that they 'are thinking of letting Dev go'. I said I thought that would be a wise decision. He asked me to fax him a list of ingredients needed for Monday's recordings. I faxed him three recipes: Giblet Pie, Baked Bullock's Heart and Economical Soup for the Poor. I was about to ask him if he would be interested in producing *The White Van*, but he said, 'Got to go. Goldie's agent is on line two. She's asking for wig parity.'

## Monday June 23rd

Pandora rang, and said, 'If the *News of the World* ring you, say, "No comment".' She wouldn't elaborate. It sounds ominous. We talked for a while about our parents' romance, using a code: A was my mother, B was her father. Pandora said that C (her mother) had rung her up in tears, saying that she had found a Kit-Kat wrapper in B's anorak pocket.

'God!' I said. 'A eats two Kit-Kats a day. But why is C so suspicious? Why shouldn't B eat a Kit-Kat?'

'He's boycotted Rowntree's products since 1989,' said Pandora. 'Something about the working conditions of the cocoa-workers.'

'They're getting careless,' I said. We agreed to review the ABC situation next week.

I went back to bed, still exhausted from yesterday's recordings. I never want to see, smell or even *touch* offal ever again.

Dev Singh had not been 'let go', far from it. If anything he had been let loose! Everyone in the studio was convulsed with laughter at his tiresome antics – apart from me and Cath.

When he juggled with the chicken gizzards and caught them in the wok I almost walked out of the studio. However, I pride myself on my professionalism, so I called on my inner resources and managed to maintain my composure. Plus I threw in some literary aphorisms in an attempt to raise the intellectual tone. While demonstrating how to darken gravy, by the use of PG Tips, I quoted the following *bon mot*: 'A woman is like a tea-bag – only in hot water do you realize how strong she is.' Nancy Reagan said it first. As a *mot* it's not that *bon*, but it impressed Zippo. I think.

In between shows, Zippo speed-dialled LA, sometimes switching to the conference phone so we were all party to his manic conversations about the (surely doomed) *True Love* film. Nathan Stag, the director of *Love* as they call it, screamed at one point, 'Listen up, Zippo, there ain't a wigmaker in the business who can make Burt Reynolds pass for thirty-five years of age. It's a mother f------ no-no.'

*Offally Good!* is offally bad. I will be a laughing stock.

## Tuesday June 24th

Lay awake until 4 a.m., listening to the rain and worrying about the *News of the World*. I could worry for the Olympics and win a medal. Gold.

William rang me at 5.30 a.m. to remind me that it's his birthday on July 1st. How do I tell an almost-three-year-old not to ring me before nine o'clock in the morning? I love the kid, but I wish BT had never invented automatic dial.

Humfri not seen for two days.

## Wednesday June 25th

Read about President Clinton and the sex allegations. Everybody is having sex, apart from me. Even Malcolm is enjoying a carnal relationship, with Annette, a woman who sells the *Evening Standard* on the Strand. I went to observe her today, from the opposite pavement. She makes Ann Widdecombe look like Kate Moss. Her legging-clad thighs look like those redwood trees that Americans drive their cars through. However, she's got a pretty face, and with a decent haircut would look OK.

I can always tell when Malcolm's had a good mauling from her the night before. His face, neck and chest are covered in newsprint the next morning. Malcolm is convinced that 'the Chinks' have kidnapped Humfri and turned him into beef with black bean and ginger sauce. He claims that he once found a name-tag, 'Fluffy', inside a carton of takeaway chicken chop suey, in Wolverhampton in 1993. He went to the public health with the Fluffy tag, but the officials didn't take him seriously. 'I was on the Woodpecker at the time,' he conceded, when I inquired about his general demeanour in the public-health office. 'The stuck-up git called the filth, who chucked me out.' It was obvious from his bitter tone that Malcolm still bears a grudge against the authorities.

Rosie rang me at 2 a.m. begging me to rescue her from the Glastonbury rock festival. She thinks she's got trench foot. The ground is a quagmire. She has lost her shoes and has queued for two hours to use the phone. I am her only hope. I said I had no petrol in the car and advised her to put her faith in her own caring, sharing generation.

## Saturday June 28th

Luigi rang me today and told me that several rich investors have come forward to 'save' Hoi Polloi. There is to be a complete refurbishment and the cellars are to be turned into an oxygen bar (!). The present restaurant is to be refitted in a 1950s working-class kitchen style, using Utility furniture, and the upstairs (including my flat) is to become a Members Only club for smokers.

Luigi said that smokers applying to join will have to provide a doctor's letter to prove that they are serious and not opportunistic clean-lunged wannabes.

Michael Caine is rumoured to be one of the invest-ors. Not many people know that, and I am sworn to secrecy. None of the present staff have been retained. Luigi is helping his brother-in-law with his window-cleaning round in Cadogan Gardens. I have started looking for somewhere else to live in London. I don't want to move back to Wisteria Walk: I have outgrown the provinces.

## Sunday June 29th

The Savoy Hotel has been invaded by a small plague of mice. They are offering a free drink to any guest who spots one. I sat in the American Bar, nursing a glass of sparkling water, for an hour and a half tonight. I paid particular attention to the skirtings and floor, but saw no vermin of any kind. This is just my luck.

## Monday June 30th

I am lonely. The only person I spoke to at any length today was a Japanese tourist, who stopped me outside Tesco's in Covent Garden (where I was bulk-buying Opal Fruits). She asked me how to get to Torquay. I was pleased to be able to direct her to Paddington station where she would be able to buy a ticket to Devon. I offered to accompany her in a black cab, but she declined.

I fantasized in bed about her on the beach at Torquay, wearing a black Lycra bikini, but nothing came of it. Even my penis has gone off me. Have I inherited flaccidity from my father, together with hair loss? Perhaps it's time I visited Dr Ng again. If I ring today I might get an appointment three weeks hence.

136

*7 p.m.* I am seeing Dr Ng on July 17th at 10.10 a.m. It's a good job that of my multifarious ailments none is immediately life-threatening.

Chris Patten and Prince Charles gave Hong Kong back to Communist China today. I predict that, by tomorrow night, Hong Kong will be attacked by the pillaging Chinese, desperate for Levi's and Sony Walkmen. Hong Kong will be aflame. Question: Why didn't Chris Patten wear a uniform for such a solemn occasion? There must have been something (a cocked hat) he could have borrowed. You can't hand back our Empire in a lounge suit – it's simply not appropriate.

## Tuesday July 1st

I was waiting outside Hamleys at 9 a.m. As soon as the doors opened I escalated myself up to the dressing-up clothes department, where I asked about a Jeremy Clarkson outfit. The personage in charge, Kevin, sneered at my inquiry, saying, 'We only do fictional characters.'

I immediately pointed out to him a garish Robin Hood outfit (ages four and a half to eight years), which came complete with a feathered hat, and bow and suctioned arrow. Kevin said that Robin Hood 'was a fictional character', and went on to say that his dissertation, 'Men and Myths in Sixteenth-century Nottinghamshire', which gained him an MA from

Nottingham University, explored society's need for heroes.

I asked Kevin why he was flogging kids' dressing-up clothes when he was in receipt of a Master's degree. He said, 'To pay for my PhD.' He's already mapped out his subject: 'Coffee: Its Introduction and Effect on English Literary Life, from Dr Johnson to Martin Amis'.

My heart was beating fast with jealous rage. I asked him how such a subject would help him find a fulfilling and well-paid job. He fiddled with the Sleeping Beauty boxes and said, 'Well, Nescafé might take me on.' I bought the Robin Hood outfit. William must learn to be proud of his East Midlands heritage.

### Ashby-de-la-Zouch – William's Third Birthday

My father got out of bed for the blowing-out-of-the-candles-on-the-cake ceremony, which is such an important part of our English culture. William tried hard, but couldn't blow the candles out in one go. It took five of his little puffs and a little surreptitious help from me before he extinguished the tiny flames. It's my mother's fault. He's tied too tightly to her apron strings. He needs to toughen up. It's a hard world out there.

Jo Jo sent him some traditional silken garments, as worn by the Yoruba people. He preferred these to the Robin Hood outfit, and refused to take them off when it was time for bed. My mother told me that she is thinking of suing Imperial Tobacco for one million pounds. She blames them for her nicotine addiction, persistent smoker's cough and wrinkles.

## Thursday July 3rd

It was in the paper today that a Japanese woman had been found wandering around Torquay 'in a state of distress'. Apparently she had wanted to go to Turkey and had been misdirected to the Devon resort by a Londoner unable to understand her heavily accented English. Coincidence!

## Friday July 4th
*At the Bar Italia*

Two Americans are celebrating Independence Day by ordering straight coffee, rather than decaff. But now that the cups are put in front of them I notice that they are sipping the coffee as though it were liquid nitroglycerine.

## Saturday July 5th

Savage used his key to let himself into the flat today. He was accompanied by an architect, who was wearing what appeared to be a round-collared dentist's overall, though I suppose it was a shirt. They walked in and out of my bedroom as if the room were empty whereas, in fact, I was there in bed. My slight depression worsened into misery. I almost wept when they'd gone.

It rains unendingly.

## Sunday July 6th

I must get out of bed and find somewhere to live. Savage brought three builders round today for quotes. They didn't have a noble or honest facial feature between them.

Rain continues.

## Monday July 7th

Nigel rang to say that his mother had taken the news badly that he was gay. She was still 'in denial' about Rock Hudson, and was convinced that Nigel would turn heterosexual as soon as he met the right girl. His father had muttered something about 'horseplay in the showers at Catterick' then gone out to his shed.

## Wednesday July 9th

Malcolm came round to see if Humfri had returned. I was forced to tell him that the cat had not been seen for days. I quipped, 'It's probably drowned in all the rain!' To my horror, Malcolm burst into tears. I know that we late-nineties men are allowed to cry in public, and to show our emotions now, but it still doesn't feel right to me. I had to resist the urge to tell him to pull himself together. I gave him £20 and told him to buy a Tamagotchi computer pet.

*2 a.m.* I've just remembered that Malcolm won't be able to read the instructions on how to care for his Tamagotchi. It's probably already dead.

## Thursday July 10th

Pandora has been attacked in the press for 'crimes against the environment'! She admitted in an interview with *Chat* magazine to wearing Chanel No. 5, and the Green Party were down on her like a felled oak. It seems that Chanel No. 5 contains an oil which is extracted from a rare and exotic tree found in endangered Brazilian forests. I rang Edna to commiserate, and she told me that Alastair Campbell has ordered Pandora to go to her constituency and plant some trees. English oaks, preferably. There is a press call outside the KP nut factory in Ashby-de-la-Zouch on Sunday at 10.30 a.m. I might be there, I need to talk to Pandora in person.

I bought an electronic organizer today on the Tottenham Court Road. I spent all night typing my personal data into it. It's time I streamlined my affairs and became cutting-edge. The thing is amazing in what it can do, yet it's small enough to fit in my pyjama pocket.


**Friday July 11th**

Harriet Harman, the Social Security secretary, has been on radio and television trying to explain about the government's 'Welfare to Work' scheme. Several times she called it a 'crusade'. It has to be said that Mrs Harman has the look of the zealot about her, as well as a constant air of irritation. She should let her fringe grow out, stop wearing smocks and buy an uplift bra. Also, she should stop complaining about sexism in politics. It's most annoying.

## Sunday July 13th

I was outside the KP nut factory by 10 a.m. with a reporter and photographer from the *Leicester Mercury*, and a photographer bloke from the *Independent*, who told me that Pandora was the thinking man's Princess Di.

A small crowd of constituents were watched by eight policemen, who sat in two patrol cars.

A helicopter appeared in the sky over the soap works, hovered about a bit, then landed in the grounds of the nut factory. Pandora jumped out, wearing Rohan-labelled clothes in khaki. She was carrying a gleaming stainless-steel spade. She is the only woman I've ever seen who looked good in outdoor-pursuits wear.

Pandora's entourage emerged from the helicopter with a scruffy man, in a stained jacket and crumpled trousers, called Charlie Whelan. He lit a fag and said, 'Where's the rest of the f------ press?'

The photographer from the *Independent* said, 'They're staking out Kensington Palace. Princess Diana's got a new squeeze, an Arab bloke.'

Pandora said, 'Charlie, where are the trees I've got to plant?'

Charlie slapped his nicotined fingers to his rumpled forehead and said, 'I've left the bleeders at the heliport.'

At this point I took off my baseball cap and dark glasses and made myself known to Pandora. She didn't look thrilled to see me. She said, 'Adrian! Again! Are you stalking me?'

I assured her that I was just passing, on the way to see my son William. I invited her and her entourage to Sunday lunch at my mother's house. Charlie said, 'I wouldn't mind a beef and Yorkshire pudding job.' They agreed to come, providing I helped them locate some trees. I drove them to Bob Perkins Garden Centre Ltd.

The press followed, and Pandora and the eponymous Bob Perkins were photographed pretending to admire some mildewed saplings, which were leaning up against an industrial greenhouse.

The *Leicester Mercury* quizzed Pandora about her green credentials: she was all *for* recycling, clean air and Leicestershire County Council's plans to plant a New Forest, and she was very much *against* air pollution, poisoned rivers and 'profligate use of electricity and gas'.

As the interview continued, I went into a greenhouse full of hanging baskets and mobiled my mother, who didn't yet know I was in the area. When I told her that I had invited myself and three guests to Sunday lunch, she screamed down the phone. She didn't *say* anything at first, she just screamed. Eventually she shouted, 'I've got a scraggy breast of lamb, which will just about stretch to feed me, your dad, Rosie and William, I'm out of Oxos and my Yorkshire-pudding tin is badly buckled. You'll have to take them to a restaurant.'

I said, 'If this was Arabia you would give your *own eyeballs* to such honoured guests.'

My mother pointed out, quite unnecessarily, that this wasn't Arabia, it was Ashby-de-la-Zouch – and, anyway, why wasn't Pandora going to visit *her* parents, who only lived round the corner from Bob Perkins Ltd? She said, 'I know they're in because I bumped into Ivan this morning while I was *taking the New Dog for a walk*.'

I gave a hollow laugh and put the phone down. It was socially embarrassing to have to snatch back the invitation to Sunday dinner.

Charlie Whelan moaned, 'I've got the *idea* of Yorkshire pudding in my head now. My mouth's watering for it.'

When I asked Pandora if her parents would be up to cooking a traditional English roast at short notice, she laughed and said, 'A and C haven't touched meat for years. On Sundays their main meal is scrambled eggs on toast while watching *The Antiques Road Show*.'

Bob Perkins suggested *C. leylandii* trees for the KP nut roundabout. So, after Pandora had been photographed planting them, we retired to a McDonalds on the bypass. It was mainly full of access-day fathers, trying desperately to control their children.

Pandora was constantly pestered by constituents. Her Filet o' Fish remained untouched.

An old man in a golfing sweater complained that a streetlight outside his bedroom window flickered and kept him awake. An Indian bloke said he had nowhere to park his car. And a mad-looking woman said she was disgusted that Pandora had not paid public tribute to James Stewart, the actor, who had apparently died on July 2nd.

As we were leaving, a bloke in a beige car coat with a walking-stick limped up to Pandora and gave her a sob story about his evil next-door neighbour, who had planted *C. leylandii* trees along their boundary fence, five years ago. 'They're fifteen feet tall now,' he said, 'and they're blocking my daylight.'

Pandora tapped his name and address into her electronic organizer and said she would see what she could do.

There was a little crowd of schoolchildren on bikes waiting to see the helicopter take off; there was a ratio of one policeman for every two kids. I watched until the chopper was a tiny dot in the darkening sky, then I sat in my car for a long time before driving to Wisteria Walk to see my son.

## Monday July 14th

Bought an *Independent* today. Pandora's photograph was on the front. If you look very carefully you can just make out the tip of my nose in the background. I've decided to delay deciding about decision-making until I feel decidedly better. My mental state is fragile.

The manuscript of my novel, *Lo! The Flat Hills of My Homeland*, was returned today from a publisher in Osaka, Japan. He wrote that it was '*derivative*' but didn't say of what. Perhaps I should change the title to something punchier, in the *Trainspotting* mode. After a lot of thought I have settled on *Birdwatching*.

**Tuesday July 15th**

I had to leave the flat to shop for Opal Fruits this morning. Then I hurried home and parcelled up *Birdwatching* – I think I might send it off to Iceland, where I understand they are enjoying a cultural renaissance. I rang a publisher in Reykjavik using the restaurant phone. A woman answered in a language entirely foreign to my ear: Icelandic, I presume. I put the phone down. Until they adopt the English language I fear they will remain totally isolated from the rest of the world.

**Wednesday July 16th**

What am I going to do with the rest of my life? Where will I live? How will I make a living when my work with Pie Crust comes to an end? Am I now formally separated from my wife? How long can a person go

147

without a bowel movement? How much have I got in the bank? Will Savage offer me a job in one of his new enterprises? How long have I got before I am entirely bald? Which reminds me – will the Dome at Greenwich be finished on time? How does Mr Mandelson live with the worry?

## Thursday July 17th

Dr Ng said that anxiety and insecurity are entirely sane responses to a mad world. He advised me to start a pension plan. So, the National Health has come to this.

I struggled for an hour and a half to evacuate my bowels. Somebody rang on the doorbell of the flat, but whoever it was left no note. In future I will make sure that there is always a book in the lavatory. An hour and a half with my own thoughts was unbearable. A. A. Gill's 'turds' review was a particularly painful memory.

Belinda rang to say the Millennium Channel have finally given us a slot. It is 10.30 a.m. Wednesday mornings. I was bitterly disappointed and reminded her that we would be up against Richard and Judy. She said, 'Believe you me, Adrian, if it comes to a ratings war, they'll wonder what hit them.'

## Friday July 18th

I searched fruitlessly through my fail-safe electronic filing system today, trying to discover the balance of my various accounts. For some reason it wouldn't divulge the information. I went out and bought a new battery from the electrical shop on Old Compton Street. The helpful bloke in there said his electronic organizer had refused to give him his Christmas-card list last year. He went on to tell me about the family row that ensued, but I wasn't listening properly. I spotted Justine coming out of Pâtisserie Valerie opposite, so I paid the helpful bloke and ran outside to catch up with her. She took my arm as we walked towards Wardour Street. Was she signalling that she wanted to have sex with me? Or was it because she needed support? (She was wearing five-inch platforms.) You can never tell with women, these days.

A colleague of Justine's is giving Malcolm literacy lessons between shows. We arranged to meet on Tuesday and go for a Japanese meal.

## Saturday July 19th

My mystery caller on Thursday was Malcolm. He was desperate for news of Humfri. I asked him why he hadn't put a note through the door. 'I can only write "The cat sat on the lap"!' he said.

## Sunday July 20th

I spent most of the day poring over *Loot*, looking for reasonable accommodation in the Soho area. Some *joker* is asking £500 a week for a converted linen cupboard (plus access to fire escape), in Poland Street, main services not included. I need to get an update on my financial situation.

I rang my telephone bank and gave my code numbers, 9999, and my password, Yarmouth. The bank official, a pleasant-sounding woman who told me that she was called Marilyn, was horrified that I had disclosed the full password to her. She had been about to ask me what the second letter of the word was. And, had I answered 'A', she would have been able to give me the balance of my Instant Access High Interest Account. 'As it is,' she said, 'you'll need to open a new account. As from now all of your codes are null and void.'

I begged and pleaded with Marilyn to let me into the secrets of my own account, but she said, 'The computer has now closed this account. I'll put another application in the post.'

I said to her, 'Where *exactly* is my money, Marilyn? Is it in an actual *place*, like a vault?'

Marilyn said, 'Your money doesn't exist, as such.' She went on, 'Your money, *Mr* Mole, is an abstraction wafting in the air between financial institutions, at the mercy of inflation and interest rates, dependent on the health of the global economy.' She recovered herself and apologized for showing her human face. It was a kamikaze speech.

Marilyn had already told me that our conversation was being recorded. (I tried to extend the conversation, but Marilyn, who admitted to being forty-four, dark-haired, the mother of three and married, said, 'Other customers are waiting, Mr Mole.'

## Monday July 21st

I can't remember the last time I felt the warmth of a naked body.

*3 a.m.* I remember now, it was last Sunday. The New Dog sat across my lap when I read *Grimms' Fairy Tales* to William.

*4 a.m.* Can't sleep for worrying that Justine will turn up for our Japanese meal looking like a cheap tart. I know she wears expensive clothes, but she wears them in such a way that they look like *News of the World* catalogue wear.

## Tuesday July 22nd

It was as I feared. I couldn't relax in the restaurant. We were hopelessly mismatched. Justine was wearing skimpy red Versace, in honour of his memory, and I was wearing substantial grey Next. *I* knew my way around the sushi and the tempura and the chopsticks; *she* shuddered at the raw fish and asked the stern waiter for a knife and fork. She is an intelligent girl, but she hasn't read a book since leaving school. We talked about Cherie Blair, who had spent £2,000 flying her hairdresser, André Luard, out to last month's summit meeting in Denver. We agreed that this was a very American thing to do. 'It's a bit like Elvis flying his favourite cheeseburgers from Memphis to Las Vegas, isn't it?' said Justine.

I replied, 'Power corrupts and absolute power corrupts absolutely.'

Justine said, 'You're *so* clever, Adrian. Just being with you is an education.'

## Wednesday July 23rd

Received another application from my telephone bank, Money Direct. I chose 1111 as my number code, and Cromer as my letter code.

Why did I withdraw all my money from the building society in 1995? All I had to do then to check my balance was to ring old Mr Lewisham and he would tell me immediately, and he would even ask after the progress of *Lo!*. It must have broken his heart when I withdrew my £2,709.26 from the Market Harborough.

## Friday July 25th

Princess Diana's cleaning bill must be enormous. She is always wearing white clothes lately, giving her the appearance of a virgin or a saint. If I were the boss of Sketchley's I would offer to sponsor her charitable work. She has promised to buy an artificial leg for a bloke called Mohammed.

## Saturday July 26th

I rang Money Direct this morning to check the balance of my account. A non-human voice answered the phone and asked me to wait as 'The lines are busy.' I listened to four minutes of Vivaldi's *Four Seasons*, before hanging up in disgust.

Rang Front-line Insurance to request a claim form – some bastard has stolen William's tricycle while he and my mother were in the newsagent's. A robot answered and asked me to hold. It then told me that my call was 'enormously important' to Front-line Insurance. Next it informed me that I was number thirteen in the phone queue. Throughout, Chris de Burgh sang, 'Lady In Red': a song I have always hated. When Rod Stewart started warbling 'Sailing' I slammed the phone down. What has happened to England's telephonists? Has there been a cull? How long have the robots been in charge?

## Monday July 28th

Justine rang and asked why I have not called her. I could hardly tell her the truth – that I would prefer her to wear something sensible from Marks & Spencer when we are out in public. I told her instead that I was hard at work on my TV series, *The White Van*. She asked me for a part if it gets commissioned. She's got an Equity card apparently, though how Equity can give out one of its precious cards to a girl who wrestles erotically with a boa constrictor is a total mystery to me. What about the plain-faced, flat-chested drama-school graduate who longs to play Ibsen?

## Tuesday July 29th

Savage burst into my bedroom at 7 a.m. this morning and ordered me out. I said, 'When?'

He said, 'You've got an hour!'

I said, 'Peter, I've worked for you, on and off, for eight years. I've got nowhere to go. Have mercy.'

He said, 'The builders will be here at eight o'clock, so get the f--- out!'

## Friday August 1st
*Justine's Flat – Poland Street*

Many men would envy me staying here in a penthouse flat in the heart of London with a girl whose name is written in flashing neon lights outside a 'theatre' – so why aren't I happy?

After we'd finished shopping for food in Marks & Spencer, I steered Justine towards the ladies' clothing department. I suggested she try on a nice ecru twinset, in machine-washable wool, together with a pair of easy-fit jeans. She looked at me with horror in her eyes.

## Sunday August 3rd

Justine's friend, who works on the handbag counter in Harrods, reports that Princess Diana is getting engaged to Dodi Fayed, the son of Mohammed Al-Fayed, the multi-millionaire owner of the Queen's favourite store!

I scoured the press for confirmation of this ridiculous story, and found nothing. I told Justine to stop circulating the rumour.

## Monday August 4th

Large Alan dropped in today. He didn't look very keen to see me sitting at Justine's kitchen table eating a meal she'd just cooked (angel-hair spaghetti and pesto sauce). He said, 'Justine, you didn't inform me that you'd got a flatmate.'

Justine said, 'It's only Adrian,' as though I were an insentient eunuch. 'We're on separate futons.'

I left the room in some upset, but not before hearing Large Alan say, 'Justine, what do you see in him?'

She replied, 'I like intellectual men. There's more to life than sex, Al.'

Large Alan said, 'Is there?' He sounded genuinely surprised.

## Tuesday August 5th

I have decided to become celibate. Sex is very over-rated in my opinion. It's all over in a few minutes and is certainly not worth all the fuss and anguish that goes before.

Dear Stephen Fry,

My name is Adrian Mole. I once had the honour of cooking you a dish of tripe, which you pronounced 'unforgettable' (Hoi Polloi, Sept. 15th, 1996). You didn't pay us a second visit, to lunch or to dine, but no matter, I still admire your erudition and wit.

I have recently decided to become celibate, and will shortly be turning into a celebrity, and I wondered if you, as a celebrity celibate, have any tips on how to cope with both of these conditions. I expect you are busy but I'm sure you won't mind taking some time out of your schedule to advise someone who is practically your *doppelgänger*. I too am a bit of an intellectual.

Cheers, Steve,

Yours, Adrian Mole

PS. I would appreciate an early reply.

## Wednesday August 6th

An invitation card in the post, redirected from Hoi Polloi. Against a background of photographic offal was written:

*Pie Crust invites*

Adrian Mole and Guest

*to the wrap of* Offally Good!
*Attractions include posh nosh, champagne and Dev Singh.*

Justine read it and said, 'I thought you were the star, Adrian.'

I said, 'I am. There has obviously been a mistake at the printer's.'

Justine asked if she could come as my guest. She wasn't my first choice, but after ringing Pandora four times and getting no reply, I informed her that she could come with me on Friday.

She was pleased but said she had nothing to wear.

I seized the opportunity and nipped out to Marks & Spencer last night and bought a very attractive, loose-fitting, full-length dress in sludge-green viscose. I presented it to her when she came home from work at 3 a.m. I said, 'Please wear it tomorrow, at the wrap party.'

She looked at it with amusement and said, 'It's the sort of thing your mother would wear.'

It just goes to show – she has never met my mother.

## Friday August 8th

It was a mistake to take Justine to the Pie Crust studios. She was the focus of attention from the moment she stepped off the fire escape in her pink Versace slip dress and her cerise sling-back Manolos. Everyone in the studio looked at me with a new respect. Zippo said to me under his breath, 'I knew that the idiot-provincial persona you project was an act, Adrian. *Christ*, she's a wanker's dream! She's a dislocated *wrist*! She's duvet *heaven!*'

I abhorred his crude language, and told him so. Later, he confessed to me, standing at the urinals, that he had fallen in love with Justine at first sight. I know this is possible because I loved Pandora as soon as I clapped eyes on her.

Zippo said, 'Introduce me to her. Please, Adrian.'

In his excitement he splashed urine on his pale suede Gucci loafers. I kept this knowledge to myself. Why spoil the party for him?

We joined a throng of Justine's new admirers, who

were listening in some amazement to her tips on caring for the domestic python.

We pushed through and I introduced Zippo to Justine. He held on to her hand for longer than etiquette demanded.

Eventually she said, 'Can I have my hand back? I'm getting cramp.'

Zippo grabbed two glasses of champagne from Cath's tray and gave one to Justine saying, 'I've waited all my life to meet you. We must celebrate this momentous occasion.'

Justine was instantly sucked into the vortex of Zippo's smarmy talk. He did his Labrador retriever trick with his eyes, and she did her Marilyn Monroe thing with her mouth.

I asked Zippo if he thought we would get a second series, but he ignored me and asked Justine if she could cook. 'Not really,' she said. 'I just warm up ready-made meals in the micro.'

'*Warm Up with Justine!*' shouted Zippo.

I pointed out that it sounded like an exercise video. I suggested calling it *A Guide to Push-button Cookery*.

Zippo and a few Pie Crust people got very excited at this but they were all on skunk weed so none of them will remember.

Zippo took Justine aside and I heard them swapping birth signs: Scorpio him, Aries her (a disastrous conjunction, in my opinion).

Dev Singh turned up late, accompanied by a Sikh bodyguard in a turban. He was soon surrounded by a small crowd of sycophants, who hung on to his every suggestive word.

Pie Crust Productions have applied to the Lottery Fund for the money to make a documentary about Dev – called, in post-modernistic style, *Making a Documentary About Dev*. Secretly, Diary, I am still crushed by this news. How much lower can dumbing down go? It's already in the basement.

The party moved on to a restaurant in Shoreditch called Shock's. The place was full of installation artists and examples of their art. Everything seemed to be black, including the food: squid in black ink, cheap caviar, blackberry coulis, finishing with espresso coffee.

Zippo prised himself away from Justine and made a speech about filming *Offally Good!*. He mentioned me in passing, but heaped praise on Dev 'for his glorious humour, so reminiscent of that comic genius, Norman Wisdom'.

Whoops and hollers greeted this tribute – even the installation artists joined in. Wisdom is obviously big in Shoreditch, as well as Albania.

Zippo asked if I wanted to say anything. My mind went blank. Then I found myself on my feet apologizing for my performance on programme four when I had stumbled over the word 'disestablishmentarianism' eighteen times. Zippo said, 'Eighteen retakes is nothing.' He'd heard on the grapevine that Fergie, Duchess of York, held up the filming of her cranberry-juice advertisement in America 103 times because of her inability to articulate 'I like it' with conviction.

I felt vindicated by this piece of information.

Dev got up and thanked Pie Crust and me for giving him his big break. He said, 'I couldn't have done it without Adrian. He's a brilliant stooge.'

I took this compliment graciously, I hope – but my ego shrivelled up and ran out into the dark Shoreditch night. It hasn't been seen since.

I was sitting between silent Cath and the rumour-monger Belinda, who said she knew somebody who knew somebody who'd worked on *Chariots of Fire*, partly produced by Dodi Fayed. This person said that Dodi had no conversation. His only hobby was collecting baseball caps. Belinda said there was a story doing the rounds that Dodi and Diana were planning to co-produce a film about an elephant who steps on a landmine.

I nearly made a fool of myself when I mistook a piece of installation art for the men's toilet. Luckily I didn't pull my zip all the way down before realizing my mistake.


## Sunday August 10th
*Leicester*

I was shocked to my marrow to see the front page of the *Sunday Mirror* today. The headline said, 'THE

KISS'. Underneath was a blurred photograph of Princess Diana and the baseball-cap collector, Dodi Fayed. They were embracing while wearing very little clothing indeed. Prince Charles must have choked on his organic toast.

My mother and Rosie pored over the photographs, then ordered me to drive to the BP garage and buy all the scandal rags I could lay my hands on. I took William and the New Dog in the car with me. I bumped into Archie Tait, the one-legged pensioner, inside the garage shop. He was buying a Ginster's Cornish pasty for his Sunday dinner. He saw that I was buying the *News of the World* and the *People* and raised his eyebrows. I explained that they were for my mother and sister, and he said, 'Ah, the insatiable appetite that women have for trivia and gossip.' I agreed. He invited me and William for afternoon tea. I didn't want to go – in fact, it was the very last thing in the world I wanted to do – but before I could think of an excuse William had accepted for both of us. The kid doesn't get out much.

By the time our visit was over my brain hurt. Archie's conversation was very intense, and he was constantly asking me to provide the evidence for my opinions. He asked me what I was doing in London now that Hoi Polloi had been closed by the public health. (He is very well informed for a provincial.) I told him about the TV series *Offally Good!* and he took out his W. H. Smith's tartan-covered diary and wrote 'Adrian TV 10.30 a.m.' under September 10th. He doesn't have Cable, but he knows somebody who does.

When I got back from Ashby-de-la-Zouch Zippo was lolling on Justine's futon. She was heating up *moules marinière* in the microwave for him. They were laughing at a Norman Wisdom film. Their chrome mobile phones were side by side on the perspex Conran coffee table. *Wallpaper* was open at a feature about galvanized buckets (the new vases).

I felt out of place, as though I was wearing a cloak of provincialism. I offered to leave but Justine said, 'No, Adrian, please stay. We want somebody to witness the first full day of our love.'

I had eaten on the motorway earlier, so I turned down the *moules*. In between feeding Justine mussels straight from the shell, Zippo said that a focus group had been shown the first *Offally Good!* programme that morning and their response was so good that the ratings for the show were predicted to be one million. I went to bed at 11.30 and left them both propped against the futon, surrounded by shells and skunk-weed equipment.

*12.10 a.m.*. They have just consummated their love. Justine knocked on my door to tell me that Zippo was an 'incredible, caring, exciting lover'. I said I was pleased for her.

She asked if I would come into her bedroom to

reassure Zippo that she and I had never been lovers. She said Zippo was madly jealous.

I put on my dressing gown and stumbled into the bedroom. The dimmer switch was turned down to three. A lava lamp bubbled by the side of the bed. The python slithered in its tank. Zippo sat up, his loins barely covered by a white sheet. He asked me if I had 'slept' with Justine. I said truthfully that we had not had sexual intercourse, due to my vow of chastity. And also to my antipathy to Justine's python. I then went back to my own bed.

It's time to get out.

## Monday August 11th

After twenty minutes of electronic procrastination, I found out that I have got £3,796.26 in the telephone bank. This is not enough for a deposit on a London flat. And I need living expenses until my Pie Crust money comes in in September. I'm moving back to Leicester.

My mother is not pleased, but it's my family home and I *am* entitled to live there. My mother said that in her opinion, at thirty, entitlement didn't come into it. I pointed out to her that, in English law, there was no statute of limitations when it comes to returning home to live. She said, 'Perhaps not, but there should be!'

## Tuesday August 12th

As I pack I am shocked by the breaking news about Robin Cook's secret life of subterfuge with black bin-bags and parking meters, and a mistress waiting in a darkened room. All that trouble just to slake their lust! I am glad, indeed *proud*, to be celibate.

# Wisteria Walk, Ashby-de-la-Zouch

## Wednesday August 13th

Here I am again – in my old bedroom. Older, wiser, but with less hair, unfortunately. The atmosphere in this house is very bad. The dog looks permanently exhausted. Every time the phone rings my mother snatches it up as though a kidnapper were on the line.

Rosie is complaining bitterly because she is now sharing a room with William. I pointed out to her that I am *paying* for my room. Yes, my own mother is charging me £40 per week for bed and board! Once I'd moved my possessions into the bedroom I was staggered at how little I'd collected over the fourteen years of my working life. I made an inventory.

2  duvet covers and matching pillowslips, 1 black and green zigzags, 1 burgundy/cream swirls
1  high-tog-value fibre-filled duvet
4  bath towels
1  shaving mirror with magnification options

1 travelling clock
1 Anglepoise lamp + halogen bulb
1 MFI folding desk, in black ash
1 typist's chair
500 books (approx.)
1 *faux* Indian rug
2 Habitat director's chairs
1 Sony mini-stack sound system
27 compact discs (hardly used)
CD rack
TV/video (loaned by Zippo)
Dualit toaster (4-slice)
Black-ash bookcase
Willow coffee table with magazine shelf
Fruit bowl
Kettle (safety)
Ikea cutlery set
Ikea dinner service
Ikea cork noticeboard
Floor cushion (burgundy)

I thought back to the sumptuously furnished flat in Battersea which I'd shared with Jo Jo for most of our marriage. Now I'm nearly thirty and a half years of age, and I haven't got a sofa to call my own. I'm sick of lolling on a floor cushion. I said so to my mother. She said, 'Anybody over twenty-five looks ridiculous on a floor cushion.'

I agree.

I gave the thing to Rosie as a peace-offering, but she threw it back at me saying, 'Burgundy sucks. It's the colour of executives' wallets.'

William rejected it, saying that it smelled of 'something hobbollall'.

In the end I took the cushion down to the New Dog, who appeared to appreciate the gift though it is too big for the basket, so the poor animal perches on top of the cushion somewhat precariously with a nervous look in its eyes.

I have finished arranging my things. I will have to learn to live with the Barbie doll wallpaper – but I wish Rosie hadn't disfigured them with a black felt-tip pen and given them all moustaches and underarm hair.

## Friday August 15th

Justine rang. She said Alan has got a vacancy for a barman at The 165 club. Was I interested? I said no. Serving drinks to Conservative Members of Parliament was my idea of pitchfork purgatory. I asked her how her true romance with Zippo was going. She said it was over. Zippo had asked her to wear something more conservative as they were dressing before leaving the flat to visit his parents at their family seat near Cheltenham. Justine had refused, saying she had to be true to herself. He had shouted, 'My father's on borrowed time as it is. If he sees you in that skirt he'll have a heart attack and die.'

Versace has a lot to answer for.

## Saturday August 16th

Support for the Royal Family has fallen below 50 per cent for the first time. *Quelle surprise!* I remember seeing a photograph of Prince William on his first day at Eton. The poor kid was wearing a green *sports jacket!* The last time I saw a green sports jacket it was hanging on a rail in a Cancer Research charity shop.

Princess Diana flew to Athens in a Harrods Gulfstream jet, before going cruising in the Greek Islands with her friend, Rosa Monckton. I hope that in the excitement of her new romance she has not forgotten her promise to buy an artificial leg for that bloke Mohammed.

In the afternoon I took William to visit our MP's surgery, which was being held in an office at the health centre. There was a queue of ten people, mostly men. From overhearing their conversation I could tell that nearly all of them had come with trifling complaints. The majority seemed to be requesting council-house transfers because of noisy neighbours. I made sure that I was the last to go in.

I was shocked at her exhausted appearance, and said so.

'Thanks,' she said, while lighting a cigarette. 'I was up until four a.m. with Mandy.' She stifled a yawn.

'Doing the samba?' I asked. I had heard about Mr Mandelson's predilection for the rhythms of South America.

'No,' she said. 'We were writing a spoiler for Jack's disclosures in the *News of the World* next week. He's been threatening me with this since we split up on May 1st.'

I asked her why the split had occurred.

She said, 'Take your bloody pick. There was his one-and-a-half-bottles-of-Stolly-a-day habit. The hysterical midnight calls from his last ex-wife. His sexism: he would sulk if I asked him to pick up a loo brush.' She said she had heard from Alastair Campbell that Cavendish had been paid in excess of £50,000 to spill the beans about her past. He's got two of his children in the Priory and one in the Betty Ford,' she said. 'The poor sod needs the money.'

'That's no excuse to betray you, Pan,' I said. I tried to hold her hand but she slid it out of my grasp and towards her cigarette packet.

She showed me the spoiler. It was a brave document.


'I WAS FREE SPIRIT' ADMITS THE PEOPLE'S PAN
Pandora Braithwaite, 'the brightest star in Blair's firmament', issued an extraordinary statement last night, admitting that in sexual matters: 'I was a free spirit; I had

many lovers.' Speaking from her home in her constituency of Ashby-de-la-Zouch, she said, 'Yes, it's true. At one time in the eighties I was enjoying the sexual attentions of three lovers. We were all perfectly happy with the arrangement.'

### 'Erotic'

Asked if she wore erotic underwear in the debating chamber of the House of Commons she said, 'Yes, I buy my undies from Agent Provocateur in Soho. This in no way affects my ability as a politician. I work tirelessly on behalf of my constituents.'

### 'Blair Sexy'

Asked if her leader was sexy, Pandora said, 'Clearly.'

### 'Chanel – Passé'

Asked about Cavendish's allegations about financial irregularity regarding election expenses, Pandora said, 'I borrowed a couple of couture suits from Karl – I've since given them back, they were terribly passé.'

We had to fight our way out through an unruly pack of press photographers who had tracked Pandora down to the health centre.

William was excited by Pandora's Mercedes coupé and made her put the hood up and down several times as we drove to our house. My mother was excited to see her, and more excited still by the press pack, who were soon camped outside our garden gate. Even my father left his bed for a look. My mother made him change into clean pyjamas, both in honour of Pandora and in case he should be photographed accidentally.

An odd-looking boy in gangsta rap clothes stood on the opposite side of the road, staring at the house and eating crisps as though he was on a day out. I asked him to move on, but he affected not to hear me.

My mother read Jack Cavendish's copy and then Pandora's spoiler with barely contained glee. At 3 p.m. Ivan and Tania Braithwaite arrived, ashen-faced.

Ivan said to my mother, 'Pauline, my darling, I've told Tania. I had to do it before the *News of the World* did it for me.'

My father, the poor dolt, said, 'You've told Tania what?'

My heart stopped beating.

Ivan strode, in his smart casuals, up to my pyjama'd, unshaven father and said, 'I'm sorry to have to tell you this, George, but I'm in love with your wife.'

I crossed to my father and touched his shoulder. Pandora took her mother in her arms.

I watched my father's face age as the realization dawned that his wife was in love with somebody else, and that that someone else was Ivan Braithwaite, a family friend.

The New Dog slunk out of the room and went to perch on its burgundy cushion – aware, perhaps, of its role in the affair.

Tania disentangled herself from Pandora, smoothed her long, loose-fitting, floral-print frock over her hips and said, in a quavery voice, 'Ivan, I want you out of my house and garden by tonight.'

Pandora shouted, 'How could you do this to Mummy, Daddy?'

Ivan replied simply, 'Love captured us on May the first, and we have been its prisoners ever since.'

The saggy lovers exchanged a passionate glance.

I almost vomited. He should try writing for Mills and Boon.

My father sat down and lit a Rothman's. The fly on his pyjamas was open. He wasn't wearing underpants. I hastily positioned myself in front of him.

Ivan said, 'Come along with me *now*, my darling,' to my mother.

She picked up her make-up bag and they left.

I watched them pushing their way through the press at the gate. The boy was still there, eating from a bag of cheese and onion crisps.

## Sunday August 17th

It takes a long time to write a short paragraph. Pandora and I sat up until 5 a.m. composing the following, which Alastair Campbell approved at 6 a.m.

Pandora Braithwaite, MP for Ashby-de-la-Zouch, and Adrian Mole, Celebrity Chef, are delighted to announce that Mrs Pauline Mole and Mr Ivan Braithwaite (BA) are to marry in the spring.

Pandora (30) said, 'I'm thrilled for them,' and Adrian (30) said, 'Ivan is a lovely man, I couldn't be more pleased.'

The wedding will take place in Ashby-de-la-Zouch Castle, which is now licensed for marriage ceremonies. Neither Mrs Tania Braithwaite nor Mr George Mole was available for comment.

## Monday August 18th

Talk about the House of Sorrows! Dostoevsky, you should be here, in Wisteria Walk, on this day.

## Tuesday August 19th

My mother rang from the Post House Motel, two miles away, to say that she and Ivan were returning tonight.

## Wednesday August 20th

There has been an unbelievable, terrible, scandalous reversal. My mother and Ivan are living *here* at Wisteria Walk, and my father and Tania are living *there*, at The Lawns. I am absolutely furious that I was not party to these arrangements. It was done behind my back. I said to my mother, 'How could you send Dad, a sick man, to live with that gorgon Tania Braithwaite?'

She said, 'Keep your nose out of our business.'

William has already accepted Ivan into the family. Ivan bribed him with an educational pop-up book. My father mustn't find out. It will kill him.

## Thursday August 21st

Nigel fought his way through the press pack and visited today. It was brave of him: everybody who comes to the house ends up on regional television (*Midlands Today*). Tony Blair has sent a (private) letter of support to Pandora.

Dear Pandora,
    Cherie and I want to tell you how much we value your contribution to New Labour's success.

We are praying that your present personal and family difficulties will be resolved and that you will continue to serve your constituency of Ashby-de-la-Zouch for the duration of the present parliamentary term.

Yours, with love

Tony


I will never, ever get used to seeing Ivan Braithwaite's aggressively tufted toothbrush in our bathroom. Never, not in a million years.

My father's worn-down brush still stands next to it, in its customary place in the fish mug, together with his smoker's toothpaste.

Rosie can't understand why our father doesn't beat Ivan up 'so badly that the bastard ends up with a tube up his f------ nose'.


## Friday August 22nd

A reporter, called Gracie Ball, rapped on the front door today and asked for an interview with 'Pauline and Ivan'. I chatted at the door with her for a while about writing in general. I mentioned that I had written a novel, *Birdwatching*. She said she would like to see it. When I came down, she had insinuated herself into the house and was talking to my mother and Ivan at the kitchen table. The ancient lovers were holding hands and confessing their shared guilt to Gracie.


## Saturday August 23rd

I steeled myself, pushed through the reporters and drove round to The Lawns. There were three people waiting at the Braithwaites' rustic-style gates, smoking cigarettes. One of them, a girl, had a camera slung around her neck. As I got out of the car, the press shouted, 'Adrian! Adrian!' I ignored them and ran up the drive to the front door. I noticed that the shutters and blinds were closed. I knocked on the door, using the lion's-head brass knocker. My father shouted, 'Bugger off,' from the hall.

I lifted the letterbox and shouted, 'It's me – Adrian!' I heard bolts being drawn and locks turning. The door opened only wide enough to let me in, then slammed shut. My father and Tania Braithwaite stood in the spacious hallway, white-faced and haggard. Tania said, 'Do, please, come into the kitchen. I'll make coffee.' She was behaving as though the cataclysmic events of the last few days had never happened.

For once I was lost for words. What could I possibly say to them both? Less than a week ago they had thought themselves safely married; now their cuckold status was being broadcast to the nation. We sat down at the huge pine table in the kitchen. My father pulled a saucer full of fag ends and ash towards him. He lit a cigarette. Tania flapped her hand in front of her face.

'I thought this was a strictly non-smoking household,' I said.

Tania sighed. 'Yes, normally it is . . . but in the circumstances . . .' Her voice trailed away.

My father said, 'What does your mother *see* in him, Adrian?'

Tania's eyes filled with tears. 'Ivan is, *was*, a wonderful man,' she said.

'He betrayed you, Tania,' said my father. He sounded like somebody out of a Frederick Forsyth Cold War novel. It was obvious to me that they were both in shock. Tania got up to pour boiling water into the cafetière. I saw my father watching in admiration as she pushed down the plunger. He has always wanted to join the middle classes.

The phone on the wall, near the Aga, rang. Tania answered it. It became obvious that Pandora was on the line. Tania said, 'I'm taking it one day at a time. George is being a tremendous help.' There was a pause, then Tania said, 'No, darling, there's nothing you can do. Adrian's here. I'm sure he'll go to Sainsbury's for us.' Tania looked at me pleadingly. What could I say but 'Yes'?

I asked my father how long he intended staying at Tania's house.

He said, 'I dunno, I've got nowhere else to go, have I?'

Tania said, 'I've got four empty bedrooms, Adrian. George is welcome to stay for as long as he likes. He understands better than anybody what I'm going through.'

'Because I'm going through the same torment,' he said.

They exchanged a glance, and I knew, I just knew, that despite their previous mutual antipathy it wouldn't be long before they discovered that they had other things in common.

Tania wrote a shopping list, which I transferred into my electronic organizer.

2 baguettes
Tin anchovies
Tin artichoke hearts
Jar saffron strands (must be from S. America)
Coriander (fresh)
Sun-dried tomatoes
Pesto
Goat's cheese & feta
Taramasalata
Pitta bread
Fromage frais
Natural yoghurt (Greek)
Pkt Always panty-liners
Extra virgin olive oil (Italy)
2 60w lightbulbs

XL gardening gloves
2 ripe avocados
Filo pastry (frozen)
Spinach
Mange-touts

When Tania went out of the room my father glanced at the list and grumbled, 'I'll bleeding *starve* to death.' He hates foreign food, apart from chicken korma.

He gave me a £10 note and asked me to get him forty Rothman's, a white sliced loaf and a pack of pork dripping.

However, when I got to Sainsbury's I couldn't retrieve the list from my personal organizer and had to guess instead. I didn't hang around at Copse Close to watch the groceries being unpacked. I'd forgotten my father's Rothman's and I knew there'd be trouble.

## Sunday August 24th

I heard the bed creaking in my mother's room in the early hours of the morning. I banged on the party wall and the creaking stopped. I heard Rosie shout, 'Thank you, Aidy.'

## Monday August 25th

William kept asking for his grandad, so I took him round to The Lawns this morning. My father and Tania were in the garden, in deck-chairs. Apparently he'd just mown the lawn. He was wearing one of his short-sleeved Hawaiian shirts. There was a nicotine patch on his pasty left arm. He got up and played football with William, using Pandora's old netball. A passing stranger might have observed the scene and felt a pang of jealousy that they were not part of this ideal family.

When I got home the second post had arrived. There was a letter from an Arthur Stoat, editor and managing director of Stoat Books Ltd, asking if I would be interested in writing a cookery book to be called *Offally Good! – The Book!*.

As I read his letter, Rosie and Ivan clashed at the fridge. He objected to her drinking straight from the milk bottle rather than using a glass. My intervention was not appreciated by either of them. I must remove William from this hellhole.


Dear Arthur Stoat,

Yes, I would be interested. Please furnish details. Forgive this terse reply, but my time is entirely taken up with family problems at present.

Yours, etc. A. A. Mole.

PS. Do you publish fiction? I have a MS called *Birdwatching* available for publication.

## Wednesday August 27th

I found Rosie crying in the bathroom. She was holding Ivan's burgundy leather washbag over the toilet (the lid was up). I comforted her as best I could. She put the washbag back on to the cistern, where he keeps it. After a minute or two of silence I said, 'You look pink and pretty. What have you done to yourself?'

She said, 'I've washed my face. This is what I look like without make-up.'

'And your hair, it's sort of fluffy,' I said.

'Yeah, it's not gelled down,' she explained, frowning into the washbasin mirror. She lowered her voice and said, 'Ivan complimented me yesterday on my aggressive and provocative image.'

'So, you're changing it?' I checked.

'Yeah,' she said. 'I dunno what to go for,' she said. 'Any suggestions?'

'He was banging on about the "iniquities of fox-hunting" the other day,' I said. 'You could take to wearing the Quorn Hunt regalia, jodhpurs and a riding whip.'

'Yeah,' she laughed, 'that would f------ provoke him, the b------.'

I took advantage of our mutual antipathy to Ivan

the Terrible to say, 'Rosie, have you ever thought you might be suffering from Tourette's syndrome?'

'F--- off,' she said. And flushed Ivan's exfoliating hand mitt down the loo.

Drink – half a bottle of vodka
Drugs – 6 Nurofen, 2 skunk weed
Bowels – nil
Penis – 0/10

## Thursday August 28th

The plumber has only just unblocked the toilet. The mitt damage cost £275. I met my mother on the stairs. She was in a defiant mood. She said, 'I love Ivan, and he *adores me*. So try, at least, to be courteous to him, will you?'

I said, 'Has he seen you without make-up yet?'

She shouted, 'Yes, he has, and he worships every wrinkle, bag and line! He loves me to bits.'

Ivan came out of the lounge. He was halfway through the *Guardian* crossword (the difficult one – he does the quick one while he waits for the kettle to boil). He said, 'I'm *enormously* aware of the trauma you're all suffering. Perhaps when things have calmed down a little we can regroup and present ourselves for family therapy, eh?'

186

I would sooner eat *live toads* than sit in a circle with him while he drones on about our family's dysfunction.

## Friday August 29th

It is true. In times of crisis the Royal Family are a great comfort. It has certainly comforted me to think that they are even more dysfunctional than we are. Neurotic Diana is racketing around with a bloke whose family's money came from associating with arms dealers. Charles is morbidly unhappy, crippled by his unnatural childhood and his Tampax-fixation. They should scrap *The Archers* on the radio and do a soap opera based on the Royal Family. I may write it myself.

## Saturday August 30th

Relations between Rosie and my mother have now broken down completely and she has gone to live at Aaron Michelwaite's house. My mother found out that Rosie has had a monkey tattooed on her belly.

William cried himself to sleep last night (in my bed): he misses Rosie. She used to partner him when he played the boring board games he's so fond of. I am his new opponent, but I am a poor substitute. He gets fed up with me because I don't give a toss if I go up the ladders or down the snakes, and I can't be arsed to learn the rules. Quite honestly, dear Diary, I can't see the point of learning *any* rules. Nobody keeps to them any more.

William starts at Kidsplay Ltd nursery school on September 15th. It can't come too soon for me. I'm happy to pay someone to play with him.

Dear John Tydeman,

It is some years since I wrote to you but you may remember me. I offered you several chances to broadcast my work when you worked at the BBC.

Unfortunately you rejected me then and asked me not to bother you again. However, I approach you now under entirely different circumstances.

I have written a soap opera, which will replace *The Archers*. I think that all thinking people recognize *The Archers* in its present form has had its day.

The nadir for me was listening to the bedsprings when two oldie Ambridge lovers prepared for intercourse . . .

My soap opera cleverly includes the Royal Family.

I enclose a few pages of the opening episode. I have followed the 'Writing for Radio' rules and included many sound effects.

I know it is currently fashionable to record on location, but in this case permissions may not be granted.

Anyway, Mr Tydeman, cast your eye over the pages. If

you are interested perhaps we could meet up at the new Oxygen bar H$_2$O for a sniff of clean air.

Yours

A. A. Mole

## THE WINDSORS

A soap opera based on the Royal Family. To replace *The Archers.*

SCENE 1. QUEEN'S LIVING ROOM

*Sound: Richard and Judy show in the background; Sun newspaper being read; a female corgi barks.*

PRINCE PHILIP: It's appalling, what the papers are saying about Charles, our son!

*(Sound: Concorde flies over.)*

QUEEN: I know who *Charles* is, Philip.

*(Sound: A helicopter lands outside.)*

PHILIP: There was a time when you didn't. He spent so much time with his nanny that you passed him in the corridor once and assumed he was a jockey because he was so small.

*(Sound: Feet walking on priceless Persian carpet.)*

QUEEN: *(breaking into violent sobs)* Don't! Don't! I was a terrible mother.

*(Sound: A handbag is opened.)*

ANDREW: Hi there, aged parents! What's new?

QUEEN: Andrew, darling, was I a terrible mother?

*(Sound: A royal nose is blown into a damask linen handkerchief.)*

ANDREW: Dunno. I can't remember you doing any

189

mothering, Ma. You were sat all day stickin' stamps in a album.

*(Sound: A door slams.)*

CHARLES: It's *an* album, Andrew. Not *a* album. I find your grammatical errors to be quite simply er . . . unforgivable.

*(Sound: Charles frowns; a door opens.)*

ANNE: Why have you called us here, Ma? I've got an appointment with the horse doctor at eleven-thirty.

*(Sound: A door slams; a nervous cough.)*

EDWARD: Sorry I'm late, everybody.

QUEEN: Hello . . . Er . . .

EDWARD: Edward. My name is Edward.

QUEEN: So it is . . . I've called you together for a most important reason. A most important reason indeed . . .

*(Sound: Music plays, leaving listeners in suspense.)*

Copyright: Adrian Mole, August 1997

I feel in my bones that this could be a winner. Princess Diana would be the star eventually, of course. She is at present starring in her own soap opera, and the whole country wants to know what will happen to her next.

## Sunday August 31st

The soap opera of life has made a tragic mistake. You do not kill off your star halfway through a series. Now we will never know how the story ends.

*Impressions on Diana's Tragic Death*

William and Harry being driven to Crathie church, where the priest politely made no mention of the raw fact that their beloved mother had been killed only ten hours earlier.

It was a tawdry way to die. Joy-riders perish in the same way, believing themselves to be invincible against speed and a turn in the road.

Self-control on the tarmac as the Prince moved along the line, shaking the hands of those who had brought the coffin home. The woman inside it had thought that Charles would cherish a video of herself and a much smaller man, Wayne Sleep, dancing together. She didn't know how much he would hate this video. I hope she never found out.

Her only school prize was for 'Best-kept Hamster Cage'.

She once phoned Oliver Hoare, with whom she was obsessed, over twenty times in one hour. She hung up each time he answered. She was subsequently 'spoken to' by the police.

## Monday September 1st

This household has cried enough to fill several rivers, a canal and several lakes. My mother keeps saying, 'Those boys,' and dissolving into yet more tears. None of us have moved away from the television. I have even managed to watch Michael Cole, Mohammed Al-Fayed's spokesman, slither across the screen without leaving the room.

Rosie came back home and threw herself into my mother's arms. They cried together until I thought they would need medical rehydration.

## Tuesday September 2nd

Ivan Braithwaite, who is a republican, made a major *faux pas* today. He said, in front of my mother, 'I can't help feeling that this hysterical outpouring of grief is way over the top.'

She started to cry again and said, 'We're not just crying for her, we're crying for the sadness in our own lives. I'm crying for the hurt I've caused George.'

I said, to try and comfort her, 'Mum, don't worry

about Dad. He and Tania are getting on amazingly well.'

This made my mother cry even more. She asked Ivan if he would take her to Kensington Palace so that she could lay some flowers at the gates and then go to St James's Palace to pay her respects. Ivan said he was not prepared to queue up for eight hours to watch my mother sign her name in a book. My mother said, 'I'm doing more than sign my name. Adrian's going to write me a poem about Princess Di, aren't you, Aidy?'

What could I say? The poor woman is grief-stricken. I agreed to write the poem and accompany her to the various shrines. Rosie preferred to watch the Diana-mourning on television. She said it was 'more real'.

## Wednesday September 3rd

We Sellotaped my poem on to the trunk of a tree in Kensington Gardens this morning.

> *Oh Diana!*
> *Oh Diana!* Was a song, of
> my mother's youth. Sung by
> Paul Anka, who was small
> and white of tooth.

The refrain, *Oh Diana!*
Beats inside Mum's head.
A blank, a blank, a doo-dah
that her Diana is dead.

I told my mother that I needed more time to finish the poem properly, but she refused to wait. She was afraid that we would miss the space on the tree. There was a queue of poets behind us. On the way back up the M1, my mother said, 'I'm going to make something of my life.' I advised her to drop Ivan Braithwaite. She said, 'No, Ivan's going to help me. He's already offered.'

Saw the crisp-eating boy walking past our house as I was pulling the curtains at 11 p.m. He is surely too young to be out on his own.

## Thursday September 4th

My mother is furious with the Queen for not flying the flag at half-mast over Buckingham Palace, and for not coming to London to see and comfort the huge crowds of mourners who continue to throng the parks and streets near the royal palaces. The press are being blamed for her death, and my mother is threatening to cancel *Hello!*.

Over dinner tonight Ivan said, 'What Diana didn't

understand was that you can't invite photographers to put you on the cover of *Vogue* one day, then scream press intrusion the next because you're on the front of the *Sun*. You can't be a little bit famous.'

He could win a Bore of the Solar System contest. However, what he said about fame worried me. I took a sip of Tizer and said, 'Yes, I myself face the fame problem. I am broadcasting to the nation on September 10th.'

My mother said, 'I shouldn't think you'll have a problem with fame, Adrian. *Nobody* at all watches the Millennium Channel.'

I told her about the students.

She said, 'Students don't count.'


## Friday September 5th

Visited my father and Tania today. When I arrived Tania was demonstrating to my father several uses for sun-dried tomatoes. I saw my father stifle a yawn when Tania turned her back to grate some Parmesan. She told me that she was cooking some quickly heated-through food today, so that she and my father could 'maximize their time in front of the funeral coverage'.

My father's depression seems to have lifted. He is going to a Job Club on Monday. Apparently Tania has told him that he is a 'highly intelligent man'. She

195

has promised to help him 'realize his potential' if he stops smoking. This shows how little she knows my father.

He will choose Rothman's over fame and fortune any day.

## Saturday September 6th

Oh! The card on the wreath on the coffin. 'Mummy'. Oh!

We ran out of man-sized tissues very early in the day. My mother saw her friends from Groby Theatre Workshop, Alan and Abbo, walking in the procession behind the coffin. They were representing the Ashby-de-la-Zouch branch of the Terrence Higgins Trust. She said it was the first time she'd seen them without a smile on their faces.

## Sunday September 7th

Another mini-lecture from Ivan at breakfast about the virtues of New Labour. I said that I personally thought Tony Blair's reading in the pulpit at Westminster Abbey was a bit on the theatrical side. I couldn't help thinking that those endless pauses had been timed by Alastair Campbell with a stopwatch.

My mother accused me of 'heartless cynicism'. Since Ivan came to live here she has changed her vocabulary and she has now started to wear Pink Blush lipstick instead of her usual colour, Erotic Flame. *The Beginner's Guide to the Internet* is on her bedside table, next to *Pass Your Driving Test*.

## Monday September 8th

I overheard a gruesome conversation in the bathroom today. Ivan said, 'Oh, God, Pauline, you're *so* beautiful.'

My mother sniggered, then said, 'But look at my hideous cellulite, Ivy.'

'Pauline, baby,' he crooned, 'cellulite is just a thousand little dimples, and I love every one of those dimples.'

As I passed by the open bathroom door I saw him bend and kiss a patch of cellulite on her left outside thigh. Perhaps he *does* truly love her.

Only three days to go before I am a household name. Perhaps I should get a second phone line put in.

## Tuesday September 9th

Archie Tait rang from a phone box to wish me good luck – it was kind of him to remember. Why, though? I haven't given *him* a second thought.

## Wednesday September 10th

Zippo rang early this morning to say that they had shown *Offally Good!* to a focus group of Oxford undergraduates, and they had given it the thumbs up. 'They said it was great comedy,' Zippo said. After I had put the phone down I puzzled over this remark.

There was a preview from A. A. Gill in *The Times*. He wrote,

*Offally Good!* is offally bad. A wooden presenter, Adrian Mole, stumbles and bumbles through twenty minutes of *Crossroads*-quality TV. We watch with horrible fascination as he makes sheep's-head broth. (Which is not even offal, so the Tristans behind the programme are deceiving us from the start.) After twenty minutes Mole produces a pot of grey liquid, on the surface of which floats a layer of scum. Dev Singh, however, was brilliantly and genuinely funny. I sense that a star has been conceived, if not yet born.

Both sets of 'parents' have invited me to watch the programme with them. How can I possibly choose between them? Both have had Cable TV installed specifically to watch *Offally Good!*.

A compromise was reached. I watched the first half at Wisteria Walk, then got in the car during the commercial break, drove like a maniac and watched the second half at The Lawns. Both households watched in silence. The New Dog seemed to enjoy it at first, but then lost interest and went to sit on its cushion.

I overheard my mother saying to Ivan, 'I don't know if I can face showing myself in public.'

## Thursday September 11th

I stayed in bed all day with the duvet pulled over my head. Nobody rang to congratulate me. My own family cannot look me in the eye. The next five Wednesdays are going to be torment for me.

## Friday September 12th

Zippo rang to say that the ratings for *Offally Good!* showed that Richard and Judy 'should not buy a retirement property yet'. He said that 55,000 people had switched over to *Good Morning* when I cleavered the sheep's head open, leaving 57,000 watching me.

I told Zippo about the proposed book deal with Stoat. He said, 'Pie Crust own 25 per cent of any exploitation.' When I protested, he said, 'Take a peek at your contract, Aid.' I did. He is right.

I was alarmed to see that I am due to deliver the manuscript to Stoat on October 15th. He is going for the Christmas market.


## Monday September 15th

An historic day. William embarked on the first step in an educational journey that will culminate in his attending either Oxford or Cambridge. He started at Kidsplay Ltd today, a private nursery school owned by Mrs Parvez, Liberal councillor and local entrepreneur.

I resent having to pay £9 a day to Mrs Parvez. However I can't put up with the boy hanging on to my legs all day any longer. I have things to do, and places to go. (Though now I will have to do the things and go to places between the hours of 9.15 and 3.15.)

There was an emotional scene when William left Wisteria Walk wearing his burgundy sweatshirt (emblazoned with Kidsplay Ltd's slogan, 'Play As U Learn'), Gap cords, baseball cap and Velcro-fastened trainers.

My mother broke down and sobbed. 'Everything is three sizes too big for him.'

I pointed out to her that he would grow into his uniform eventually. I also asked her to try and control herself. She was carrying on as though she were Antigone. I said, 'He's going to nursery school, not to be ritually sacrificed on a slab.'

My father and Tania were waving outside The Lawns as William and I drove by, like spectators at a royal wedding. I hope the boy doesn't expect such a send-off every morning.

As we drove to Kidsplay Ltd, William asked me where birds 'hang out' (an expression he has picked up from Rosie). I asked him to rephrase the question.

'Where do they go when they're tired?' he asked, staring out of the car window at the sky.

I said, 'They go to sleep in their nests, of course.'

Kidsplay Ltd is in a converted church. There's a stained-glass window on the back wall showing Jesus on the Cross. When William saw it he said, 'That's the man who's on Rosie's necklace.'

There was no time to explain about the symbolism of Rosie's fashion-item crucifix.

Mrs Parvez bustled up in her green sari and showed William to his peg in the cloakroom. Each had an animal symbol hanging from the peg as an *aide-mémoire*. William's was an anteater. I asked Mrs Parvez if this could be substituted for something more cuddly or lovable.

She said, coldly, 'I have three left, an elk, a Thompson's gazelle and a warthog.'

I settled for the anteater.

As I drove away I couldn't help but feel that I had started off on the wrong foot with Mrs Parvez.

When I picked him up, William said, 'You told me a lie, Dad. Mrs Parvez told me that birds *don't* sleep in their nests.'

I was furious with Mrs Parvez: she had undermined my parental authority. I said, 'So where the sodding hell *do* they sleep?'

'On branches,' said William.

I gave a scornful laugh. 'Oh, branches,' I scoffed. 'All night? No, son,' I said. 'Mrs Parvez has misinformed you.' I saw him puzzling over the word misinformed. 'She lied,' I explained. I went on to press my point home. *'All birds sleep in their nests, all year round.'*


## Tuesday September 16th

William came home this afternoon with the following note.


Kidsplay Ltd
Castle Road
Ashby-de-la-Zouch
September 16, 1997

Dear Mr Mole,
    William has told me that you called me a liar, and

questioned my assertion that birds do not habitually sleep in their nests. I refer you to page 29 of *The Birds in Your Garden* by Roy Wren, published by Glauberman & Arthur Ltd, 1979.

Yours sincerely,

Mrs Parvez

PS. If you wish William to go on a trip to Brown's Farm Park Ltd on Thursday, will you please send £5.50 tomorrow morning.

## Wednesday September 17th

I rang the central reference library in Leicester. They had not heard of Mr Wren's opus. I tried to ring the RSPB but was put on hold, and made to listen to a chaffinch chaffing. It made a change from Vivaldi. A man with a gravelly voice eventually came on the line.

I asked him my nest question. 'One moment, this is Accounts. I'll put you through to Inquiries,' he said. The line went dead. Presently an owl began to hoot down the phone. Then an old woman said, 'Inquiries.'

I asked my nest question. She said, 'This is *General* Inquiries. I'll put you through to Bird Inquiries.' The line went dead again. Then a nightingale sang in Berkeley Square. Then a robot said, 'Welcome to Bird

Inquiries. Press One for identification. Press Two for migration. Press Three for feeding suggestions. Press Four for habitat. Press Five . . .'

I replaced the receiver with E. M. Forster's quotation from *Howards End* ringing in my ears: 'Only connect.'

I did not watch the second episode of *Offally Good!* (Tripe). Archie Tait rang and left a message, saying, 'Well done.' The man is practically a stranger, why does he bother? I found the following note in William's anorak pocket this evening.


Dear Mr Mole,

William has not yet brought the £5.50 for the trip to Brown's Farm Park Ltd tomorrow. If you wish William to partake of this trip, will you please remedy the situation tomorrow morning. Failure to do so will result in William being left behind in the care of Mr Lewis, the caretaker, who is not qualified in resuscitation techniques.

Yours sincerely,
Mrs Parvez


## Thursday September 18th

Dear Mrs Parvez,

I was most disturbed to be told by William that his packed lunch was stolen by a goat (Noreen) today, while he was at Brown's Farm Park Ltd. Apparently the beast ate not only the contents of the lunchbox, but the lunchbox itself. William said he was hungry and distressed, but he received no comfort (or replacement food!) from you. I have tried many times to contact Farmer Brown by telephone, but am told by voicemail that he is not at his desk(!).

It seems to me that Noreen is a menace and should be kept in isolation.

I hope you will give me your support in this matter.

Sincerely,

A. A. Mole

PS. According to the Internet, there are several species of birds that sleep in their nests. Some use feathers and down to make their nests more comfortable, rather like our human duvets and pillows.

## Friday September 19th

Kidsplay Nursery Ltd
September 18th, 1997

Dear Mr Mole,

I e-mailed Farmer Brown @ Foobar.co.uksetaside – and he e-mailed me back with the following message.

'The CCT camera next to the goat pen shows a dark-skinned lad in a red sweatshirt and brown cord trousers throwing a Postman Pat plastic lunchbox over the three-foot-high chain-linked fence towards Noreen, the goat.'

Yours sincerely,

Mrs Parvez

## Saturday September 20th

William said he did it because Noreen looked cold and hungry. He is such a soft-hearted kid. Though he is also, it has to be said, a convincing liar. I told him the story about 'Cry Wolf'. I also told him that if he didn't behave in future, a man called Jack Straw would get him and put him in prison.

The boy was outside the house today. I banged on the window and asked him to stop picking the berries off the shrub that grows on the fence. He glowered and put his hands in his pockets.

At 8.30 p.m. I sat down at my desk to begin work on *Offally Good! – The Book!*. At 11.37 I rose to my feet having written nothing. Not one word.

## Sunday September 21st

Pandora has weathered the political storm and has been promoted to something called PPS to somebody I've never heard of in the Ministry of Agriculture.

She rang to tell her father this morning, as if we didn't already know! She is plastered all over the media. She told me on the phone that her mother and my father's 'living arrangement' has definitely turned into a full-blown sexual affair. Apparently she rang Tania this morning, to find her mother still in bed. Pan said, 'I distinctly heard your father's voice whispering, "I'll put the kettle on, Tan,"' and claimed she heard his smoker's cough as he opened the bedroom door. 'So, they're definitely playing at hide the sausage,' she said.

I asked her how she felt about our parental swap. She said, 'On the one hand I'm enchanted by the synchronicity of the thing, but on the other I'm appalled and disgusted.'

It was a typical politician's reply.

Personally I am horrified by my father. He has obviously been lying about his sexual potency. I hope my mother doesn't find out that he is sexually active again. I asked Pandora if she had 'caught' *OG!*.

She said that *Offally Good!* was the talk of the Commons. She said the Federation of Master Butchers' own newspaper, *MEAT*, had given it a rave review. Sheep's heads have been 'selling like hot cakes'. Butcher's shops and supermarkets up and down the country have been inundated by students. There is a national shortage and emergency supplies are being flown in from New Zealand. The Society of the Deserving Poor has also praised the programme. I asked her how she knew all this, and she said, 'I surfed the Net, of course.' I was very touched. She obviously cares for me.

I asked her when she was coming up to Leicestershire. She said, 'Tonight, I'll be at The Lawns by three a.m. Please ask your mother and my father to attend.' I asked Pandora if someone from Relate should be in attendance. She said, 'Clearly not.'


## Monday September 22nd

It was a mistake to allow five bottles of wine into the summit meeting. At one point I thought I had stepped into a particularly acrimonious production of *Who's Afraid of Virginia Woolf?*. Pandora's conciliation skills were brushed aside while the fifty-somethings ranted and raved and came close to blows with each other. Horrible things were said. Ivan wants The Lawns to be sold and the proceeds split between them. Tania said, 'The Lawns is my life. I will never be parted from that garden.'

Ivan said, 'That's why our marriage died, Tania. You'd be out there gardening in the dark with a head torch while I was in bed, waiting for you.'

Tania screamed, 'There were slugs to kill!' with a dangerous edge of fanaticism to her voice, I thought. She then burst out with, 'How could you live with a woman whose garden is covered in *bindweed*, Ivan?'

Ivan strode down to the smoking half of the room (occupied by my mother, my father and Pandora) and took my mother into his arms. He turned to his wife and said, 'I love every nettle, every dandelion, every buttercup in Pauline's garden.'

My father shuffled down to the non-smoking section and put his arms around Tania's shaking shoulders. 'Don't worry, Tan,' he said, 'I'm here now, I'll help murder those bastard slugs.' It was an outright declaration of love. My mother was stung into casting aspersions on my father's sexual potency, at which point Pandora and I excused ourselves and went to sit outside on a bench under the apple trees. I trod on some rotten windfall apples and ruined my second-best Timberlands. Pandora said that she disapproved of my mother's boasting about Ivan's potency. I confessed to Pandora that I had been disgusted at her father's refusal to observe the two minutes' silence for Diana.

Zippo rang me on my mobile. He is back in London. He said the ratings for *Offally Good!* were rising 'like fish in a bucket'. He said Dev's postbag was 'amazing'. I asked if I had any fan mail, he said, 'Yeah, we'll post it on to you when there's enough to fill an A4 envelope.'

Worked all night on *OGTB* yet had little to show for it. I simply couldn't get the pig's trotters recipe to sound exciting.

## Thursday September 25th

The lamb sweetbreads with black bean sauce episode went out yesterday morning. I watched alone: everyone else in my household was out on more important business, apparently. Am I a consummate television professional, or am I an embarrassing amateur? I don't know. There isn't a single person I know whom I can rely on to give me good, impartial advice. I need an agent. I rang Brick Eagleburger's office. Boston's voicemail answered. I said, 'Adrian Mole from *Offally Good!*. Ring me back, will you?' I forced myself *not* to say please. Assertiveness is the new manners.

Brick himself rang back fifteen minutes later. 'I *lurve* that *show*,' he boomed. 'I practically *peed* my pants when that sheep's testicle fell out of the wok. Adrian, you – are – so – funnee!'

Once again I was baffled. Sweetbreads are not testicles, are they?

When he stopped laughing, I explained that I was in desperate need of an agent. 'You got one!' said Brick.

I'm going to have lunch in London with him tomorrow, to plan my career, my publicity, my writing ambitions, my financial planning, my divorce, my tax. *My life.*

## Friday September 26th

Brick looks like a gangster who has read Proust. He towered above me and nearly stopped my circulation with his handshake. I'm almost sure he wears a black wig. He chews constantly on an unlit cigar. We went to the Ivy. A. A. Gill saw me walk in and raised a hand in greeting, as though we were equals! Has he forgotten that he has twice now given me execrable reviews?

I wasn't sure what was the correct response to Gill, so I confined myself to smiling ruefully at him and raising my eyebrows. When I went into the gents' later I encored these facial expressions in front of a washbasin mirror. I looked like Coco the Clown, one person I have always loathed.

Brick encouraged me to drink four White Ladies then to talk about myself for two and a half hours. He didn't look bored once – apart from when he was signing the bill. I agreed to give him 20 per cent of my income for life.

## Saturday September 27th

When I picked up the *Guardian* from the BP shop today, I was astonished to see Dev Singh's photograph at the top of the front page, alerting readers to an interview on page four of the G2 section. I sat in my car on the forecourt and read it. I was only mentioned once: 'Dev's dazzling wit and uproarious physical comedy is in glorious contrast to the dour televisual presence of Adrian Mole, a pedant from Middle England.'

When I got home I found an invitation from the Leicester Tortoise Society to open their Christmas Fayre on Saturday November 1st. My first public engagement.

## Sunday September 28th

A bombshell! My mother has told me that she is no longer prepared to look after William when I go back to work! Ivan has asked her to travel the world with him. She said, 'Adrian, I've got to go, haven't I? I can't say no to the world, can I?' I suggested that they take the lad with them. It would broaden his mind. She said, 'You don't get it, do you, you selfish sod? I'm through with childcare.'

I said, 'What about Rosie?'

She said, 'Rosie's tall enough to reach the stove and the fridge and the ironing-board and, anyway, she's got her dad.'

## Monday September 29th

Ivan and my mother have taken over the kitchen table with their maps, guidebooks and brochures. They told me that they intend to *cycle* around the world. They are obviously suffering from *folie à deux*: neither of them has cycled further than the local shops before today.

I received a postcard today from Arthur Stoat. On one side was a photograph of a Norwegian peasant woman riding on a pig's back. On the other side was written, 'Please send me assurance that you have started work on the book. Yours, A. Stoat. PS. New deadline, October 21st.'

*11.30 p.m.* Rosie came to see me in my bedroom tonight. She asked me to promise, on William's life, to keep the secret she was about to divulge. I promised.

She is two months pregnant.

I did all the traditional things – said, 'Oh, my God!' clapped a hand to my forehead, got up and paced the available space between my bed and the window. 'How did it happen?' I asked.

'The usual way. Like, I wasn't visited by an angel or nothing,' she sneered. She then attempted to justify her condition. 'We've only done it four times,' she said.

'Minus contraception, I presume?' I asked.

'You sound like Jack *Straw*,' she said, accusingly.

I ignored the insult and asked her if she was sure.

'Yeah, I'm sure, I told Dad I needed money for Nike trainers, which is sixty quid, but I got a cheaper pair and bought a pregnancy test with the difference.'

I felt a pang of jealousy that she was able to con my father out of sixty quid with such apparent ease. She has always been his favourite. The news of her pregnancy could plunge him back down into the pit of depression. I said, 'He'll go mad when he finds out.'

'He won't find out,' she said, irritably. 'He doesn't know what Nike trainers *look* like.'

I went to bed earlier than usual and lay in the dark thinking about Rosie and the little tadpole baby she had inside her. I like to think that I am a civilized man, but I wanted to run round to Aaron Michelwaite's house, drag him into the street and beat him up for what he'd done to my little sister. He's bigger than me, but I reckoned that an unexpected and well-timed blow to the back of his head with my hardback edition of *War and Peace* would knock him off his feet.

I was present in the delivery room when Rosie was born, on November 11th, 1982. I hadn't planned to be there, I was only a lad, but I was trapped by ghastly circumstances and forced to watch and listen as my mother gave birth. The sights! The sounds! I tried to escape several times, but my mother wouldn't let go of my right hand (it still plays me up when the weather is cold). She kept shouting, 'Don't leave me, Adrian'

– she was estranged from my father at the time. In fact, there was gossip about Rosie's paternity, led by Edna May Mole, my grandma. She died still convinced that Rosie's dad was *not* George Albert Mole, the name on her birth certificate, but Mr Lucas, the man who lured my mother away to Sheffield.

As far as I know Rosie is completely unaware of the question mark surrounding her conception and birth. I saw her seconds after she left my mother's body, before she took her first breath. She was half bald and angry-looking and resembled my father. She looked nothing like Lucas, but of course she had no teeth then. It was me who held her for the first time, after she'd had the slime removed, and me who taught her to click Lego bricks together. She used to follow me around like a small shadow, until she turned twelve, then something horrible happened to her and she transmogrified into a demon.

I know I promised to keep her secret, but I can feel it growing like an abscess inside me. It is longing to burst out. Even Aaron Michelwaite is unaware that he has fathered a foetus.

I asked her tonight if she *wants* a baby. She said, 'I might.' This surprised me. She had never shown the slightest sign of maternalism. Her dolls were treated disgracefully. She chopped their hair and eyelashes off, scribbled on their faces with biro, and performed horrible experiments on them with the contents of my father's toolbox. She was like a torturer's apprentice. I felt it my duty to warn her that New Labour strongly disapproved of single parents, and that should she choose to tramp that particular road in life, she would find it 'stony and full of potholes'. I said, 'Tony Blair will make you go out to work, Rosie. Any dream you have of breastfeeding your baby in front of *The Big Breakfast* will stay just that, a dream.'

She said, 'I can't *stand* Denise Van Outen, and there's no *way* I'd breastfeed.'

I felt my temples begin to throb. I urged her to talk to a professional with a diploma about her dilemma, but she refused.

We sat in silence: I looked around her room and noted that she had turned all her Barbie dolls to face the wall.

I asked her if her school provided parenting classes. She said, 'Yeah, like, they teach us how to, like, fill a single-parent benefit form in.'

I retired for the night. How can Rosie have a baby? She is a baby herself.

## Tuesday September 30th

I was driving William to his nursery when I heard a woman on a local radio station talking about teenage pregnancy. I turned the volume up in time to hear her say, '. . . and these dolls are extremely lifelike, they weigh eight and a half pounds. They are programmed to cry and they must be fed and changed regularly. The teenager either has to take it everywhere with them or find a babysitter.'

After I'd dropped William off I rang the radio station's helpline and obtained the fax number of the supplier of the *faux* babies. I'm hiring one for two weeks. The rubber kid should be here by ten o'clock tomorrow if Parcel Force keeps its promise.

Rosie said today that if she decides to have the baby she wants me to lend her the money to have the tattoo lasered off her belly. She said, 'By the time I get to the labour ward my little monkey will have stretched to look like King Kong.'


## Wednesday October 1st

Everybody wanted to know what was in the parcel. I was forced to lie and said I'd started my Christmas shopping. My mother rolled her eyes and exchanged an amused glance with Ivan. I saw her lips form the word 'anal'.

When William was at Kidsplay Ltd, and Ivan and my mother were out training for their circumnavigation of the world, I called Rosie into my bedroom and we unpacked the baby doll. It was unsettlingly realistic – it looked like a prettier William Hague. It was wearing a yellow Babygro, and had a label around its neck, which said:

Hello, I'm five weeks old, I weigh eleven pounds and I need to be 'fed' every four hours around the clock. I have been programmed to cry at antisocial times. If I am roughly handled an ear-splitting alarm will be activated, which may disturb your neighbours.

*Warning!* Do not attempt to tamper with my solar-powered batteries. Do not bathe me. Do not ingest my eyeballs.

*Contents*
Doll
Electronic bottle
Transportation sling
Bottle-cleansing solution
Six diapers
1 comforter

I unfastened the Babygro. The doll was of indeterminate sex. Rosie was disappointed, she had been hoping for a girl.

It took me over an hour last night to persuade her to look after the doll for a fortnight. In the end I had to bribe her with the promise that I would pay for her to have hair extensions fitted at Toni and Guy.

Rosie redressed the doll and said, 'I'm gonna call her Ashby.'

She put Ashby in the sling and went to school. We have decided to tell our mother that Rosie is participating in a research project. We haven't bothered with a cover story for the school. They have been preparing for an Ofsted inspection and so are unlikely to notice.

My mother and Ivan didn't get home until after dark. It had taken them most of the day to get to Coalville and back, a distance of seven miles on mostly flat terrain. They were *très* shocked to find Ashby lying face down on the draining-board, where Rosie had dumped her while she fed the New Dog. I had a quiet word with Rosie later. I stressed that unless she kept to the rules I was not going to fork out for the hair extensions. I watched the video of the third *Offally Good!* (Belgian Faggots), with my family and Ivan. Unfortunately, Ashby bawled throughout. I was most annoyed, though not as annoyed as Rosie, who eventually left the room muttering, 'She's doin' my 'ead in.'

William behaved atrociously at bedtime. He flounced around his bedroom like Little Lord Fauntleroy. I was forced to shout at him. My mother poked her head round the bedroom door and said, 'Don't be too hard on him, he's bound to be jealous of the new baby.'

I heard Rosie get up twice in the night to see to Ashby.

## Thursday October 2nd

The household (and the neighbourhood) were woken at 6.15 this morning by what sounded like the klaxon used for summoning the Lowestoft lifeboat crew. It was Ashby. Rosie denied that she had handled the doll roughly, but I knew otherwise. I had heard her snarling at Ashby through the plasterboard wall that separates her bedroom from mine. The klaxon noise only stopped when I took the baby in my arms, and walked her up and down the landing. William stood at the door of his bedroom watching us; his face was suffused with jealous rage.

## Friday October 3rd

Zippo rang. Pie Crust have been inundated with complaints from various Belgian gay organizations about this week's episode of *Offally Good!*.

I phoned Mr 20-per-cent-for-life and asked his voicemail for advice. He rang me back in person, but I was feeding Ashby so I had to ask him to call back. Unless you get the electronic bottle into her mouth at the precise angle, she refuses to 'feed'.

Brick advised me to go for what they call in the PR trade 'The Full Grovel'. He drafted the following press release.

Adrian Mole is sincerely sorry if he gave offence to any person of any nationality, colour, creed, or sexual orientation. He would like to point out that his best friend, Nigel, is gay.

Belgian Faggots are a traditional dish and the recipe is adapted from *A Plain Cookery Book for the Working Classes* by Charles Elme Francatelli, Chief Cook to Her Majesty Queen Victoria.

## BELGIAN FAGGOTS

These may be prepared with sheep's pluck (intestines) or even with bullock's liver, but a pig's pluck would be the personal preference of most top chefs.

Chop up the heart, liver, lights and kidneys; season well and divide into balls the size of a small apple. Traditionally these should each be secured in shape with a piece of pig's caul, fastened with a wooden twig then baked for about half an hour in a brisk oven. If watching your cholesterol levels, pour half the grease from the faggots into the waste-bin before ensuing. If using a twig as a fastening device, check for splinters before inserting the faggot into the mouth. If you live in a flat and twigs are not easily available, wooden skewers can be purchased at most Greek supermarkets.

### Friday October 10th

Rosie asked me to babysit Ashby today. She wanted to go to the multiplex to see Leonardo DiCaprio in *Shakespeare's Romeo and Juliet*. I refused. None of the grandparents were available. They were having yet another of their interminable meetings about divorce, remarriage and finance. Rosie stayed at home and looked after her baby.

Nigel rang. He was furious at being 'outed' by me. He said his grandmother was terminally ill and that I had 'probably put the lid on her coffin'.

### Saturday October 11th

I found Ashby in the back garden this morning. She was wet and cold and had a dent in her head. Rosie admitted throwing the baby out of the window last night. 'It's ruining my life,' she said. 'I'm gonna go *mad* if I don't get some *sleep*.'

*The afternoon*

I was in the garden hosing the New Dog down (don't ask, just don't ask, Diary), when Rosie came out to

222

join me. She had her arms wrapped round herself in the way women do when they venture outside. She watched the hosing operation for a while and said, 'I've decided not to have it.'

I turned off the hose and the New Dog shook itself dry before escaping through a hole in the fence. I said, 'I think we'd better tell Mum, then.'

We both looked down the garden to the kitchen window where my mother was to be seen washing up. Ivan was standing behind her with a tea towel and they were both laughing. Only that morning they had received official permission from the Mongolian government to cycle across part of the Gobi desert.

Rosie said, 'No, don't let's.'

She has been told by the NHS that she can have the operation on Wednesday 15th. The day before the cyclists are due to start their world tour.


## Monday October 13th

I couldn't bear to mention it before today, dear Diary, but Barry Kent's fifth novel, *Blind*, has been nominated for the 1997 Bookworm Prize. I pray with every fibre, every molecule, every strand of DNA in my body that *Blind* does not win. I forced myself to read Ivan's copy last night. It's about a working-class boy, Ron Angel, who is blinded in the trenches of the First World War, and goes on to have a sexual romance with his eye-surgeon, Cedric Palmer-Tomkinson.

*Blind* is the favourite at Ladbrokes. Melvyn Bragg called it 'haunting', Hanif Kureishi said it was 'cool', Kathy Lette that it was a 'hoot'. I quote Dr E. E. G. Head, writing in the *Literary Review*: 'Kent's book is a sustained metaphorical *tour de force*.' I faxed Arthur Stoat a recipe for my book. I hope it will pacify him.

## Tuesday October 14th

The living-room floor is littered with lightweight camping equipment. Ivan has repacked his panniers five times. He has been ruthless with my mother and has forbidden her to take her hair-dryer or travelling iron.

I asked Ivan how they were getting to Dover.

He said, 'We're cycling, of course.'

My mother said, 'Couldn't we put the bikes in the guard's van and go by train?'

Ivan threw the tent poles on to the carpet and said, 'If you're having second thoughts, Pauline, now is the time to express them.'

My mother ran up to him and put her arms around his chest. She was wearing Lycra cycling shorts; her bum looked like two balloons fighting in a black bin-bag.

I left them to it and went to find Rosie. She was upstairs in her room. Ashby was dressed in a pair of William's old Baby Gap dungarees, and Rosie was cleaning the doll's ears with a cotton bud. I said, 'Rosie, I've got to send Ashby back today – the hire time is up.'

She put Ashby into the box herself and watched while I Sellotaped it shut. Then she asked me to reopen the box so that she could say goodbye properly. When the postmistress, Mrs Porlock, put the parcel on the scales at the post office, Ashby's mechanism started to cry. It was very disconcerting. The colour drained from Mrs Porlock's face. She insisted on me unpacking the parcel. I said, 'Do you seriously think that I would consider sending a *live baby* via Parcel Force?'

## Wednesday October 15th

It's my fault that the whole family knows that Rosie had a termination today. Before we set out in the car I phoned the clinic for directions. Apparently, as soon as we left the house my mother's insatiable curiosity prompted her to dial 1471; when she pressed Redial a receptionist answered at the clinic in Leamington Spa. My mother badgered the woman for information but, to her fury, the receptionist refused to disclose any details 'pertaining to clients'.

My mobile was ringing constantly all the way to Leamington Spa. Rosie begged me not to answer and I respected her wishes.

I went inside with her and held her hand, but Rosie whispered, 'Aidy, you're showing me up.' I looked around and quailed at the rows of female faces, all waiting to be 'processed' and all staring at me with varying degrees of contempt. It wasn't a good place to be a man. I went outside, sat in the car and listened to Radio Four.

I then went for a walk in the grounds. There were some very expensive cars in the staff car park.

On the way back to Ashby-de-la-Zouch I pulled into the BP garage and bought Rosie a Magnum ice cream in an attempt to cheer her up.

We arrived home to a storm of accusations and recriminations. We opened the front door to hear my mother yelling, 'How can I set off on a world tour tomorrow when my little girl needs me?'

Ivan muttered, 'Pandora had a termination during her lunch break once. There was none of this bloody *hysteria*.'

My mother sobbed, hysterical, 'It's not hysteria, Ivan, it's called *emotion* – something you and your tight-arsed family know nothing about.' The decibel level rose when the New Dog joined in, barking loudly. The only person not making a noise was William. My heart stopped. In the chaos, no one had remembered to collect him from Kidsplay. I dashed to the car and drove to the nursery, exceeding the speed limit several times.

Mrs Parvez was sitting with her coat on by the entrance. William was asleep on her lap. The nursery was silent; all the little chairs had been turned upside down and placed on the child-sized tables. When she saw me rushing in she glared, then said, 'He cried himself to sleep. He thought you'd gone away, like his mum.'

## Thursday October 16th

I have made remarkable progress on my radio soap opera script.

THE ROYAL ARCHERS

*Agricultural bagpipe music plays.*

QUEEN: Phil, was that the vet's van I saw driving away, with Eddy Grundy trapped amusingly between the back wheels?

PHIL (*deep sigh*): Yes, it was, and I'm afraid it's bad news, Liz. The corgis have gone down with scab foot.

QUEEN: The whole herd?

PHIL: 'Fraid so. I'll have to shoot them all.

QUEEN: Then this is the end for us, Phil. We'll have to sell the farm.

SHULA: Hello, Mum, I've just dropped into your farmhouse kitchen to sigh and stand by the Aga, and tell you that I'm having an affair with my best friend's husband, the village doctor.

QUEEN: Does Andrew Morton know, Shula? (*Pause*) Does he? (*Pause*) Tell me, tell me now.

(*Agricultural bagpipe music plays.*)

## Friday October 17th

Arthur Stoat rang me in person today to ask for clarification on the pigs' trotters recipe I faxed to him on Monday 13th. He said, 'Are the actual trotters – the bits that make contact with the shit in the pigsty – left on during cooking, or are they filleted out before, and thrown away?'

I informed him that the trotters were a vital ingredient of the dish, and that if he tried to edit them out I would remove my name from the book.

He said, 'Keep your hair on.' (Has he heard about my incipient baldness?) 'All I wanted was a yes or a no. As it stands your recipe is open to ambiguity.'

I didn't like the sound of him. I asked him if he came from Cardiff; I pride myself on my ability to spot a regional accent. He said, 'No,' he originated from South Africa, but conceded that he listened to a lot of Welsh-hill-farmer plays on the BBC World Service. He said, 'Do I take it that you will not be delivering your completed manuscript within the next few days?'

I said that I'd had a lot of family business occupying my mind lately.

He said, 'So you'll be missing your deadline, will you?'

I admitted that I was highly unlikely to be able to write the book in a week.

My new deadline is November 1st; Stoat is determined to have the tome in the bookshops in time for Christmas. He reckons he can 'turn a book round' in three weeks. He said, 'I did it with *Diana at My Fingertips*, by her personal manicurist, and I'll do it for *Offaly*.'

If I work non-stop and cease all sleeping and eating and non-essential activities, I should be able to do it.


## Saturday October 18th

Aaron Michelwaite has finished with Rosie. He told her that he was not ready for a 'long-term commitment' because he wants to study marine engineering at Plymouth University. I was outraged at the callous timing of his announcement and said so.

Rosie is lolling about the house in her Knickerbox satin pyjamas. She refuses to get dressed because she doesn't intend going outside 'ever again'.

A recorded message at the Michelwaite residence informs callers that 'The family have gone to Devon with the caravan, to recharge our batteries.' This is a timely move on their part, because my father, sub-sequent to the news of Rosie's termination, is still threatening to punch Aaron's lights out. If he does, they'll need their batteries.

William came into my bed last night. Rosie woke him up crying for Ashby.

## Sunday October 19th

A researcher from *Kilroy* rang this morning to ask me if I would appear on the show tomorrow morning to talk about the theme 'mixed marriages'. I pointed out to her that my African wife was divorcing me. 'Due to racial intolerance?' she asked, sounding excited.

'No,' I replied. 'Due to her intolerance of my personal habits.'

She said they were doing a show in November called, 'My Partner's Habits are Driving Me Mad'. Would I be interested?

I said, 'No.'

The researcher then asked to speak to my mother, saying she had read in the press about her colourful private life. I handed the phone over with more than a few misgivings. An hour later, when she came off the phone, I warned my mother about the dangers of TV exposure, but I could tell that my warning fell on deaf ears. She is talking of booking herself a six-week course of non-surgical face-lifts at the place where she gets her hair done.

## Monday October 20th

I shall not be making any more entries in my diary until my book is finished. I *must* keep the deadline or risk losing all credibility. I have written to the Tortoise Society to say that I am unable to open their Christmas Fayre 'due to pressure of work'.

## Friday October 31st

A horrible thing happened today. I was unable to control myself when William found and scoffed my last packet of Opal Fruits. I went berserk, shouted at him and told him that he would end up in prison if he carried on stealing other people's property. He fled in tears to my mother.

Later, Ivan came into my room, sat down on my bed in a caring way, and said, 'Adrian, do you think you may be sort of getting *dependent* on Opal Fruits?'

I pushed his hairy wrist off my shoulder, drove to

the cash-and-carry warehouse and bought a multi-pack of OFs. I have hidden them under my bed. I have fitted a bolt to my door. I have not finished or even started the book, despite sitting at my desk for sixteen hours a day.

---

FAX MESSAGE

**To:** Boston Goldperson – Brick Eagleburger Associates
**From:** Adrian Mole
**Date:** 31.10.97

Dear Boston,

First may I say how much I admire your decision to change your surname from Goldman to Goldperson. In these times when so many women are renouncing their feminist principles, it is heartening to know that you still carry the flame.

Now for the bad news. It has become apparent to me that I will be unable to meet my latest deadline of November 1st for the delivery of *Offally Good! – The Book!*. Family matters have occupied my time and attention to the detriment of my creative impulse.

In your role as agent's assistant will you please break the news to Arthur Stoat of Stoat Books Ltd. I will, of course, return my advance of £250, though I will need to give one month's notice to my bank or risk losing the accumulated interest. I hope to see you when I am next in London. I am slightly concerned that *Birdwatching* and *The White Van* remain unsold despite their obvious mass-market appeal.

Yours, A. Mole

## Saturday November 1st

---

FAX MESSAGE

**From:** Boston Goldperson
**To:** Adrian Mole

Listen, kiddo, The f------ offal book has been *sold* already. W. H. Smith have made it their *Book of the Week*! The cover has been sent to *The Bookseller*! Stoat Books have had advance orders for 25,000 copies in hardback! This book is a f------ bestseller! It has to be written! Stoat is threatening to sue this agency for every cent we have if you don't deliver. So write the mother!

Boston

## Sunday November 2nd

William seems to have forgiven me for the Opal Fruits incident, though my mother is unrelenting and has not laid a place at the table for me for three days.

Ivan is negotiating with Tania over his Tyrolean-style garden shed. He wants to take it down and reassemble it here, in the back garden of Wisteria Walk. I objected, saying that it would take up nearly all of the lawn. 'Where will William play?' I asked my mother.

'In *your* garden?' she said.

'I haven't got a garden,' I pointed out.

'Then *get* a garden,' she said.

I think this is a hint that she wants me and William to move out.

### Monday November 3rd

I went to see my father and Tania today. I took William with me. My father was on the back lawn digging a hole for Tania's Koi carp pool. A black Labrador puppy called Henry was watching him. 'Our baby,' said Tania.

I asked if we could move into the Tyrolean shed until I found something permanent. Neither of them looked very keen. Unfortunately, at that moment, William had a spectacular tantrum because I refused to sing the Teletubbies song, there and then. After five minutes of watching him scream, drum his heels and roll around on the grass, Tania said, 'Should we call an ambulance?'

My father said, 'No, Adrian was just the same when

he was three. You had to do "Incy Wincy Spider" fifty times a day.'

Eventually Tania said, 'I don't think it would work out, Adrian, not with the dog and the carp. Your father and I have a domestic routine that suits us and, anyway, we're not insured for small children.'

This was patently ridiculous, but I let it pass. William, now recovered from his tantrum, asked for Coco Pops. My father, who used to eat three bowls a day himself, said, 'Coco Pops are full of additives and E numbers, William. How about a nice glass of carrot juice?'

We went into the kitchen where my father demonstrated the juicer machine to an indifferent William. Henry, however, watched my father's every move with rapt attention.

Tania asked me how the book was progressing.

Perhaps if I stay awake for three days and nights on the trot I will be able to write it. Noël Coward wrote *Private Lives* over a long weekend with the aid of stimulants. I rang Nigel for help on how to track down some Pro-plus, but he was out at his grandma's funeral.

Started on the introduction at midnight, when the household was relatively quiet.


Hello Offal lovers,

Man has lived on offal since time began: petrified offal has been found in ancient caves in France, proving that offal was once the staple diet of French cavemen. This legacy can still be seen today in the world-famous French cuisine, to which flock gourmets from throughout the world.

There is something about the last sentence that is not quite right. The syntax? The grammar? After spending an hour staring down at it, I went to bed, exhausted.

## Wednesday November 5th

Ivan has put a veto on a bonfire or fireworks in the garden, saying, 'They're primitive, barbaric and dangerous. It's time that Guy Fawkes Night was abolished.' The government seem to agree with him. The population of Britain are being urged to attend organized events with paramedics in attendance. I bought William some sparklers and he waved them about a bit on the patio. The New Dog watched through the patio doors.

Worked on the introduction until 3 a.m.

The gourmets today still flock from their homes throughout the world to partake of the legacy which is offal!

It's still not quite right.

## Thursday November 6th

William has a mega-tantrum in Clarks. He wanted a
pair of mini Doc Martens in red patent leather with
twelve lace-holes. I wanted him to have a pair of
black-leather Velcro-fastening 'school shoes'. He sank
on to Clark's carpet and screamed. At the manager's
request, I dragged him out of the shop. I ended up
buying him some Bugs Bunny slip-on plimsolls from
Woolworths. They are totally unsuitable for winter,
but if he wears thick socks with them his feet should
be warm enough.

When we got home my mother said, 'I thought
you went out to buy *winter* shoes. He'll catch his
death in those.' She looked down at the plimsolls
disdainfully. I felt my parental confidence seep out
of the house.

## Friday November 7th

I now have no income. I am eating into my capital.
Rang the bank call centre in a panic, but forgot code
word. I told the woman on the line that it was the
name of a seaside resort on the east coast, but she
simply repeated, 'I am afraid I must ask you for the
fifth letter of your password, sir.'

I pleaded with her for my balance, but to no avail.

237

Have our financial services been colonized by extra-terrestrials? Is it all a plot to send us mad and take over the world? I am not given to paranoid fancies normally, dear Diary, but I confide in you that I am seriously thinking of withdrawing all my money and placing it in a box under my bed. I've worked hard for that money and no Martian is going to get its slimy green hands (tentacles?) on it.

Sent the introduction and one further offal recipe to Arthur Stoat. A sense of achievement.

## Saturday November 8th

What was I thinking of, dear Diary? I wouldn't *dream* of keeping my money under my bed. I shall hide it in several *faux* baked-bean tins, and keep them on the top shelf of the pantry.

## Sunday November 9th
*Poppy Day*

I dropped a pound coin in a collecting tin by mistake today. I'd meant to give 20p. The old man shaking the tin was quite rude. He almost *slammed* the 80p change into my hand.

238

## Monday November 10th

Brick rang at 3 p.m., he said he'd had a fax from Arthur Stoat.

---

FAX MESSAGE

**To:** Mr Brick Eagleburger
**From:** Arthur Stoat
**Date:** 10.11.97

Dear Mr Eagleburger,

Your client Mr Adrian Mole has reneged on his agreement with Stoat Books Ltd, to deliver the completed manuscript of *Offally Good! – The Book!* by 1st November.

I seriously doubt that Mr Mole is capable of writing this book and suggest that you and Mr Mole find a ghost-writer with the ability to complete the task. He will, of course, be expected to meet any expenses incurred.

Given the somewhat 'hand-to-mouth' nature of Stoat Books' finances and the fact that we have missed a crucial opportunity to capitalize on the Christmas market, Mr Mole's failure to deliver means that the staff of Stoat Books will not now be enjoying their end-of-year bonus. This is especially disappointing as research conducted by Stoat Books Ltd has shown that one in ten male student viewers intended buying the book for their mother or stepmother.

I have moved the delivery date to the third week of

December and hope to publish on January 14th to coincide with the first transmission of *Ping with Singh*.

Yours sincerely,

A. N. Stoat

Managing Director – Stoat Books Ltd

What is this *Ping with Singh*? It's the first I've heard of it.

## Tuesday November 11th

I was in Safeway for the one-minute silence. The cash registers were turned off. An assistant on the cheese counter giggled nervously after thirty seconds.

Apparently Dev Singh has written a book on microwave cookery. Serialization rights have been bought by *Good Housekeeping* and there is already talk of a stage adaptation to be directed by Ned Sherrin.

## Wednesday November 12th

Ivan asked me in the kitchen this morning to get my own phone/fax line installed. He said that he is starting up a new business as a website designer and needs to use his line exclusively. I pointed out to him that the line did in fact belong to my mother, who was my blood relation; therefore I had more authorization over the line than he did.

He spluttered, 'That's patent nonsense. Your mother and I are life partners, and what's more *I* paid the last bloody phone bill, and fitted a new fax roll.'

When I reminded him that I paid £40 a week to live in this house he said, 'We heavily subsidize you and William, who's constantly leaving the lights on and wasting food.'

Rosie came in, looking upset. She wiped the bread-knife on the corner of her pyjama jacket and said to Ivan, 'If you don't like it here, why don't you go home to your wife?'

Ivan said, 'I happen to be in love with your mother, and she happens to be in love with me, check?'

He went outside to sort his recycling bags before the dustbin men came. Rosie watched him from the window as she waited for her toast to cook. She said, 'Which do you hate *most* about him? His Birken-stocks, his hairy wrists, or the cap he wears when it rains?'

I said, 'The way he says, "Enjoy," before every meal.'

## Thursday November 13th

After taking William to school I went to the Housefinder centre and informed them that I urgently

241

required a three-bedroomed detached house with a garden to rent for no more than £60 per week. I stipulated that it must be in a superior area where there were no rough people. It must have trees and the garden should face south. The person behind the desk, a moustachioed youth wearing a too-big suit, said, 'We don't cover the Highlands of Scotland.' I gave him my card, but as I was passing the window I saw him drop it into the wastebin.

When I picked William up from Kidsplay Ltd, he said, 'Your breath smells like poo, Dad.'

This was only half an hour after I had rigorously brushed my teeth. For how long has my breath smelled like poo?

I mobiled for an appointment and drove to the surgery, where Mr Chang the dentist broke the news to me that I have got a gum disease called pyorrhoea. Unless I have £1,000 worth of treatment immediately I could be toothless in a year.

Mr Chang used to be NHS but he no longer caters for the poor: 'They bring tooth decay on themselves,' he said. 'They are always eating the confectionely.' So, Opal Fruits have brought me to this.

Mrs Wellingborough, Chang's receptionist, whispered to me that it might be worth getting a second opinion. Apparently Chang is up in front of the dentists' self-regulatory council next week for overcharging a woman for a clean and polish. Mrs Wellingborough recommended Jeffrey Atkins. 'He's the *crème de la crème,*' she said. I am seeing Atkins next Tuesday.

Rosie has found a fiendish method of causing Ivan pain. During a discussion at the dinner table about our lack of outings as children, Rosie said to my mother, 'You never took us nowhere.' She saw Ivan wince and whisper, 'Double negative,' to himself.

She has been torturing him grammatically ever since.

## Saturday November 15th

I took William to Twycross Zoo today. It was a terrible mistake. When he saw that the lions were in cages, he wept and pleaded, 'Let them out, Dad, please, let them out.' He seemed to be under the impression that they were cartoon creatures, rather than live beasts capable of tearing his head from his shoulders.

## Sunday November 16th

It has been revealed that a millionaire with a fringe and aviator glasses – Bernie Ecclestone – has donated £1,000,000 to the Labour Party's funds. The tiny Formula One boss is anxious to keep tobacco sponsorship for his noisy sport. Tony Blair is baffled and hurt by public criticism and charges of corruption. 'I'm a pretty straight kinda guy,' he said. I have been pondering this statement. Break the sentence down and much is possibly revealed.

Bowels – blocked
Mood – black
Prospects – hopeless
Breath – foul

## Monday November 17th

People have been flinching away from me all day. My gums have turned me into a social pariah.

## Tuesday November 18th

Jeffrey Atkins was shocked at the shoddy state of my mouth and Chang's fillings. He examined me and said that my bad breath is the result of 'impacted food in *one* tooth only'.

As he probed my mouth he held forth on the state of the arts in Leicester. It was, of course, a one-sided conversation (though I hope my eye-rolling was eloquent). I stumbled into the reception area where I asked Hazel the receptionist if it was possible to give Jeffrey a tip. She said, no, dental etiquette forbids tipping.

## Friday November 21st

Michael Hutchence of INXS is dead, choked by his own belt, which was tied to a hotel doorknob. My mother said she couldn't understand why men choke themselves in order to achieve heightened sexual satisfaction. She said, 'He made love to some of the most beautiful women in the world, so why would he want to hang off a door?'

Ivan said, 'Because it's less *complicated* than having a relationship with a woman. One doesn't have to tell a *door* twenty times a day that one loves it.'

Well! Well! Well! Is Ivan tiring of my mother's emotional neediness?

## Saturday November 22nd

Pandora graced Wisteria Walk with her presence after her surgery at the health centre. She was tired and irritable and complained about the long hours she was working. She hates her constituents. Their incessant complaints about council-house transfers and on-in-the-day street lights are driving her crazy. She said, 'If it wasn't for Mandy and our Grand Plan I would go back to Oxford.'

Naturally I asked her what the 'Grand Plan' was. She said, 'I'm to be the first woman Prime Minister in Britain.'

I said, 'And *Mrs Thatcher*? She never existed?'

'Mrs Thatcher is a man in drag, everybody knows that,' she said contemptuously.

I reeled back at this revelation. 'What's her/his real name?' I asked, agog.

'Leonard Roberts,' she said. 'His parents disliked boys, so he was rechristened Margaret by a crooked vicar in Grantham and re-registered in the next district by a registrar who forged a new birth certificate. Leonard was dressed like a girl and treated like a girl.'

'And his genitalia?' I questioned.

'Abnormally small,' she said.

There were so many questions I wanted to ask. Did Denis *know* his wife was really a man?

And how did Thatcher give birth to the twins, Carole and Mark? I told Pandora about my 'William Hague is Thatcher love-child theory'. She said, 'No, William Hague is the result of a cloning experiment conducted in the sixties. The sperm was taken from Churchill and the eggs were donated by Thora Hird.'

She then went into the kitchen to have a 'girly' talk with Rosie and my mother. They laughed solidly more or less for an hour and a half, only stopping when I went in to complain about the cigarette smoke pouring out from under the door.

## Sunday November 23rd

To The Lawns to set fire to William's Christmas list in their open fireplace. This method of sending the list to Santa is a Mole tradition that I am determined to keep up. I won't easily forgive my parents for boarding up our own fireplace and putting a storage heater in the gap between the plywood and the fender.

William wants:

1. Po
2. Tinky Winky
3. Laa-Laa
4. Dipsy
5. And the other one whose name always escapes me.

My father said, 'You do realize, don't you, that there's none to be had?' He pronounced the aitch in 'had'. He pronounced 'that' as *thet*. He was wearing Timberland deck-shoes, and stroking Henry's glossy head. He is Eliza Doolittle to Tania's Henry Higgins.

## Monday November 24th

Took the New Dog to the vet's to get its nails cut. It keeps skidding across the kitchen lino like Torville or Dean, whichever is the hairiest.

An envelope containing my fan mail came today. A man in Wolverhampton, Edwin Log, wrote to tell me that he has eaten offal every day of his life for forty-five years and 'enjoys perfect health'. A woman in Battersea said I was encouraging the 'mass murder of the innocents'. She said she would like to see me hung by my intestines from Blackfriars Bridge.

## Tuesday November 25th

William asked me why I don't go to work 'like other daddies do'.

I told him that I am a published author and a TV presenter – a personality in fact. I pointed to the five fan letters on my desk/dressing-table and said, 'People out there love me.'

William went to the window and looked down on the street. 'There's nobody out there,' he said.

## Thursday November 27th

*3.30 a.m.* I am at William's hospital bedside. He is being kept in overnight for observation after placing a coffee bean in his left ear 'to see if it would rattle'.

It has been removed, but they had to give him a general anaesthetic. It has been the most harrowing night of my life, it took me, my mother and two nurses to hold him down while a tiny woman doctor, called Surinder, examined his ear with an illuminated probe. The casualty department at the Leicester Royal Infirmary was rent with his screams. When the decision was made to operate I turned on my mother in my anguish saying, 'I hold Ivan Braithwaite responsible. It was he who introduced the coffee bean to Wisteria Walk.'

She didn't respond in the way I expected. Instead she said, 'I hear what you're saying, I hear your anger.'

I was in the recovery room with William when he came round from the operation. He cried for my mother. A nurse saw that I was upset by this and said, 'He doesn't know what he's saying.' But I think he did know. I now realize that I'm not the most important person in his life, as he is in mine.

## Friday November 28th

William is a lovely boy – especially when slightly sedated by prescription drugs. I am writing this in the hospital restaurant – Nightingales. I am alone in the seventy-seat non-smoking section. Whereas the small smoking section is crammed full of doctors and nurses. Why don't they see the light and give up? Had an All-Day Breakfast, was annoyed when they forgot my black pudding. Went to counter to complain, was told it was *either* mushrooms *or* black pudding. I offered to pay extra for the black pudding, but was told the computerized till wouldn't allow this. Raised voice to fat girl with pretty face behind counter.

She said, 'It's not my fault.'

I said, 'Nobody accepts responsibility for anything any more. Nobody apologizes, nobody resigns.'

She looked mystified.

Went back to non-smoking section to find smokers goggling and All-Day Breakfast congealed on the plate.

*3 p.m.* Still here, at bedside. Nurses in love with William. He has told them that he is having all four Teletubbies for Christmas. A very nice staff nurse called Lucy came up to me and said, 'If you've got a source, I'm desperate for a Po.'

I confessed that I had no Teletubby 'insider knowledge'. This is quite worrying: perhaps I should start a search.

I asked why William had not been discharged yet. Staff Nurse Lucy (blonde, slim, fair hairy arms, breasts 5/10) said, 'Dr Fong is slightly concerned about the bruising on his lower back.' I explained that William had fallen off the arm of the sofa while pretending to take a corner as Jeremy Clarkson. Lucy, who has a three-year-old daughter, said, 'They're mad at that age, aren't they?' and laughed. However, Dr Fong had never heard of Jeremy Clarkson, and obviously didn't believe my explanation.


## Saturday November 29th
*Royal Infirmary – Nightingales*

Still here. William's body and mind are under investigation. I have pleaded with him to stop saying, 'No, Dad, no,' etc., but he has turned into a fiend. I left him surrounded by his adoring grandparents and step-grandparents, who are showering him with toys and sweets and pop-up books. No wonder he doesn't want to come out.

Lucy is a single parent like me. Her daughter is called Lucinda. Staff Nurse Lucy said that Lucinda can also be a fiend, and once shouted, 'Are you going to lock me in the cupboard when we get home, Mummy?' in the queue at Homebase. Lucy's relationship with a policeman has just broken up because of his deception when on a late shift. She said, 'I really enjoy talking to you, Mr Mole, or can I call you Adrian?'

*Ten reasons why I am not attracted enough to Staff Nurse Lucy to ask her out.*

1. Hairy arms – *blonde* hairs but far too many of them.
2. Has seen Sir Cliff Richard in *Wuthering Heights*, eleven times.
3. Thought Tolstoy wrote *Love in a Cold Climate*.
4. Lucinda.
5. Prefers normal to lemon Jif.
6. Thinks it's exciting that Chris Evans has bought a radio station from Richard Branson for eight million pounds. She thinks they are 'two fun guys'.
7. Likes Princess Anne because she is 'hard-working'.
8. Failed the Auberon Waugh test.
9. Unwittingly let on that she has a neon sign in her lounge window, which flashes 'Merry Yuletide' every three seconds.
10. Claims never to have *even* heard of the *Independent*, let alone read it.

## Sunday November 30th

Dr Fong has allowed William to go home, even though William shouted, 'Please, Dad, please, I want to stay with staff nurse Lucy.'

My father was there. He said, sounding like his old self, 'If you don't shut your trap, lad, I'll shut the bleeder for you.'

William shut his trap and allowed me to dress him in his outdoor clothes. He was escorted out of the hospital by his entourage, consisting of me, Rosie, my father, my mother, Ivan and Tania.

He held my hand in the car and refused to let it go. It was a bit awkward changing gear, but I didn't mind.

## Monday December 1st

Phoned bank successfully! I have got £7,961.54 in a high-interest account. I know it's correct because a robot called Jade told me.

My mother has written a poem called, 'A Weeping Womb'. She is sending it to the *Daily Express*, to a bloke called Harry Eyres. I told her that it stood no chance of being published. Harsh, I know, but I can't bear her to be disappointed.

> *The Weeping Womb by Pauline Mole*
> Hush! Is that weeping? Listen awhile –
> 'Tis something within me –
> Not distant (a mile)
> Quiet! Is that sobbing?

From whence does it come?
My pelvis *is* throbbing
Quite near to my bum,
Hark to the crying!
Pay heed to the pain
My womb – it is dying!
Ne'er fertile again!

She slipped this under my door last night.

When I saw her at breakfast I made no reference to it. What could I possibly say? Ivan is behind all this: he believes that 'Everybody has a talent, it's just that our society cannot encompass . . .' etc., etc., etc., blah, blah, blah.

## Tuesday December 2nd

Jesus Christ almighty! God save me from this biblical-like curse which has fallen on me!

A letter from Sharon Bott, with whom I once had a frenzied sexual relationship.

Dear Aidy,

This must come as a bit of a downer. I belong in the past, I know, but it weren't me who wanted to send this letter. It is my son Glenn. He is a big lad of 12 now and he wants to know who his father is. And the thing is, Aidy, I don't know. As you found out I was having relations with you and Barry Kent at the same time. I have written to Barry the same as you. Glenn says that you and Barry should take a DNA test to find out who is his dad. He is a good lad at home, never no trouble. I don't know why the teachers are against him at school. I'm sorry to bother you with this only I had to do it for Glenn. Can you give me a ring? I work shifts at Parker's Poultry, but I'm home at ten. Me and Glenn have seen you on Cable. You were quite good. Did you see that Barry has won a prize for writing a book about a blind man? It was in the *Mercury* last night.

Yours faithfully,

Sharon L. Bott


No way! No way! No way is she forcing me to accept Glenn 'The Teachers Are Against Him' Bott as my son. I've *got* one son. Another is surplus to requirements.

I showed the letter to Rosie, who said, 'I know Glenn Bott. He's a psycho, but he has got your nose. He helps out on a stall at Leicester market on Fridays after school. The one opposite Walker's, the pork butcher's.'

I phoned the Bott house. A little kid told me that 'Mam's gone to work.'

## Wednesday December 3rd

William returned to Kidsplay today. He was greeted like a returning hero by the other children, though the teachers were distinctly cool. There have been several copy-cat incidents of children placing foreign objects in their ears (lentils, beads). Mrs Parvez is away with a stress-related illness.

Phoned Sharon late tonight. It was hard to concentrate due to the old sexual frisson and the background noise of television and yelling of children. It was an awkward conversation. I kept getting flashbacks of the two of us engaging in sexual intercourse on the pink velour sofa in my parents' house on Thursday nights while they were out having marriage guidance.

I told Sharon that I was unlikely to be Glenn's father due to an abnormally low sperm count, but she asked if I would take the test 'for Glenn'. What could I say but yes? She put the phone down, saying, 'Douggie's just come in.'

## Thursday December 4th

At four o'clock I drove to Leicester, parked in the Shires car park and walked through the Christmas shoppers to the market place. I stood outside

Walker's, the pork butcher's, and watched the fruit stall opposite.

It didn't come as a complete shock to find that Glenn is the same boy who's been hanging about outside our house for the last few months. He's tall for his age, and if he had a decent haircut and stopped glowering he'd be quite a handsome lad. He was dressed as though he lived on the streets of Hell's Kitchen, New York, in ludicrously baggy trousers and a Puffa jacket. When he came round to the front, to tidy the fruit, I saw that he was wearing trainers the size and shape of small bulldozers.

The owner of the stall, a weasel-faced man, with earrings and a grey ponytail, seemed content to let Glenn do most of the work, apart from handling the money. I presumed this was Douggie, apparently Sharon's live-in partner.

As I watched Glenn I tried to get in touch with my emotions. What exactly did I feel?

Diary, I felt nothing.

I could tell even from a distance that the boy didn't have a single strand of intellectual DNA in his body.

Sharon lives on the dreaded Thatcher Estate. I parked outside 19 Geoffrey Howe Road and decided to activate the car alarm *and* fit the steering lock on the Montego. The battered wooden gate scraped on the concrete path as I pushed it open. There was a picture of a large Devil Dog saying, 'Go Ahead, Make My Day,' propped against the front-room window.

Sharon opened the door before I could knock. She

looked like Moby Dick with a perm. I could barely discern the Sharon I once knew from the flesh mountain she had become. The cigarette between her podgy fingers looked tiny, like the ones made of confectionery I used to 'smoke' as a boy.

She led me into the front room where two shaven-headed little boys were sitting on a sofa, watching a video. The TV screen showed a maniac with a hedge-trimmer pursuing a girl with large breasts down the steps of a dark cellar. The smallest boy picked up a cushion and hid his face behind it.

I was not introduced to them and, after a swift glance at me, they turned their attention back to the screen. Sharon indicated that I was to sit in one of the two matching armchairs. The carpet felt sticky beneath my feet.

She stubbed out her cigarette in a saucer. It was inconceivable to me that I had ever had carnal knowledge of this woman. A loud atonal cacophony from the television prompted me to ask Sharon if we could talk in the kitchen, though once we'd arrived there, I wished we'd stayed where we were.

'I've not 'ad time to wash up yet,' she said, looking around at the spectacular chaos.

I looked through the grimy window into the garden. A sodden mattress lay in the long grass. Glenn's bike was out there, padlocked to the concrete post of the washing-line. The spillage of light from the kitchen window showed that the bike was well maintained: the chrome trims and the spokes sparkled. I was pleased to see that the boy had fitted a padlock and chain to one wheel, and a cycle lock to the other.

Sharon handed me a piece of paper, which told me where and when to go for a blood test: 10.30 Monday December 8th at the clinic in Prosper Road. 'Barry's solicitor 'as arranged it all,' she said. She kept glancing nervously at the narrow, gold-coloured watch which lay between the folds of fat around her wrist.

I said, 'Has Glenn shown any preference as to who his natural father is?'

Sharon was rinsing a mug under the cold tap. '*He's* not,' she said. 'But it might be better for me if it's Barry, maintenance wise.'

'And certainly better for *me*, if it's Barry, maintenance wise,' I said.

She offered me tea, but I declined. She told me that I would receive a copy of the results from a laboratory, and then we could 'take it from there'.

When I got home I asked my mother if she could locate any photographs of me at the age of twelve. She sorted through a few shoeboxes and brought out a school photo. On the back was written 'Adrian, aged eleven and a half' in my father's anal handwriting. When I turned it over I was shocked to see a picture of Glenn Bott looking up at me. My mother wanted to know why I wanted a photograph of myself at that age. I could not answer her.

## Sunday December 7th

Staff Nurse Lucy rang to say that I'd left A. N. Wilson's biography of Tolstoy in William's bedside locker. She was passing our house; she lives in Clematis Close – should she drop it in? I said I didn't think it would squeeze through the letterbox. 'If Tolstoy had died at thirty-five you might have stood a chance,' I joked. She asked how old Tolstoy was when he died. 'In his nineties,' I said. I waited for her to say that she was busy on the ward, but she seemed to have plenty of time to talk. She said that after work she would walk round to Wisteria Walk with Lucinda. I begged her not to. I wanted to sit and read the *Observer* in peace – but she insisted.

Rosie and my mother got themselves into a lather of excitement, and Ivan went upstairs and came down in a shirt and toning tie. I told them all not to waste so much nervous energy. I am not in the least attracted to Staff Nurse Lucy.

I tried to keep her and Lucinda on the doorstep, but William pulled Lucinda inside to play with his farmyard, which is stocked with dinosaurs and other prehistoric animals, so I reluctantly showed Staff Nurse Lucy into the kitchen, where I found a Sainsbury's chocolate gâteau thawing in her honour. In the subsequent conversation it emerged that her favourite poet is Barry Kent, her favourite singer Liam Gallagher. I had to get up and leave the table. She stayed two long hours. She pronounced the gateau 'yummy'. Just before she left, she went upstairs with me and my mother to watch William and Lucinda putting the dinosaurs to bed in the farmhouse.

'Ah, bless,' said Lucy. 'They get on so well, don't they?'

I looked at my mother's face and saw that, in her mind's eye, she had me and William installed in Clematis Close with Lucy and Lucinda. When they'd gone I disabused her of this idea, citing the hairy blonde wrists. My mother said, 'A tube of Nair would sort that problem out.'

An air of heavy disappointment hangs over the house.

As I was putting him to bed William asked when Lucinda was coming to play again.

I replied, 'Never.'

## Monday December 8th

I needn't have changed my underwear. I wasn't asked to remove my clothes, just roll my sleeve up. I felt rather weak when I spotted the syringe and I looked away while a fat bloke in a white coat took my blood. To distract myself I muttered the words of the Lord's Prayer. The blood-taker said, 'Pardon?'

I opened my eyes and saw him syringing my dark red blood into a little plastic bottle. 'I didn't speak,' I said.

'You did,' he said. 'You said, "Amen." Have *you*, too, found the Lord?'

As I was fastening my cuff, he took a leaflet from the drawer in his desk and placed it in front of me. He belongs to a sect called Godhead. They believe that the world is going to end a second after the stroke of midnight on January 1st in the year 2000. I put my coat on and stood by the door, but he wouldn't let me go until he'd explained that the Dome at Greenwich was to be the site of 'Satan's Last Stand'. According to him, Mr Peter Mandelson is the Prince of Devils, and the entire Cabinet is made up of demons. He said that Jack Cunningham has cloven hoofs and has to have his shoes made bespoke. I thanked him for the information and he thanked me for listening, saying, 'A lot of people think we're cranks.'

I was glad when he handed me my blood and asked me to give it to the clinic receptionist, ready for collection. I didn't like the thought of him tinkering with it after I'd gone.

When I got home my mother reported gleefully that Arthur Stoat had rung, demanding the name and telephone number of my ghost-writer. She said, 'I don't understand why you can't write the bloody thing yourself. It's only a few recipes. It wouldn't take you more than a week if you got stuck in.'

I said, 'You non-writers don't *understand*. There's

the question of *tone* and tense and clarity. And which word to put in front of another, and when to use a semicolon and how to know when only a *colon* will do!'

The DNA results will be sent to me by registered letter on Friday. Barry Kent has paid for the express service.

## Tuesday December 9th

I went to Toys 'Я' Us this afternoon in my thankless quest for a Teletubby. I asked a boy (who inexplicably wore a badge saying 'Gary Heppenstall, Assistant Manager') where the Teletubbies were to be found. He smirked and said, 'In China, sir, where they make 'em.' He said they'd had a few La-Las on Monday, but they'd gone within minutes. I asked him why they couldn't manufacture the Teletubbies in this country. He smiled pityingly at me and said, 'They'll work all week for a bowl of rice in China, sir. We can't compete.'

Trawled to town for Teletubbies. There are none to be had. I am now on the waiting list of seven shops and have my mobile everywhere with me at all times should a consignment arrive in the middle of the night. Nigel is also on the case.

*2 p.m.* Is there no end to the suffering of Paula Yates? The latest tragedy to befall her is that DNA testing has proved she is the daughter of the dead right-wing aviationist and sinister quizmaster Hughie Green. Personally, I curse the day DNA was discovered. Weren't we all happier in our ignorance?

In the evening Ivan went round to The Lawns to start dismantling his hardware and software. He is going to set up a home office in an alcove in our dining room.

Tania is insisting on keeping the chalet as part of the divorce settlement. While he was out we decorated the house with paper chains and balloons, and I held the ladder while my mother climbed into the loft to retrieve the Christmas tree and the box of decorations. The fairy-lights fused after only half an hour but, as I said to my mother, 'It is traditional in our culture.'

## Wednesday December 10th

There's been a big row about the Christmas tree. Ivan said, 'I've got to be frank with you, Paulie, I think it's far too early to put a tree up and I can't bear that kitsch stuff you've thrown on it. The effect is nauseating.'

My mother rounded on him with a knife in her hand (she was peeling potatoes at the sink), and said,

'Who the hell do you think you are? Sir Terence bleeding Conran?'

He said, 'Pauline, please don't swear, it demeans you.'

She said, 'Then don't criticize my baubles, Ivan.'

The tree row led to the who-will-be-where-and-with-whom-at-Christmas row. I took charge and asked each person what their ideal Christmas would be. My mother said, 'Ideally, I want to watch William open his presents on Christmas morning and then go abroad, somewhere hot, with Ivan.'

Ivan said ideally he wanted to invite his ninety-two-year-old mother, who is in a residential home in Rutland, to spend Christmas week at Wisteria Walk. 'It could be her last Christmas,' he said.

Rosie said, 'Ideally I want to stay in bed eating tortilla chips all day and watch my Christmas present: a new portable colour television.'

William said he didn't care what he did, so long as he did it with a full set of Teletubbies.

I phoned my father to canvass his opinion. He said, 'Ideally we'd like to watch William open his presents with us at The Lawns on Christmas morning and then spend the rest of the day quietly with Henry.' He said that they had received a press release from Pandora which said that she would be visiting Leicester Royal Infirmary on Christmas Day and was planning to carve a turkey for the tragic youngsters on the children's ward.

The Sugdens, my mother's parents, said they would ideally like to drive up from Norfolk on Christmas morning and spend 'a quiet two days at Wisteria Walk, eating and drinking in moderation'.

I said, 'In an ideal world I would like to take William to a hotel with a log fire for the duration.'

Ivan, who had been inputting all the 'ideal Christmases' on his computer, looked up from the screen and said, 'The computations are beyond it.' However, he did find a week self-catering in Tenerife, which left on December 24th from Stansted at 3 p.m. My mother asked me if I was prepared to break with Mole tradition and let William open his presents on Christmas Eve instead of Christmas morning.

I said, 'No.'

## Thursday December 11th

My mother sent me round to The Lawns to cut some greenery for the holly wreath she is making as per the instructions in the Christmas supplement of *Good Housekeeping*. I asked Tania if I could borrow some gardening gloves and secateurs, but she said, 'I'm afraid I can't have a non-gardener just slashing at my conifers and evergreens willy-nilly.'

My father looked up sheepishly from the marble slab where he was cutting out gingerbread men, eventually to be varnished and hung on the tree that

Tania had so sensibly reserved at a specialist nursery.

I said, 'I'll go elsewhere for my greenery, then.'

My father said, 'Don't go, son . . .'

But Tania said, 'Don't you see, George? This is just Pauline's way of *tormenting* me.'

I left them to it and headed for Sainsbury's car park, where I used my Swiss Army knife and filled two carrier-bags with their green prickly stuff.

While I was out my mother had made the skeleton of a wreath by twisting three coat-hangers together. We managed to fashion the green stuff and holly into a roundish shape and hung it all on the door with a red ribbon. Ivan said it had an 'anarchic spirit' to it. I could see my mother was unsure whether this was a compliment or not.

## Friday December 12th

I was woken at dawn this morning by an urgent ringing on the doorbell. Thinking it to be the registered letter, I stumbled downstairs dressed only in my boxers, to find the milkman on the doorstep clutching a handkerchief to his left eye. Two broken bottles of milk lay on the doorstep. 'I've been poked in the bleddy eye by a piece of f------ holly,' he said.

As we watched, a piece of recalcitrant holly fell from the wreath and landed among the shards of glass in a little white lake. I had no choice but to give him a lift to Eye Casualty at the Royal Infirmary in Leicester. When I got home I found my mother anxiously reading the household-insurance policy. There was nothing in it about cover for third-party holly-wreath accidents. She has cancelled the milk 'until further notice' and removed the wreath from the front door.

I waited for the postman with a thumping heart and a dry mouth, praying that Barry Kent would be the one to stump up the maintenance, but the only thing that came was a Christmas *letter* from George 'n' Tania circulated to their 'many friends and family members around the world'.

Dear Loved Ones,

1997 has been a turbulent year for us both. Most of you have been informed about the breakdown of Tania and Ivan's marriage, due to his love affair with Pauline, George's wife. For those of you who are finding out for the first time, phew! Sorry! Take a breather!

Let's go back to the start of the year, shall we?

*January* saw Ivan and Tania in Norwich where they attended a get-together of the Redundant Dairy Workers Association. Ivan enjoyed seeing some of his old colleagues and catching up on the news.

In *February* Tania started a night-school course in Citroën car maintenance, after receiving a horrendous bill for a service from Honest Jack's (Railway Arches) garage. Tragically, Bismarck, Ivan and Tania's adorable marmalade cat, died of leukaemia. She remains sadly missed to this day.

In *March* Tania took on more responsibility at De Montfort University – she formed a gardening club, *Doigts Verts*, which meets fortnightly in the physics department from 7 p.m. to 9 p.m. and already has a thriving membership. In the same month, George won a Spot the Ball competition in a local trade paper – £25 for placing a cross correctly! But not as easy as it looks!

*April* saw Ivan and Tania drifting apart somewhat, though they enjoyed a weekend visit to Stratford and had a lovely meal in the Dirty Duck.

*May:* Pandora, bless her, was elected the Member of Parliament for Ashby-de-la-Zouch. We're so very proud of her. She has since been appointed a PPS to Julia Snodworthy at the Department of Agriculture. Pandora's ex-husband, Julian, has also been making a name for himself, becoming a leading campaigner for a bill to lower the homosexual age of consent to sixteen.

In late May Ivan began a clandestine affair with Pauline Mole. Meanwhile, Tania was working hard to pay the mortgage, the household bills and also to repay the loan on the garden chalet from which Ivan was going to freelance as a dairy management consultant, but as it turned out hardly ever did. Tania was devastated by Ivan's betrayals; she had meant *every* word of her wedding vows. However, in June she and George found that their relationship was more than friendship, and Tania is slowly accepting that it is possible to love again.

In *September*, Brett, George's only son by Doreen Slater, a.k.a. 'Stick Insect', wrote to his father from Rugby School, where he has been awarded a scholarship. George was pleased and not a little proud! Brett has since had several meals with us, and is a charming, good-looking boy, with exquisite manners!

Dear Diary, this is news to me! Why are all these sons suddenly creeping out of the woodwork? I put it down to the millennium. Why didn't my father tell me about Brett's success? After all, he is my half-brother.

I read on . . .

Adrian, George's elder son, has been away working in London's Soho! He once met Ned Sherrin in the street!

Is that it? Is that the full sum of my considerable achievements this year, to have met Ned Sherrin in the street? In fact I more than 'met' Ned in the street. I engaged him in conversation just as he was about to step into a black cab.

We have embarked on an ambitious plan to landscape the garden at The Lawns. The lawns are to be replaced and gravel laid in their place. We hope ultimately to re-create the Emperor Hirohito's palace gardens, though on a more modest scale! George will shortly be attending a course on Zen gardening at Dartington College, Devon, run by Isokio Myanoko, garden master to the Japanese Royal Family.

Lastly, but certainly not leastly, Henry, an adorable black Labrador puppy has arrived to share our lives. So, together with the Koi carp, Yin and Yang, we have become a family!

Happy Christmas,

Love to all,

Tania and George

I couldn't wait for my mother to get out of the bath. When she read the letter she laughed until she cried. Even Ivan smiled at the thought of my father raking gravel in a meaningful way. Tania 'n' George's round robin has been pinned up above the bread-bin. Every time I extracted a slice of organic white at breakfast I laughed quietly to myself.

Most of the World War II baby-boomer generation are to be pitied. My mother has often spoken about the overcrowded classrooms: 'Three of us to a desk, four of us to a book.' She claims that even the pavements were crowded when she was a girl, and that she had to queue to go on the swings in the park.

At 10.10 a.m. a post-office van drew up outside, then

the doorbell rang and the New Dog began to bark. I took this to be an ominous portent. The New Dog never barks. (It cost me £26 at the vets in April to have its vocal cords checked.)

The New Dog obviously sensed, with its canine intelligence, that the letter the postman was holding out to me contained bad news. I scrawled my name on the postman's clipboard and wished him a merry Christmas, then went upstairs to my bedroom. I locked the door and opened the letter.

Labtest Ltd
Unit 1, Branson Trading Estate
Filey-on-Sense
Essex

Dear Mr Mole,

Tests carried out on blood samples by this laboratory show conclusively that you are the father of Glenn Bott, who currently resides at 19 Geoffrey Howe Road, Thatcher Estate, Leicester.

Should you wish to query the test results, there will be a further charge of £150 plus vat. As requested, copies of this report have been sent to Barry Kent, Mrs Sharon Bott, and Mrs Bott's solicitor, Ms Miranda Pankhurst of Justice for Children.

Yours sincerely,
Amanda Trott
(Director of Parental Attribution Tests)

I have now read the letter several times, including the enclosed lab report, which might as well be written in Welsh for all the sense it makes to me. I have hidden it under a pile of handkerchiefs, next to my rolled-up socks.

I am in shock.

## Saturday December 13th

Spent the morning searching for a word or phrase to express my feelings. I tried to imagine what Tony Blair would do under the circumstances, and was certain that tears would not be very far away.

> *Glenn Bott*
> Seen from a distance
> Tall, frowning, twelve.
> Gangsta clothes
> In an English market.
> Half of Sharon, half of me.
> Fully himself.

## Sunday December 14th

I phoned Sharon this morning. Douggie answered. He said that Sharon was out Christmas shopping. He said, 'She'd better be back soon. I'm stuck here with the bleddy kids, waiting to go out for a few bevvies.'

I said that I would ring later. He said, 'Bad luck on the blood test, eh?'

I said icily that I was looking forward to making my son's acquaintance. He laughed a smoker's laugh and put the phone down.

## Monday December 15th

The New Dog had a sudden burst of energy this morning and attacked the Christmas tree, almost destroying it. Ivan offered to repair the damage. It is now back up, but many of the old decorations seem to have disappeared. I searched the waste-bins and the wheelie-bin, but found no evidence, yet I know that the cardboard star I made for my mother twenty-two years ago is in the house somewhere.

As I was loading the washing-machine tonight, I found a note in the pocket of William's anorak; it was dated Thursday December 3rd.

Dear Parent, Guardian/Primary Carer

Your son/daughter has been allocated a part in the Kidsplay Nativity enactment.

He/she will require a costume for the following character: _____goat._

The performance will begin at 4 p.m. sharp on Tuesday December 16th.

Yours sincerely,

Mrs Parvez

Tomorrow!

I was outraged. William is to play a lowly goat! Mrs Parvez obviously still bears a grudge over the farm visit incident.

And how am I supposed to find a goat costume before tomorrow morning? And, anyway, what role does a goat play in the Nativity? I checked the Christmas cards hung by a string on the living-room wall, but didn't see a single goat in any of the mangers.

My mother has refused to have anything to do with the goat costume, so I was forced to ask for Tania's help.


## Tuesday December 16th

William was easily the best performer in the Nativity play. He was the essence of goatiness. My mother whispered, 'How is he getting his eyes to protrude like that?'

He looked magnificent in his goat outfit – though Ivan was furious to see that Tania had cut up his old grey car-coat for the body, four legs and goatee beard. He had a little trouble with the 'horns' made of painted carrots, but the cloven hooves that my father had fashioned from four empty Flora tubs were a triumph.

Pauline 'n' Ivan and George 'n' Tania ignored each other and also the printed notices left on our seats.

Please do not take flash photographs.
Kidsplay will be selling official photographs @ £27.50 per pack in the new term.
NB. Please note, it is not possible to split packs.

I thought the other children gave a distinctly lacklustre performance. Joseph looked particularly gormless.

During the children's long and atonal rendition of 'Away In A Manger', my thoughts drifted to Glenn Bott; the type of child who was unlikely to be chosen to play anything ever in a Nativity play, not even a goat.

I phoned the Bott household when I got back home, but there was no reply.

## Wednesday December 17th

A Christmas card from Pandora. It began 'Dear Constituent,' and was signed with a rubber stamp.

I drove to Sharon's tonight and sat in the car rehearsing what I would say to the boy. Would I be expected to hug and kiss him, or merely shake his hand in a manly way?

As I sat there, a battered white van drew up at the kerb. Glenn and Douggie emerged. Douggie pointed at my car and laughed, and Glenn put his head down and went into the house, slamming the door behind him. I turned the engine on and drove away.

## Thursday December 18th

Brick Eagleburger rang to say that he'd had an irate Arthur Stoat on the phone, demanding the manuscript of *Offally Good! – The Book!*.

Brick said, 'Level with me, Aidy, I'm your agent for Chrissake, I lie for a f------ living. I can ring Stoat and tell him you've been in a f------ *coma*. But I wanna know the *truth*. I'm gonna ask you two questions. One: have you written the f------ book?'

'No,' I said.

'OK, so now we're getting somewhere. Two: is a ghost-writer writing the f------ book?'

'No,' I admitted.

Arthur Stoat is threatening to sue me for breach of contract and claim compensation for lost income and damage to his professional reputation. I asked him how much Stoat was demanding. Brick said, 'The guy was quoting a ballpark figure of sixty K.'

After I'd replaced the receiver I sat on the stairs for a full five minutes trying to imagine the life that lay ahead of me. I did a quick calculation on the telephone message pad.

| | |
|---|---|
| Stoat Books | 60,000 |
| Legal fees | 6,000 (approx) |
| | £66,000 |

I would be forced to live in penury in my mother's house with two sons to support and my professional reputation in tatters. It was my darkest hour.

When my mother came in from Christmas shopping I told her everything: about Glenn, and Stoat Books, and the hopeless future that lay ahead of me.

She put her arm round me and said, 'Don't worry, pet, you've still got your mother. I can be strong for both of us.'

She then went to her bedroom and lay down with a cold white flannel over her face.

## Friday December 19th

I heard my mother get up at five this morning and then start clacking on her computer keys in the alcove. My bedroom lies directly above Ivan's work-station and I was forced from my bed by the disturbance. I went down to complain. She swung round guiltily on her typist's chair and said, 'I'm writing *our* round-robin Christmas letter. Go back to bed.'

She is so inconsiderate: I need all the sleep I can get at a time like this.

## Sunday December 21st

Am I the only person in this house who is remotely interested in the arrangements for Christmas? There isn't a candle, a mince-pie or a bag of nuts in the house. And I need to focus my little remaining energy on tracking down a Teletubby.

## Monday December 22nd

I have bought book tokens from Waterstones for everybody, apart from my mother, for whom I already have a gift. It is a set of mini toiletries I took from a boarding house I stayed in last year: shampoo, conditioner, bath gel, sewing kit, cotton buds and a shoeshine pad. I plan to place them in a wicker bread-basket and cover them with clingfilm. She will never know it is not a *bona fide* shop-bought present.

## Tuesday December 23rd

My mother has still not bought a turkey, even though we are apparently to host the entire family on Christmas Day. She is spending sixteen hours a day at the keyboard writing her interminable round robin.

## Wednesday December 24th
*Christmas Eve*

I rose at dawn and went downstairs to find my mother still seated in front of the screen, the ashtray next to her overflowing. I pointed out to her that this was a pointless exercise as she had long missed the last posting day for Christmas and she said that she had turned it into a New Year greeting. When I told her that, after a tip-off from Nigel, I was going to queue outside Safeway's for a Teletubby, she said, 'Pick a turkey up while you're there, and a Christmas cake and stuff.' As I slammed the door she shouted, 'Don't forget the bread-sauce mix.'

The Teletubby queue was at least thirty people long by the time I arrived; some had been there all night. I cursed God, went inside, filled two trolleys with Christmas Fayre, drove home, unpacked, put the turkey in the bath to defrost, drove to Toys 'Я' Us, threw a lot of plastic rubbish suitable for a three-year-old into a trolley, and drove home again.

I was wrapping the book tokens in my room when the doorbell rang with an aggressive urgency. My mother shouted from the computer alcove, 'For Christ's sake! Will somebody please answer that bloody *door*?'

William got there before me.

Glenn Bott stood on the doorstep looking down at his half-brother. He was holding a large envelope. Wordlessly he handed it over to me.

Wordlessly I took it. He would not look me in the eye.

William said, 'Do you want to see my dinosaur farm?'

Glenn nodded, and William led the way up the stairs. I followed, tearing open the envelope. Inside was a Christmas card. A picture of a pipe-smoking-dad type, in a cardigan, sitting by a roaring fire in an armchair with a decanter and a glass on a small round table next to him. Across the top was gold-embossed writing: 'To Dad at Christmas'.

May Yuletide cheer
Be yours this year
And may your Christmas
Dreams come true
If e'er I'm sad
I think of Dad
And I'm so pleased
My Dad is you!

He had signed it – 'To Dad, from Glenn'.

I thanked him and he frowned. He doesn't go in for smiling much. He looks like a cross between William Brown (the same tuft of hair sticking up at the back) and a younger, blonder, thinner, more authentic version of Gordon Brown. The Chancellor of the Exechequer.

I couldn't think of anything to say to the boy, and thanked God for William's obvious social skills. But when William went to the toilet and we were alone, I confided in him my despair at being unable to give William his most devout wish, a set of Teletubbies.

Was I subconsciously warning the boy about my inadequacies as a parent?

Eventually, Glenn said, 'What shall I call you? Dad or Adrian?'

I said, 'Dad,' and he now calls me Dad at least once every sentence. I never call my father anything.

When William came back, Glenn got to his feet and said, 'I've gotta go, Dad.'

My mother was waiting at the foot of the stairs. Her face crumpled slightly when she saw him. Glenn blushed a deep red as they were introduced and my mother was uncharacteristically lost for words, so I hurried the boy out of the door. He said, 'I'll be back, Dad.'

After he'd gone I drove to the BP garage, where I panic-bought a plastic football. I hoped that the boy had at least a passing interest in the game.

I got back to the house to find my mother in the kitchen with Ivan. She kept saying, 'Just you wait until you *see* him,' in a kind of despairing way. Ivan said, 'Pauline, the child has had none of the advantages of our children: library tickets, nourishing food, etc.'

This is a joke: I was brought up on boil-in-the-bag.

Rosie said, 'He's riding around on a £200 BMX.'

'It's probably stolen,' said my mother.

I defended Glenn, saying, 'He is my son, a member of the Mole family. We must grow to love him.'

My mother said, 'I'll try to like him, Adrian, but *love* may take some time.'

Rosie had prejudiced my mother against Glenn by telling her that he is a psycho and has been suspended from school three times, once for throwing his shoes over the oak tree in the grounds (one got caught in a lower branch), once for saying that the moussaka he had for school dinner was 'crap', and once for asserting to his comparative religion teacher that God

283

was 'a bit of a bastard' for allowing famines and plane crashes to happen.

## Thursday December 25th
*Christmas Day – Bank Holiday*

The day has been exhausting. William was up at 5.30. I tried to fob him off with his Christmas stocking and then to persuade him back to bed, but the kid was in a frenzy of excitement and made several attempts to break into the living room, where Santa had left his presents. As arranged I telephoned my father and Tania, and told them that William was about to 'open'. Next I knocked on my mother 'n' Ivan's door and told them the same. I shouted to Rosie and went down to put the kettle on. This was only the first of my many domestic duties on this day. I sometimes wish I lived in pre-feminist times when if a man washed a teaspoon he was regarded as 'a big Jessie'. It must have been great when women did all the work, and men just lolled about reading the paper.

I asked my father about those days when we were preparing the Brussels sprouts, the carrots and the potatoes, etc., etc. His eyes took on a faraway misty look. 'It was a golden age,' he said, almost choking with emotion. 'I'm only sorry that you never lived to see it as an adult man. I'd come home from work, my dinner would be on the table, my shirts ironed, my socks in balls. I didn't know how to turn the stove *on*, let alone cook on the bleeding thing.' His eyes then narrowed, his voice became a hiss as he said, 'That bloody Germaine Greer ruined my life. Your mother was never the same after reading that bleeding book.'

The Norfolk Sugdens, my mother's parents, turned up at 1 p.m. I'm amazed that the Swansea licensing authorities allow Grandad Sugden to drive. He's got cataracts and narcolepsy, a condition that sends him to sleep every twenty minutes.

'He ain't asleep for long,' said Granny Sugden, 'no more 'n a second or so.'

They sat down in front of the television five minutes after arriving, and watched everything on the screen with the same open-mouthed fascination. The signal is weak where they live. I asked my mother if she'd told the Sugdens about the Great Mole/Braithwaite Partner Swap.

'No,' she said, 'they're retired potato farmers. It would only confuse them.'

I certainly saw confusion in Grandma Sugden's eyes when Ivan took my mother into his arms under the mistletoe and French-kissed her for a good two minutes. I was glad to leave them all to it and get into the kitchen. Though I was enraged to find out that the turkey hadn't defrosted properly!

Why not? It had been in the bath at least sixteen hours.

Rosie sat for an hour with her new Rowenta hair-dryer on full, directing heat into the turkey's cavities. By the time it came out of the oven, the light was fading and everyone had stuffed themselves full of chocolates and mince-pies. I must admit, my dear Diary, that the last ten minutes before dishing up the Christmas dinner were possibly the most pressured of my life. Serving dinner for sixty at Hoi Polloi was a doddle by comparison. I have been nagging my mother to have the large ring on her electric cooker repaired for months but, oh, no, that would have been too sensible!

Finally, when all the vegetables were in their serving dishes, and the roast potatoes and chipolatas and stuffing balls were clustered around the turkey, I realized the horrible truth: I had forgotten to make the gravy! In a normal household this would hardly matter – a dollop of Bisto and a few pale Oxos would suffice. But the Christmas Gravy in the Mole house has over the years taken on the stuff of myth and legend.

My dead grandma, Edna May Mole, is responsible for setting the standard. First the turkey giblets are stewed for twenty-four hours, and when the stock has been reduced and the scum has been removed, then and only then are proprietary gravy brands added, slowly and carefully, until exactly the right shade of light brown liquid, not too thick, not too thin, simmers in the Christmas Gravy Saucepan.

I tore some kitchen paper from the roll and buried my face in it, only to be jolted from my feelings of inadequacy by Tania, who burst into the kitchen and asked irritably, 'How much longer must we wait? I'm hypoglycaemic you know.'

I said, through gritted teeth, that I had forgotten to make the Christmas Gravy.

'I'll do it,' she said.

This would be tantamount to having Charles Manson give the Pope's Easter Blessing. I tried to stop her but before I could she had pulled the chicken Oxos out of my hand and crumbled them into the turkey roasting-pan. She was stirring it (quite viciously, I thought) when my mother arrived on the scene. 'What do you think you're doing?' she asked.

'I'm making gravy,' said Tania.

'Only a person who carries the Mole name is allowed to make the Christmas Gravy,' said my mother, whose lips, always thin, had now all but disappeared. 'Give me that spoon.'

Tania said, 'Whether you like it or not, Pauline, I will soon *be* a Mole. George and I are getting married as soon as we're all divorced.'

'Fine! Fine!' shouted my mother. 'You can make your own Christmas Gravy in your own house, but until then get out of my kitchen!'

Everybody then congregated in the kitchen to join the row, apart from William who was putting his plastic insects (a present from Rosie, 30 for £1 from Poundstretcher) to bed in various containers.

Meanwhile, the Christmas dinner, over which I

had toiled for most of the day, grew cold. I went upstairs, slammed shut my bedroom door and threw myself on to my bed. I waited for the sound of feet on the stairs; surely somebody would come to me and beg me to rejoin the company? But the next sounds I heard were pings from the microwave, then crackers being pulled, corks being popped, and eventually, to my disgust, laughter!

Several times I heard the word 'gravy' shouted in tones of hilarity!

I must leave this house at the earliest opportunity.

I woke at 7.30 in the evening to find Glenn Bott shaking me roughly. 'Thanks for the football,' he said. Then, 'You've got dribble on the side of your mouth, Dad.' He gave me a badly wrapped and Sellotaped parcel, which bore an ill-written label: 'To Dad, from Glenn'. I opened it and found a bottle of anti-freeze and a mitt for scraping ice off a car windscreen. I was very touched. I'm going to try to persuade the boy to grow his hair. Apart from the tuft his scalp is intimidating.

Tania patronized Glenn for a few minutes, 'I say Glenn, those trainers are terribly cutting-edge,' then left to join Pandora at a hospice carol service. I was glad to see the back of her. She had made it obvious all day that Christmas Day at the Moles' had been a walk on the wild side for her.

My father, maudlin on Johnnie Walker, invited us to The Lawns tomorrow for Boxing Day 'Brunch'.

Glenn helped me to sort out the Sugdens' camp

beds. We worked quite well as a team. Before he went home on his bike he said, 'I was just thinkin', Dad, Jesus is 1,997 years old today, ain't he?'

It was a rhetorical question, which, thank God, I didn't need to answer. Is the boy a religious obsessive? How will he react when he finds out that his father is a radical agnostic?

## Friday December 26th
*Boxing Day – Bank Holiday*

Brunch at The Lawns was a tense affair. It started off badly when Grandad Sugden slipped and fell into the Koi carp pool and damaged the lining. Tania's mouth turned into a slit and stayed that way throughout lunch. The atmosphere was not helped by my mother laughing openly at their Christmas tree, on which were arranged twenty-five gingerbread men, each hanging by their necks from a noose-like silver ribbon. 'I thought you were against the death penalty, Tania,' she said.

'George forgot to put the holes in their heads for the ribbon,' Tania said, as she handed round a plate of home-made sushi; it looked suspiciously like bits of the Koi carp, which were gasping for breath outside as my father tried desperately to repair the pool lining.

I saw Ivan look wistfully around at his old spacious home.

Things livened up a bit when the Labrador puppy woke up and caught one of Rosie's hair extensions in his paws, but as soon as she was disentangled we left.

In the late afternoon I took William for a walk with his wheelbarrow, and bumped into Archie Tait outside the BP garage, where he'd just been to buy a turkey burger for his dinner. I asked him how he'd spent Christmas Day.

'Alone,' he said.

He asked me how I'd spent the day.

'Lonely, but not alone,' I replied.

Some insane impulse prompted me to say that if he felt like coming to Wisteria Walk at 6 p.m. there would be Christmas cake, pickles, leftover turkey, etc. He looked at the turkey burgers and said, 'I wonder if they would consider a refund.' Talk about mean!

10 p.m. I have just realized that the refund remark was almost certainly a joke, because Archie is far from mean. He arrived at the house festooned with presents. He gave me a copy of Boswell's *Life of Doctor Johnson* that I admired when I was last in his house. To William he gave a set of Lakeland drawing pencils, sixty of them in a wooden box, graded colour by lovely colour. It is far too handsome a present for a three-year-old. William will almost certainly lose or destroy them within hours. I said so to Archie.

He bent down to William and said, 'William, these pencils each have their own place in the box and they must be replaced exactly before you go to bed each night.'

William spent the rest of the day taking the pencils in and out of the box. I asked Archie where he had bought such a lovely present at such short notice. He said he'd had the pencil box for fifteen years. His face showed that he didn't want to go into further details.

## Saturday December 27th

Thank God it's all over and there's only the New Year to get through.

## Monday December 29th

My mother received the following note from Archie Tait today.

Dear Mrs Mole,

It was most kind of you to have me to your Boxing Day celebration. I enjoyed myself enormously; it was so refreshing to be among people with whom one feels an affinity. As a young man I campaigned for the principles of free love, and the rejection of bourgeois values. It was good to see these values being practised so assiduously in your family.

Yours, with best wishes,

Archibald Tait

PS. Adrian is a fine young man. Congratulations.

My mother has taken this short note to be a total vindication of her louche and undisciplined behaviour since she came to sexual maturity.

Glenn turned up (again) this evening to wish us all a happy New Year. And to give me a Hogmanay card from his mother, Sharon. I put it unread on top of the refrigerator. 'You oughta read inside it, Dad,' said Glenn.

I opened it and read,

Dear Adrian,

I hope you had a very happy Christmas and that you will have a happy and preposterous New Year.

I presumed she meant *prosperous*; a moment with the dictionary would have saved her considerable embarrassment. There was an invoice inside the (bag-piper-with-mountains-in-background-Labrador-in-foreground) card.

To arrears of child maintenance @ £15,000
Payment to be made immediately, to Pankhurst, Barnwell,
Brewin, Laker, Medwin, O'Keefe, Family Law Centre.


I did some mental arithmetic. The £66,000 I owe
Arthur Stoat plus £15,000 equals £81,000!!!!

I leaned against the fridge.

'Sorry, Dad,' said Glenn. 'It's nothin' to do with
me.'

I felt like saying, 'On the contrary, Glenn, it has
*everything* to do with you.'

This is such an horrific development in the traject-
ory of my life that I can't see how I am going to
recover from it. I have a morbid horror of debt. My
parents have never, to my knowledge, been *out* of
debt. Indeed, my father claims to have been in debt
since he was a small child (a loan to buy a Corgi
Ferrari).

I can do nothing at the moment: all the Crisis
phone lines are clogged up. I've tried the Help With
Debt line several times. I even tried to get through
to Talk Radio's Anna Raeburn, but I was only one of
many to be disappointed.

Later, me and William and Glenn went to Leicester
Town Hall square, although I was in no mood to
celebrate. There were hundreds of people there. Some
in fancy dress. The council had switched all the Christmas decorations off. The place was in total darkness.
The only light that could be seen was the red one on

the police video camera, which was filming the crowd from the Lord Mayor's balcony.

At the stroke of midnight the crowd went mad with excitement and the policemen got out of the vans where they'd been sitting waiting. We sang 'Auld Lang Syne'. There was no trouble, just an air of terrible anticlimax and sadness that the council and the police had such a poor opinion of their citizens.

At 1 a.m. I took my boys home. I was pleased to see that Sharon came to the door to welcome Glenn back. We waved, but didn't speak. She looked fatter than ever.

## Thursday January 1st, 1998

These are my New Year resolutions:

1. I will be charitable. Not give money, just be kinder to those less fortunate than myself.
2. I will support *both* my sons.
3. I will find somewhere to live.
4. I will take out insurance.
5. I will get *The White Van* produced.
6. I will resume sexual relations with women.
7. I will give Mr Blair another six months.
8. I will throw all my white socks away.

9. I will stop obsessing about my hair loss.
10. I will join a gym.

## Friday January 2nd

I arranged to meet Sharon Bott in McDonald's 'Restaurant', as she calls it, in Leicester city centre. I was a little early and caught her with her mouth full of a triple something or other.

There was an awkward pause, during which she chewed like mad and I tried to think of something to say that wouldn't require her to speak. I commented that Glenn and I were getting along quite well, considering our short acquaintance. She nodded. I added that he would look better if he allowed the shaved bits of his scalp to 'grow out'. She chewed and nodded frantically. Her fingers look like Walker's thick sausages.

Eventually she swallowed and we talked about the £15,000 her solicitors were demanding. I pointed out that, unlike Barry Kent, I was not a rich man. I said I would give Sharon an interim payment of £1,000 if she would not reveal to the Child Support Agency where I lived. 'They will only claw it back,' I said, 'and you could lose your Income Support.'

She agreed to take £1,000 by bank transfer.

## Saturday January 3rd

I went to see Pandora at her surgery this afternoon. I needed advice about my entitlement to legal aid. It's no good, Diary, I can't lie to you. The truth is I just wanted to *see* her.

There were dark shadows under her eyes, but she still looked beautiful in her pink cashmere twinset. She took a packet of Ultra Low from out of her grey patent Prada bag. I commented on the handbag. Shouldn't she be seen to be buying British?

She said, 'It was a Christmas present.'

'From a rich man, obviously,' I said, trying to control my jealousy.

She smiled enigmatically.

I went on to tell her about my failure to write the book, the impending legal action from Stoat, and my maintenance problems *re* Glenn Bott.

At the end she burst out laughing! And said, 'Your life is a situation comedy! You're over thirty, you're living at home with your mother, you're frightened of women – you're a Ronnie Corbett for the nineties!'

When I'd recovered my composure, I asked how she was enjoying the world of Agriculture and Fisheries. She grimaced and said, 'I should be at the Foreign Office. I speak fluent Mandarin and Serbo-Croat, for Chrissakes! I could be *useful*. As it is, I'm wasting my bloody time on *whelks*!'

Her paper bleeped and a message flashed across –

RING ALASTAIR. She paled a little and reached for her mobile.

I left with a heavy heart.


Bowels – loose
Alcohol – bottle of Niersteiner, 2 vodkas
Pains – right knee, neck, left testicle
Sleep – v. little
Phobias – licking postage stamps, netting, ring-pulls, Psion Organizer


## Sunday January 4th

Now I truly understand the meaning of the phrase 'mother-love'. I am fortunate to have the most wonderful mother in the world. I blush with shame when I re-read these diaries. There is hardly a positive entry about this truly kind and self-sacrificing woman. Pauline Mole is a saint – she has saved me not only from humiliation, but also from a lifetime of debt.

MY MOTHER WROTE *OFFALLY GOOD! – THE BOOK!.* WHAT'S MORE, SHE SENT IT TO STOAT ON DECEMBER 24TH! AND IT HAS MY NAME ON THE FRONT PAGE.

I found out this morning after a baffling call from Arthur Stoat. I picked up the phone thinking I was safe from him at 7.30 a.m. on a Sunday morning.

Stoat said, 'Good, caught you. I'm reading the proofs of *Offally Good!*. On page forty-three you say, "Take an *otter* tail." Should that be, "Take *another* tail"?'

I didn't know what he was talking about: there was *no* page forty-three. However, I remembered some advice my grandma gave me once: 'If in doubt, say nowt.' So I kept quiet, apart from making noncommittal grunts every now and then.

Stoat ended by saying that *Offally Good!* was a 'fine piece of work, funny, informative, compassionate, even'. He said he hadn't realized quite how much of a feminist I was, so chapter ten, 'The Future For Men Is Bleak', came as 'quite a surprise in a book about offal'.

He said he was 'enormously touched' by the dedication at the front of the book. 'To my beloved mother, Pauline Mole, who has nurtured me and inspired me throughout my life. Without this magnificent woman's wisdom and erudition I could not have written this book.'

Stoat sighed and said, 'You're a very lucky man, Adrian. My own mother is a dreadful disappointment. She's a dowdy, whining hypochondriac.'

There was joy in my heart when I put the phone down. When I heard my mother moving about upstairs I put some bacon in the pan to fry, so that when she eventually came downstairs to feed the New Dog she was greeted by the sight of a full English breakfast laid out on the table for her, complete with a pot of freshly brewed coffee and de-crusted toast. I even placed an ashtray within reach of her place setting. I said, 'Thank you for writing the book,' and pulled a chair out for her.

She said, 'I did it for myself. I couldn't stand another *minute* of you whingeing on about the bloody thing.'

I said, 'I can't wait to read it. Have you got a copy?'

She padded into the alcove and pressed a few knobs on the computer. The printer started to whir and throw out neatly typed pages. By the time she'd finished her breakfast, and smoked a fag, *Offally Good! – The Manuscript!* was sitting there, waiting to be read. My mother said, 'I shall expect 50 per cent of any monies due or earned, including royalties, a percentage of any merchandising deals and foreign-rights sales and, of course, residuals.'

I was in no position to argue.

*10 p.m.* I have just finished reading the manuscript. It's not bad, though there is far too much emphasis on gender politics for my taste. Germaine Greer appears fourteen times in the index.

## Monday January 5th

Zippo rang today. He wanted to congratulate me on the book I didn't write. Pie Crust intend to repeat the first TV series 'on the back of the book'. He said that it has huge cult potential, especially since the beef-on-the-bone ban. 'We should pick up some right-wing, beef-eating *Telegraph* types,' he said, 'which will broaden the advertising potential enormously.' He listed the advertising profile of *Daily Telegraph* readers. Apparently they go in for: garden sheds, incontinence pants, secateurs, erotic underwear, liquid manure, Egyptian cruises, pergolas, cutlery sets, denture fixatives and anything to do with dogs.

Zippo is liaising with Stoat Books. Publication date is February 24th, which, according to Zippo, is a dead time in publishing. 'Nobody publishes then,' he said. 'It's a black hole as far as buying books is concerned.' When I asked why *Offally Good! – The Book!* was being published in this 'dead time', he said, '*Offally Good!* isn't a *book* as such, is it, Aidy? It's a TV tie-in.'

### Wednesday January 7th

Archie Tait is dead. A policeman called Darren Edwards rang to tell me. He found my telephone number under a jar of Haywood's piccalilli. He thinks Archie died on Monday night. I asked the policeman why he'd rung me – I'm not Archie's next of kin. PC Edwards said that my phone number was the only one they could locate in the house.

## Thursday January 8th

I told William about Archie last night. I asked my mother for advice first. How *do* you explain death to a three-year-old?

She said, 'I don't know, it used to be easy when we all believed in God. You just told little kids that dead people had gone to heaven to see Jesus.'

Ivan said, 'We may have to re-invent God. He served a useful purpose at times.'

Rosie suggested an ecological approach. She said, 'Tell William that Archie's dead body is, like, gonna sorta fertilize the ground and make, like, vegetables grow bigger, an' that.'

In the end I told William that Archie had gone to sleep and didn't want to wake up. He understood that. He has often seen me unable to get out of bed in the morning.

## Saturday January 10th

Do the baby boomers have no sense of morality?

Robin Cook, the Foreign Secretary, has been revealed to be a *serial* adulterer! How can this be? I am at least *twice* as good-looking as him. It must be true that power is an aphrodisiac. How else do you explain the fact that Gaynor Regan is in love with the elf?

## Sunday January 11th

I sat out in the garden in the sun today and had a cup of tea! The weather has gone mad. The novelty fruit thermometer I bought from Spain for my mother, which is still nailed to the side of the house, showed the temperature to be two oranges past a banana – 63°F.

## Wednesday January 14th

The bloke in the BP shop told me that Archie Tait is to be buried by Social Security unless somebody comes up with an alternative by Friday. It's not my problem. I hardly knew the bloke. And, anyway, death is death. Archie won't know, or care, whether he's cremated by Social Security or Harrods' Funeral Service. The BP bloke said he died of pneumonia. He asked me if I wanted Archie's copy of the *London Review of Books*, which had come on Saturday. I said I'd take it off his hands.

## Friday January 16th

Archie is being cremated on Tuesday morning at 11 a.m. I'm doing the music and the words. The BP bloke is supplying Ginster's Cornish pasties and sausage rolls.

## Saturday January 17th

Poor President Clinton has had to put up with a lot since he was elected. The Ku Klux Klan, the Survivalists and the Daughters of the Revolution have all been out to discredit him. Now they had come up with a ludicrous story about him sexually harassing a woman called Paula Jones in a hotel room in Arkansas in 1991. As if! He is a good-looking bloke, he doesn't *need* to sexually harass any woman. I asked my mother if she had heard about the Paula Jones case. She looked back at me with pity in her eyes. 'The whole world has heard about Paula Jones,' she said. 'Where have you *been*? On the planet Zog?'

I said it wasn't possible to keep up with *all* the news.

She said, 'We're not talking about a three-car pile-up in Market Harborough, Adrian. This is top of the broadcast, world-class, CNN, BBC, headline *news*.' She advised me to see a neurologist: she thinks I may be suffering from selective memory loss.

## Tuesday January 20th

There were only eight people at Archie's funeral. Me, my mother, Rosie, the bloke from the BP shop, Archie's neighbour (a student called Liam), a representative from the Socialist Labour Party, Archie's solicitor Mr Holden, and a man from the crematorium. I'd only known him since May, yet here I was conducting his funeral service. My mother had made a nice job of desk-top-printing the funeral service.

*11 a.m. Louis Armstrong: 'It's A Wonderful World'*
*11.02 Adrian Mole: 'The Archie Tait I Knew'*
*11.05 Liam O'Casey: Reading from Tom Paine*
*11.08 Hymn: 'Jerusalem', William Blake*
*11.10 Open for Archie's friends to comment on his life*
*11.15 As coffin slides into oven, 'Ode to Joy', Beethoven*
*Wake to be held at Wisteria Walk, Ashby-de-la-Zouch*
*Refreshments sponsored by BP*

Everybody said that it was a lovely occasion. There was none of that morbid Church of England stuff about being 'born into sin and dying in sin'. The BP bloke came to the lectern to say that Archie came in every day for his groceries and was always polite, even when his *London Review of Books* hadn't been delivered. He said that Archie never complained about his artificial leg, even when the pavements were icy. Mr Holden, the solicitor, said that he had only met Archie a couple of times, but had found him to be a true gentleman who had made great personal and professional sacrifices in the cause of socialism. But it was a terrible thing to be at a funeral where nobody cried. I sometimes long for a bit of Mediterranean blood.

Only the Socialist Labour Party man and Liam, the student, came back to Wisteria Walk. The BP bloke had to go back to the shop, and Mr Holden was due in court. William returned from nursery school and entertained the company with his rendition of traditional nursery rhymes until the company tired and went away.

*2 a.m.* Have I got any principles I would sacrifice my personal and professional life for? I don't know the answer to this question.

*4.30 a.m.* Due to Mr Blair's obvious hatred for war I am never going to be tested in battle. A shame.

## Wednesday January 21st

An elaborate brochure from Peter Savage today, promoting his latest venture, an oxygen bar called $H_2O$. A piece of stiff white card with $H_2O$ written in tiny silver print in the centre. Inside a list of what I presumed to be a selection of the oxygens available.

Mont Blanc
Bracing Skegness
California Dream
Cape Cod night
Hindu Kush

All oxygens @ £25 per litre inclusive of VAT.
All masks are sterilized between users.

I showed it to my father when he came to visit Rosie and William tonight. He was horrified. He said, 'Twenty-five quid for sniffing fresh air! Some people would stick tenners up their bums if you told them it was fashionable.'

I reminded him that it cost him at least £45 a week to suck on burning carcinogenic leaves.

He protested that he'd cut down to fifteen fags a day now Tania was pressurizing him to give up, though conceded that he was spending 'another six quid a day on nicotine patches'. He said, 'You're lucky you haven't got an addictive personality, Adrian.'

He obviously doesn't know about my alarming daily consumption of Opal Fruits, and my increasing dependence on the green ones.

Mr Holden, Archie's solicitor, rang today and asked if I could meet him at his office at 2.30 on Friday afternoon. I expect he's going to ask me to stump up for part of the funeral expenses – which is not fair. As I've said many times, I hardly knew the bloke.

Stoat has faxed through four pages of editorial corrections. My mother is working on them as I write. Ha! Ha! Ha!

## Thursday January 22nd

Glenn in trouble at school for farting in maths. His maths teacher, Miss Trellis, says that the fart was deliberate. Glenn claims that his mother is feeding him 'too many beans'.

I rang the school today and made an appointment to see Miss Trellis (4.30 p.m. on Monday).

## Friday January 23rd

Mr Holden smiled, baring his yellow teeth. Then he handed me a document and said, 'This is Mr Tait's will, which he amended only three weeks ago.'

*The Last Will and Testament of Archibald Erasmus Tait*

I made the acquaintance of Adrian Mole on May 1st when he was kind enough to give me a lift to the polling station. The two journeys were quite short, yet we covered a great deal of conversational ground and found despite the disparity of our ages that we had some interests in common.

He was gracious enough to compliment me on my cat, Andrew, of whom I am very fond. I am a difficult man, I have never had the gift of friendship and I have spent most of my life engaged in the cause of revolutionary politics – where so often friendship has to be sacrificed to principle.

Contact with my family was terminated at the time of the Suez Crisis when I led a pro-Nasser rally through the streets of Downham Market, where my wife and I were living at the time.

I have little to leave, apart from the house and a small insurance policy, which will cover funeral expenses. After careful consideration I have decided to leave my house, 33 Rampart Terrace, Ashby-de-la-Zouch, and its contents to Adrian Mole, of 45 Wisteria Walk, with the proviso that he resides in the house and cares for Andrew, my cat, until such time as Andrew dies. Mr Mole will then be free to do as he wishes with the property.

I leave my silver cigarette case to Rajit c/o the BP garage, Kedlestone Road, with thanks for his many small kindnesses to me.

To William Mole, of Wisteria Walk, I leave my folding binoculars.

To Glenn Mole, I leave the signed photograph of Sir Stanley Matthews, which he recently admired.

If Adrian Mole does not wish to reside at Rampart Terrace under the above conditions then the house is to be sold by my solicitor, Mr Holden, and the proceeds to be donated to the Socialist Labour Party of Great Britain.

Archie Tait


I looked up when I'd finished reading and said, 'How old is the cat, Mr Holden?'

He smiled and said, 'I've never had the pleasure of meeting the creature, Mr Mole.'

I get the keys on the 27th. My mother burst into tears of joy at the news. We drove to Rampart Terrace but it was too dark to see very much.

## Saturday January 24th

Liam helped me to get Andrew into his travelling basket. The cat certainly put up a fight. I had white and ginger hair all over my navy chinos. I took him to morning surgery at the Pet Centre where the New Dog is registered. The vet examined the struggling, spitting animal.

'How long will he live?' I asked.

'Don't worry, Mr Mole,' said the vet jocularly. 'He'll live to a good old age.'

Andrew is lying on my bed as I write. He's been banned from downstairs since he jumped on Ivan's back and drew blood.

## Sunday January 25th

I took the family to see the outside of Archie's house this morning. My mother peered through the letter-box and said it needed a lot doing to it. Rosie pointed out that there was no sign of central heating.

Ivan crossed the road, looked up at the roof and said that there were 'a quantity of tiles missing' and that, in his opinion, the chimney-stack 'looked unstable', and that the guttering could 'go at any time'. William said he liked the colour of the front door (red). His was the only positive statement.

Later I took Glenn and William. Glenn disappeared down the side passage and climbed over the gate, which he then unbolted. We went into the back yard and found a paved patio and trees growing in tubs, a tiny lawn and a picnic bench with a cup and saucer on it. There was a bird table near the kitchen window. Glenn said, 'It's all right, in't it, Dad?'

There was a shed at the bottom of the yard. Glenn pushed the door open and said, ''Ere, William, this'd make a great den.' They played inside the shed until it grew too cold. Later, I dropped Glenn off at Geoffrey Howe Road. 'Mam will have me dinner ready,' he said.

I've only just realized that Glenn can't read properly. Inside the shed was a bag that clearly said 'John Innes Potting Compost'. When William asked Glenn what was inside the bag, Glenn was at a loss.

'I can't read words like that,' he said.

I didn't say anything to him at the time, but I will take the matter up with Miss Trellis on Monday. The boy is intelligent and has received compulsory schooling for *seven* years. In the car he asked me if I thought he should get an earring. I said, 'No, I absolutely forbid it.' He looked quite pleased.

I wish sometimes I wasn't a parent, even when I am alone I carry him and William with me, across my shoulders and inside my heart.

## Monday January 26th

Miss Trellis is a mousy little creature in a beige cardigan. She lacks many things: personality, humour, style, charm. I informed her of my recent entry into Glenn's life and told her I would be keeping a close eye on his future behaviour.

On the way out I made an appointment to see Roger Patience, the headmaster.

Glenn was waiting outside in the school car park.

'How'd you get on, Dad?' he said.

I said, 'All right.' I advised him to practise farting quietly. I assured him that it was possible.

He said that he would 'give it a go, Dad'.

On the way home I took him into the library where I used to work and enrolled him as a member. He was amazed to learn that the library service was free. He said, 'How do they know you're not gonna nick the books, Dad?' He took four out. All picture books about football.

## Tuesday January 27th

I was given the key to Archie's house today. It doesn't seem right somehow. Archie was present in every room. His bed unmade, a pair of socks on the floor. A sinkful of washing-up. A plate, a bowl, a cup, a saucer. A knife, a fork, a dessertspoon, a teaspoon, an eggcup. I opened all the windows, then examined the bookshelves. What treasure! What joys ahead of me! Somebody called Eric Blair had inscribed Orwell's *Homage to Catalonia*: 'To Archie, Best wishes, Eric Blair'. I didn't tell anyone else that I have the key.

## Wednesday January 28th

Roger Patience is a deeply neurotic person. He is under the delusion that Chris Woodhead, the Chief Inspector of Schools, is out to get him.

Patience is more obsessed with tables than a Premier League football manager. I asked him why his school is near the bottom of the league. He blamed 'the catchment area, the riff-raff from the estates'. He blamed the teachers. 'They won't stay.' He blamed the caretaker. 'He undermines my authority.' He blamed 'Glenn Bott', whom he said was a 'borderline remedial'.

Apparently the last time the school was inspected Glenn was selected at random by an inspector to name three successful British manufacturing industries.

He couldn't name one.

I asked Roger Patience to arrange for Glenn to have extra help with his reading and writing. 'I believe it's called *teaching*,' I said, sarcastically.

While I was there the school secretary rang through and said, 'Roger, Ofsted on the line.'

Patience took a bottle of Prozac out of his desk drawer, opened it with difficulty (a childproof cap) and slipped a capsule under his tongue before saying, 'Patience here.' After he had completed a grovelling phone call he called through and instructed his secretary to ask if 'Ms Flood is free'.

While we waited for Ms Flood, we spent five awkward minutes of conversation about my sister Rosie and her foul mouth. 'I think she has undiagnosed Tourette's syndrome,' I said.

There was a knock at the door and Eleanor Flood was ushered in. She is pale and thin, with thick black hair. She was dressed in a black polo-neck sweater and a black trouser-suit. She carried a large black-leather shoulder-bag. Her eyes are grey. The sight of her fragile wrists almost brought tears to my eyes.

When she spoke her voice was soft. 'I'm very sorry, Mr Patience, but my remedial reading class is already full to overflowing,' she said, after Patience had asked her if she could 'squeeze Bott in'. 'And, anyway,' she said, turning her eyes on me, 'Glenn needs one-to-one tuition for at least a couple of hours a week.'

Patience snorted at the impossibility of providing this service in school.

'I do give private tuition, in the evening,' she said.

Patience said, 'Ms Flood, I can't have you *importuning* Mr Mole during school-time.'

I explained to Ms Flood that I did not agree with private education. However, given the parlous state of Glenn's reading skills, perhaps I ought to take a more pragmatic view. She charges £9 per hour. She is going to ring me to tell me when she can start. I thought about her wrists all the way home.

## Thursday January 29th

President Clinton has denied in the strongest possible terms that he ever had sex with a White House intern called Monica Lewinsky. Looking into the camera and stabbing his finger for emphasis, he said, with burning honesty, 'I did not have sexual relations with that woman.' He then added, with his charming Southern manners, 'Miss Lewinsky'. I, for one, believe him totally.

My mother and Ivan seem to know all about the Lewinsky affair. When I said that I had never heard of the young woman before today, they looked at me incredulously. Ivan said, 'I once had a secretary at the dairy who'd never heard of Van Gogh. She thought Van Morrison had painted *Sunflowers*.'

My mother said, 'You seem to filter out anything remotely detrimental to President Clinton.'

I said I admired the man.

She said, 'He's a sex addict.'

I pointed out that his wife, Hillary, was an attractive woman. Why would he need to look elsewhere for sexual gratification?

They looked at each other; 'I think we've got a Mary Archer "fragrant" situation here,' said Ivan.

My mother said, 'Adrian, you'll be thirty-one in a couple of months. I know you've had sex at least twice, but you don't seem to know the first thing about *lust.*'

I went upstairs to watch *Newsnight* on my portable. Pandora's on now quite often.


## Friday January 30th

I have watched President Clinton's 'Lewinsky statement' endless times. The man is not lying. The truth cries out from his eyes, his nostrils and his lips.


## Saturday January 31st

Troubled by dreams about Monica Lewinsky in which she lives in Eleanor Flood's house, and we begin a lustful relationship after a game of Cluedo.


Penis function – 10/10
Drugs – 2 Nurofen

## Monday February 2nd

After reading some fan mail that came in from Pie Crust today, I'm convinced that the big Victorian mental hospitals should be reopened. A woman from Dorset is collecting the 'toenail clippings of the famous' for a charity auction. She enclosed a tiny self-seal plastic bag with *Adrian Mole* written on it, and asked me to post it back to her in the SAE she'd also enclosed. Rosie clipped the New Dog's claws and put them into the little bag. The New Dog looked happy for a change after its pedicure, so some good came of it.

I am moving out of this house next Sunday. Nigel is providing his van. He has forgiven me for outing him since he found out that one of his uncles had a sex change in 1979 – information that his family had kept from him.

## Wednesday February 4th

I am not moving out a minute too soon! I came perilously close to a row with my mother today. She is very cool towards Glenn. When I said, 'You've hardly spoken to Glenn since Christmas Day when you told him to take his elbows off the table,' she shouted, 'One of his elbows was in the *Brussels sprouts dish*, for Chrissake!'

Ivan, of course, defended my mother and in a sudden rush of rage I accused him of being a cuckoo in the nest of Wisteria Walk.

'It's *you* who's the cuckoo,' yelled my mother. 'Sunday can't come too soon for me!'

I said she hadn't given Glenn a chance. She screamed, 'I've never known a boy to fart so often. It's like being on the edge of a sulphurous *volcano!*' I explained about the beans, but she didn't want to know.

Sunday can't come too soon for me either.


## Saturday February 7th

Glenn told me he wished I would marry his mother. We were putting empty Walker's crisps boxes into the back of Nigel's van at the time. I almost laughed out loud at the absurdity of the idea, then I looked at his face and was glad that I hadn't. I said that Sharon and I would never marry.

'Why not, Dad?' he said.

Out of the thousand and one reasons I could have given the lad, I chose one that I knew he would understand. 'I'm in lurve with somebody else, son,' I said, trying to sound like Grant Mitchell from *East-Enders* (his hero).

'Right, Dad,' said Glenn, and we spoke no more of it.

# Rampart Terrace, Leicestershire

## Sunday February 8th

It only took one van journey to move my possessions to Archie's house. When the last box had been lugged out of the van and dumped on the front-room floor, Nigel said, 'The rolling stone gathers no moss, eh, Moley?'

It was freezing in the house. I had to keep going outside to get warm. I found some firelighters and some chopped-up sticks in the kitchen and I lit a fire in the little grate. Nigel drove round to the BP garage, bought some compressed sawdust logs and a bag of smokeless fuel, and the fire (and the heat) were soon roaring up the chimney.

Archie had not been a meticulous housekeeper. The floors are covered in Andrew's hair. Nigel advised me to buy a Dyson vacuum cleaner and a cat comb. We went upstairs to examine what was to be my bedroom. Nigel shuddered at the sight of Archie's unmade bed with its grey sheets and light green candlewick bedspread. 'Did he die in bed?' he asked, pulling on a pair of rubber gloves. I admitted I didn't know. Nigel said, 'I won't let you sleep in that bed tonight, Moley. It's like something out of *Les Misérables*.'

We went to Bed City, where we took off our shoes and lay side by side on every king-sized bed in the shop.

'Have you tested the Queen's, sir?' asked a smarmy salesman of Nigel, who was wearing a diamond stud in one ear.

We chose a four-drawer divan that had the approval of the British Bed Council. I also treated myself to four new foam-filled pillows and a 15-tog duvet.

When we got home Andrew was hogging the fire. He watched with his usual indifference as we lugged the old bed out and the new bed in. He has shown absolutely no signs of grief. William is still at Wisteria Walk: my mother is refusing to let her first grandchild go until I've done something about the damp and cold at Rampart Terrace. So I will spend my first night here alone.

My address is now 33 Rampart Terrace, Ashby-de-la-Zouch, Leicestershire.

Ms Flood rang on the mobile and said that she had 'a window in her schedule' and could start Glenn's tutorials on Friday 13th at 7.30.

## Monday February 9th

I still can't decide between having an upstairs study in the spare bedroom or making it into a room for Glenn. My indecision is creating a bottleneck of unpacked boxes in the living room, hall and kitchen. The kid has never had a room of his own – he shares with his two younger brothers, Kent and Bradford. On the other hand, I long to sit at a desk under an Anglepoise and write and think. Wasn't it Leonard Woolf who said, 'Every man should have £100 a year and a room of his own?' I've been neglecting my intellectual life lately. I haven't seen *Titanic* yet, for instance.

## Tuesday February 10th

Sharon Bott has gone into hospital because her blood pressure is sky high. I thought she was just fat, but I find, in fact, she is eight months pregnant. Glenn told me that her bloke, Douggie, 'has done a runner, Dad'.

Her younger kids have been farmed out and Glenn has opted to come here. He could have gone to his Bott grandmother, but he said, 'She's mean with the spuds, Dad.' Sharon phoned me from her hospital bed to say how grateful she was. I asked her how long she was likely to be in hospital. She said, 'Until the baby's born. It could be a month if I go full term.' She sounded hopeful.

This clashes with the publication and promotion of *Offally Good! – The Book!* I asked her if Douggie was likely to come back. She broke down and said, 'No, he's took all me money out the tea caddy and moved to Cardiff with the girl from the video shop.'

THIS IS NOT HOW I EXPECTED MY LIFE TO PAN OUT! I AM TOO YOUNG TO BE BRINGING UP TWO BOYS! AND ANYWAY I ONLY EVER WANTED *ONE* CHILD, A *DAUGHTER*. SHE WAS TO BE CALLED LIBERTY AND PANDORA BRAITHWAITE WAS TO HAVE BEEN HER MOTHER!

GOODBYE, UPSTAIRS STUDY! GOODBYE, WRITING! GOODBYE, THINKING! GOODBYE, FREEDOM! HELLO, WASHING-MACHINE! HELLO, DYSON! HELLO, STOVE! HOW CAN I POSSIBLY BE RESPONSIBLE FOR THE UPKEEP OF TWO CHILDREN! I CAN'T DO IT! I HAVEN'T BEEN TAUGHT! I DON'T KNOW HOW TO BE A FATHER! I CAN'T PLAY FOOTBALL! I'VE NEVER READ A TERRY PRATCHETT *DISCWORLD* BOOK! I CAN'T CONTROL A BLACK AND DECKER DRILL!

What I want is to live with Pandora, to work in the day at something interesting (novel-writing preferably) and then to have cocktails in the bath with her at seven before we go out to eat at eight. This is what I want! Why can't I have it?

## Wednesday February 11th

Calmer today. Called a helpline – Single Fathers. The bloke on the end of the line said my reaction was quite common. 'We're still cavemen,' he said. 'We want to be out there, killing things. We don't want to be in the cave, tidying up and looking after the kids.'

## Thursday February 12th

My money and I are slowly but surely parting company. Accepted an estimate of £1,405 to install central heating. Another of £795 to mend roof and supply new guttering. Went to Bed City and bought another bed, for Glenn. William still fits his plywood racing-car bed, thank God.

Made a payment into Sharon's bank of £1,000. The bank clerk asked if I was all right (my hands were trembling, my cheeks were wet with tears, as I passed the banknotes over). I said I had an allergy to pot plants; the bank is full of them.

Took Glenn to see his mother in the maternity

hospital. Her moronic relations were crowded round her bed. Nobody greeted us. Apparently the Botts don't go in for greetings or introductions. Sharon gave Glenn two pound coins for his pocket money and said she hoped he was 'being good'. I said he was 'behaving impeccably'. Several of the Botts sniggered at this. I took the boy away as soon as was decent. I called in at Wisteria Walk on the way back and told my mother that she must release her tenacious hold on William. I said that there was a fan heater in his bedroom, should he need it.

She went upstairs to pack his things with the air of a woman on her way to the gallows.

William loves his room, which overlooks the back yard. He especially likes the racing-car posters that Glenn drew with felt-tip pens from the Everything's A Pound shop, and which now adorn his walls.


## Friday February 13th
*Rampart Terrace*

My mother made a point of keeping her Puffa jacket on throughout her visit here this afternoon. She said, after looking around, 'Those fan heaters are a waste of space. It's as cold as a polar bear's bum in here.'

William said he liked wearing his anorak in bed. I

wanted to smite him. She was critical of my food supplies, and said pointedly, 'I bet *that* big lummox costs a fortune to feed.'

I said, 'Are you referring to Andrew, or to Glenn?'

She claimed she was talking about the cat. I asked her why she was in such a bad mood.

She said, 'I miss my baby,' and pulled William to her. He struggled free and she left soon afterwards.

Glenn and William and I cleaned the kitchen in honour of Ms Flood's visit. At 7.15 Glenn took off his baseball cap, combed his hair and sat at the kitchen table, waiting.

She arrived at exactly 7.30. She was wearing a long black leather coat and tiny black suede boots, which could have been fashioned by a fairy cobbler under a toadstool somewhere. I helped her off with her coat. She has no breasts to speak of, though her nipples were surprisingly discernible behind her dark grey sweater. The end of her nose was slightly pink from the cold outside. It was the only touch of colour about her.

I hovered about in the kitchen for a while, watching as she unpacked books and writing materials from her capacious black handbag. Then she sat down at the table next to Glenn, who said, 'Are you goin' or what, Dad?'

I took William upstairs to bed and told him a story about a quiet dark-haired princess who falls in love with a dinosaur. The boy completely accepted this unlikely scenario. After he'd gone to sleep, I took advantage of the peace to do a little of my own writing. I think the Archers/Royal Family idea has legs.

Pandora was grilled on the question of beef-on-the-bone by Jeremy Paxman on *Newsnight* last night. She kept to the Party line: 'Must protect the public, blah, blah, blah!' Though in the last conversation I'd had with her she said, 'It's all quite absurd. Statistically the average Briton is more likely to die from falling off a f------ step-ladder.'

She did show the woman behind the politician once during her interview. After Mr Paxman had said, 'Oh, come off it, Ms Braithwaite,' she said, dropping her voice, 'Jeremy, you're so very forceful,' then laughed her husky laugh and appeared to poke her tongue out at him.

It was almost the most erotic thing I've seen or heard since Barbara Windsor lost her bra in *Carry On Camping*.

The newspapers are full of it this morning. Brutus in the *Express* alleged that Paxman ran straight from the studio into a cold shower and stayed there for twenty minutes.

## Saturday February 14th
*Valentine's Day*

*10 a.m.* Not a single card in the first post. Not one. Is this all I've got to show for nearly thirty-one years on this earth? An empty mantelpiece on Valentine's Day?

However, William and Glenn made me a card this afternoon. William used the Lakeland pencils. It was nice enough, a big heart with stick arms and legs, with a bubble coming out of its 'mouth' saying, 'To Dad, your grate'.

At 9 p.m. or thereabouts a Valentine card was dropped through the letterbox. I immediately opened the door and looked up and down the street, but there was no one to be seen. The card was everything a Valentine should be: a big red padded heart. Inside there was a single letter E. I don't know anybody whose name begins with an E. Who can it be, dear Diary?

## Sunday February 15th

Les Banks, the builder I have engaged to do the work on Archie's house, phoned today to say that he can't start tomorrow as promised. His mother-in-law died suddenly last night.

## Monday February 16th

A person called Nobby called round to ask if he could 'leave the ladders round the back'. He claimed to work for Les Banks. I asked for some ID. He said, 'Phone Les on his mobile.'

I did so. Les confirmed that Nobby was one of his labourers and said that the work at Rampart Terrace could start on Wednesday 'once the funeral is out of the way'. He didn't sound grief-stricken. In fact, he sounded as though he was outdoors somewhere, on a roof, with Radio One playing.

*3 a.m.* Aren't the Banks family burying the dead woman with indecent haste?

## Tuesday February 17th

Glenn said to me today, 'Do you think Glenn will play Michael, Dad?' I had no idea what he was talking about. I thought the boy had started to refer to himself in the third person, as Thatcher used to do. A sure sign of madness, or megalomania.

After watching the news, I now know that 'Michael' is Michael Owen, an eighteen-year-old footballer, and 'Glenn' is Glen Hoddle, the England football manager. From now on I will have to read the sport pages of the *Independent*. Until this day I have used them to line the waste-bin under the sink.

Eleanor Flood came again tonight. She was wearing lipstick and she smelled of ripe mangoes. It was all I could do to stop myself from stroking her delicate wrists.

I realize now that I have always been attracted to women's joints: I am a knee, shoulders, neck, ankle and wrist man. Though I can take or leave their fingers.

Eleanor told me after Glenn's lesson that she thinks he is 'a very intelligent boy, though culturally impoverished'.

I said that I was trying to address the problem. We were talking in the front room, sitting either side of the fire. She glanced around the room at the books and my print of Matisse's goldfish and said, 'He's very fortunate to have you as his father. My own father was an . . .' She lowered her grey eyes and looked into the flames of compressed sawdust logs, unable to finish her sentence. The firelight made her black hair shine. The phrase 'raven's wing' came into my mind.

I said, 'Alcoholic?'

'No,' she replied, but maddeningly she wouldn't say *what* he was. Then she left as she had an appointment to have her bikini line waxed. At this hour?

Glenn said, when I went in to say goodnight, 'D'you reckon I'll be readin' in time for the World Cup, Dad?'

I said, 'When is the World Cup?'

Glenn frowned and said, 'You *gotta* know that, Dad, surely?'

I said the date had slipped my mind, but I could tell that he was disappointed in me.

*2 a.m.* I am in lust with Eleanor Flood. I can't stop thinking about her bikini line.

## Wednesday February 18th

No sign of Les Banks. Nobby called at 5 p.m. and took the ladders away. I phoned Les's numbers but only got his message service.

Gateshead City Council has erected a sixty-foot statue called *The Angel of the North* next to the A1. My mother and Ivan are cycling up to see it, stopping off at bed-and-breakfast places on the way. Ivan said, 'I'm a long-term fan of Anthony Gormley's.'

My mother said, 'Didn't he used to be married to Joan Collins?'

## Thursday February 19th

Les Banks rang to say that he couldn't start work today because he was 'at Casualty with the wife. She's gone and cut her fingers up on an electric carving-knife.'

Nobby brought the ladders back.

## Friday February 20th

Mrs Banks's fingers have turned septic, necessitating another visit to the hospital. Les is obviously devoted to her. He promised to start work on Monday, 'without fail, Mr Mole'.

## Saturday February 21st

My mother rang from Gateshead and said, 'What day is my book being published?'

I said, 'It's *my* book, I think you'll find.' I told her it was the 24th. She said, 'Are we celebrating?'

I replied that I would be too busy with publicity.

She said, 'It should be *my* publicity.' Is this the 'ghost' coming out of the woodwork? She is desperate for fame! Being in the tabloids last year has only fuelled her hunger. I asked her what *The Angel of the North* was like. She said, 'It's heartbreaking, like everything else in my life.'

*3 p.m.*: Stop press! Securicor delivered five copies of *Offally Good! – The Book!* this afternoon. Dev Singh

333

is on the cover! I am a photographic blur next to him. My name is partially obscured by a saucepan, his is not.

## Sunday February 22nd

Took my Next suit and my Boss overcoat into Safeway's dry-cleaners this morning. I requested the express service. I stressed to the youth behind the counter, 'Darren Lacey, Executive Dry Cleaning Manager', how important it was that the articles be immaculately cleaned and pressed. I told him that I was intending to appear in front of the public in them. As I left the counter with my receipt I heard an old git who had been waiting beside me say to 'Darren', 'Where does he usually wear his clothes then? In a cupboard?'

## Monday February 23rd

Mrs Banks' fingers have turned gangrenous. 'She could lose 'er 'and.' Meanwhile the house is freezing and the roof is leaking. Will Mr Banks' domestic misfortunes ever allow him to start work on my house?

**Tuesday February 24th**
*Publication Day*

Today should have been a great day in my life. *Offally Good! – The Book!* may be 80 per cent mother-written and it is certainly not literature but, even so, it *is* a book and it bears my name. Yet could I enjoy this considerable achievement unfettered by domestic and child-care worries? No! I could not. Publication Day found me ransacking the house looking for Glenn's trainers, which he claimed to have kicked under his bed but which 'disappeared in the night, Dad'.

William's school shoes had also disappeared. I was forced to take him to school in his red wellingtons. For once I prayed for rain, though none came. Glenn had to wear a pair of my own Marks & Spencer's trainers, which were three sizes too big, obliging him to wear two pairs of wool socks with them. I dropped him off at the school gates and watched as he reluctantly sloped into school. If he wasn't exactly dragging his feet, he was certainly dragging his trainers.

Why are schoolday mornings at Rampart Terrace so fraught with domestic tension? Even Andrew twitches with nerves from 7.30 until 8.45 a.m. Never once have William, Glenn and I sat down to breakfast together with that glow on our faces that the families in advertisements are blessed with. William carries on like the Last Emperor, petulantly rejecting all the cereals offered until it's too late and he has to eat a piece of fruit in the car. And Glenn is so *slow*. It infuriates me to watch him spreading butter on his toast; how he covers the four corners of the bread, then goes back to the centre and starts the whole tedious business again.

This morning in the car, Glenn said, 'You're doin' a lot of shoutin', Dad.'

I shouted, 'Don't talk with your mouth full. You're dropping toast crumbs all over the upholstery.'

William was peeling a satsuma in the back seat and I noticed that his Kidsplay sweatshirt was on inside out. And how does the house get itself into such a state? I only have to turn my back and it's littered itself with *objects*.

At 10.30 I was live on air, broadcasting from Zouch Radio. The presenter, Dave Wonky (surely not his real name), introduced me 'as the latest talent to emerge from Ashby-de-la-Zouch. Who is he, listeners?'

I was puzzled by this introduction until Mr Wonky played an inane jingle.

> Mystery Guest
> That's the test
> Play the game
> If you know the name.

Nobody rang, so Mr Wonky gave out a further clue. 'OK, clue number two. He's a celebrity chef.'

The lines remained silent. Mr Wonky played the jingle and read out the traffic news. A lorry had overturned on the Billesdon bypass, spilling its load of goldfish food. Still nobody rang. I had now been in the studio, totally silent, for ten minutes. I was forbidden to speak until my identity had been guessed at by a listener.

After Wonky had read out a list of rummage sales to be held 'in the upcoming week', a woman rang to ask if I was Delia Smith.

Five minutes later Wonky gave out his third clue. 'He married into the Nigerian aristocracy.'

Even I wouldn't have recognized myself from this description. A moronic youth, Tez, from Coalville, asked if I was Lenny Henry. Wonky got slightly irritated and said, 'Tez, Dawn French is *not* a Nigerian aristocrat, is she?'

Tez said he didn't know and Wonky cut him off quite abruptly, without saying thank you. Wonky has aspirations to be the first Midlands Shock Jock. He told me this while playing Max Bygraves' 'Windmill in Old Amsterdam'. When it finished he said, 'That was for Mrs Agnes Golightly, who is eighty-nine years young today, God bless her.'

His fourth clue was that 'My mystery guest's family has been in the news lately. His parents have been embroiled in a love-swap tangle, involving a certain lady called Pandora.'

337

The lines were jammed, though nobody remembered my name properly. Was I 'James Vole'? 'Adrian Sole'? 'Lance Pole'? I was hurt and humiliated, especially when Wonky told the listeners that since nobody had got my name right, he would be rolling today's prize, a Radio Zouch T-shirt, over to tomorrow's programme.

He allowed me to speak briefly for two minutes on *Offally Good! – The Book!*, but I was not at my most articulate. He then invited listeners to phone in and ask me questions. A vegetarian called Yvonne rang to ask why I was encouraging the mass genocide of animals by advocating the cooking of offal. I told her that I was an animal lover and a cat owner, and said that it was a well-known fact that vegetables and fruit screamed in agony when pulled from the ground, or cut from the bough. Yvonne then got hysterical and accused me of being a man.

Wonky said, 'It's not a crime to be a man yet, is it, Yvonne?'

Yvonne then broke down and confessed that her ex-husband, a womanizing carnivore, had left his goodbye note under a plate of calves' liver in the fridge. Wonky began to counsel the woman and indicated to me that I was to leave the studio. I was glad to do so.

William came home with a note from Mrs Parvez:

Dear Mr Mole,

If you require help in purchasing school shoes for William, may I draw your attention to the enclosed Social Security leaflet, 'Help with Footwear'.

Sincerely,

Mrs Parvez

There was a message on the answerphone to say that Glenn had not attended morning or afternoon registration. When I tackled him on this, he said, 'I couldn't do it, Dad. There was no way I could go walkin' in that school in Marks & Spencer's trainers.' Tears sprang to his eyes. He looked surprised at this.

I took him and William to the out-of-town shopping complex The Pastures, where it is now possible to shop until 10 p.m. seven days a week. We went to Footlocker. A handsome black shop assistant said to Glenn, 'These equal respect, man.' He handed Glenn a pair of trainers that to my eye looked like those vehicles that pick up minerals from the surface of the moon. Glenn tried them on and I could tell he had a moment of epiphany. He said, 'Oh, Dad, they're *top!*' They were £75.99.

I said, 'Almost £76 for two bits of rubber! It would kill me, Glenn.'

He handed them back to the shop assistant, who put them back in the box. Then I remembered the grey slip-ons I was made to wear to school, instead of the Doc Martens that everyone else in my year was

339

wearing. I heard Barry Kent's taunts in the playground and went back into the shop and bought the trainers. £75.99! It has made me ill.

Bought William some Lion King slip-ons. He wanted some Titanic zip-up boots, but I said no. We looked around the bookshop on the complex. There was no sign of *Offally Good – The Book!* My sons were disgusted.

I buried Barry Kent's book, *Blind*, under a pile of Stephen Kings.

### Thursday February 26th

Nobby came round for the ladders.

Radio Leicester interview at 12.30. Larry Graves, the interviewer, said he had tried the pig's trotters recipe at home last night, but he had found them inedible. He'd watched the TV series and thought that Dev Singh was 'a comic genius'. He asked me if I would get Dev to sign his copy of the book.

### Friday February 27th

Eleanor very gloomy tonight after the lesson. I said that I hoped Glenn was not to blame. She told me

Roger Patience was not going to renew her contract at Neil Armstrong Comprehensive. I asked why, but she was curiously evasive. She put her oversize black coat on and left in rather a hurry.

Patience is a fool: she is a brilliant teacher. Glenn's reading age has improved by two years in as many weeks. He is now almost on a par with the average nine-year-old.


## Saturday February 28th

Heard on Radio Leicester that several cars were set alight in the staff car park at Neil Armstong Comprehensive at lunchtime yesterday. 'Mindless vandalism' is thought to be the cause.

I hope Eleanor's Fiat wasn't damaged. The headmaster's Volvo was a write-off.

Sharon Bott has given birth to a girl. She has called the poor child Caister, after the place where conception took place. Took Glenn to see his half-sister. On the way home he said, 'I'm worried about me mam, Dad. How's she goin' to manage?'

I diverted the conversation to Gazza. 'Will Hoddle play him?' I asked.

'No, Dad, he's too fat,' he predicted.

## Sunday March 1st

Glenn and I both got pinched and punched 'first day of the month' by William. I noticed that Glenn has already started instinctively to cover his genitals when William is within hurtling distance. Women don't know how lucky they are to have their sexual paraphernalia tucked inside their bodies.

A review in the *Sunday Times* Book Section. Under 'Briefly' it said:

*Love by Lamplight* – Hermione Harper
Gritty tale of Crimean War romance.

*Filth* – Spike McArtney
Thinly veiled autobiography of life in Glasgow's sewers.

*Offally Good! – The Book!* – Adrian Mole
100 ways with offal – a hoot.

Went to the BP garage and bought six copies of the *ST*. The boys were so proud to see my name in what Glenn called 'one of them long newspapers'. My mother phoned at 10 p.m. to ask if I'd seen 'her' review.

## Tuesday March 3rd

Met Les Banks buying cigarettes in the BP shop tonight. I asked after his wife. He looked me in the eye and said, 'She's not good, her father dropped down dead last night.' I laughed a bitter, cynical laugh and walked away.

Banks shouted after me, 'You callous bastard.'

## Thursday March 5th

Was shocked to see a photograph of Les Banks and his family in tonight's *Leicester Mercury*. A headline said, ' *"What Next?" Asks Tragic Banks Family*'.

I couldn't bring myself to read the article. I wished I hadn't noticed that Mrs Banks was described in the caption under the photograph as 'Lydia Banks, 41, Brave Amputee'.

Glenn asked where Kosovo was tonight. I handed him the *Times Atlas of the World* and told him to look it up in the index. He looked at me blankly. He doesn't know what an index is.

I rang Les Banks and apologized. He said he'd come round tomorrow, 'weather permitting'. I asked him what would preclude him from starting. He said, 'Anything that's gonna blow me off the roof.'

## Friday March 6th

Gale force winds all day. Attended the small-claims court with my mother this morning for her hearing: Mole versus Shoe Mania!.

That legal buffoon Charlie Dovecote had led her to believe that she stood a good chance of winning sizeable damages for injury, stress and trauma suffered when the heel of a stiletto broke off as she reached the summit of Snowdon, believing Sir Anthony Hopkins to be making a public appearance there on that day. When asked in court why she was wearing such unsuitable shoes she said, 'I only wore them for the final stages, I didn't want Sir Anthony to see me in my hired climbing boots.' Charlie Dovecote cross-examined Justin Swayward, representative of Shoe Mania!. 'Did the said stilettos bear a health warning, Mr Swayward?'

'Of course not.'

'Of course not? Why not?'

'Because any *reasonable* person could see at a glance that these shoes are unsuitable for – '

'Ah, yes! A *reasonable* person might. But, Mr Swayward, my client, Mrs Mole, was *not* a reasonable person at the time. She was a middle-aged woman in the grip of a menopausal fixation about Sir Anthony

344

Hopkins, the film actor, who had recently donated one million pounds towards the purchase of the said mountain.'

She won damages of £2,000 plus costs. The judge/magistrate said that Shoe Mania! 'intended, by the use of the word "mania" followed by an exclamation mark, to excite and encourage vulnerable women into making unwise and unsuitable purchases'.

I am, quite frankly, disgusted at this flagrant misuse of our overcrowded civil courts.

Eleanor has started another job at the Keith Joseph Community College. She is head of remedial studies. She said, 'But nothing will come between me and my weekly visits to Rampart Terrace. I *live* for Fridays.'

## Sunday March 8th

Les Banks rang to say that an articulated lorry reversed over his dog yesterday. I was careful to sympathize. He said he would send a subcontractor round: Bill Broadway. He said, 'He's sound, Mr Mole.'

I said I hoped his dog made a full recovery.

## Monday March 9th

Dev Singh was on with Richard and Judy this morning, promoting *Offally Good! – the Book!*.

I got on the phone to Brick Eagleburger immediately and left a message on his voicemail protesting in the strongest possible way about Dev's usurping of my role.

Bill Broadway is on the roof playing Radio Two at full volume. I'd guess from his accent that his parents come from Jamaica. His hair is almost entirely grey, yet he's only thirty-seven. He blames the stress of being in the building trade. He doesn't like heights.

## Friday March 13th

While the boys were in bed I did some work on my Royal Archers Radio series. Experimented with adding the Blairs.

### THE ROYAL ARCHERS
*Agricultural bagpipe music which fades to*
*Sound: Helicopter landing in barleyfield.*
QUEEN: More bacon, Philip?
PHIL: (*Grumbling*) Who's that landing a helicopter in my barleyfield, just as I'm eating my breakfast?
QUEEN: I'll just cross from the Aga to the window, while

still carrying the frying-pan, and look out and tell you. Oh, it's Charles and there's somebody with him . . . a woman in jodhpurs.

PHIL: Who is it, Liz? Who? Who is with our eldest son?

*Cut to:*

CHERIE AND TONY'S DIARY

*Sound: Of yoghurt pots being washed.*

CHERIE: (*Deep sigh*) I can't get the yoghurt scab virus out of the yoghurt pots, Tony (*sigh*).

TONY: Does it matter, Cherie?

CHERIE: (*Screaming*) If I don't, the whole of Ambridge could go down with yoghurt scab!

TONY: Oh, let them, Cherie. Let them.

*(Agricultural bagpipe music.)*

The End


A strong start, I think.

When the hour was up I went downstairs and paid Eleanor. I offered her a glass of Bull's Blood. She accepted. We sat by the fire and discussed Glenn's progress. He is doing well, and can now read nearly everything in the sport pages of the *Sun*. Eleanor gazed into the flames and gave a loud sigh. I asked her what was wrong. She said, 'I've been wrestling with my personal demons.' But she didn't go into details. I told her of my netting phobia. Something I have never spoken of to another human being. *Baby and Child Care* was my parents' bible. They followed Spock's advice to the letter. When at the age of eighteen months I started to climb out of my cot several times a night, they looked up the appropriate remedy in the index. Spock advised my gormless parents to imprison me at night by throwing a badminton net over the side of the cot, securing it to the legs. (The cot's legs, not my legs.) My parents followed this advice slavishly, though it is on record* that my grandma Mole objected violently. She maintained that 'A good hard slap across the back of his legs would have helped him to settle down at night.'

I well remember trying to fight myself out of that badminton net. Spock may have been sound on Vietnam, but he was oh-so-wrong on badminton nets. I have never been able to enjoy Wimbledon because of him. Even the sound of Virginia Wade's voice makes me break into a light sweat. Because of this childhood trauma I let William sleep where he drops, then carry him to bed.

### Tuesday March 17th

Glenn has now been here at Rampart Terrace for over four weeks. I asked him last night where he wants to live and who he wants to live with. He said, 'Here, with you, Dad.'

---

* Source letter from Edna May Mole, mother of George Mole, to Mrs Sugden, mother of Pauline, May 2nd, 1968.

It wasn't especially what I wanted to hear. I'm fond of the boy but . . .

I phoned Sharon this morning and asked her if I could come round and talk to her about Glenn's future. It was a difficult conversation: Caister was crying in a distant room and Bradford and Kent were quarrelling somewhere very near to the telephone. Not surprisingly, Sharon sounded distracted. When I first mentioned Glenn's name, she said, 'Who?' We agreed I'd go round on Thursday night.


## Wednesday March 18th

A police patrol car pulled up outside the house at three o'clock this afternoon. A policeman came to the door and said, 'Did you know, sir, that there's a black man on your roof?'

I said, 'Yes, I do know, I'm paying him £20 an hour to be there.'

Glenn *v.* unhappy. Man U out of European Cup after drawing 1–1 with Monaco. I said to him, 'Glenn, football is like life, you must have a goal. But some-times you win and sometimes you lose.'

He said, 'But why couldn't Man U get *another* goal and win, Dad?'

He doesn't know about metaphors.

## Thursday March 19th

My father rang me today, which is an unusual occurrence. His voice was lowered, so I knew that Tania was in the vicinity. He said, 'Have you seen the papers, Adrian?'

I said that, no, I hadn't, I had been too busy scraping burned stuff from the hotplate of the steam iron to go out for a paper.

He said, 'They've gone too bleeding far now. They've gone and put a *woman* in charge of a *warship*. HMS *Express*. Think of the *carnage* that woman could cause.'

I heard Tania call from the garden, 'Darling, come and hear the blackbird.'

My father muttered, 'Got to go.'

My mother once steered a canal boat into the wall of a deep lock, causing my father to nearly fall overboard. This incident was watched by drinkers in the garden of the Lock-keeper and Camel public house. I will never forget their jeers.

*1 a.m.* Sharon was so tired she fell asleep twice while I was talking to her about Glenn's future. Caister is the type of baby who prefers to be fed every three-quarters of an hour. Unfortunately Sharon is breast-feeding. This may be beneficial to the baby but it did me no good whatsoever. I once enjoyed gazing at her eighteen-year-old breasts, but now she is aged thirty they are vast, intimidating, blue-veined edifices. Sharon Bott is a walking dairy. Her nipples look like Liquorice Allsorts.* She looks more like fifty than thirty.

I asked her how she would feel if Glenn came to live with me permanently. She said, 'I know he'd have a better life with you. I can't give him nothing.'

I said that, on the contrary, she had given him a lot. I told her that she had done a good job of bringing him up and that I was very fond of the boy.

She looked relieved, and said, 'He could come to me for the weekends sometimes, couldn't he?'

I said that I would be glad to have the occasional weekend free.

I looked around her living room. There were no books, or magazines, or even newspapers. I looked forward to the day when I could introduce my eldest son to the world of literature. When I got home we celebrated by sending out for a Chinese takeaway. They forgot William's prawn crackers, but he didn't have his usual tantrum. He was happy because Glenn is going to be living with us for ever.

When I went upstairs to carry William to bed, I saw that there was a notice pinned on Glenn's bed-room door. It said, 'Glenn Bott privet'.

* I meant, of course, liquorice *torpedoes*.

## Friday March 20th

Left Bill Broadway pointing up the chimney-stack and drove into Leicester. I miss big-city life. Bought William some Power Ranger underpants from the Everything's a Pound shop. Was disturbed to see that somebody has opened an Everything for 50p! shop. Things are going downhill fast. This is a sure sign that city-centre shopping is in its death throes.

I was examining some *Baywatch* eggcups, with a view to purchase, when a man in a green-knitted bobble hat approached me and said he had seen me on the telly. He asked me for my autograph, saying it was for Phyllis, his mentally ill sister, who was my 'biggest fan'. On the back of his gas bill I wrote: '*To Phyllis, It was Offally nice to meet your brother. Best wishes to you, From Adrian Mole.*'

The man looked at the back of the bill and said, 'She won't like *this*.'

I asked why. Apparently the cause of Phyllis's mental problems centred around her being the first-born and having her 'nose put out of joint' when he, her brother, was born. 'She never recovered,' he said. 'You writing, "It was nice to meet your brother," could tip her over the edge.'

He gave me his bus ticket and on the back I wrote: '*To Phyllis, Best wishes from A. Mole.*'

He looked at it for a minute, then said, 'She might think that A Mole meant one of them little burrowing animals. She's got a thing about small mammals.' He handed me a dry-cleaning ticket and I wrote on the back, 'Hello Phyllis, This is Adrian Mole, the TV chef. Get well soon!'

He shook his head. 'No, you can't write, "Get well soon",' he said. 'She doesn't know she's ill.'

I snatched at the Bhs receipt he held out and scribbled, 'Best wishes, Adrian Mole', on the back. He said a grudging thank-you, adjusted his bobble hat and sloped out of the shop. I was too flummoxed to be able to concentrate on the Baywatch eggcups, and I left the shop without buying anything.

To calm down I had a cappuccino at a pavement café in the high street. This place, the Brasserie, has only been open a week, and has been viewed with suspicion by some sections of Leicester society. An OAP passed my table, saying to her companion, 'It's obstructing the pavement, in't it? What about blind folk and them in wheelchairs?'

In the afternoon I went to see my father and Tania, to inform them that Glenn was living with me permanently. They had just been to the sexual dysfunction unit at the hospital. Unfortunately they felt the need to tell me, in minute detail, about their joint consultation. Tania held my father's hand and said to me, 'I've tried to reassure him that penetrative sex is not the be all and end all.'

When she got up and went to the kitchen to make some herbal tea, my father's gaze followed her ample hips out of the room as he said, 'Penetrative sex is

353

the be all and end all with *me*. I can't be doing with all that bleddy tongue-wagging stuff – I even failed the oral when I took my driving test.'

I changed the subject by informing him that learner drivers now had to take a written test, but he returned like a homing pigeon to the topic of his private parts by telling me that Tania was treating his piles with aromatherapy. He shifted uncomfortably on his chair. I suggested that a rubber ring or an *operation* might give more effective relief than a whiff of lavender oil. He glanced at her fearfully as she re-entered the room and said loudly, 'I've got great faith in aroma-therapy. You shouldn't mock it, Adrian.' Tania smiled down at him as though he were a well-behaved toddler.

Eleanor mobiled me to say she can't come tonight, she had 'an emergency appointment' to see her therapist.

On the way home I did some shopping at the BP garage and bought Glenn a World Cup fixtures chart for his bedroom.


## Saturday March 21st

Glenn said today, 'Shall we do the lottery, Dad?' I almost gave him my standard anti-lottery lecture. Then I heard myself saying, 'Why not, son?' Our numbers are 3, William's age, 13, Glenn's age, 31, soon

354

to be my age, 16, Rosie's age, 30, Sharon's age, and 5, the New Dog's age.

## Sunday March 22nd

A weekend of non-stop toil. The washing, ironing, folding, putting away of clothes! The washing, drying and putting away of crockery! The sucking up of dirt from the floors! The endless wiping of surfaces! The constant preparation of food! I should have a woman to do all this for me. A woman I don't have to pay. A wife.

After the housework there was the mind-numbing boredom of reading aloud to Glenn from his World Cup wall chart. He is determined to have memorized the fixtures by June.

## Tuesday March 24th

Over dinner we discussed what we would do if we won the lottery. Glenn said, 'What does a million pounds look like, Dad?' I wrote out a cheque for a million pounds and made it payable to 'Glenn Bott Esquire'. He was dead chuffed and put it in the breast pocket of his school shirt.

## Wednesday March 25th

Roger Patience rang me at 11.30 this morning. He asked me to go into school immediately, there was a serious problem. I was so alarmed I drove well over the speed limit (39 m.p.h.). I was escorted to his office by the duty pupil of the day, a charming girl called Nell Barlow-Moore.

Patience was sitting behind his mock mahogany desk staring at a computer screen.

'Ah, Mr Mole,' he said, rising from his back-sufferer's chair. 'Sorry to call you in, but there's been an incident.'

*Incident.* The word hung in the air, pregnant with menace.

'Glenn brought a cheque for a million pounds to school today,' he said. 'There is a strict rule that anything over a monetary value of £10 has to be given to the school secretary for safe-keeping. However, when Miss Trellis, his maths teacher, tried to take the cheque from Glenn he became abusive and called her a drongo. I won't have my female staff abused and intimidated, Mr Mole. I have suspended Glenn for a week.'

I said, 'The cheque was for a *million pounds*, Mr Patience. What did you think it was? His pocket money?'

Patience said, 'He was waving it around in the

playground. Some of the first-years were sick with excitement.'

I threatened to take Glenn away from the school.

Patience said, 'You won't get him into another school round here. Bott is known to staff rooms up and down the county. He is infamous.'

Glenn was sitting on a scratched-up wooden bench outside the office. He stood up as I came out and said, 'Sorry, Dad.'

## Saturday March 28th

William and Glenn asked me what we were going to 'do' over the weekend. I said that when I was a boy I didn't *do* anything. I just hung about the house until it was time to go back to bed.

## Monday March 30th

My mother rang and asked me what I would like for my birthday on Thursday. I said, 'I would like a lilac lavatory brush and holder from the Innovations catalogue.'

She said, 'Don't be ridiculous!'

I said, 'I'm perfectly serious. Archie's brush has lost all of its bristles.'

She said, 'I'll get you a book token as usual.'

She asked how William was. I said, 'He's extremely well,' then pointedly, 'as is my other son, Glenn.'

She said, 'I'm trying very hard with Glenn, Adrian, but I have to admit that . . .' There was silence, then she burst out with, 'I can't *bear* the way he breathes through his *mouth*, and I can't *stand* to watch him with a knife and fork.'

I said that I couldn't bear the way that Ivan's eyebrows met in the middle, or the way he knotted his tie or the way he pushed himself up against her when she was at the sink. But I replaced the receiver with a heavy heart. We had both gone too far. Dishonesty is obviously the best policy.


## Tuesday March 31st

A panic attack at 3.17 a.m. What had I done with my life?

I am an unsuccessful husband.

I am a disappointing son.

I am a failed writer.

I have failed to master the Psion Organizer.

I prayed fervently that I wouldn't fail with my sons.

## Wednesday April 1st
*April Fools' Day*

Oh, joy! Oh, precious rapture! A letter has arrived from the BBC!

Dear Adrian Mole,

I will cut to the chase. I have just finished reading *The White Van* (never mind how it got into my hand, suffice it to say that it has a large cult following here at the BBC). I am bowled over by this magnificent piece of work, and I would like to make a TV series out of it. I envisage 20 hour-long episodes.

The casting, of course, is crucial, but early thoughts include Robbie Coltrane, Dawn French, Pauline Quirke, Richard Griffiths.

I am away today on a Stress Awareness Course (mobile phones are banned). I will be back in my office tomorrow. Please telephone me then.

Yours sincerely,
John Birt
Director General

Then, handwritten,

PS. I can't tell you how excited I am by this.

I immediately telephoned Brick Eagleburger and left a message on his voicemail asking him to ring me back. Then, after supplying the boys with food and clean clothes and conducting the now almost obligatory search for shoes, I drove round to my mother's and photocopied the letter.

I have faxed copies to George 'n' Tania, Brick Eagleburger, Pandora, Barry Kent, Peter Savage and the *Leicester Mercury*. I then posted copies to the faxless: Nigel, Grandma and Grandad Sugden, Auntie Susan and her wife.

Dear Diary, I will sleep well tonight. John Birt has given me a wonderful thirty-first birthday present.

### Thursday April 2nd

I was woken by William throwing himself on to my bed and poking the sharp corner of a birthday card into my neck. He had made the card at nursery school under the supervision of Mrs Parvez. There was a crude approximation of me on the front: a stick man with huge teeth and wild hair. Seven fingers on each hand, and wearing high-heeled shoes. Inside, Mrs Parvez had made William copy 'To Daddy, best wishes from William'. 'Best wishes!' It speaks volumes about Mrs Parvez's relationship with her own father.

Glenn hung about in the bedroom doorway, glowering and smiling in turn. His hair has grown considerably, but he still looks like a thug. I will be glad when he has outgrown his thug clothes and I can introduce him to the Next range of junior menswear.

Eventually he came forward and thrust a shop-bought card into my hand. I took it out of its lurid red envelope. The illustration on the front was of a pipe-smoking, jutting-jawed fly fisherman who was up to his waders in a river. Jut-jaw's vintage car was parked on the bank. The boot of the car was open, showing that Jut-jaw had already caught five large fish, and placed them in a wicker basket. There was a black Labrador gazing up at its master. On the front of the card it said, 'To A Special Father On Your Birthday'. Inside there was a verse printed in Gothic script:


Father, it's your Special Day,
Time for fun and pleasures gay.
The sporting life it is for you, tramping through the
    morning
Dew, with dog and rod and fishing-line,
then home to bathe and sup and dine.


It could hardly have been more inappropriate. I loathe the great outdoors, and the thought of encouraging a harmless fish to impale itself on a sharp hook fills me with horror. However, when I saw that the boy had written 'Love from Glenn' in not too bad handwriting, and had scrawled thirty-one kisses on a blank interior page, I was touched.

Glenn also handed me a snake ashtray he'd made in Pottery at school. It consisted of a long thin coil of baked clay, ending in a snake's face. He said, 'In case you want to start smokin', Dad.' The post brought cards from Pandora (Happy Birthday, Constituent), Nigel (a card that said, 'Come out of the closet, you know you're gay,' with a drawing of a man stuck in a wardrobe), the Sugdens (a jut-jaw washing a sports car).

When I was in the shower somebody came round and pushed the Mole family's cards through the front door. My mother's card was tactless in the extreme: a cartoon balding man (who looked uncommonly like me, actually) had a bubble coming out of his mouth saying, 'I'm over thirty, can you direct me to the Hill?' My father's card was of a village green cricketing scene, and several black Labradors were watching the match from various vantage-points. A woman was coming down the pavilion steps with a tray of sandwiches. The women spectators were wearing pretty frocks, hats and high-heeled shoes. My father had written: 'Those were the days! Happy Birthday, Adrian, from Dad and Tania.'

I rang John Birt but his secretary said he was in a meeting. I was surprised to find that she didn't know about *The White Van*! I rang at various intervals throughout the day, but Mr Birt seemed to go from meeting to meeting. There was a small birthday celebration at my mother's at 4 p.m.: a Spice Girls cake and a Marks & Spencer's party-food pack, which my mother hadn't properly defrosted. A toast was drunk to me in sparkling wine. Rosie gave me a boot-fair find, a leatherbound copy of Chekhov's short stories. She said, 'It smells f------ mouldy, but it might clean up.'

I thanked her from the bottom of my heart. She is obviously the only member of my family who understands me. My mother started whimpering when Glenn levered a mini-pizza into his mouth with the flat of his knife, so I took him and William home.

At 11 p.m. an extraordinary thing: there was a knock on the door. I laid aside my copy of Lee Salk's *What Every Child Would Like His Parents to Know* and went downstairs. On the doorstep was a box. I took it inside and opened the lid. A balloon floated out and hovered near the ceiling. A card inside the box said, 'I burn for you, I yearn for you.' Who *can* this be from, dear Diary?

## Friday April 3rd

*6.30 p.m.* John Birt is now out of the office, again, on a 'Visions and Values' course. His secretary was unable to give me an account of his movements. I rang Brick, but he had heard nothing either. I asked to speak to Boston. Brick said, 'She don't work here no longer, Aidy. She kinda flipped and I had to let her go. She's back on the East Coast.'

Ms Eleanor Flood arrived at her usual hour; she admired the balloon and said, 'I didn't know it was your birthday.'

I was quite relieved.


## Tuesday April 7th

Apparently the sales figures for *Offally Good! – The Book!* are disappointingly low. The publishers are talking about remaindering some and pulping others. Apparently W. H. Smith have got a machine somewhere that turns books into fertilizer. My father, the book-phobic, would no doubt enjoy seeing this literature-crushing machine in operation.

Pie Crust rang and asked me to go on the *Late Night with Derek and June* show on Thursday. Dev Singh had to cancel due to stress. He has booked into the Priory for a week. *Derek and June* is filmed at studios in Soho at midnight. I said I would require a hotel room, as I was reluctant to drive both up and down the M1 on the same night due to the danger of falling asleep at the wheel.

Rosie is going to babysit.

Nothing from the BBC. A bloke called Richard Brookes, from the *Observer*, rang me and asked for details about the BBC deal. He told me that he had first read the treatment for *The White Van* three weeks ago. When I asked him how he had got his hands on it, he said that it had been passed around in the Groucho Club. I don't know whether to be flattered or outraged.

I prayed throughout my interview that nobody of my acquaintance would watch *Late Night with Derek and June* tonight. First I had to go along with the lie that I was sitting at their own kitchen table, whereas in fact we were in a crappy little 'studio' in the red-light district. Then, to my astonishment, Derek said to me, live on camera, 'We've been friends for years, haven't we, Adrian?'

He appeared to be doing an impression of Mr Bean. He took a copy of *Offally Good! – The Book!*, turned to the recipe for chicken giblets in parsnip coulis, and began to read aloud.

June's fat shoulders shook throughout. The whole interview was risibly amateurish. Derek and June made personal remarks about my appearance, then appeared to ignore me and chatted between themselves about their caravan holiday at Ingoldmells. The studio crew seemed to find their every banal utterance hysterically funny. When they turned their attention back to me it became obvious to me that Derek and June were having fun at my expense. They were, in fact, totally uninterested in offal. I felt angry and humiliated. I left the studio as soon as the filming was finished.

A spotty girl in denim shorts and thigh boots was leaning against my car smoking a cigarette. 'Hand job?' she said.

'No, it's fully automatic,' I replied, got in and drove to the Temple Hotel in Haven Hill Gardens, W2.

*Temple Hotel*

2 *a.m.* This place is a minimalist nightmare of Japanese design. My room is white and cream, and is decorated with old Japanese petrol cans. I can't find a way to open the wardrobes, or discover how to flush the lavatory. I will have to sleep with the lights on as don't know how to switch them off. When I finally managed to turn the shower on it was so powerful that it hurled me out of the cubicle, then flooded the floor and gushed into the sleeping pit, where it was soaked up by the futon.

I should have paid more attention when the hall porter showed me around the room but, to be honest, I was too intimidated by his severe black uniform and French accent to concentrate.

8 *a.m.* I found it hard to sleep for worrying about the flood from the shower. Would they charge me for water damage to the futon? Then there were the contents of the lavatory bowl: how would I dispose of them? I made another search for the flushing

mechanism, but failed to find anything remotely like a handle, a knob, a switch or a floor pump. I took a tumbler and used it to pour water into the lavatory. It took twenty minutes before the contents finally disappeared.

**Saturday April 11th**

Glenn told me that it's his birthday next Saturday. 'I'm becomin' a teenager, Dad.' He is very excited. I didn't like to tell him that my own teenage years were utterly desolate and miserable. However, he has one advantage over me: he can in no way be described as an intellectual. Glenn does not lie awake pondering on the nature of existence. He lies awake wondering who Hoddle will field in the World Cup.

**Monday April 13th**

A postcard from Cape Cod, America! I know no one in those parts! Blank, apart from my address on one side, and on the other 'April Fool, Nebbish!'
   A mystery.

## Tuesday April 14th

The shame of it! No wonder John Birt failed to ring me back. I have studied the handwritten PS endlessly, but don't recognize the prankster's handwriting. How will I ever overcome my terrible humiliation and disappointment?

Glenn tried to console me with a joke. 'At least you know it weren't me, Dad, on April 1st. I didn't *have* no handwritin'.'


## Wednesday April 15th

Tonight, with Eleanor's assistance, Glenn copied out his name and address and also 'Gazza', 'Hoddle' and 'World Cup'.

I opened a bottle of Mateus Rosé and asked Eleanor to join me in celebrating his progress. I almost wished I hadn't – after half a glass she began to gaze at me very intensely. I think I am going off her a little.


## Thursday April 16th

Eleanor rang at 7.30 a.m. (a touch early, I felt) to apologize for her melancholic behaviour. Apparently she is in therapy due to 'inadequate nurturing and a subsequent lack of self-esteem'. I didn't ask for details. I said that I, too, had been in therapy due to my parents' neglect of me when young.

In thirty-one years I can remember only two acts of parental self-sacrifice from my father. The first was when I was six years old, and dropped my raspberry ripple on the sand at Wells-next-the-Sea. He gave me his own (slightly eaten). The second was when I was suspended from school for contravening the rules by wearing red socks. He took time off work and went to see the headmaster, the fearsome Mr Scruton, and forced him to make a grovelling apology.

*2 a.m.* Regarding the Red Socks Row. I've just remembered the true facts.

1. My father *did not* take time off from work. He was unemployed at the time.
2. He *did not* confront Scruton at the school. He telephoned him.
3. Scruton *did not* make a grovelling apology.
4. On the third day I capitulated and wore black socks to school.

## Saturday April 18th

*Glenn's birthday*

Glenn came into my bedroom this morning and thanked me for the *'You're a teenager, Son!'* card. (Picture: a blond boy with a baseball cap on back to front, sitting in front of a computer.) He asked me to read the verse inside. After I'd done so I wished I'd read the inscription thoroughly in the shop. I would almost certainly have bought another card.

'It's a boy!' the midwife said. Emotions went from A to Z.

All your life I've guided you, taken you to school and zoo,

Helped you with your ABC, been there when you needed me.

Now you are an in-between, not child, not man, but new-turned teen.

As you make your way through life, there may be days of woe and strife

Remember I am always here to give, advise and lend an ear.

I'm your dad and you're my son. When most is said, and all is done.

I thought Glenn was moved by these sentiments, though it's hard to tell, with his face being as it is. He liked the England strip I bought him from JJB Sports, and went to the bathroom straight away to change into it. He's got my legs: he doesn't look good in shorts. William gave him a card he'd made at nursery: a cardboard football decorated in glued and painted polenta. When we were sitting eating break-fast (I insist we sit around the table for all meals – I grew up watching my mother eat standing up with her back to the sink and my father sitting on top of the pedal bin), Glenn said, 'Am I havin' a surprise party, Dad?'

I said, 'No.'

Glenn said, 'But you'd have to be sayin' that, wouldn't you, Dad?'

When he'd gone outside to kick his football up and down the yard with William, I phoned Sharon and asked her to come to a party with her children.

She sounded pleased – she's never been to Rampart Terrace before. I then rang round my family and begged them to attend at 5 p.m., and to bring cards and presents.

I left a message on Eleanor's machine.

I spent most of the day shopping for the 'surprise' party. I bought a Jane Asher football cake and thirteen candles. At 4.45 p.m. I made a huge cauldron full of mashed potatoes and put thirty-five links of Walker's sausages into the oven. I cut up two pounds of Spanish onions and fried them slowly. I then spent the next quarter of an hour on the doorstep, looking anxiously up and down the street, praying that the guests would turn up.

Eventually, Sharon, Caister, Kent and Bradford arrived on foot, then my own family. I asked them all to wait outside until I'd lured Glenn into the yard by telling him I wanted him to help me hone my footballing skills – an unlikely story, but he fell for it. After five minutes of tedious footballing pretence I led him into the living room, which was now crowded with his friends and relations. He blushed to the roots of his hair and fell silent as the assembled company sang 'Happy Birthday To You'.

Eleanor's voice soared above the others; she was like a song-thrush fallen amongst crows. Tania Braithwaite said, in a loud whisper to my father as tea was served, 'Sausages, mashed potatoes and fried onions? How very basic.' My mother overheard and said to her, 'What have you got against sausages?'

Tania said, 'I've nothing against sausages *per se.*'

My mother nodded towards my father and said, 'I expect by now you've settled for chipolatas.'

Tania turned away angrily and spent the next half-hour talking to Eleanor about cashmere. 'It's scandalous,' I heard her say.

When she'd gone I said to Eleanor, 'If Tania thinks it's a scandalous price she shouldn't buy it.'

Eleanor looked back at me, baffled. Then she said, 'We weren't talking about *cash*mere. We were discussing the situation in Kash*mir*.'

I'm glad I'm no longer fixated with her. No full-blooded man wants a relationship with a flat-chested woman who talks about Kashmir in the late afternoon. Caister was passed around and admired by all the guests, except Eleanor. Privately I think the kid is a bit of a Woody Allen lookalike, though without the glasses, of course.

Sharon looked pleased when Glenn asked my mother to take a photograph of him with his mum and dad.

My mother took several shots of us with her disposable camera. She was not happy when Glenn thanked her, saying, 'Thank you, Grandma.' She likes William to call her Granny Paulie.

## Sunday April 19th

This morning I asked Glenn if he knew what 'Sabbath' meant. He screwed up his face in concentrated thought, then said, 'Would I be right in thinkin' it's an olden days' band?'

I said, 'That's *Black* Sabbath, who glorified in mocking Christianity and middle-class mores.' I explained about *the* Sabbath, saying that it represented the seventh day, when God had a day off from designing the world.

He was fascinated. He told me that they've done Judaism, Hinduism, Sikhism, Buddhism and Paganism at school, but they haven't got round to 'doin'' Christianity yet, Dad'.

He has never heard of Moses and the Ten Commandments. As we cleared the Sunday-lunch table, I told him and William about Jesus turning water into wine. 'Did he have a drinkin' problem, Dad?' he asked, when I finished.

Most of the people in Glenn's previous life had an official problem, which the state was helping them to cure. I didn't tell him about the Opal Fruits, and my netting phobia. He thinks I'm entirely sane. I don't want to disabuse him of that opinion. After lunch, I slept on the sofa while the boys played with the PlayStation that Sharon bought from a catalogue for Glenn's birthday.

Had an erotic dream about stripping Eleanor of cashmere in Kashmir. It was some minutes before I could move from the sofa with any dignity.

## Wednesday April 22nd

Bill Broadway is in Paris tracking down a pair of World Cup tickets. I rang the ticket hotline to buy a few as an investment, but apparently 20 million people had the same idea. Only 15,000 got through. I wasn't one of them.

*3 a.m.* Glenn has just had a nightmare that Alan

Shearer, his hero, is dropped by Hoddle for being an atheist.

## Friday April 24th

There is a drug on the market (not Leicester market) called Viagra. It gives a man an hour-long erection.

My father is already in a state of ecstasy at the prospect! He has persuaded Tania to withdraw some of her pension-plan money and buy two return tickets to New York to track down a supplier! More 1950s baby-boomer madness!

At 6 p.m. I drove my father and Tania to Birmingham Airport. They both sat in the back with their seat belts on. The M6 was particularly awful so I drove slowly, but got trapped between two huge articulated lorries. At one point my father shouted, 'For crying out bleddy loud, get a move on. Overtake! We'll miss the duty-free at this rate.'

Tania looked even more tense than usual. I expect she was nervous about the effect the Viagra drug would have on their relationship. I loaded their luggage on to a trolley – they've both got bad backs from gardening. My father muttered to me, 'Nine thousand miles and two thousand quid for a bit of pork swordsmanship! It had better be worth it.'

Due to the unseasonable heatwave I promised to water their garden twice a day. Global warming is playing havoc with our English horticulture. 'Please don't let the containers dry out,' begged Tania. It's pathetic how enslaved people become to a few plants. I hope it never happens to me.

## Saturday April 25th

I saw my love on the news tonight: she was addressing a small crowd of whelk workers on a quay somewhere. She looked totally ravishing. Her hair was blowing in the stiff east-coast breeze. She spoke about the government's pledge to protect whelks with passion and intensity, as others might speak of Bach or early-English poetry.

## Sunday April 26th

My father rang from New York at 3 a.m. this morning, oblivious to the fact that in England people were sleeping. He asked about the garden. I lied and said that I had given it a good soaking. 'Good,' he said, 'because when we saw CNN the weather girl said that Britain was having freak hot weather for April.' To change the subject I asked him if he had managed to track down some Viagra. He said, 'Yeah, I've found a supplier. He's dropping some off at the hotel tonight.' He sounded like Al Pacino.

As soon as we'd had breakfast, we drove round to The Lawns. The gravel was OK, it was very nicely raked, but the plants in the pots were wizened and drooping. I dragged the hose out and ordered the boys to saturate the grass and the galvanized containers, which contained the various ex-flowers. The water just ran off the impacted surface. 'It's too late,' said Glenn. 'Everythin''s dead, Dad.'

We debated whether it would be better to remove the wilting plants, or leave them where they were. In the end we pulled them up and replaced them with some nice cheerful stuff from Homebase.

We were invited to Wisteria Walk for Sunday lunch. I was pleased to accept. I'm sick of cooking and trying to cater for the very different tastes of the boys. William will now only eat Coco Pops, Marmite on white bread with the crusts removed, seedless grapes and yoghurt with no bits.

Glenn has opted for vegetarianism after watching a *World in Action* documentary called 'Slaughter on Perkins Avenue', an exposé of an abattoir in Upper Norwood. As the programme came to its horrific conclusion, freeze-framing the face of a stun-gunned cow, Glenn pushed away the beef sandwiches I'd prepared for supper and said, 'I shan't be eatin' meat ever again, Dad. Have we got any cheese?'

377

I seem to exist on a diet of boiled, mashed, fried, roasted, sautéd and baked potatoes, as did the greatest writers in the history of literature, Dostoevsky and Joyce, both of whom hailed from countries where the potato was a staple foodstuff. There is obviously something in the humble spud that aids the creative process.

Ivan is looking increasingly stressed out. As we laid the table my mother told me that he is spending sixteen hours a day at his terminal in the alcove of the dining-room. She said, 'Information pours into this house twenty-four hours a day. There's e-mail, and voicemail, and data from the Web, then there's faxes and the ordinary phone and letters through the door. The human brain can't cope with it all, Adrian. Even his bloody *car* tells him what to do.'

I agreed that it sounded as though Ivan was suffering from sensory overload. I asked her, 'What exactly *is* it that Ivan does for a living?'

She confessed that she didn't exactly know.

When I went to tell Ivan that lunch was ready, he was at his terminal, white-faced and sweating. I asked him what was wrong. He said, 'I've done a Web search for drinking-straw manufacturers and received 17,000 entries.'

I steered him gently towards the dining end of the room, but I noticed that, as he carved the chicken, he constantly glanced towards the terminal where the names and e-mail addresses of manufacturers of drinking straws throughout the world were rolling ceaselessly down the screen.

Over lunch I tried to pin down what he did. 'I process information,' he said, tetchily.

'For whom?' I asked.

'For *whomsoever* will buy the information I process,' he said, raising his voice. The table fell silent, apart from the sound of cutlery on the plates and Glenn's noisy demolition of a roast turnip.

Later, as the boys and I washed up, I heard my mother say to Ivan, 'If this relationship is going to work, I'll have to have my own terminal and a dedicated phone line.' I asked her why she needed her own equipment, and she said that she was hoping to start up a business, desk-top printing greeting cards for the millennium. Divorce cards, love-child cards, I'm Gay cards and in-vitro-fertilization cards.

I was glad to get back inside my own house, where the only cutting-edge thing is Archie Tait's old bread-knife.

## Monday April 27th

Brick forwarded a letter from a bloke in Belgrade with an unpronouncable name full of Ks and Js who wants to translate *Birdwatching*, should it ever be published in the former Yugoslavia.

Dear Mr Mole,

I am reading your most wonderful good writings *Bird-watching* and I am thinking that this will be good for Serb people to read also. Are you permission giving for my translate this into English form Serbian language?

I am translating too *The Catcher in the Wry*, *The Lord of the Files*, and of my latest *Bridget Jones Dairy*.

If your agreement with this preposition you will send fax to mine office. As shows this at above.

I am send you in hope good wish.

Jajkj Vljkjkjv

I rang Brick. He wasn't as enthusiastic as I had hoped. He said, 'I ain't got no faith in Vljkjkjv's English. The guy don't got no feeling for the language.'

William blabbed the truth about the horticultural disaster at The Lawns to Tania as soon as we spotted them in the arrivals hall of Birmingham Airport. She visibly paled. 'Did you manage to salvage any of the herbaceous stuff?' she said.

'Describe them,' I said.

'When in bloom, they're rather lovely, pale and subtle,' she said.

Glenn said, 'You've gotta use another tense now, Mrs Braithwaite. *Could have been* rather lovely, you gotta be sayin' now.' He has obviously benefited from private education.

*10.30 p.m.* Tania has phoned my mother to complain. Apparently she thinks I ruined her garden deliberately. She has pulled up all my colourful replacement plants and replanted with her herbaceous weed look-alikes.

My mother told me in the strictest confidence that Tania is sick to death of my father's new sexual demands. Apparently (according to my mother, who is not always a reliable witness) Tania lies back for an hour and thinks about her seed catalogues. She told my mother that she will be glad when my father's supply of Viagra runs out. She is praying that the NHS refuses to prescribe it to impotent men. She said, 'I'd hoped that gardening would sublimate George's sex drive.'

I don't want my mother and Tania to be friends: it's against the natural order of things. It would be like Ian Paisley and Gerry Adams going to Ibiza together.

## Tuesday April 28th

Pandora was on the news tonight. She has been outed as a whelk-hater by an anonymous enemy! My love was secretly filmed in conversation with Peter Mandelson in a restaurant in Notting Hill. There was no sound, but the enemy had employed the services of an expert lip-reader and the following transcript was shown on the screen as 'Pandy' and 'Mandy' stuffed themselves on Tex-Mex delicacies.

MANDY: You know how much I love Tony, Pandy. I'd do anything for him. Anything.

PANDY: Yeah, yeah, but you can't expect him to have to choose between you and Gordon, can you? Wow! The salsa is sublime.

MANDY: I've tried to like Gordon but ... Is that Robin Cook in the corner with Gaynor?

PANDY: No, relax, it's just another ugly bearded git with a young girl.

MANDY: Talking of ugly bearded things, I caught you on the news on Saturday night. You know, that whelk thing.

PANDY: You're thinking of oysters, Mandy darling. *They* have beards. *Whelks* are those revolting things that look like diseased genitals. How *anybody* could put one in their mouth! (*Laughter.*)

MANDY: Anyway, Pandy, you were magnificent. Are you happy at Ag and Fish?

PANDY: No. I want Robin's job. I speak Serbo-Croat, Russian, Mandarin, French, Italian and Spanish. I'm made for the Foreign Office. And I'd look great addressing the United Nations. In Vivienne Westwood.

MANDY: I'll put a word in Tony's ear, Pandy.

PANDY: Shall we have a pudding?

MANDY: Not for me, just a decaff.

**Wednesday April 29th**

The headline in the *Sun* said, 'WHELKS – "DISEASED GENITALS", SAYS PAN'

**Thursday April 30th**

WHELK STORM GROWS

Pandora Braithwaite MP has denied saying that whelks remind her of diseased genitals. She said in a statement today, 'Lip-reading is not an exact science.'

The Whelk Association Trust have called for Braithwaite's resignation. 'Her position is untenable,' said a TWAT spokesman.

*Independent*

The British Association of Lip Readers has joined others in calling for Dr Pandora Braithwaite's resignation. A spokeswoman for the Society for the Deaf said today, 'She has put us back in the Dark Ages.'

Rick Stein, renowned fish chef, has commented, 'When I look at a whelk, sex is not the first thing that springs to mind.'

Brutus – *Express*

My mother said that Pandora has been summoned to an emergency meeting of the Ashby-de-la-Zouch Labour Party tonight. Their first-anniversary celebration, where she was to have been a guest of honour, is to go ahead without her.

## Friday May 1st

*6.30 a.m.* Pandora has just left my bed! She turned up at midnight last night, totally distraught after resigning from her job at Ag and Fish. She said, 'I don't know why I'm here,' and fell into my arms on the doorstep. I led her inside and said that it was a tragedy that a few stinking whelks had led to her downfall. We sat by the fire; she took a bottle of Stolichnaya from her briefcase and asked me to fetch two glasses. I went into the kitchen, I arranged some Twiglets in a bowl, cut some cheese up into chunks, added ice to two glasses and found a bottle of tonic. I put everything on a tray and took it through.

'I want to get drunk,' she said, as I came in.

She had kicked off her shoes and was curled up in Archie's manky armchair. A portrait of Beatrice Webb gazed sternly down on her as she lit a cigarette. 'Whelks bloody well *do* look like clapped-out genitals,' she said, defiantly. Then, 'Why should I have to lose my job for simply telling the truth?'

It was a naive question from an elected MP. I knelt

384

by her side and took her wrist in my hand. She said, 'Why are you taking my pulse?' Then burst into tears and said, 'You've always been there for me, Aidy.'

We finished the vodka, and I opened a bottle of champagne I'd been keeping for Millennium Night. After that had been drunk I searched Archie's pantry and found a half-bottle of Martell brandy. Andrew spat at me as I slopped some into Pandora's glass.

At 2.30 a.m. the telephone rang, but there was only the faint sound of shallow breathing.

Shortly afterwards Pandora and I struggled up the stairs to bed. She slept in my arms all night. We both kept our underwear on (hers was disappointingly functional). I had been looking forward to making love to her in the morning, when we were both sober, and had bolted the door from the inside to prevent interruption, but at 6.15 a.m. her pager bleeped and she leaped out of bed to check it.

She was on message again.

She dressed hurriedly, mumbled, 'Thanks,' unbolted the door and ran downstairs. I heard her Saab turn the corner a moment later. She telephoned at 7 a.m. from her car on the M1. 'I must know, Aidy, did we *do* it?'

I assured her that we were no further forward in our carnal knowledge of each other than we had ever been. I asked her where she was going in such a hurry. She said, 'I've got a meeting with Alastair, to plan my comeback. Then we're lunching at Wilton's, the fish restaurant, with a photographer.'

I can guess what she'll choose from the menu.

*9.30 p.m.* An extraordinary outburst from Eleanor tonight! I must say, she did look rather wild when she arrived and swept past me through the front door without a word. After Glenn's lesson was over, I offered her a cup of tea. She nodded, biting her lip and looking a bit like Anna, in *The King and I*, when she tells Yul Brynner she is going back to England. I made the tea to complete silence, apart from the thwack of the football on the yard wall. I handed her the mug, which said, 'Having a bad hair day?' (Picture of a stick woman with hair on end.) She looked at the mug and said tersely, 'Why *this* mug?'

I said, 'No reason. It was chosen off the mug tree quite at random.'

Eleanor said, 'Why have you stopped gazing at my wrists?' She then told me, in a choked-up voice, that she'd waited outside my house all night and witnessed Pandora leaving at 6.20 a.m. What could I say, dear Diary? Caught in the act! Unfortunately I slurped noisily on my tea, then tried to disguise it by coughing. I inhaled some of the liquid, which went down my windpipe. This led to a protracted and messy coughing fit, complete with snot and running eyes and a slight leak of urine from my full bladder.

Glenn came in and said, 'Why are you cryin', Dad?'
I was still unable to speak.
Eleanor said, 'The world is a sad place, Glenn.'
This was a gross misrepresentation of the reason

for my tears. Glenn said, 'I think the world's all right.'

To think I once fantasized about lying on top of Eleanor and covering her pale body with kisses!

When I'd recovered and Glenn had gone upstairs to have a bath, I said to Eleanor, 'I'd rather you didn't give Glenn the impression that I'm in the habit of weeping for the world.'

She said, 'Everything looks black to me now.'

I said, 'Everything about you *is* black. Why don't you introduce a bit of colour into your life? A pink shirt or a white jumper might cheer you up.'

She said, 'My numerologist warned me that I would meet a new lover through my work, and that it would end in tears.'

I said, 'Eleanor, you are constantly adding up two and two and making five. We've never *been* lovers.'

She looked me in the eyes and said, 'Do you *want* to be lovers?'

I explained that, like Stephen Fry, I had taken a vow of chastity.

She said, 'I don't believe you. The real reason is that you've been talking to Roger Patience and the police.'

'What about?' I said, alarmed at the turn the conversation had taken.

She ignored my question and said, 'You're in love with that MP tart. You had her in *our* bed.'

I said, 'Pandora and I slept together. However, nothing of a sexual nature took place. We kept our underwear on at all times.'

She then dropped the bombshell that Stephen Fry had renounced chastity and was going about saying that sex was 'absolutely marvellous'.

Glenn shouted from the bathroom that William had run off with the World Cup soap-on-a-rope. I went upstairs to sort the boys out. When I came downstairs I noticed that Eleanor had opened a button on her black silk shirt. I asked her casually about the rather worrying police reference she had made earlier.

She said, 'If you really must know I have a police record, though why it should impact on my effect-iveness as a teacher –'

I cut her off. 'What kind of police record?' I asked.

She shook her head and said, 'Why does this happen to me over and over and over again? Why can't I find a man who would walk through *fire* for me, as I would for him?' She lifted the hem of her long black dress and dabbed at her eyes.

I saw that she had a tattoo on her left knee, a phoenix with wings outstretched. She obviously never wears miniskirts.

She said, 'My father rejected me when I was thirteen years old and men have been casting me aside ever since.'

I said, 'Just because your father ran away doesn't mean . . .'

She rose from her chair. 'He didn't *run* away,' she said, 'he died, in an accident.'

'I'm sorry,' I said. 'Was it a car crash?'

She gave a bitter smile. 'Oh no, that would have been acceptable.' She looked defiantly at me. 'A small dog fell on his head from a balcony, in Torremolinos.'

Diary, I tried not to laugh. And for at least five seconds I kept my composure but then I cracked. I turned my head away but she obviously saw my shoulders shaking and said, 'Yes, laugh, laugh at the most tragic event in my life.' I struggled to control myself and blurted out, 'Was it a pedigree?'

Why? Why? I knew perfectly well that there *are* no pedigree dogs in Torremolinos. I was there five years ago.

I paid her £9, then asked her to leave and not come back.

Before she slammed the door she said, 'I will be back!'

If she does come back I won't open the door to her.


## Saturday May 2nd. The Lawns

*11.59.* I have nothing left. No house, no money, no car, no manuscripts. Eleanor burned the lot. William's insects. Glenn's trainers. The BP bloke apologized for selling her the petrol. He had joined the crowd of excited onlookers as they watched my house burn down.

We stayed and watched until the flames had been extinguished. Then a Chief Inspector Baron told me that Eleanor Flood had been arrested and that in his opinion she should never have been 'let out of that secure unit'. Apparently her career as an arsonist started at teacher training college with a small fire in the bar after she'd been refused a late-night drink.

My mother turned up in her towelling bathrobe and the grey socks she wears in bed. She leaped out of Ivan's car and ran towards where we stood behind the police barrier at the end of the street. The excitement and the reflective glow from the fire made her look ten years younger.

'Adrian, please tell me you were insured!' were her first words.

I couldn't bring myself to reply. Eventually Glenn said, 'Dad kept forgettin' to buy any, didn't you, Dad?' He clumsily patted my shoulder. I patted his.

A fireman came out of the house carrying something carefully in his helmet. I hoped it was some of my fifty-pound notes, but it turned out to be Andrew. He is quite thin when his fur is wet and flattened down.

My father tried to comfort me by saying, 'Houses and possessions can tie you down, lad.'

Things are undoubtedly bad. However, I have William and Glenn and Andrew and a smoke-damaged diary that a fireman found under the mattress of Glenn's bed. On the cover are the words: 'The Top Secret Diary of Glenn Mole (13)'.

On the first page is written: 'When I grow up I wood like to be my dad.'

I have often wondered how I would stand up against fire, flood and tempest. Would I run in panic and try to save my own life? Until tonight I suspected that I would do exactly that. But when I woke to the exploding glass and the choking smoke and the sharp flames on the stairs, I found that my own life was unimportant to me. Nothing else mattered apart from removing my sons from danger.

I expect that by tomorrow I will have embellished the story and given myself a heroic status I do not deserve, but all the same, on this night at this hour, I am pleased to record that I acquitted myself well.

# The
# Baltimore
# Waltz

## and other plays

# The Baltimore Waltz

### and other plays

## Paula Vogel

THEATRE COMMUNICATIONS GROUP

*The Baltimore Waltz and Other Plays* is published by Theatre Communications Group, Inc., 355 Lexington Ave., New York, NY 10017-0217.

Vogel, Paula.
The Baltimore waltz and other plays / Paula Vogel.
Contents: The Baltimore waltz—The oldest profession—Desdemona, a play about a handkerchief—And baby makes seven—Hot 'n' throbbing.
ISBN 1-55936-109-3
I. Title.
PS3572.0294A6   1995
812'.54—dc20   95-45986
     CIP

Cover art by Gustavo de Leon
Cover design by Cynthia Krupat
Book design by Lisa Govan

First Edition, April 1996
Third Printing, May 2000

THIS BOOK IS DEDICATED
TO ANNE STERLING —

with gratitude for the brilliance of her days,
the warmth of her nights.

# Contents

# Loose Screws

BY DAVID SAVRAN

Shortly after I met Paula Vogel—twenty years ago in a seminar room at Cornell University—she told me a story I have never forgotten. Although I couldn't know it at the time, it proved to be the best possible introduction to the extraordinary plays that she would go on to write. The story involves Paula, her mother Phyllis and her older brother, Carl, and takes place somewhere in the suburban sprawl between Baltimore and Washington.

When Paula was thirteen years old, her mother, recently divorced and with a reputation for being something of a trouble-maker, complained to the Board of Health about the trash col-lection—or lack of it—in their apartment complex. The Board investigated and, sure enough, conditions were unsanitary and the landlord was charged. As might be expected, the Vogels were promptly delivered an eviction notice, but rather than contest it, they found another apartment. The night they moved into their new lodging, however, Phyllis bundled the children into the car and drove back to their old flat. Once in the empty rooms, Phyllis pulled three screwdrivers out of her purse and instructed the two children to unscrew every screw in the apartment. She then drew an imaginary circle on the living room rug and asked them to place the screws inside the circle. Without damaging anything, they deftly unscrewed all the lights and electric sockets, unhinged all the doors, took apart all the kitchen cabinets, the refrigerator and oven. Every fixture, every appliance in the apartment, was carefully disassembled and every door, every switchplate, was neatly, almost lovingly, lined up against the wall. On the living room rug, meanwhile, grew a mountain of screws of every shape and size. Finally, when everything was dismantled, Phyllis drew a piece of paper from her purse, wrote "SCREW YOU" on it in bold letters, and artfully positioned it on top of the pile.

This story, which could very easily be a scene in a Paula Vogel play, is in fact amazingly revealing about Paula's strategies as a playwright. Like her unusually resourceful mother, she characteristically directs her energies toward responding to, critiquing and dismantling someone else's work. Each of her plays (with the notable exception of *The Baltimore Waltz*) is an act of retaliation. It questions, resists and teases a particular dramatic text and, more important, the text's guiding assumptions in regard to (among other things) gender, family, sexual identity, love, sex, aging and domestic violence. Going quite literally behind the scenes, *Desdemona* suggests that Shakespeare's women are not quite the innocent victims of masculine desires they appear to be but active makers—and unmakers—of each others' destinies. Talking back to *Who's Afraid of Virginia Woolf?*, *And Baby Makes Seven* celebrates fantasy and the power of narrative—and gives a new meaning to "family values." Responding to both the structure and the quaintly elderly protagonists of David Mamet's *The Duck Variations*, *The Oldest Profession* reimagines old age as a time of sensual delight. Taking on the plays of John Patrick Shanley and Sam Shepard with a vengeance, *Hot 'N' Throbbing* demonstrates that behind their poor, misunderstood male protagonists lies a romanticization of violence against women that proves both dangerous and irresponsible. And although *The Baltimore Waltz* is a commemoration of Paula's brother, Carl, it also is a masterful reworking of Ambrose Bierce's "An Occurrence at Owl Creek Bridge," in which all of the action takes place in the mind of a soldier during the moment in which he is being hanged. Analogously, all of Anna's memories and fantasies can be understood to transpire in that split second after the doctor tells her that her brother has died.

Paula's method of critiquing, or if one prefers, deconstructing the work of her forebears comes from her reading of the theories of Bertolt Brecht and, even more significantly, of Viktor Shklovsky, the Russian Formalist from whom Brecht purloined the Alienation Effect. Shklovsky recognized that over time our perceptions become increasingly habitual and automatic: We no longer see what is around us. The purpose of art, according to Shklovsky, is to restore visibility, to *defamiliarize* the commonplace so that we notice it again. In adapting Shklovsky, Brecht added a political dimension to this notion of defamiliarization: Brecht's theatre attempted to demonstrate that that which we take for granted and assume to be universal and eternal is, in fact, the product of human labor and history—and thus subject to change. Like Brecht's, Paula's theatre is one in which the commonplace is insistently made strange, in which five grandmotherly women sitting on a park bench turn out to be prostitutes, or three obstreperous little boys turn out to be the imaginary children three adults manipulate to work out an ingenious and extravagant *ménage à trois*. The effect of this defamiliarization is to allow spectators and readers to see these characters and their situations in a new light, to reevaluate the meaning of women's work outside the home, or to celebrate the elements of fantasy that necessarily structure all relationships.

Like Brecht, Paula writes from a deeply rooted political sense. Unlike her illustrious predecessor, however, Paula is an avowed feminist. All of her work is devoted to exposing not just how women are entrapped and oppressed, but the possibilities that figures like Desdemona or the oldest professionals have to contest, subvert and redefine the roles they have been assigned. Yet Paula's feminism is itself a complex phenomenon. As these plays suggest, she reacted strongly against the first wave of feminist theatre that surfaced during the 1970s, the "let's-celebrate-ourselves-as-women" brand of feminism that Paula regards not just as simplistic and ahistorical but also as exclusionary because certain kinds of women (depending on their class or racial or occupational position) inevitably get left out of the celebration. She has carved out her own distinctive feminist theatre in these five plays by recognizing, in her own words, that feminism means being politically incorrect. It means avoiding the easy answer—that isn't really an answer at all—in favor of posing the question in the right way. It means refusing to construct an exemplary feminist hero. It means writing speculative rather than polemical plays. It means turning Desdemona into a whore for real, or constructing two lesbians who use imaginary *boy* children as the conduits for their desires, or showing a woman titillated not just by writing pornography but by using her own children as the bases for her sexual fantasies.

Paula's complex relationship to feminism, as well as to Brecht, is in part the result of the very real contradictions that molded her when she was growing up. The daughter of a Jewish father from New York and a Catholic mother from New Orleans (her father left home when she was eleven), Paula has always been just a little bit schizoid. Passionately identifying with Mary Martin as Peter Pan, she confesses that she was always, well, confused about sexual identities—she expected that she, too, could get the girl. A lesbian who, by her own accord, loves men (and John Waters movies), she came out when she was seventeen. Brought up in a working-class family (her mother would move the household about once a year), she nevertheless entered academia, graduating from Catholic University and spending three years in the doctoral program in theatre at Cornell. A devotee of Büchner and Sigmund Romberg, Maria Irene Fornes and Judy Garland, *In the Summer House* and *The Bad Seed*, she is a fierce defender of the theatre in an era when it is under fire, seemingly, from all quarters. Since 1985, she has been director of the Graduate Playwriting Program at Brown University and has fashioned it into one of the very best in the country. Modeling herself in equal parts Joseph Papp and Max Bialystock (Zero Mostel in *The Producers*), she has transformed the annual New Plays Festival at Brown into one of the most exciting showcases for new work in the country (although I still look forward to the realization of a project she and I have long fantasized, the Dinner Theatre of Cruelty). A brilliant mentor, she inspires students and

gives the most penetrating—and supportive—critiques I have
ever seen. As in her own work, Paula is intent on getting her students to write not about what they are sure of, but what they
don't know, what terrifies them, what they desire madly, what
they have to fight to comprehend. As she explains it, she longs,
both in her own writing and that of her students, to unleash the
confusion in the hope that this will lead both writer and reader
to understand the confusion, to make sense out of a world—and
a society—gone terribly awry.

The reader turning to Paula's plays expecting that they will
provide a straightforward narrative of her life will be disappointed. Although all are rooted in her experiences and all, in
effect, tell her own story, none, not even *The Baltimore Waltz*,
does so directly. And while she is the first to admit that her writing is deeply autobiographical, she has reacted strongly against
the intensely personalized actor training methods she observed
in graduate school. She writes by focusing not on autobiographical content but on questions of dramatic form, trusting that the
content will take care of itself. She is obsessed with various theatrical devices and all of her plays use a formal device as their
starting point, be it the "five blackbirds" principle of *The Oldest
Profession* or the jump cuts of *Desdemona*. The device she uses
most commonly is circular form, which she understands as an
attempt to defamiliarize what Brecht calls Aristotelian drama,
drama organized by the law of cause and effect and dependent
upon a spectator's strong empathic response to a protagonist.
*The Baltimore Waltz*, *And Baby Makes Seven* and *Hot 'N'
Throbbing* are all circular in their organization. They are all
about a repetition of the beginning, a return to the scene of the
crime, as it were, that signals that everything has remained the
same and, simultaneously, changed radically. All three texts play
out and inhabit that contradiction. Paula's defamiliarization of
Aristotelian drama also requires a strict limitation on empathy.
And while all of her characters inspire a certain amount of identification, Paula is more concerned that the spectator come to
recognize and deal with the necessarily problematic position of

each protagonist. As a result, these five plays do not make easy reading—or playing. They demand that readers, actors and directors approach them with a genuine commitment to exploring their desires and fears as well as the laws, both spoken and unspoken, of the society in which they live (in the understanding that it is the law that produces desire and fear in the first place).

Of the five plays in the collection, the most unequivocally comic one, *And Baby Makes Seven*, is also the one with the most ill-fated production history (Paula refers to it as her "Scottish play"). For me, however, it remains a source of pure delight. In production, the three imaginary children always steal the show—as they were designed to do. (Paula carefully avoids providing much information about their three adult keepers.) And although the play's focus is clearly on the relationship between the adults and the children, and, specifically, on how the adults use the children to say and do what they are unable to do, *Baby* is really a play about narrative, about the stories that people make up to construct their identities, to deal with the people they love, and to divert themselves. Anna and Ruth are playwrights of sorts (to that extent, they both stand in for Paula), expert plotters who use their imaginary children to negotiate their relationship with each other and with Peter, and to deal with the impending arrival of a real child. Despite the play's psychological acumen and its formal brilliance (its three extraordinary death scenes leading up to the birth), however, *Baby* is perhaps the most original and important for its redefinition of family. For me, the play's rather eccentric nuclear family functions as a utopian fantasy, an ideal community in which even the wildest desires can be satisfied, in which personal histories can be invented on the spot, and in which adults are free to play like children. And although the first draft of the play was written in 1982, it uncannily anticipates the new "queer politics" of the 1990s because of the ways in which it destabilizes sexual identities. For although the three adults clearly self-identify as lesbian or gay, both the nature of their *ménage* and the content of their fantasies (at least as enacted by the imaginary children) question those designations. What is one to make of a family in which the boundaries between illusion and reality, power and subjection, friendship and love, female and male, are so porous, and in which family members freely materialize and dematerialize.

Like the other plays in this collection, *Baby* is more concerned with asking these questions than answering them. Like *The Baltimore Waltz*, it is a celebration of narrative, of the power of the theatre to make fantasy real. It commemorates the childhood one never had, the friends wished for but never gained, the desires never acknowledged. In their very different ways, all of these plays are acts of commemoration, both exhuming and reimagining the past—Paula's past for sure, but also that of the culture of which she is a part. Thus, *The Oldest Profession* looks back to a time when there was a palpable connection between people and both the work they performed and the things they consumed. And *Hot 'N' Throbbing* rereads the stories that constitute the canon of great literature and exposes what has been omitted in the telling. Yet these plays look back without nostalgia. They represent less an idealization of the past than a return to the scene of the crime. Like Phyllis taking Paula and Carl back to their vacant apartment, they are intent upon revisiting the past in order to take it apart, to analyze it, to undermine it, and so to wreak a truly creative revenge. In this volume, Paula leaves us not just a pile of loose screws (although there are plenty of those jangling about), but the pieces of the rooms in which we live, the closet doors, the marriage beds, the sources of light—and darkness—in the hope that we will discover how to put them to better use.

*June 1995*

David Savran has published widely on post-World War II American theatre. His most recent book is *Communists, Cowboys, and Queers: The Politics of Masculinity in the Work of Arthur Miller and Tennessee Williams* (Minneapolis: University of Minnesota Press, 1992). He is a professor of English at Brown University.

ACKNOWLEDGMENTS

First and foremost, thanks are due to my late brother, Carl Vogel. My heart has given him all its glittering prizes.

And to family members—my mother, Phyllis Vogel, who gamely reads each new play; and my brother Mark. The entire Marks and Manos family who keep the Maryland home fires burning.

Thanks as well belong to my agent, Peter Franklin for shielding me from the slings and arrows and sharing the champagne. The following artists have generously given me their artistry and opened their artistic and personal homes: Molly Smith and the casts and companies of Perseverance Theatre; Tanya Berezin, Anne Bogart, Cherry Jones and the casts and companies of Circle Repertory Theatre; the company of Bay Street Theatre; Robert Brustein and the cast and company of American Repertory Theatre and Andrew Manley and the Harrogate Theatre. Gratitude to constant advisors, supporters and friends who, over the past decade, have read first drafts of my plays and the letters to critics and foes they convinced me never to send: Joanne Zippel, Ellen Schwartz, Stephen Ciesluk, Tish Dace and Stephen Weeks. I am fortunate to have the dramaturgy and the friendship of Ronn Smith and David Savran.

My writing is indebted to a decade of Brown University playwrights: Eliza Anderson, Doyle Avant, Debbie Baley, Michael Barnwell, Adam Bock, David Bucci, Heidi Carla, Claire Chafee,

Bridget Carpenter, Karen Cronacher, Nilo Cruz, Edwidge Danticat, Dennis Davis, Donna DiNovelli, Paja Faudree, Thalia Field, Juliann France, Tony Gerber, Rob Handel, Azande Mangeango, Ruth Margraff, Keith Mayerson, Bonnie Metzgar, Honor Molloy, Rebecca Morris, Gale Nelson, Lynn Nottage, Madeleine Olnek, Jena Osman, Aishah Rahman, Rick Rankin, George Rattner, Sung Rno, Sarah Ruhl, Kate Rushin, John C. Russell, Rachel Sheinkin, Rob Shin, Adam Sobsey, Dominic Taylor, Shay Youngblood. Plus many more talented writers, students and colleagues in Creative Writing and English who have instructed this instructor to dance on the page by their example.

Support for these plays has been generously provided by the MacDowell Colony, Yaddo, the National Endowment for the Arts fellowships, The Bunting Institute, The Bellagio Center of the Rockefeller Foundation, the Fund for New American Plays, The Harold and Mimi Steinberg Charitable Trust and the AT&T OnStage program. I am grateful for this support.

In March of 1994, Gustavo de Leon was commissioned by the Yale Repertory Theatre to design and create the artwork concept for their upcoming production of *The Baltimore Waltz*. When Gustavo began work on the play, his brother, Antar de Leon, was going through the final stages of AIDS. On the night of April 30, a week before opening night, he died. The artist would like to dedicate the artwork for the Yale production and the cover of this anthology to his memory.

# The
# Baltimore
# Waltz

*The Baltimore Waltz* was workshopped October–November 1990 at the Perseverance Theatre in Douglas, Alaska, under Molly D. Smith, Artistic Director and Deborah B. Baley, Producing Director. The production was directed by Annie Stokes-Hutchinson, with sets by Bill Hudson, costumes by Barbara Casement and Kari Minnick, lights by John E. Miller and sound by Katie Jensen. The cast was as follows:

| | |
|---|---|
| ANNA | Deborah Holbrook |
| CARL | Rick Bundy |
| THE THIRD MAN/DOCTOR | Charles Cardwell |

*The Baltimore Waltz* was produced February 1992 at the Circle Repertory Company in New York City under Tanya Berezin, Artistic Director and Terrence Dwyer, Managing Director with a grant from AT&T OnStage. It was directed by Anne Bogart, with sets by Loy Arcenas, costumes by Walker Hicklin, lights by Dennis Parichy and sound and score by John Gromada. The dramaturg was Ronn Smith. The cast was as follows:

| | |
|---|---|
| ANNA | Cherry Jones |
| CARL | Richard Thompson |
| THE THIRD MAN/DOCTOR | Joe Mantello |

TO THE MEMORY OF CARL —
BECAUSE I CANNOT SEW.

I always saw myself as a surrogate who, in the absence of anyone else, would stand in for him. And even now, when I'm in
front of an audience and I feel good, I hearken back to that feeling, that I'm standing in for them.

—*Ron Vawter*
(From *Breaking the Rules*
by David Savran)

In 1986, my brother Carl invited me to join him in a joint excursion to Europe. Due to pressures of time and money, I declined, never dreaming that he was HIV positive. This is the letter he wrote me after his first bout with pneumonia at Johns Hopkins Hospital in Baltimore, Maryland. He died on January 9, 1988.

As executor of his estate, I give permission to all future productions to reprint Carl's letter in the accompanying program. I would appreciate letting him speak to us in his own words.

*The Baltimore Waltz*—a journey with Carl to a Europe that exists only in the imagination—was written during the summer of 1989 at the MacDowell Colony, New Hampshire.

—*Paula Vogel*

*March 1987*

*Dear Paula:*

I thought I would jot down some of my thoughts about the (shall we say) production values of my ceremony. Oh God—I can hear you groaning—everybody wants to direct. Well, I want a good show, even though my role has been reduced involuntarily from player to prop.

First, concerning the choice between a religious ceremony and a memorial service. I know the family considers my Anglican observances as irrelevant as Shinto. However, I wish prayers in some recognizably traditional form to be said, prayers that give thanks to the Creator for the gift of life and the hope of reunion. For reasons, which you appreciate, I prefer a woman cleric, if possible, to lead the prayers. Here are two names: Phebe Coe, Epiphany Church; the Rev. Doris Mote, Holy Evangelists. Be sure to make a generous contribution from the estate for the cleric.

As for the piece of me I leave behind, here are your options:

1. Open casket, full drag.
2. Open casket, bum up. (You'll know where to place the calla lilies, won't you?)
3. Closed casket, interment with the grandparents.
4. Cremation and burial of my ashes.
5. Cremation and dispersion of my ashes in some sylvan spot.

I would really like good music. My tastes in these matters run to the highbrow: Fauré's "Pie Jesu" from his *Requiem*, Gluck's "Dance of the Blessed Spirits" from *Orfeo*, "La Vergine degli Angeli" from Verdi's *Forza*. But my favorite song is "I Dream of Jeannie," and I wouldn't mind a spiritual like "Steal Away." Also, perhaps, "Nearer My God to Thee." Didn't Jeanette MacDonald sing that di-vinely in *San Francisco*?

Finally, would you read or have read A. E. Housman's "Loveliest of Trees"?

Well, my dear, that's that. Should I be lain with Grandma and Papa Ben, do stop by for a visit from year to year. And feel free to chat. You'll find me a good listener.

*Love,*
*Brother*

CHARACTERS

ANNA

CARL: Her Brother.

THE THIRD MAN/DOCTOR, who also plays:

HARRY LIME
AIRPORT SECURITY GUARD
PUBLIC HEALTH OFFICIAL
GARÇON
CUSTOMS OFFICIAL
THE LITTLE DUTCH BOY AT AGE 50

MUNICH VIRGIN
RADICAL STUDENT ACTIVIST
CONCIERGE
DR. TODESROCHELN
and all other parts

*The Baltimore Waltz* takes place in a hospital lounge in Baltimore, Maryland.

PRODUCTION NOTES

The lighting should be highly stylized, lush, dark and imaginative, in contrast to the hospital white silence of the last scene. Wherever possible, prior to the last scene, the director is encouraged to score the production with music—every cliché of the European experience as imagined by Hollywood.

Anna might be dressed in a full slip/negligee and a trench coat. Carl is dressed in flannel pajamas and a blazer or jacket. The stuffed rabbit should be in every scene with Carl after Scene VI. The Third Man should wear latex gloves throughout the entire play.

**I.**

*Three distinct areas on stage: Anna, stage right, in her trench coat, clutching the* Berlitz Pocket Guide to Europe; *Carl, stage left, wearing pajamas and blazer; The Third Man/Doctor, in his lab coat, with stethoscope, is center.*

*Anna reads from her book. Her accents are execrable.*

ANNA: "Help me please." *(Recites from memory)* Dutch: "Kunt U mij helpen, alstublieft?" "There's nothing I can do." French: *(Searches in vain)* I have no memory. *(Reads from the* Berlitz*)* "Il n'y a rien à faire." "Where are the toilets?" "Wo sind die Toiletten?"

I've never been abroad. It's not that I don't want to—but the language terrifies me. I was traumatized by a junior high school French teacher, and after that, it was a lost cause. I think that's the reason I went into elementary education. Words like brioche, bidet, bildungsroman raise a sweat.

Oh, I want to go. Carl—he's my brother, you'll meet him shortly—he desperately wants to go. But then, he can speak six languages. He's the head librarian of literature and languages at the San Francisco Public. It's a very important position.

The thought of eight-hundred-year-old houses perched on the sides of mountains and rivers whose names you've only seen in the Sunday *Times* crossword puzzles—all of that is exciting. But I'm not going without him. He's read so much. I couldn't possibly go without him. You see, I've never been abroad—unless you count Baltimore, Maryland.

CARL: Good morning, boys and girls. It's Monday morning, and it's time for "Reading Hour with Uncle Carl" once again, here at the North Branch of the San Francisco Public Library. This is going to be a special reading hour. It's my very last reading hour with you. Friday will be my very last day with the San Francisco Public as children's librarian. Why? Do any of you know what a pink slip is? *(Holds up a rectangle of pink)* It means I'm going on a paid leave of absence for two weeks. Shelley Bizio, the branch supervisor, has given me my very own pink slip. I got a pink slip because I wear this. *(He points to a pink triangle on his lapel)* A pink triangle. Now, I want you all to take the pink construction paper in front of you, and take your scissors, and cut out pink triangles. There's tape at every table, so you can wear them too! Make some for Mom and Dad, and your brothers and sisters. Very good. Very good, Fabio. Oh, that's a beautiful pink triangle, Tse Heng.

Now before we read our last story together, I thought we might have a sing-along. Your parents can join in, if they'd like to. Oh, don't be shy. Let's do "Here We Go Round the Mulberry Bush." Remember that one? *(He begins to sing. He also demonstrates)* "Here we go round the mulberry bush, the mulberry bush, the mulberry bush / Here we go round the mulberry bush, so early in the morning.

"This is the way we pick our nose, pick our nose, pick our nose / This is the way we pick our nose, so early in the morning."

Third verse! *(He makes a rude gesture with his middle finger)* "This is the way we go on strike, go on strike, go on strike / This is the way we go on strike, so early in the—"

What, Mrs. Bizio? I may leave immediately? I do not have to wait until Friday to collect unemployment? Why, thank you, Mrs. Bizio.

Well, boys and girls, Mrs. Bizio will take over now. Bear with her, she's personality-impaired. I want you to be very good and remember me. I'm leaving for an immediate vacation with my sister on the East Coast, and I'll think of you as I travel. Remember to wear those pink triangles.

*(To his supervisor)* I'm going. I'm going. You don't have to be rude. They enjoyed it. We'll take it up with the union. *(Shouting)* In a language you might understand: Up-pay ours-yay!

ANNA: It's the language that terrifies me.

CARL: Lesson Number One: Subject Position. I. Je. Ich. Ik. I'm sorry. Je regrette. Es tut mir leid.

ANNA: But we decided to go when the doctor gave us his verdict.

DOCTOR: I'm sorry.

CARL: I'm sorry.

DOCTOR: There's nothing we can do.

ANNA: But what?

CARL: How long?

ANNA: Explain it to me. Very slowly. So I can understand. Excuse me, could you tell me again?

DOCTOR: There are exudative and proliferative inflammatory alterations of the endocardium, consisting of necrotic debris, fibrinoid material and disintegrating fibroblastic cells.

CARL: Oh, sweet Jesus.

DOCTOR: It may be acute or subacute, caused by various bacteria: streptococci, staphylococci, enterococci, gonococci, gram-negative bacilli, etc. It may be due to other microorganisms, of course, but there is a high mortality rate with or without treatment. And there is usually rapid destruction and metastases.

CARL: Anna—

ANNA: I'm right here, darling. Right here.

CARL: Could you explain it very slowly?

DOCTOR: Also known as Löffler's Syndrome, i.e., eosinophilia, resulting in fibroblastic thickening, persistent tachycardia, hepatomegaly, splenomegaly, serious effusions into the pleural cavity with edema. It may be *Brugia malayi* or *Wuchereria bancofti*—also known as Weingarten's Syndrome. Often seen with effusions, either exudate or transudate.

ANNA: Carl—

CARL: I'm here, darling. Right here.

ANNA: It's the language that terrifies me.

**II.**

CARL: Medical Straight Talk: Part One.

ANNA: So you're telling me that you really don't know?

DOCTOR: I'm afraid that medical science has only a small foothold in this area. But of course, it would be of great benefit to our knowledge if you would consent to observation here at Johns Hopkins—

CARL: Why? Running out of laboratory rats?!

ANNA: Oh, no. I'm sorry. I can't do that. Can you tell me at least how it was...contracted?

DOCTOR: Well—we're not sure, yet. It's only a theory at this stage, but one that seems in great favor at the World Health Organization. We think it comes from the old cultus ornatus—

CARL: Toilet seats?

ANNA: Toilet seats! My God. Mother was right. She always said—

CARL: And never, ever, in any circumstances, in bus stations...

ANNA: Toilet seats? Cut down in the prime of youth by a toilet seat?

DOCTOR: Anna—I may call you Anna? You teach school, I believe?

ANNA: Yes, first grade. What does that have—

DOCTOR: Ah, yes. We're beginning to see a lot of this in elementary schools.

Anna—I may call you Anna? With assurances of complete confidentiality, we need to ask you very specific questions about the body, body fluids and body functions. As mature adults, as scientists and educators. To speak frankly...when you needed to relieve yourself...where did you make wa-wa?

ANNA: There's a faculty room. But why—how—?

DOCTOR: You never, ever used the johnny in your classroom?

ANNA: Well, maybe once or twice. There's no lock, and Robbie Matthews always tries to barge in. Sometimes I just can't get the time to—surely you're not suggesting that—

DOCTOR: You did use the facilities in your classroom? *(The Doctor makes notes from this)*

CARL: Is that a crime? When you've got to go, you've got to—

ANNA: I can't believe that my students would transmit something like this—

DOCTOR: You have no idea. Five year olds can be deadly. It seems to be an affliction, so far, of single schoolteachers. Schoolteachers with children of their own develop an immunity to ATD—Acquired Toilet Disease.

ANNA: I see. Why hasn't anybody heard of this disease?

DOCTOR: Well, first of all, the Center for Disease Control doesn't wish to inspire an all-out panic in communities. Secondly, we think education on this topic is the responsibility of the NEA, not the government. And if word of this pestilence gets out inappropriately, the PTA is going to be all over the school system demanding mandatory testing of every toilet seat in every lavatory. It's kindling for a political disaster.

ANNA *(Taking the Doctor aside)*: I want to ask you something confidentially. Something that my brother doesn't need to hear. What's the danger of transmission?

DOCTOR: There's really no danger to anyone in the immediate family. You must use precautions.

ANNA: Because what I want to know is...can you transmit this thing by...by doing—what exactly do you mean by precautions?

DOCTOR: Well, I guess you should do what your mother always told you. You know, wash your hands before and after going to the bathroom. And never lick paper money or coins in any currency.

ANNA: So there's no danger to anyone by...what I mean, Doctor, is that I can't infect anyone by—

DOCTOR: Just use precautions.

ANNA: Because, in whatever time this schoolteacher has left, I intend to fuck my brains out.

DOCTOR: Which means, in whatever time is left, she can fuck her brains out.

## III. Carl and the Doctor.

CARL *(Agitated)*: I'll tell you what. If Sandra Day O'Connor sat on just one infected potty, the media would be clamoring to do articles on ATD. If just one grandchild of George Bush caught this thing during toilet training, that would be the last we'd hear about the space program. Why isn't someone doing something?!

I'm sorry. I know you're one of the converted. You're doing...well, everything you can. I'd like to ask you something in confidence, something my sister doesn't need to hear. Is there any hope at all?

DOCTOR: Well, I suppose there's...always hope.

CARL: Any experimental drugs? Treatments?

DOCTOR: Well, they're trying all sorts of things abroad. Our hands are tied here by the NIH and the FDA, you understand. There is a long-shot avenue to explore, nothing, you understand, that I personally endorse, but there is an eighty-year-old urologist overseas who's been working in this field for some time—

CARL: We'll try anything.

DOCTOR: His name is Dr. Todesrocheln. He's somewhat unorthodox, outside the medical community in Vienna. It's gonna cost you. Mind you, this is not an endorsement.

ANNA: You hear the doctor through a long-distance corridor. Your ears are functioning, but the mind is numb. You try to listen as you swim toward his sentences in the florescent light in his office. But you don't believe it at first.

This is how I'd like to die: with dignity. No body secretions—like Merle Oberon in *Wuthering Heights*. With a somewhat becoming flush, and a transcendental gaze. Luminous eyes piercing the veil of mortal existence. The windows are open to the fresh breeze blowing off the moors.

Oh. And violins in the background would be nice, too.

*(Music: Violins playing Strauss swell in the background.)*

## IV. The Phone Call.

THE THIRD MAN: Lesson Number Two: Basic Dialogue. The phone call. Hello. I would like to speak to Mr. Lime, please.

CARL: Entschuldigen Sie, bitte—operator? Operator? Hello? Guten Tag? Kann ich bitte mit Herr Lime sprechen?

Harry? Harry? Wie geht es dir?! Listen, I...can you hear...no, I'm in Baltimore...yeah, not since Hopkins...no, there's—well, there is something up. No, dear boy, that hasn't been up in a long time. No, seriously—it's my sister. ATD.

THE THIRD MAN: ATD? Jesus, that's tough, old man. You've got to watch where you sit these days. She's a sweet kid. Yeah. Yeah. Wait a second.

*(Offstage)* Inge? Inge, baby? Ein Bier, bitte, baby. Ja. Ja. You too, baby.

*(Pause)*

Okay. Dr. Todesrocheln? Yeah, you might say I know him. But don't tell anybody I said that. There's also a new drug they've got over here. Black market. I might be able to help you. I said might. But it's gonna cost you.

*(Cautiously, ominously)* Do you still have the rabbit?

CARL: I'll bring the rabbit.

THE THIRD MAN: Good. A friend of mine will be in touch. And listen, old man...if anybody asks you, you don't know me. I'll see you in a month. You know where to find me.

THE THIRD MAN AND CARL *(Simultaneously)*: Click.

## V.

THE THIRD MAN: Lesson Number Three: Pronouns and the Possessive Case. I, you, he, she and it. They and we. Yours, mine and ours.

VOICE OF ANNA: There's nothing I can do. There's nothing you can do. There's nothing he, she or it can do. There's nothing we can do. There's nothing they can do.

ANNA: So what are we going to do?

CARL: Start packing, sister dear.

ANNA: Europe? You mean it?

CARL: We'll mosey about France and Germany, and then work our way down to Vienna.

ANNA: What about your job?

CARL: It's only a job.

ANNA: It's a very important job! Head of the entire San Francisco Public—

CARL: They'll hold my job for me. I'm due for a leave.

ANNA: Oh, honey. Can we afford this?

CARL: It's only money.

ANNA: It's your money.

CARL: It's our money.


## VI.

THE THIRD MAN: Lesson Four: Present Tense of Faire. What are we going to do? Qu'est-ce qu'on va faire.

ANNA: So what are we going to do?

CARL: We'll see this doctor in Vienna.

ANNA: Dr. Todesrocheln?

CARL: We have to try.

ANNA: A urologist?

CARL: He's working on a new drug.

ANNA: A European urologist?

CARL: What options do we have?

ANNA: Wait a minute. What are his credentials? Who is this guy?

CARL: He was trained at the Allgemeines Krankenhaus during the Empire.

ANNA: Yeah? Just what was he doing from, say, 1938 to 1945? Research?

CARL: It's best not to ask too many questions. There are people who swear by his work.

ANNA: What's his specialty?

CARL: Well, actually, he's a practitioner of uriposia.

ANNA: He writes poems about urine?

CARL: No. He drinks it.

ANNA: I'm not going.

CARL: Let's put off judgment until we arrange a consultation— my god, you're so messy. Look at how neat my suitcase is in comparison. You'll never find a thing in there.

ANNA: I refuse to drink my own piss for medical science.

*(Carl grabs a stuffed rabbit and thrusts it in Anna's suitcase.)*

ANNA: What are you doing?

CARL: We can't leave bunny behind.

ANNA: What is a grown man like you doing with a stuffed rabbit?

CARL: I can't sleep without bunny.

ANNA: I didn't know you slept with...stuffed animals.

CARL: There's a lot you don't know about me.

## VII.

THE THIRD MAN: Lesson Five: Basic Dialogue. At the airport. We are going to Paris. What time does our flight leave? Nous allons à Paris. A quelle heure depart notre vol?

*(The Third Man becomes an Airport Security Guard.)*

AIRPORT SECURITY GUARD: Okay. Next. Please remove your keys and all other metallic items. Place all belongings on the belt. Next.

(*Carl and Anna carry heavy luggage. Carl halts.*)

CARL: Wait. I need your suitcase.

(*He opens Anna's luggage and begins to rummage around.*)

ANNA: Hey!
CARL: It was a mess to begin with.
    Ah...(*He retrieves the stuffed rabbit*) There.
ANNA: Are you having an anxiety attack?
CARL: You hold it.

(*Carl and Anna stamp, sit and stand on the baggage. Carl manages to relock the bag.*)

ANNA: What is wrong with you?
CARL: X rays are bad for bunny.
AIRPORT SECURITY GUARD: Next. Please remove all metallic objects. Keys. Eyeglasses. Gold fillings.
CARL: Go on. You first.
AIRPORT SECURITY GUARD: Metallic objects?
    (*Anna passes through, holding the stuffed rabbit. Carl sighs, relieved. Carl passes through. The Airport Security Guard stops him*) One moment, please.

(*The Airport Security Guard almost strip-searches him. He uses a metallic wand which makes loud, clicking noises. Finally, he nods. He hands Anna and Carl their bags, still suspiciously looking at Carl.*)

ANNA: Okay, bunny—Paris, here we come!

## VIII.

THE THIRD MAN: At the hotel.

> (*Simultaneously with Carl's next lines*) Lesson Six: Direct Pronouns. I am tired. And my sister looks at herself in the mirror.

CARL (*Simultaneously with The Third Man*): Sixieme Leçon: Pronoms—Compléments Directs. Je suis fatigué. Et ma soeur elle se regarde dans la glace.

> (*Carl climbs into a double bed with the stuffed rabbit. Anna stares into a mirror. The Third Man, apart, stands in their bedroom.*)

THE THIRD MAN: The first separation—your first sense of loss. You were five; your brother was seven. Your parents would not let you sleep in the same bed anymore. They removed you to your own bedroom. You were too old, they said. But every now and then, when they turned off the lights and went downstairs—when the dark scared you—you would rise and go to him. And he would let you nustle under his arm, under the covers, where you would fall to sleep, breathing in the scent of your own breath and his seven-year-old body.

CARL: Come to bed, sweetie. Bunny and I are waiting. We're going to be jet-lagged for a while.

ANNA (*Continues to stare in the mirror*): It doesn't show yet.

CARL: No one can tell. Let's get some sleep, honey.

ANNA: I don't want anyone to know.

CARL: It's not a crime. It's an illness.

ANNA: I don't want anybody to know.

CARL: It's your decision. Just don't tell anyone...what...you do for a living.

> (*Anna joins Carl in the bed. He holds her hand.*)

ANNA: Well, there's one good thing about traveling in Europe...
and about dying.

CARL: What's that?

ANNA: I get to sleep with you again.


**IX.**


CARL: Medical Straight Talk: Part Two.

*(The Third Man becomes a Public Health Official.)*

PUBLIC HEALTH OFFICIAL: Here at the Department of Health and
Human Services we are announcing Operation Squat. There
is no known cure for ATD right now, and we are acknowl-
edging the urgency of this dread disease by recognizing it as
our 82nd national health priority. Right now ATD is the
fourth major cause of death of single schoolteachers, ages
twenty-four to forty—behind school buses, lockjaw and
playground accidents.

    The best policy, until a cure can be found, is of education
and prevention.

    *(Anna and Carl hold up posters of a toilet seat in a circle
with a red diagonal slash)*

    If you are in the high-risk category—single elementary
schoolteachers, classroom aides, custodians and playground
drug pushers—follow these simple guides.

    *(Anna and Carl hold up copies of the educational
pamphlets)*

    *Do*: Use the facilities in your own home before departing
for school.

    *Do*: Use the facilities in your own home as soon as you
return from school.

    *Do*: Hold it.

    *Don't*: Eat meals in public restrooms.

    *Don't*: Flush lavatory equipment and then suck your digits.

If absolutely necessary to relieve yourself at work, please remember the Department of Health and Human Services' ATD slogan: Don't sit, do squat!

## X.

*Music: Accordion playing a song like "La Vie en rose."*
*Anna and Carl stroll.*

CARL: Of course, the Left Bank has always been a haven for out-casts, foreigners and students, since the time that Abelard fled the Île de La Cité to found the university here.

ANNA: Oh, look. Is that the Eiffel Tower? It looks so...phallic.

CARL: And it continued to serve as a haven for the avant-garde of the twenties, the American expatriate community that could no longer afford Montparnasse.

ANNA: My god, they really do smoke Gauloise here.

CARL: And, of course, the Dada and Surrealists who set up camp here after World War I and their return from Switzerland—

*(The Third Man, in a trench coat and red beret, crosses the stage.)*

ANNA: Are we being followed?

CARL: Is your medication making you paranoid?
*(Pause)*
Now, over here is the famous spot where Gertrude sup-posedly said to her brother Leo—

*(The Third Man follows them.)*

ANNA: I know. "God is the answer. What is the question?"—I'm not imagining it. That man has been trailing us from the Boulevard St. Michel.

CARL: Are you getting hungry?

ANNA: I'm getting tired.

CARL: Wait. Let's just whip around the corner to the Cafe St. Michel where Hemingway, after an all-night bout, threw up his shrimp heads all over Scott's new suede shoes—which really was a movable feast.

*(The Third Man is holding an identical stuffed rabbit and looks at them.)*

ANNA: Carl! Carl! Look! That man over there!

CARL: So? They have stuffed rabbits over here, too. Let's go.

ANNA: Why is he following us? He's got the same—

CARL: It's your imagination. How about a little déjeuner?

*(Anna and Carl walk to a small table and chairs.)*

## XI.

GARÇON *(With a thick Peter Sellers French)*: It was a simple bistro affair by French standards. He had le veau Prince Orloff, she le boeuf à la mode—a simple dish of haricots verts, and a médoc to accompany it all. He barely touched his meal. She mopped the sauces with the bread. As their meal progressed, Anna thought of the lunches she packed back home. For the past ten years, hunched over in the faculty room at McCormick Elementary, this is what Anna ate: on Mondays, pressed chipped chicken sandwiches with mayonnaise on white; on Tuesdays, soggy tuna sandwiches; on Wednesdays, Velveeta cheese and baloney; on Thursdays, drier pressed chicken on the now stale white bread; on Fridays, Velveeta and tuna. She always had a small wax envelope of carrot sticks or celery, and a can of Diet Pepsi.

Anna, as she ate in the bistro, wept. What could she know of love?

CARL: Why are you weeping?

ANNA: It's just so wonderful.

CARL: You're a goose.

ANNA: I've wasted over thirty years on convenience foods.

*(The Garçon approaches the table.)*

GARÇON: Is everything all right?

ANNA: Oh god. Yes...yes—it's wonderful.

CARL: My sister would like to see the dessert tray.

*(Anna breaks out in tears again. The Garçon shrugs and exits. He reappears a few minutes later as The Third Man, this time with a trench coat and blue beret. He sits at an adjacent table and stares in their direction.)*

ANNA: Who is that man? Do you know him?

CARL *(Hastily looks at The Third Man)*: No, I've never seen him before.

*(The Third Man brings the stuffed rabbit out of his trench coat.)*

ANNA: He's flashing his rabbit at you.

CARL *(Rises)*: Excuse me. I think I'll go to les toilettes.

ANNA: Carl! Be careful! Don't sit!

*(Carl exits. The Third Man waits a few seconds, looks at Anna, then follows Carl without expression.)*

ANNA: What is it they do with those rabbits?

*(A split second later, the Garçon reenters with the dessert tray. Anna ogles him.)*

GARÇON: Okay. We have la crème plombière pralinée, un bavarois à l'orange, et ici we have une Charlotte Malakoff aux framboises. Our specialité is le gâteau de crêpes à la Normande. What would mademoiselle like?

*(Anna has obviously not been looking at the dessert tray.)*

ANNA *(Sighing)*: Ah, yes.
GARÇON *(Smiles)*: Vous êtes américaîne? This is your first trip to Paris?
ANNA: Yes.
GARÇON: And you do not speak at all French?
ANNA: No.

*(The Garçon smiles.)*

GARÇON *(Suggestively)*: Bon. Would you like la specialité de la maison?

## XII.

CARL: Exercise: La carte. La specialité de la maison.
   Back at the hotel, Anna sampled the Garçon's specialité de la maison while her brother browsed the Louvre.
   *(Anna and the Garçon are shapes beneath the covers of the bed; Carl clutches his stuffed rabbit)*
   Jean Baptiste Camille Corot lived from 1796 to 1875. Although he began his career by studying in the classical tradition, his later paintings reveal the influence of the Italian style.
ANNA *(Muffled)*: Ah! Yes!
GARÇON *(Also muffled)*: Ah! Oui!
CARL: He traveled extensively around the world, and in the salon of 1827 his privately lauded techniques were displayed in public.
ANNA: Yes—oh, yes, yes!
GARÇON: Mais oui!

CARL: Before the Academy had accepted realism, Corot's progressive paintings, his clear-sighted observations of nature, revealed a fresh, almost spritely, quality of light, tone and composition.

ANNA: Yes—that's right—faster—

GARÇON: Plus vite?

ANNA: Faster—

GARÇON: Encore! Plus vite!

ANNA: Wait!

GARÇON: Attends?

CARL: It was his simplicity, and his awareness of color that brought a fresh wind into the staid Academy—

GARÇON: Maintenant?

ANNA: Lower—faster—lower—

GARÇON: Plus bas—plus vite—plus bas—

CARL: He was particularly remembered and beloved for his championing the cause of younger artists with more experimental techniques, bringing the generosity of his advancing reputation to their careers.

ANNA: Yes—I—I—I—I—!

GARÇON: Je—je! Je!! Je!

*(Pause.)*

CARL: In art, as in life, some things need no translation.

GARÇON: Gauloise?

CARL: For those of you who are interested, in the next room are some stunning works by Delacroix.

## XIII. Back at the Hotel.

CARL: Lesson Seven: Basic Vocabulary. Parts of the Body.

*(Carl, slightly out of the next scene, watches them.*
*Anna sits up in bed. The Garçon is asleep beneath the sheet.)*

ANNA: I did read one book once in French. *Le Petit Prince*. Lying here, watching him sleep, I look at his breast and remember the rose with its single, pathetic thorn for protection. And here—his puckered red nipple, lying poor and vulnerable on top of his blustering breast plate. It's really so sweet about men.

*(She kisses the Garçon's breast. The Garçon stirs.)*

GARÇON: Encore?

ANNA: What is the word—in French—for this? *(She fingers his breast)*

GARÇON: For un homme: le sein. For une femme: la mamelle.

ANNA: Le sein?

GARÇON: Oui. Le sein.

ANNA *(She kisses his neck)*: And this?

GARÇON: Le cou.

ANNA: Et ici?

GARÇON: Bon. Décolleté.

*(Anna begins to touch him under the sheet.)*

ANNA: And this?

*(The Garçon laughs.)*

GARÇON: S'il vous plâit...I am tickling there. Ah. Couille.

ANNA: Culle?

GARÇON: Non. Couille. Le cul is something much different. Ici c'est le cul.

ANNA: Oh, yes. That's very different.

GARÇON *(Taking her hand under the sheet)*: We sometimes call these also Le Quatrième État. The Fourth Estate.

ANNA: Really? Because you press them?

GARÇON: Bien sûr.

ANNA: And this?

GARÇON *(With pride)*: Ah. Ma Tour Eiffel. I call it aussi my Charles de Gaulle.

ANNA: Wow.

GARÇON: My grandfather called his Napoléon.

ANNA: I see. I guess it runs in your family.

GARÇON *(Modestly)*: Oui. Grand-mère—qu'est-ce que c'est le mot en anglais? Her con—here—ici—do you know what I am meaning?

ANNA: You're making yourself completely clear.

GARÇON: We called hers the Waterloo de mon grand-père—

ANNA *(Digs under the sheet more)*: And this?

GARÇON *(Scandalized)*: Non. There is no word en français. Pas du tout.

ANNA: For this? There must be—

GARÇON: Non! Only the Germans have a word for that.


*(Carl enters and casually converses with Anna. Startled, the Garçon covers himself with the sheet.)*


CARL: Hello, darling. Are you feeling better?

*(Carl walks to the chair beside the bed and removes the Garçon's clothing.)*


ANNA: Yes, much. I needed to lie down. How was the Louvre?

*(The Garçon carefully rises from the bed and takes his clothing from Carl, who is holding them out. He creeps cautiously stage left and begins to pull on his clothes.)*


CARL: Oh, Anna. I'm so sorry you missed it. The paintings of David were amazing. The way his paintbrush embraced the body—it was just incredible to stand there and see them in the flesh.

ANNA: Ah yes—in the flesh. *(She smiles at the confused Garçon)*

CARL: Well, sweetie. It's been a thoroughly rewarding day for both of us. I'm for turning in. How about you?

*(The Garçon is now fully dressed.)*

ANNA: Yes, I'm tired. Here—I've warmed the bed for you. *(She throws back the sheet)*
CARL: Garçon—l'addition!
ANNA *(To the Garçon)*: Merci beaucoup.

*(Anna blows him a kiss. The Garçon takes a few steps out of the scene as Carl climbs into bed.)*

## XIV.

THE THIRD MAN: Anna has a difficult time sleeping. She is afflicted with night thoughts. According to Elizabeth Kübler-Ross, there are six stages the terminal patient travels in the course of her illness.
     The First Stage: Denial and Isolation.

*(The Third Man stays in the hotel room and watches Carl and Anna in the bed. They are sleeping, when Anna sits upright.)*

ANNA: I feel so alone. The ceiling is pressing down on me. I can't believe I am dying. Only at night. Only at night. In the morning, when I open my eyes, I feel absolutely well—without a body. And then the thought comes crashing in my mind. This is the last spring I may see. This is the last summer. It can't be. There must be a mistake. They mixed the specimens up in the hospital. Some poor person is walking around, dying, with the false confidence of my prognosis, thinking themselves well. It's a clerical error.
     Carl! I can't sleep. Do you think they made a mistake?
CARL: Come back to sleep.

*(Carl pulls Anna down on the bed to him, and strokes her brow.*

*They change positions on the bed.)*

THE THIRD MAN: The Second Stage: Anger.

ANNA *(Sits bolt upright in bed, angry)*: How could this happen to me! I did my lesson plans faithfully for the past ten years! I've taught in classrooms without walls—kept up on new audio-visual aids—I read Summerhill! And I believed it! When the principal assigned me the job of the talent show— and nobody wants to do the talent show—I pleaded for cafeteria duty, bus duty—but no, I got stuck with the talent show. And those kids put on the best darn show that school has ever seen! Which one of them did this to me? Emily Baker? For slugging Johnnie MacIntosh? Johnnie MacIntosh? Because I sent him home for exposing himself to Susy Higgins? Susy Higgins? Because I called her out on her nose-picking? Or those Nader twins? I've spent the best years of my life giving to those kids—it's not—

CARL: Calm down, sweetie. You're angry. It's only natural to be angry. Elizabeth Kübler-Ross says that—

ANNA: What does she know about what it feels like to die?! Elizabeth Kübler-Ross can sit on my face!

*(Carl and Anna change positions on the bed.)*

THE THIRD MAN: The Third Stage: Bargaining.

ANNA: Do you think if I let Elizabeth Kübler-Ross sit on my face I'll get well?

*(Carl and Anna change positions on the bed.)*

THE THIRD MAN: The Fourth Stage: Depression.

CARL *(Sits on the side of the bed beside Anna)*: Anna... honey— come on, wake up.

ANNA: Leave me alone.

CARL: Come on, sweetie...you've been sleeping all day now, and you slept all yesterday. Do you want to sleep away our last day in France?

ANNA: Why bother?

CARL: You've got to eat something. You've got to fight this. For me.

ANNA: Leave me alone.

*(Carl lies down beside Anna. They change positions.)*

THE THIRD MAN: The Fifth Stage: Acceptance.

*(Anna and Carl are lying in bed, awake. They hold hands.)*

ANNA: When I'm gone, I want you to find someone.

CARL: Let's not talk about me.

ANNA: No, I want to. It's important to me to know that you'll be happy and taken care of after...when I'm gone.

CARL: Please.

ANNA: I've got to talk about it. We've shared everything else. I want you to know how it feels...what I'm thinking...when I hold your hand, and I kiss it...I try to memorize what it looks like, your hand...I wonder if there's any memory in the grave?

THE THIRD MAN: And then there's the Sixth Stage: Hope.

*(Anna and Carl rise from the bed.)*

CARL: How are you feeling?

ANNA: I feel good today.

CARL: Do you feel like traveling?

ANNA: Yes. It would be nice to see Amsterdam. Together. We might as well see as much as we can while I'm well—

CARL: That's right, sweetie. And maybe you can eat something—

ANNA: I'm hungry. That's a good sign, don't you think?

CARL: That's a wonderful sign. You'll see. You'll feel better when you eat.

ANNA: Maybe the doctor in Vienna can help.

CARL: That's right.

ANNA: What's drinking a little piss? It can't hurt you.

CARL: Right. Who knows? We've got to try.

ANNA: I'll think of it as…European lager.

CARL: Golden Heidelberg.

*(Carl and Anna hum/sing the drinking song from* The Student Prince.*)*

## XV.

THE THIRD MAN: And as Anna and Carl took the train into Holland, the seductive swaying of the TEE-train aroused another sensation. Unbeknownst to Elizabeth Kübler-Ross, there is a Seventh Stage for the dying. There is a growing urge to fight the sickness of the body with the health of the body.

The Seventh Stage: Lust.

*(Anna and Carl are seated in a train compartment. Carl holds the stuffed rabbit out to Anna.)*

ANNA: Why?

CARL: Just take it. Hold it for me. Just through Customs.

ANNA: Only if you tell me why.

CARL: Don't play games right now. Or we'll be in deep, deep do-do.

*(Anna reluctantly takes the stuffed rabbit and holds it.)*

ANNA: You're scaring me.

CARL: I'm sorry, sweetie. You're the only one I can trust to hold my rabbit. Trust me. It's important.

ANNA: Then why won't you tell me—?

CARL: There are some things you're better off not knowing.

ANNA: Are you smuggling drugs? Jewels?

CARL *(Whispers)*: It's beyond measure. It's invaluable to me. That's all I'll say.

> *(In a louder tone)* Just act normal now.

CUSTOMS OFFICIAL: Uw paspoort, aistublieft.

> *(Anna and Carl give him their passports. Carl is nervous. Anna smiles at the Customs Official a bit lasciviously.)*

CUSTOMS OFFICIAL: Have you anything to declare?

ANNA *(Whispering)*: Yes, Captain, I'm smuggling contraband. I demand to be searched. In private.

CUSTOMS OFFICIAL *(Blushes)*: Excuse me?

ANNA: Yes. I said—waar is het damestoilet?

CUSTOMS OFFICIAL: Oh…I thought…

> *(The Customs Official Giggles.)*

ANNA: Yes?

CUSTOMS OFFICIAL: First left.

> *(He returns their passports)*
> Have a very pleasant stay.

> *(Anna waves bunny's arm goodbye. The Customs Official looks at her, blushes again and retreats. Carl relaxes.)*

CARL: You're good at this. Very good.

ANNA: When in Holland, do like the Dutch…Mata Hari was Dutch, you know.

## XVI.

CARL: Questions sur le dialogue. Est-ce que les hommes hollandais sont comme les français? Are Dutch men like the French?

*(Anna and The Little Dutch Boy at Age 50. He wears traditional wooden shoes, trousers and vest. His Buster Brown haircut and hat make him look dissipated.)*

THE LITTLE DUTCH BOY AT AGE 50: It was kermis time, the festival in my village. And I had too much bier with my school friends, Piet and Jan. Ja. Soo, Piet thought we should go to the outer dyke with cans of spray paint, after the kermis. So we went.

Here in Noord Brabant there are three walls of defenses against the cruelty of the North Sea. The first dyke is called the Waker—the Watcher; the second dyke is de Slaper—the Sleeper; and the last dyke, which had never before been tested, is known as the Dromer—the Dreamer.

And when we got to the Dreamer, Piet said to me: "Willem, you do it." Meaning I was to write on the walls of the Dreamer. This is why I was always in trouble in school— Piet and Jan would say, "Willem, you do it." And whatever it was, I would do it.

Soo, I took up a can of the paint and in very big letters, I wrote in Dutch that our schoolmaster, Mijnheer Van Doorn, was a gas-passer. Everyone could read the letters from far away. And just as I was finishing this, and Piet and Jan were laughing behind me, I looked—I was on my knees, pressed up against the dyke—and I could see that the wall of the Dreamer was cracking its surface, very fine little lines, like a goose egg when it breaks from within.

And I yelled to my friends: Look! And they came a bit closer, and as we looked, right above my head, a little hole began to peck its way through the clay. And there was just a small trickle of water. And Jan said: "Willem, put your thumb in that hole." And by that time, the hole in the dyke was just big enough to put my thumb in. "Why?" I asked of Jan. "Just do it," he said. And so I did.

And once I put my thumb in, I could not get it out. Suddenly we could hear the waves crashing as the Sleeper began to collapse. Only the Dreamer remained to hold off the savage water. "Help me!" I yelled to Jan and Piet—but they ran away. "Vlug!" I cried—but no one could hear me. And I stayed there, crouching, with my thumb stuck into the clay. And I thought what if the Dreamer should give in, too. How the waves would bear my body like a messenger to the village. How no one would survive the flood. Only the church steeple to mark the spot where we had lived. How young we were to die.

(Pause)

Have you ever imagined what it would be like to be face to face with death?

ANNA: Yes...yes I have.

THE LITTLE DUTCH BOY AT AGE 50: And have you ever prayed for deliverance against all hope?

ANNA: I—no. I haven't been able to get to that stage. Yet.

THE LITTLE DUTCH BOY AT AGE 50: But the Dreamer held. And finally there came wagons with men from the village, holding lanterns and sand and straw. And they found me there, strung up by my thumb, beside the big black letters: Mijnheer Van Doorn is een gas-passer. And they freed me and said I was a hero, and I became the boy who held back the sea with his thumb.

ANNA: Golly. You were very brave.

THE LITTLE DUTCH BOY AT AGE 50: I was stupid. Wrong place, wrong time.

ANNA: How long ago did this happen?

THE LITTLE DUTCH BOY AT AGE 50 (Sadly): Let us just say it happened a long time ago.

ANNA: You've faced death. I wish my brother were here to meet you.

THE LITTLE DUTCH BOY AT AGE 50: Where is he? Wo ist dein bruder?

ANNA: Oh, he stayed in Amsterdam to see the Rijksmuseum and the Van Gogh Museum.

THE LITTLE DUTCH BOY AT AGE 50: And you did not go? You should see them, they are really fantastic.

ANNA: Why? What's the use? I won't remember them, I'll have no memory.

THE LITTLE DUTCH BOY AT AGE 50: So you are an American?

ANNA: Yes.

THE LITTLE DUTCH BOY AT AGE 50: So do you want to sleep with me? All the women toeristen want to sleep with the little Dutch boy who put his thumb in the dyke.

ANNA: Do you mind so much?

THE LITTLE DUTCH BOY AT AGE 50 *(Shrugs)*: Nee. It's a way to make a living, is it niet?

ANNA *(Quietly)*: Let's go then.


## XVII.


CARL: Répétez. En français. Where is my brother going? Où va mon frère? Bien.

ANNA: I had just returned from my day trip and left the Centraal Station. The sun sparkled on the waters of the canal, and I decided to walk back to the hotel. Just then I saw my brother.

*(Carl enters in a trench coat, sunglasses, holding the stuffed rabbit.)*

ANNA: I tried to catch up with Carl, dodging bicycles and pedestrians. And then, crossing the Amstel on the Magere Brug, he appeared.

*(The Third Man enters, in a trench coat, sunglasses, and with black gloves, holding a stuffed rabbit.)*

ANNA: I trailed them from a discrete distance.

*(The Third Man and Carl walk rapidly, not glancing at each other. Carl stops; The Third Man stops a few paces behind. Carl walks; The Third Man walks. Carl stops; The Third*

*Man stops. Finally, they face each other and meet. Quickly, looking surreptitiously around, Carl and The Third Man stroke each other's stuffed rabbits. They quickly part and walk off in opposite directions.*

*Anna rushes to center stage, looking in both directions.)*

ANNA: I tried to follow the man in the trench coat, and crossed behind him over the Amstel, but I lost sight of him in the crowd of men wearing trench coats and sunglasses.

I want some answers from my brother. Whatever trouble he's in, he has to share it with me. I want some answers back at the hotel. He's going to talk.

## XVIII.

CARL: Questions sur le dialogue. You must learn. Sie müssen lernen.

*(Anna enters the empty hotel room. On the bed, propped up on pillows, lies a stuffed rabbit.)*

ANNA: Carl? Carl? Are you back? Carl?

*(Anna stops and looks at the stuffed rabbit.)*

CARL *(From the side)*: You were not permitted to play with dolls; dolls are for girls. You played with your sister's dolls until your parents found out. They gave you a stuffed animal—a thin line was drawn. Rabbits were an acceptable surrogate for little boys. You named him Jo-Jo.

You could not sleep without him. Jo-Jo traveled with you to the seashore, to the hotel in New York City when you were seven, to your first summer camp.

He did not have the flaxen plastic hair of your sister's Betsey-Wetsy, but he had long, furry ears, soft white on one side, pink satin inside. He let you stroke them. He never

betrayed you. He taught you to trust in contact. You will
love him always.

ANNA *(Moves toward the stuffed rabbit)*: My brother left you
behind, did he? Alone at last. Okay, bunny, now you're
going to talk. I want some answers. What have you got that's
so important?

*(Just as Anna reaches for the stuffed rabbit, The Third Man
[in trench coat, sunglasses and black gloves] steps out into
the room.)*

THE THIRD MAN *(Threateningly)*: I wouldn't do that, if I were you.
   *(Anna screams in surprise)*
   Now listen. Where is your brother? I have a message for
him. Tell him he's running out of time. Do you understand?
   *(Anna, scared, nods)*
   Good. He'd better not try to dupe us. We're willing to
arrange a swap—his sister for the rabbit. Tell him we're
waiting for him in Vienna. And tell him he'd better bring the
rabbit to the other side.

*(The Third Man disappears. Anna, shaken, sits on the bed
and holds the stuffed rabbit. She strokes it for comfort. Carl
enters, in a frenzy. He carries his stuffed rabbit. Anna stares
as Carl tosses the decoy rabbit away.)*

CARL: Don't ask me any questions. I can't tell you what's hap-
pening. Are you able to travel? Good. We have to leave
Amsterdam tonight. There's a train in an hour. We'll go to
Germany. Are you packed?

## XIX.

ANNA AND THE THIRD MAN *(Simultaneously)*: Wann fahrt der
nächste Zug nach Hamburg?

*(German band music swells as Anna and Carl sit in their rail-road compartment, side by side. Anna, pale, holds the stuffed rabbit in her lap.)*

CARL: Ah, Saxony, Bavaria, the Black Forest, the Rhineland...I love them all. I think perhaps now would be a good time to show the slides.

ANNA: I'm so sorry. I hate it when people do this to me.

CARL: Nonsense. People like to see slides of other people's trips. These are in no particular order. We'll only show a few, just to give a taste of the German countryside.

ANNA: Carl took over two hour's worth of slides.

CARL: If you'll just dim the lights, please.

*(The Third Man wheels in the projector and operates it throughout the travelogue.)*

CARL: Well. Bonn's as good a place to start as anywhere. This is the view from our snug little hotel we stayed in. The gate-way to the Rhine, the birthplace of Beethoven and the resting place of Schumann.

*(SLIDE: The view of downtown Baltimore from the Ramada Inn near Johns Hopkins Hospital, overlooking the industrial harbor.)*

ANNA: Looks a lot like Baltimore to me.

CARL: My sister jests. As you can see in the slide, one night we splurged and stayed in a rather dear inn near the Drachenfels Mountains, where Lord Byron had sported.

*(SLIDE: A close-up of the balcony railing looking into the Ramada Inn hotel room.)*

ANNA *(Deadpan)*: This is the room I slept in while I stayed with my brother Carl.

(SLIDE: *Gutted ruins of inner-city Baltimore near the Jones-Fall Expressway; rubble and obvious urban blight.*)

CARL: Alas, poor Köln. Practically wiped out by airplane raids during World War II, and yet, out of this destruction, the cathedral of Köln managed to survive—one of the most beautiful Gothic churches in the world, with a superb altar painted by the master artist of Köln, Stefan Lochner.

(SLIDE: *An impoverished storefront church, a black Evangelical sect in Baltimore.*)

CARL: Let's see—what do we have next?

(SLIDE: *A Sabrett hotdog cart with its blue and orange umbrella in front of Johns Hopkins Hospital.*)

CARL: Oh, yes. Let's talk about the food. Whereas I snapped mementos of the regal pines of the Black Forest, Anna insisted on taking photos of everything she ate.
ANNA: I can remember things I feel.
CARL: Well, then, let's talk about the food. Germany has a more robust gustatory outlook than the delicate palate of France. The Germans positively celebrate the pig from snout to tail. I could not convince Anna to sample the Sulperknochen, which is a Rheingau concoction of ears, snout, tail and feet.
ANNA: Ugh.

(SLIDE: *A close-up of a vendor placing a hotdog on a bun and lathering it with mustard; there are canned sodas in a wide variety.*)

CARL: And of course, everything is washed down with beer.

(SLIDE: *Anna sipping a Bud Light.*)

ANNA: It was delicious.

CARL: Enough of food. May we talk about culture, sister, dear? Next slide, please.

(SLIDE: *The Maryland National Armory; the state penitentiary.*)

CARL: Ah, Heidelberg. Dueling scars and castles. Spectacular ruin which serves as the locale for open-air concerts and fireworks...

(SLIDE: *The Baltimore smokestack.*)

CARL: And by a quaint cable car, you can reach the peak at Königstuhl, 2,000 feet high, with its breathtaking view of the Neckar Valley.

(SLIDE: *The Bromo Seltzer tower in Baltimore.*)

(SLIDE: *The interstate highways viewed from the tower.*)

CARL: Every cobblestoned street, every alleyway, was so pristine and clean.

(SLIDE: *The rowhouses on Monument Street.*)

(SLIDE: *A corridor of Johns Hopkins Hospital, outside the basement laboratories.*)

CARL: Wasn't it, Anna?

ANNA (*Deadpan*): Yes. Sterile.

(SLIDE: *A hospital aide washing the floor.*)

CARL: Even the Black Forest looked swept. We splurged once again and stayed at the Waldhorn Post here, outside of Wildbad.

(SLIDE: *Exterior of Johns Hopkins Hospital.*)

CARL: The hotel dates back to 1145—the chef there is renown for his game dishes.

(SLIDE: *Anna in front of a vending machine dispensing wrapped sandwiches in the Johns Hopkins Hospital cafeteria.*)

ANNA: I wasn't too hungry.

CARL: I was ravenous.

(SLIDE: *Route 95 outside the harbor tunnel; the large toll signs are visible.*)

CARL: Let's see—the Romantic Road...Die Romantishe Strasse...a trek through picture-book Bavaria and the Allgau Alpen... Füssen to Wurzburg.

ANNA: Honey, perhaps they've seen enough. It's hard to sit through this many—

CARL: Wait. Just one more. They've got to see Neuschwanstein, built by mad King Ludwig II. It's so rococo it's Las Vegas.

(SLIDE: *The castle at Disneyland.*)

CARL: I believe that Ludwig was reincarnated in the twentieth century as Liberace.

    Wait a moment, that's not the castle.

ANNA: Yes, it is.

CARL *(Upset)*: It looks like—how did that get in here?

ANNA: I don't know which castle you're referring to, but it's definitely a castle.

(SLIDE: *A close-up of the castle, with a large Mickey Mouse in the picture.*)

CARL: That's not funny, Anna! Are you making fun of me?
ANNA: Don't get upset.

(SLIDE: *Donald Duck has joined Mickey Mouse with tourists.*)

CARL: I went to Europe. I walked through Bavaria and the Black Forest. I combed through Neuschwanstein! I did these things, and I will remember the beauty of it all my life! I don't appreciate your mockery!
ANNA: It's just a little—
CARL: You went through Germany on your back. All you'll remember are hotel ceilings. You can show them your Germany!

(*He rushes off, angry.*)

ANNA: Sometimes my brother gets upset for no apparent reason. Some wires cross in his brain and he—I'm sorry. Lights, please.

(*The Third Man wheels the projector offstage.*)

ANNA: I would like to show you my impressions of Germany. They were something like this...

## XX. In Munich.

*Anna is under the sheet beside the Munich Virgin, who is very young.*

ANNA: Are you comfortable?
MUNICH VIRGIN: Ja, ja...danke.
ANNA: Good. Have you been the bellhop here for a long time?

MUNICH VIRGIN: Not so very long a time. My vater owns the hotel, and says I must learn and work very hard. Soon I will be given the responsibility of the front desk.

ANNA: My. That's exciting.

*(Pause)*

Are you cold?

MUNICH VIRGIN: Nein. Just a...klein nervös. My English is not so very good.

ANNA: Is this your first time? You always remember your first time.

*(Pause)*

I'm very honored.

*(Pause)*

Listen. I'm a schoolteacher. May I tell you something? A little lesson? When you're a much older man, and you've loved many women, you'll be a wonderful lover if you're just a little bit nervous...like you are right now. Because it will always be the first time.

MUNICH VIRGIN: You are a very nice woman.

ANNA: The human body is a wonderful thing. Like yours. Like mine. The beauty of the body heals all the sickness, all the bad things that happen to it. And I really want you to feel this. Because if you feel it, you'll remember it. And then maybe you'll remember me.


## XXI.


*Anna and the Munich Virgin rise. Carl gets into the bed with his stuffed rabbit. Anna gets ready to leave.*


THE THIRD MAN: Conjugations of the verb *verlassen*. To leave, to abandon, to forsake. The present tense.

CARL: Are you leaving me alone?

ANNA: Yes. Just for a little while. I need to take a walk. I'm restless. It's perfectly safe.

CARL: Okay, sweetie. Don't be too long. Bunny and I are ready for bed.

ANNA: I won't stay out long. I'll be right back.

THE THIRD MAN: The future tense of the verb *verlassen*.

CARL: Will you be leaving me alone again tonight? I'm ready for bed.

ANNA: I will be leaving you alone. Just for a little while.

CARL: Who will it be tonight? The bellhop? The desk clerk? Or the maître d'?

ANNA: Don't be mean. You said you didn't make judgments.

CARL: I don't. I just want to spend time with you.

ANNA: I'll be back in time for a bedtime story.

THE THIRD MAN: The past tense of the verb *verlassen*.

CARL: Again? Again? You went out last night. And the night before.

ANNA: I can't help it. I've been a good girl for the past thirty years. Now I want to make up for lost time.

CARL: And what am I supposed to do while you're out traipsing around with every Thomas, Deiter und Heinrich?

ANNA: Hug bunny.

THE THIRD MAN: There are three moods of the verb *verlassen*: the indicative, the imperative and the subjunctive. Anna and Carl are never in the same mood.

CARL: Leave me alone.

ANNA: Carl, don't be like that.

CARL: Why? It doesn't matter what I want. You are going to leave.

ANNA: I never stay out very long.

CARL: All I can say is if this establishment charges us for room service, they've got some nerve—

ANNA: I've got to take what opportunities come along—

CARL: I wish you wouldn't go—

ANNA: Please understand. I don't have much time. I spend as much time with you as I can, but while I still have my health…please?

## XXII.

THE THIRD MAN: As children they fought.

CARL: We never fought, really.

ANNA: Not in a physical way. He was a sickly child.

CARL: She was very willful.

ANNA: No roughhousing. But he knew all of my weak points. My secret openings. He could be ruthless.

CARL: She'd cry at the slightest thing.

ANNA: He has a very sharp tongue.

CARL: But when one of you is very, very sick, you can't fight. It's not fair. You've got to hold it in. We never fight.

ANNA: But we had a doozy in the hotel room in Berlin.

CARL: Well, my god, Anna, even though you're sick, I have the right to get angry.

ANNA: We'd been traveling too long. We were cranky. The rooms were closing in.

CARL: I'm just saying that we should spend a little more time together. I don't get to see you alone enough. You're always restless.

ANNA: Fine. You go out without me for a change.

CARL: I'm going out for a walk.

ANNA *(Starting to weep)*: I don't care.

CARL: When she was little, this would be the time I'd bribe her. With a comic book or an ice cream. I always had pennies saved up for these little contingencies.

ANNA: But sometimes, for the sake of my pride, I would be inconsolable. I would rush off and then feel just awful alone. Why didn't I take the bribe?

*(To Carl)* I'm going out.

CARL: To fuck?

ANNA: No, dear. The passive voice is used to emphasize the subject, to indicate the truth of the generalization. I'm going out. To get fucked.

**XXIII.**

*Music: Kurt Weill.*

*Anna goes over to a small cabaret table. There is a telephone on the table. The Radical Student Activist sits at another identical table, smoking, watching her.*

ANNA: I'm going to enjoy Berlin without him. I'll show him. I'm going to be carefree, totally without scruples. I'll pretend I've never taught first-graders.

*(Beat)*

I'm going to have a perfectly miserable time.

*(The Radical Student Activist picks up the telephone. The telephone at Anna's table rings.)*

ANNA: Oh my goodness. My miserable time is calling me.

*(Picks up the phone)* Yes?

RADICAL STUDENT ACTIVIST: Are you alone, Fraülein?

ANNA: Well, uh, actually...yes, I am.

RADICAL STUDENT ACTIVIST: Gut. Du willst mal richtig durchgefickt werden, ja?

ANNA: I'm sorry. I don't speak a word of German.

*(The Radical Student Activist laughs.)*

RADICAL STUDENT ACTIVIST: Ja. Even better. I said, would you like to get fucked?

ANNA: Do you always come on to single women like that?

RADICAL STUDENT ACTIVIST: Would you like it better if I bought you tall drinks with umbrellas? Told to you the stories of how hard a time my parents had during the war? Tell you how exciting I find foreign women, how they are the real women, not like the pale northern mädchen here at home? How absolutely bourgeois.

ANNA: I see. Why do you come here?

RADICAL STUDENT ACTIVIST: I don't come here for the overpriced drinks. I come here because of the bored western women who come here, who leave their tired businessmen husbands in the hotel rooms behind.

ANNA: You're cute. In a hostile way.

RADICAL STUDENT ACTIVIST: Fucking is a revolutionary act.

ANNA: Your hovel or my hotel?

## XXIV.

*In the hotel room. Anna, awake, lies in the middle of the bed. To her left, Carl sleeps, curled up. To her right, the Radical Student Activist, curled on her breast, slumbers.*

*Anna is awake with an insomniacal desperation.*

ANNA *(Singing softly)*: Two and two are four; four and four are eight; eight and eight are sixteen; sixteen and sixteen are thirty-two...

RADICAL STUDENT ACTIVIST *(Groggy)*: Wo ist die Toilette?

*(The Radical Student Activist rises and stumbles stage left.)*

ANNA: In lovemaking, he's all fury and heat. His North Sea pounding against your Dreamer. And when you look up and see his face, red and huffing, it's hard to imagine him ever having been a newborn, tiny, wrinkled and seven pounds.

That is, until afterwards. When he rises from sleep and he walks into the bathroom. And there he exposes his soft little derrière, and you can still see the soft baby flesh.

*(As the Radical Student Activist comes back into the room)* I've got a put a name to that behind. What's your name? Wie heissen Sie?

RADICAL STUDENT ACTIVIST *(Starts dressing in a hurry)*: Auf Wiedersehn. Next thing you'll ask for my telephone number.

ANNA: No, I won't. I was just curious—

RADICAL STUDENT ACTIVIST: Ja, ja...und then my sign of the zodiac. I'll get cards from Hallmark und little scribblings like "I'll never forget the night we shared."

ANNA: Forget it.

RADICAL STUDENT ACTIVIST: There is something radical in two complete strangers committing biological necessity without having to give into bourgeois conventions of love, without breeding to produce workers for a capitalist system, without the benediction of the church, the family, the bosses—

ANNA: I have something to confess to you. I lied to you.

RADICAL STUDENT ACTIVIST: About what?

ANNA: I'm not here on business. I don't specialize in corporate takeovers. I don't work on Wall Street. I only told you that because I thought that was what you wanted to hear.

RADICAL STUDENT ACTIVIST: Okay. So you do estate planning? Income tax?

ANNA: No. You just committed a revolutionary act with a first-grade schoolteacher who lives in low-income housing. And I'm tired. I think you should go.

RADICAL STUDENT ACTIVIST: And your husband?

ANNA: Not too loud. And he's not my husband. He's my brother. A maiden librarian for the San Francisco Public.

*(As the Radical Student Activist starts to leave)* And by the way—the missionary position does not a revolution make.

*(The Radical Student Activist leaves. Anna, depressed, lies down. Carl rises from the bed.)*

## XXV.

CARL: And as she lay in the bed, sleepless, it swept over her—the way her classroom smelled early in the morning, before the children came. It smelled of chalk dust—

THE THIRD MAN: It smelled of Crayola wax, crushed purple and green—

CARL: The cedar of hamster cage shavings—

THE THIRD MAN: The sweet wintergreen of LePage's paste—

CARL: The wooden smell of the thick construction paper—

THE THIRD MAN: The spillings of sticky orange drink and sour milk—

THE THIRD MAN AND CARL *(Simultaneously)*: And the insidious smell of first-grader pee.

CARL: It smelled like heaven.

ANNA: And the first thing I did each morning was put up the weather map for today on the board under the flag. A bright, smiling sun or Miss Cloud or Mr. Umbrella. On special days I put up Suzy Snowflake. And when I opened my desk drawer, scattered like diamonds on the bottom were red, silver and gold stars.

> *(Beat)*

> I want to go home. Carl, I want to go home.

CARL: Soon, sweetie. Very soon.

ANNA: I've had enough. I've seen all of the world I want to see. I want to wake up in my own bed. I want to sit with you at home and we'll watch the weather. And we'll wait.

CARL: We've come so far. We have to at least go to Vienna. Do you think you can hold out long enough to meet Dr. Todesrocheln?

> *(Anna, miserable and homesick, nods)*

> That a girl. I promise you don't have to undertake his…hydrotherapy unless you decide to. I have a friend in Vienna, a college chum, who might be able to get us some blackmarket stuff. It's worth a shot.

ANNA: Then you'll take me home?

CARL: Then I'll take you home.

## XXVI.

*Music: A song such as the zither theme from* The Third Man.
*Carl and Anna stand, with their luggage, in front of a door buzzer.*

CARL: First we'll just look up Harry. Then we'll cab over to Dr. Todesrocheln.

*(Carl rings the buzzer. They wait. Carl rings the buzzer again. They wait. An aging Concierge comes out.)*

CARL: Entschuldigung. Wir suchen Harry Lime? Do you speak English?

CONCIERGE: Nein. Ich spreche kein Englisch.

*(Carl and the Concierge start to shout as if the other one was deaf.)*

CARL: Herr Lime? Do you know him? Herr Harry Lime?

CONCIERGE: Ach. Ach. Ja, Herr Harry Lime. You come...too spät.

CARL: He's gone? Too spät?

CONCIERGE: Fünf minuten too spät. Er ist tot—

CARL: What?

CONCIERGE: Ja. Ein auto mit Harry splatz-machen auf der Strasse. Splatz!

ANNA: Splatz!?

CARL: Splatz?!

*(It dawns on Carl and Anna what the Concierge is saying.)*

CONCIERGE: Ja, ja. Er geht über die Strasse, und ein auto... sppplllaattz!

ANNA: Oh, my god.

CONCIERGE *(Gesturing with hands)*: Ja. Er hat auch eine rabbit. Herr rabbit auch—spplllaattz! They are...diggen ein grab in den Boden. Jetz.

CARL: Now? You saw this happen?

CONCIERGE: Ja. I...saw it mit meinen own Augen. Splatz.

    *(As he exits)* Splatzen, splatzen, über alles...

CARL: Listen, darling. I want you to take a cab to the doctor's office.

ANNA: Where are you going?

CARL: Ich verlasse. I'll find out what happened to Harry.

ANNA: I wish you wouldn't leave...

CARL: I'll come back. Okay?

## XXVII.

*Anna climbs onto a table and gathers a white paper sheet around her. She huddles.*

ANNA: Some things are the same in every country. You're scared when you see the doctor, here in Vienna just like in Baltimore. And they hand you the same paper cup to fill, just like in America. Then you climb up onto the same cold metal table, and they throw a sheet around you and you feel very small. And just like at home, they tell you to wait. And you wait.

*(As Anna waits, dwarfed on the table, the scene with Harry Lime and Carl unfolds. Music, such as* The Third Man *theme, comes up.)*

## XXVIII.
### On the Ferris Wheel in the Prater.

*Carl holds the stuffed rabbit closely.*

CARL: Why are we meeting here?

HARRY LIME: Have you looked at the view from up here? It's quite inspiring. No matter how old I get, I always love the Ferris wheel.

CARL: I just came from your funeral.

HARRY LIME: I'm touched, old man. Was it a nice funeral?

CARL: What are you doing?

HARRY LIME: It's best not to ask too many questions. The police were beginning to do that. It's extremely convenient, now and then in a man's career, to die. I've gone underground. So if you want to meet me, you have to come here. No one asks questions here.

CARL: Can you help us?

*(Harry Lime at first does not answer. He looks at the view.)*

HARRY LIME: Where is your sister? She left you alone?

CARL: She's—she needs her rest. You were my closest friend in college.

HARRY LIME: I'll be straight with you. I can give you the drugs— but it won't help. It won't help at all. Your sister's better off with that quack Todesrocheln—we call him the Yellow Queen of Vienna—she might end up drinking her own piss, but it won't kill her.

CARL: But I thought you had the drugs—

HARRY LIME: Oh, I do. And they cost a pretty penny. For a price, I can give them to you. At a discount for old times. But you have to know, we make them up in my kitchen.

CARL: Jesus.

HARRY LIME: Why not? People will pay for these things. When they're desperate people will eat peach pits or aloe or egg protein—they'll even drink their own piss. It gives them hope.

CARL: How can you do this?

HARRY LIME: Listen, old man, if you want to be a millionaire, you go into real estate. If you want to be a billionaire, you sell hope. Nowadays the only place a fellow can make a decent career of it is in Mexico and Europe.

CARL: That's...disgusting.

HARRY LIME: Look. I thought you weren't going to be...sentimental about this. It's a business. You have to have the right perspective. Like from up here...the people down on the street are just tiny little dots. And if you could charge a thousand dollars, wouldn't you push the drugs?

I could use a friend I can trust to help me.

CARL: When we were at Hopkins together, I thought you were God. You could hypnotize us into doing anything, and it would seem...charming. "Carl, old man," you'd say, "just do it." Cutting classes, cribbing exams, shoplifting, stupid undergraduate things—and I would do it. Without knowing the consequences. I would do it.

THE THIRD MAN: Oh, you knew the consequences, old man. You knew. You chose not to think about them.

CARL: I've grown old before my time from the consequences, I'm turning you in.

HARRY LIME: I wouldn't do that, old man.

*(Pats a bulge on the inside of his trench coat)* By the time you hit the ground, you'll be just a tiny little dot. *(Carl and Harry Lime look at each other, waiting)*

And I think you have something I want. The rabbit, bitte.

CARL: No. You're not getting it. I'm taking it with me.

*(Harry Lime puts his arms in position for a waltz and begins to sway, seductively.)*

HARRY LIME: Come on, give it up. Come to my arms, my only one. Dance with me, my beloved, my sweet—

*(Carl takes the stuffed rabbit and threatens to throw it out the window of the Ferris wheel. A Strauss waltz plays very loudly, and Harry Lime and Carl waltz-struggle for the rabbit. Carl is pushed and Harry Lime waltzes off with the rabbit.)*

## XXIX.
## Meanwhile, Back at Dr. Todesrocheln.

ANNA: You begin to hope that the wait is proportionate to the medical expertise.

My God. My feet are turning blue. Where am I? An HMO?

*(Waits)*

The problem with being an adult is that you never forget why you're waiting. When I was a child, I could wait blissfully unaware for hours. I used to read signs and transpose letters, or count tiles in the floor. And in the days before I could read, I would make up stories about my hands—Mr. Left and Mr. Right.

*(Beat)*

*(Demonstrates)* Mr. Left would provoke Mr. Right. Mr. Right would ignore it. The trouble would escalate, until my hands were battling each other to the death.

*(Beat)*

Then one of them would weep. Finally, they became friends again, and they'd dance.

*(Anna's two hands dance together. She is unaware that Dr. Todesrocheln has entered and is watching her. He clears his throat. He wears a very dirty lab coat with pockets filled with paper and a stale doughnut. He wears a white fright wig and glasses. He also wears one sinister black glove. With relish, he carries a flask of a golden liquid.)*

ANNA: Oh, thank goodness.

DR. TODESROCHELN: Ja. So happy to meet you. Such an interesting specimen. I congratulate you. Very, very interesting.

ANNA: Thank you.

DR. TODESROCHELN: We must have many more such specimens from you—for the urinocryoscopy, the urinometer, the urinoglucosometer, the uroacidimeter, uroazotometer, und mein new acquirement in der laboratorium—ein urophosphometer.

ANNA: My goodness.

*(Dr. Todesrocheln has put the flask down on a table. Quietly, his left hand reaches for it; the right hand stops the left.)*

DR. TODESROCHELN: Ja. Nowadays, we have learned to discover the uncharted mysteries of the fluids discharged through the urethra. We have been so primitive in the past. Doctors once could only analyze by taste and smell—but thanks to the advancement of medical science, there are no limits to our thirst for knowledge.

ANNA: Uh-huh.

*(Dr. Todesrocheln's left hand seizes the flask. Trembling, with authority, his right hand replaces the flask on the table, and soothes the left hand into quietude.)*

DR. TODESROCHELN: So much data has been needlessly, carelessly destroyed in the past—the medical collections of Ravensbruck senselessly annihilated—and that is why as a scientist, I must be exacting in our measurements and recordings.

ANNA: What can I hope to find out from these...specimens?

DR. TODESROCHELN: Ah, yes—the layman must have his due! Too much pure research und no application makes Jack...macht Jack...*(Loses his train of thought)*

Fräulein Anna—I may call you Fräulein Anna? Let us look at the body as an alchemist, taking in straw and mud und schweinefleisch and processing it into liquid gold which purifies the body. You might say that the sickness of the body can only be cured by the health of the body. To your health!

*(His left hand seizes the flask in a salute, and raises the flask to his lips. In time, the right hand brings the flask down. A brief struggle. It appears the flask might spill, but at last the right hand triumphs.)*

ANNA: You know, even though I really grew up in the suburbs of Baltimore, I like to think of myself as an open-minded person—

DR. TODESROCHELN: The ancient Greeks knew that the aromatic properties of the fluid could reveal the imbalances of the soul itself...

*(The left hand sneaks toward the flask.)*

ANNA: I'm always very eager to try new foods, or see the latest John Waters film—
DR. TODESROCHELN: Its use in the purification rites of the Aztecs is, of course, so well known that it need not be mentioned...

*(The hand has grasped the flask and begins to inch it off the table.)*

ANNA: And whenever I meet someone who cross-dresses, I always compliment him on his shoes or her earrings—
DR. TODESROCHELN: It is the first golden drop that marks the infant's identity separate from the womb.

*(The hand has slipped the flask beneath the table; his right hand is puzzled.)*

ANNA: But still, it's important to know where your threshold is...and I think we're coming dangerously close to mine...
DR. TODESROCHELN: Until the last precious amber releases the soul from the body—ashes to ashes, drop to drop—excuse me—

*(His left hand, with the flask, swings in an arc behind his body. He swivels his body to the flask, his back turned to us. We can hear him drink in secrecy.)*

DR. TODESROCHELN *(With his back turned)*: Ahhh...

*(He orders himself. Composed, he turns around to face Anna again, and demurely sets down the flask. Its level is noticeably lower.*
  *Anna is aghast.)*

DR. TODESROCHELN: I can sense your concern. I have been prattling on without regard to questions you must surely have—

ANNA: Is that your real hair?

DR. TODESROCHELN: Of course. I can not promise results, but first we must proceed by securing samples—

ANNA: I don't believe that's your real hair.

DR. TODESROCHELN: I will need first of all twenty-four hours of your time for a urononcometry—

ANNA *(Increasingly scared)*: You look familiar to me—

DR. TODESROCHELN: Although I can tell you from a first taste— er, test—that your uroammonica level is high, not unpleasantly so, but full-bodied—

ANNA: Oh, my god...I think I know who you are...you're... you're...

*(Anna rises to snatch his toupee. Dr. Todesrocheln suddenly stands, menacing.*
*The light changes.)*

DR. TODESROCHELN: WO IST DEIN BRUDER?

*(He takes off his wig and glasses and appears as the Doctor in the first scene, peeling off the black gloves to reveal latex gloves underneath.)*

DR. TODESROCHELN: You fool! You left your brother in the room alone! WO IST DEIN BRUDER?

*(Music: The Emperor Waltz plays at a very loud volume.*
*Anna, frightened, races from Dr. Todesrocheln's office to the hotel room. We see Carl, lying stiff beneath a white sheet. To the tempo of the Strauss, Anna tries to wake him. He does not respond. Anna takes off the sheet and forces him into a sitting position, the stuffed rabbit clenched beneath his arm. Carl remains sitting, stiff, eyes open, wooden. He is still in his pajamas. Then he slumps. Anna raises him again. He remains upright for a beat, and begins to fall. Anna stops*

*him, presses his body against hers, pulls his legs over the bed, tries to stand him up. Frozen, his body tilts against hers. She tries to make him cross the floor, his arms around her neck. She positions him in a chair, but his legs are locked in a perpendicular angle and will not touch the floor. She presses his legs to the floor. He mechanically springs forward. Then suddenly, like the doll in E. T. A. Hoffmann, the body of Carl becomes animated, but with a strange, automatic life of its own. Carl begins to waltz with Anna. Gradually, he winds down, and faltering, falls back to the bed. There is the sound of a loud alarm clock; the Doctor enters, and covers Carl with a sheet. Then he pulls a white curtain in front of the scene, as the stage lights become, for the first time, harsh, stark and white.)*

## XXX. In the Hospital Lounge.

*The Doctor holds the stuffed rabbit and travel brochures in his hands. He awkwardly peels off his latex gloves.*

DOCTOR: I'm sorry. There was nothing we could do.

ANNA: Yes. I know.

DOCTOR: I thought you might want to take this along with you.

*(The Doctor hands Anna the stuffed rabbit.)*

ANNA *(To the stuffed rabbit)*: There you are!
     *(Hugs the stuffed rabbit and sees the Doctor watching her)* It's Jo-Jo. My brother's childhood rabbit. I brought it to the hospital as a little surprise. I thought it might make him feel better.

DOCTOR: Sometimes little things become important, when nothing else will help...

ANNA: Yes.
     *(They pause and stand together awkwardly)*
     At least Carl went in his sleep. I guess that's a blessing.

DOCTOR: If one has to die from this particular disease, there are worse ways to go than pneumonia.

ANNA: I never would have believed what sickness can do to the body.

> *(Pause)*

> Well, Doctor, I want to thank you for all you've done for my brother.

DOCTOR: I wish I could do more. By the way, housekeeping found these brochures in your brother's bedside table. I didn't know if they were important.

ANNA *(Takes the brochures)*: Ah, yes. The brochures for Europe. I've never been abroad. We're going to go when he gets— *(Stops herself)*

> *(With control)* I must learn to use the past tense. We would have gone had he gotten better.

DOCTOR: Anna—I may call you Anna? I, uh, if there's anything I can do...

ANNA: Thank you, but there's nothing you can do—

DOCTOR: I mean, I really would like it if you'd call me for coffee, or if you just want to talk about all this...

*(The Doctor trails off. Anna looks at him. She smiles. He squirms.)*

ANNA: You're very sweet. But no, I don't think so. Not now. I feel it's simply not safe for me right now to see anyone. Thanks again and goodbye.

*(Anna starts to exit. The Doctor, wistful, watches her go. The lighting begins to change back to the dreamy atmosphere of the first scene. Softly, a Strauss waltz begins. Carl, perfectly well, waits for Anna. He is dressed in Austrian military regalia. They waltz off as the lights dim.)*

END OF PLAY

# And Baby Makes Seven

*And Baby Makes Seven* was produced January 1984 by Theatre with Teeth at the 18th Street Playhouse in New York City. The director was Paula Vogel and the cast was as follows:

| | |
|---|---|
| PETER | Ted Montague |
| RUTH | Sondra Allen |
| ANNA | Cary Bickley |

The play was produced February 1986 at Theatre Rhinoceros in San Francisco. The director was Kris Gannon, with sets by Vola Ruben, lights by Cayenne Wood and costumes by Ann Marie Leimer. The cast was as follows:

| | |
|---|---|
| PETER | Michael DeMartini |
| RUTH | Sandra Langsner |
| ANNA | Karen Lynn Seaton |

*And Baby Makes Seven* opened at the Lucille Lortel Theatre in New York City, May 1993. It was produced by Circle Repertory Company under Tanya Berezin, Artistic Director. It was directed by Calvin Skaggs, with sets by Derek McLane, lights by Peter Kaczorowski and costumes by Walker Hicklin. The cast was as follows:

| | |
|---|---|
| PETER | Peter Frechette |
| RUTH | Mary Mara |
| ANNA | Cherry Jones |

FOR DAVID

CHARACTERS

PETER LEVEN: Has the appearance of a precocious child.

RUTH ABRAMS: Short, dark and intense.

ANNA EPSTEIN: A little overweight right now.


THE CHILDREN

CECIL BARTHOLOMEW: Age 9, genius IQ. Played by Anna.

HENRI DUMONT: Age 8, French accent. Played by Ruth.

ORPHAN MCDERMOTT: Age 7, with a stutter. Played by Ruth.


THE SETTING

A loft apartment in New York City. A window,
which leads onto a fire escape.


THE TIME

The play takes place in the present.

## Prologue to Act One

*In the darkness, we hear three children talking in their beds. There is a glow from a clown night-light.*

HENRI: And so that is how babies come to be made.

CECIL: Oh, God.

HENRI: Well, it is!

CECIL: You've got it all wrong, Henri.

HENRI: No, I do not. Do I Orphanne?

ORPHAN: I-I-I d-d-don't kn-know.

HENRI: Well, Cecil, if you're so smart, how do you think babies are made?

CECIL: Well, it's actually a complicated, sophisticated process. A marvel of human technology.

ORPHAN: Umm-hmm.

CECIL: The process starts with intercourse between two humans— a male and a female.

HENRI: Get to the good part. *(Laughs raucously)*

CECIL: The male inserts his erect member into the female's vagina and then begins to...uh, oscillate the member with increasing rapidity until the...uh, friction causes orgasm.

HENRI: Oh, barf.

CECIL: At orgasm, thousands of millions of sperm are released and swim their way upstream to the egg. Only one survives. It's kind of a microcosm of Wall Street.

HENRI: This is boring.

CECIL: This is science. The sperm fertilizes the egg, which becomes a fetus, which becomes a baby, until finally, the female goes into contractions—

HENRI: Wait a minute, Cecil. Are you telling us that the baby comes out of the lady's wee-wee hole?

CECIL: It's not a wee-wee hole. It's a vagina.

HENRI: Do you expect us to believe this?

CECIL: It's the truth!

HENRI: Orphanne? What do you vote for?

ORPHAN: I vote for th-the eggplant.

HENRI: Okay. That makes two votes for the eggplant. You're wrong, Cecil.

CECIL: You can't vote down the truth!

HENRI: Yes, we can...This is a democracy. Maybe you came from a wee-wee hole. We came from the eggplant.

ORPHAN: W-w-wee-wee!

*(Henri and Orphan begin to laugh.)*

HENRI: Cecil's a wee-wee head!

*(Henri and Orphan erupt in laughter again.)*

CECIL: Stop it!! Stop it!! Or I'll make you stop!!

HENRI: Wee-wee head!!

*(The kids continue to laugh. Suddenly, a door stage right cracks open in a stream of light. We see the figure of Peter, who closes the door behind him.)*

PETER: All right, boys. What's going on?

HENRI: Cecil's a wee-wee head!

PETER: Henri. Orphan. Settle down. It's time to go to sleep.

CECIL: Uncle Peter! Tell them! Make them stop! Tell them!

PETER: Tell them what, Cecil?

CECIL: How babies are made.

PETER: Oh. Well, uh, I think that's something you should discuss with Anna.

HENRI: Uncle Peter, Cecil used the V-word.

PETER: The V-word?

HENRI: For a lady's—you know.

CECIL: Vagina. Vagina. It's not a dirty word. It's clinical.

HENRI: That makes you a vagina head.

*(Henri and Orphan erupt again.)*

CECIL: Uncle Peter! Tell them! Please! Man to man!

ORPHAN: M-m-man t-t-to m-man! Mmm-hmm.

PETER: If I tell you how, will you boys settle down and go to sleep?

HENRI: All right. Just make it good...

PETER: All right. It's your bedtime story. Okay? Well, when a man—

HENRI: Sit on my bed, please, Uncle Peter!!

PETER: All right.

*(Pause)*

Now, then, babies are made when a man—Hey! Henri!! What are you doing! Stop that!!

HENRI: I'm just hugging you.

PETER: Well, don't hug me there! Now then, when a man and a woman really, really love one another, they decide to make a baby to share that love—

CECIL: Oh, brother. Just tell it straight, will you, Uncle Peter?

PETER: Okay. A man rams his hot throbbing member into a woman and humps so hard that he explodes just as she's screaming: "Don't stop, don't stop!"—Is that straight enough for you?

*(Pause.)*

CECIL: Uncle Peter...you're not a well man.

*(Pause.)*

HENRI: Uncle Peter?

PETER:  Yes, Henri? What is it?

HENRI: I want to have your baby!!

*(Nursery music tinkles as lights fade up to Scene One.)*

## Scene One

*Day One.* A.M. *The kitchen. Peter, Anna and Ruth sit around the table. They are in the middle of a discussion.*

PETER: I think they have to go. That's all I'm saying!

RUTH: Look, Peter, you just waltz in here—

PETER: What's with the "waltz!" I've been here for a solid six months now—

RUTH: The boys have been here for a long, long time! And they'll be here for a long, long time to come—

ANNA: Honey, we should just hear Peter out—

RUTH: Peter—if they go, I go!

PETER: Look, this is nothing to get emotional about.

RUTH: This is something between Anna and me.

PETER: Not anymore it's not. We entered into a contract; now the three of us have equal say in the bringing up of our child.

ANNA: Honey—Peter doesn't think we're…well, that the way we talk to our children is healthy.

PETER: Imaginary children.

RUTH: What do you mean, not "healthy"?

PETER: I've just noticed that you're both doing it a lot more. Going into character. Now whenever I'm around those… "kids" are always with us.

RUTH: Well, Peter, you're one of the family now. Isn't that right, Anna?

ANNA: Honey—I think Peter has a point. We are doing the kids more often. All the time now.

PETER: Yes—it's become an obsession.

RUTH: I wouldn't call it that.

PETER: But you're doing it all the time!

RUTH: So what!! And it's not all the time. It's just a way of releasing anxieties…

PETER: Don't you think it would be better to address those anxieties directly?

RUTH: What the hell are you paying a hundred dollars an hour for?

PETER: I pay someone to listen to me. I don't go around talking to myself in a high tiny voice…Cecil, the child genius. Henri, from that movie—

RUTH: *The Red Balloon*—

PETER: Whatever it was. And on top of it all, this wild child raised by a pack of dogs. I say they have to go.

RUTH/HENRI: And I say to you—you—you are a big, fat wee-wee head!

PETER *(To Anna)*: You see? That's just the kind of thing I'm talking about.

ANNA: Look, the three of us have to work this out like mature, rational adults—

RUTH/HENRI: Wee-wee head!!

ANNA: Ruth. Please.

> *(Shifts her weight)* Ow. Damn. I don't believe it. I have to go to the bathroom. Again.

*(Anna gets up heavily to her feet; she is very pregnant. She exits. Pause.)*

PETER: We have to remember that she's peeing for two now.

*(Suddenly Ruth becomes Henri again.)*

RUTH/HENRI *(With great significance)*: Uncle Peter? I loved the bedtime story you told me last night. You know.

PETER: Oh.

RUTH/HENRI: Will you tell us the same story...tonight? And sit on my bed?

PETER: Ruth, I'm really not in the mood right now to play—

RUTH/HENRI: Can I sit in your lap?

PETER: Well, I'd really rather that you wouldn't—

*(Ruth/Henri sits in Peter's lap, wriggling suggestively.)*

PETER: What in the hell are you doing?

RUTH/HENRI: I'm finding a comfortable spot.
> *(Henri laughs)*
> It's so lumpy, Uncle Peter.

PETER: Ruth—get up—

RUTH/HENRI: But, Uncle Peter, don't you like little boys?

PETER: Well, of course I—no! Not like that—come on, get up, Henri—

RUTH/HENRI: But first you have to...give me something...

*(Anna comes into the room and sees Ruth in Peter's lap. As soon as Ruth sees Anna, she jumps up as Henri and throws her arms around Anna.)*

RUTH/HENRI: Anniah!

ANNA: Henri!! What were you doing to Uncle Peter?

RUTH/HENRI: Nothing.

ANNA: Were you bothering him again?

RUTH/HENRI: No. I didn't do nothing!

ANNA: Petey? Was Henri...bothering you again?

*(Henri appeals to Peter silently.)*

PETER: Ah...no.

ANNA: Okay. Because you know, Henri, that we had that talk about no g-r-o-p-i-n-g. Remember? Not even if Uncle Peter wants you to.

RUTH/HENRI: I would like to go to my room, please!

PETER: By all means, be our guest.

*(Ruth makes sounds of an offended Henri leaving the room, and slamming the door. Pause. Anna sits. Pause.)*

PETER: Look, maybe it's me...But I just think that the...the line between reality and you know...well, it's getting dangerously thin around here.

RUTH: We never do it out of the house. You know that.

PETER: That's not the point. What about when the baby comes? What kind of effect is it going to have on Emma or Nathan—

RUTH: What do you mean, Emma or Nathan? We haven't decided that yet. It might be Sigourney or Christopher—

ANNA: Oh, please, not this again. I don't give a damn what it's called. Just let it come out healthy.

RUTH/ORPHAN: I-I l-l-like th-the name Lassie.

ANNA: Yes, Orphan. That's a sweet name. But that's a name for a dog, honey.

RUTH/ORPHAN *(Cooing agreement)*: Mmm-hmm.

ANNA: You want to name your baby sister in honor of the stray dogs of Port Authority who found you and took care of you?

RUTH/ORPHAN *(Again, cooing)*: Mmm-hmm.

ANNA: Yes, sweetie, but we're bringing up the baby differently than you were. Remember when we found you behind a Greyhound bus last winter? Running on all fours and scratching with your hind legs? Well, your sister's going to have a much different upbringing than the dogs gave you.

PETER: That's for sure. No fleas for little baby Emma. Or Nathan.

*(Suddenly Ruth/Orphan leans over and bites Peter savagely.)*

PETER: Ow!! Goddamn!—

ANNA: Orphan, no!! Bad Boy!! You don't bite people! Now go to your room!!

PETER: Look at that! The skin is practically broken! Now they're biting me!!

RUTH: A flesh wound.

PETER: You bit me!

RUTH: Not me. Orphan. He's never going to break that habit.

PETER: I'm sitting here, bitten, and nobody cares! I'm trying to have a talk! I'm trying to take my responsibility seriously, like a grown man, and you two are—

ANNA/CECIL: Listen, Uncle Peter, calm down. You have to understand that you're hyperventilating from a very common syndrome.

PETER: Oh, Jesus. Now I get counseling from a nine-year-old doctoral candidate—

ANNA/CECIL: Okay, buddy. But I'm here. I just want you to know that. When you're having problems coping with those feelings of...of being extraneous in the face of—

ANNA AND RUTH: Woman Creating—

PETER: Shut the fuck up!!

*(There is silence.)*

ANNA/CECIL: Golly.

RUTH: Cecil, why don't you go join your other brothers in the other room? I think "Sesame Street" is on.

CECIL: Do you think I'm a child?

*(Noises of a wounded Cecil leaving the room. Pause.)*

ANNA: Petey? Do you want to talk?

PETER: No! No...I've got to get out.

RUTH: Oh, come on, Peter. We were only playing around—

PETER: I've got to go. I'm late. I'll...I'll see you later.

*(Peter storms out of the room. Pause. The women look at each other.)*

RUTH: He's got to learn how to relax.

## Scene Two

*Day One. Late that night. Anna sits at the table playing solitaire. There is a key in the door, and Peter enters, very softly, so as not to wake the women.*

ANNA: Peter?

*(Peter jumps. Looks very sheepish and somewhat guilty.)*

PETER: Oh...Hi.
    *(Pause)*
    You didn't have to wait up, you know.
ANNA: I didn't. Ruthie got worried when you didn't show for dinner.
PETER: Oh. Ah—I ate out.
ANNA *(Looking at him carefully)*: Uh-huh.
    *(Laughs)*
    I'll bet you did. Did you have a good time with the boys?

*(Peter becomes beet red.)*

PETER: Umm...well, not a bad time, you know...
ANNA: Promise me you're being careful...
PETER: I'm being so careful.
ANNA: How's your wound?—Are you still mad at us?
PETER: I wasn't mad. Just...just concerned.
ANNA: It's all going to work out fine.

PETER: I...have my doubts sometimes.

ANNA: Why?

PETER: Well, sometimes, with you and Ruth...I feel like I'm in the way.

ANNA: That's nonsense. We don't feel that way.

PETER: Maybe we made a mistake...threesomes never work.

ANNA: Now is not the time to get cold feet. You've been saying since college that you wanted to have a child...

PETER: I know, but—

ANNA *(In an intimate way)*: Wasn't it fun?

PETER: It was pretty funny, too.

ANNA: Oh, but also romantic. No turkey baster for little Emma. The bottle of champagne from Ruth, that little inn—

PETER: The innkeeper thinking we were newlyweds—

ANNA: Our little plots...The Nubian boy spread on a Persian rug, the English schoolboy being disciplined—which was your favorite?

PETER: Well, personally I liked the one you told me about the young Greek sailor, swabbing the deck on his knees in the hot Mediterranean sun...

ANNA: Oh, yes, that one was good, too.

*(Pause.)*

PETER: Anna? I just wanted you to know...that the fantasies weren't...necessary.

ANNA: Oh, Petey. How sweet.

PETER *(Shyly)*: I just wanted you to know...I really miss breasts.

ANNA: Really? That must be awful...

*(Anna looks down and strokes her breast.)*

PETER: It's so alien to me. That softness...

ANNA: Well, you know, Petey, whenever you get hit by the urge, you can always feel one...

PETER: Can I?

ANNA: Of course you can. Be my guest. Go ahead, it won't bite you...

*(Peter hesitantly puts out his hand to stroke Anna's breast. Ruth, still half-asleep, enters in her pajamas.)*

RUTH: Petey? Are you home? You okay?
PETER: Yes.

*(He starts to remove his hand, but Anna holds it to her breast.)*

RUTH: What are you two up to?
PETER: I'm, um, stroking Anna's breast.
RUTH *(Totally unconcerned)*: Oh. That's nice.
ANNA: There's room for one more here.
RUTH *(Enthused)*: Okay.

*(Ruth goes to Anna's other side and gently puts her hand on Anna's breast. Peter and Ruth look at each other. Ruth smiles. Anna smiles, and sighs.)*

ANNA: Ahhh.

## Scene Three

*Day Two. Ruth and Peter in the kitchen. On the table is a large rubber tub filled with water, towels, a baby bottle, diapers and a life-sized doll. Ruth holds a baby-care book, from which she reads.*

RUTH: Ready?

*(Peter is rolling up his sleeves, and looking grim.)*

PETER: Let's go.

RUTH: Where do you want me to start from?

PETER: The beginning of the book!

RUTH: Okay.

*(Reads)* "Parenthood is many things to many people—a new beginning, a new definition of self, a challenge and a—"

PETER *(Irritably)*: Oh, skip that crap!

RUTH: You said from the beginning.

*(Pause)*

You know, Petey, is this really necessary? When the baby comes home—

PETER: I asked you to help me!

RUTH: I'm helping, I'm helping…I just don't think parenthood is something you bone up on from a book—

*(Peter gives her a look.)*

RUTH: Okay.

*(Flips through the index)*

How about starting with...let's see—"Positions, comma, proper, comma, for carrying newborns"?

PETER: All right. Now we're cooking with gas.

RUTH: Okay. Do you have Junior? Right. Page nineteen.

*(Peter picks up the doll)*

"It is important to carry the baby so that its neck is always supported. Do not touch the soft spot at the top of the baby's head, and hold it in such a fashion so that your hand supports the weight of the head."

*(Peter tries to accomplish this, leaving the body dangling at a strange angle.)*

PETER: Shit. That's not right.

RUTH *(Trying to continue with a straight face)*: "One hand should cushion the back of the baby's head and the thumb and wrist of the adult will provide a bulwark for the infant's neck..."

PETER: Christ! Can't they write these things in plain English? Here—take this—let me see that book!

*(Peter thrusts the doll at Ruth, while grabbing the book. Ruth tenderly takes the doll, demonstrates perfect carrying position and smiles at Peter.)*

RUTH: You're at a disadvantage. You never played with dolls.

PETER: Says you.

RUTH: Hold this thing. *(Thrusts the doll at Peter)* The right way.

*(Peter holds the plastic doll like a pro.)*

RUTH: That's great, Peter!

PETER: You really think so?

RUTH: The Madonna herself couldn't do better.

PETER (*Pleased; with renewed confidence*): Okay. Hit me with the hard stuff.

(*Ruth flips to the back of the book again.*)

RUTH: Okay. "Bathing, comma, newborns."

PETER: I'm ready.

RUTH: Well, take its little tutu off first.

PETER: Oh. Right.

RUTH: Now then. "Nothing can be more slippery and capricious to hold then the newborn infant, soapy and wriggling like an eel on the proverbial hook—" (*Stops*)

    What moron wrote this?

PETER: Come on.

RUTH: "The first bath is every parent's nightmare. To avoid tragic consequences—" blah-dy, blah-dy, blah... "Carefully lower the child into the water, with one hand supporting the child's—" blah, blah, blah. "With the other hand, wet the child's—" blah, blah, blah...

    Now comes the tricky part.

PETER: It's all a matter of concentration.

RUTH (*With increased sadism*): "When removing the baby from the bath water, have a towel ready to wrap the infant's tiny body in so that the child will not slip from your grasp, and possibly injure its delicate, tissue-thin membranes..."

(*Peter begins to slip with the doll. We see him frantically grasp its little plastic parts to no avail. The doll eludes his hold, and crashes into the tub.*)

PETER: AHH—AHH—Goddamn!!

(*Beat. Ruth and Peter watch the doll float. They try to control themselves, but erupt in laughter. Peter holds the doll's face underwater, then tosses the doll into the air.*)

PETER: Thirsty? Glub, glub, glub, glub, glub...Good baby! Daddy's baby! Baby go boom? Don't Touch the Soft Spot!! Wheeee! Go to Ruthie—

*(Peter tosses the doll to Ruth, who catches it. In a split second, we hear Henri's maniacal giggle. Then before Peter can respond, Ruth calls:)*

RUTH: Hut One and Hut Two!

*(Peter and Ruth break out into football fantasy.)*

PETER *(Simultaneously with Ruth)*: Hike! He drops back to pass, he's forced out, out of the pocket, he's rolling to the right, reading the defense, now he's scrambling, it looks like he's going long! Yes! He's going to throw the bomb—

RUTH *(Simultaneously with Peter)*: Hike! She's splitting the defense, she's crossing into the flat, the crowd's going wild, can you hear that excite—she fakes a move to the corner— penalty for traveling! She's open and there's—

*(Peter tosses the baby doll across the room at Ruth just as Anna enters and catches the doll in surprise. Calmly Anna moves downstage with the baby; the other two are embarrassed. With motherly care, Anna sets the baby down on the table.)*

## Scene Four

*Henri is in the kitchen, humming softly.*

HENRI: And now pour le dejeuner. A little poisson? Or peut-etre—a little poulet—cordon bleu? Or maybe steak Dijon?

*(Stands in front of the refrigerator, contemplating the choices. He opens the refrigerator door and gasps in disgust)* Peanut Butter and Jelly! Peanut Butter and Jelly! Avec Wonderbread!

RUTH *(Calls to the offstage Anna)*: Anna, you want a PBJ?

ANNA *(Offstage)*: No thanks. I'm going to take a nap.

*(Ruth becomes Henri again.*

*Henri sighs, then begins to work. He gathers the bread, peanut butter, jelly and knife on the table, arranges them. He looks at them. He takes out a nice plate and linen napkin, grabs a silk rose in a vase, and rearranges it all into a still life. Satisfied, he begins to create his sandwich, making a sensuous meal out of his peanut butter and jelly. As he works, he sings a medley of Maurice Chevalier hits. [Since it's really Ruth doing Henri imitating Maurice Chevalier, it's not as awful as the real thing.] He hums "Louise," occasionally substituting with "Henri.")*

HENRI: "Every little breeze seems to whisper 'Henri'—da dada da, da dada da—'Henri'—da da da da—da da da da—'I love you, love you—'"

*(Henri modulates into "Mimi," changing lyrics freely for "Cecil." As Henri sings, he completes his sandwich, does a light soft-shoe with the plate, puts the plate back on the table. Then Henri dances from the room for a second.*

*Ruth returns as Orphan, walks into the kitchen. Orphan sees the peanut butter sandwich; stops. Looks around, sees no one. Orphan goes to the table, and sniffs the sandwich. Orphan likes what he smells.)*

ORPHAN: Mmm-hmmm!

*(Orphan takes a huge bite of the sandwich. Orphan stops, looks around, furtively leaves the room. Ruth returns as Henri, and comes sauntering back into the room still singing vintage Chevalier. Sees sandwich. Stops. In rage, picks it up and sees big bite gone from its middle.)*

HENRI: WHO…Who…Who did this? What big, fat, humongous couchon did this to me?

*(Henri/Ruth ducks under the kitchen table and waits. We see a hand sneak from under the edge of the table toward the sandwich, and hear:)*

ORPHAN: Ahhh-hhhah!!

*(Ruth/Orphan stands, takes the sandwich, smiles; and just as he's about to take a bite:)*

HENRI: All right, Orphanne! Hold it right there! That's my peanut butter sandwich!
ORPHAN *(Snarl)*: NAA-NOOOOOOH!

*(Orphan starts to eat. Orphan/Henri struggle with both of Ruth's hands.)*

HENRI: Put It Down—
ORPHAN *(Baring fangs)*: Sahh-sssahhh!!!
HENRI: I'm going to…

*(Henri makes bopping noises; Orphan starts to cry.)*

ORPHAN: GRR…

*(Orphan bites the air several times.)*

HENRI: OOWW!

*(Henri starts to cry. Ruth's hand does a Dr. Strangelovian battle with her other hand, fighting for possession of the peanut butter and jelly. In the midst we hear her sing Wagner, etc. Finally, Ruth, as Orphan, pops the entire sandwich in her mouth in triumph.)*

ORPHAN: MMMM-MMMMMMMM!!!

*(Ruth suddenly stops, with peanut butter crammed in her mouth, turning to see Anna watching her from the hallway. Ruth tries to manage a smile with her PBJ-smeared mouth.)*

## Scene Five

*In the morning. Anna sits at table, drinking coffee. Peter sits, smoking and brooding.*

PETER: I feel bad about our fight the other day. But…

ANNA: What fight?

PETER: About the kids.

ANNA: Oh, forget it. That wasn't a fight. That was a discussion. It's only a fight when something gets broken.

*(Just then, there's a tremendous crash offstage. Anna does not blink. We hear Ruth, offstage, overlapping as Henri and Orphan.)*

HENRI *(Offstage)*: Now look what you've done, Orphanne!

ORPHAN *(Offstage)*: T-tough n-n-noogies.

*(Offstage noise continues.)*

PETER: I…I shouldn't have yelled at Cecil like that.

ANNA: Well, you know. Peter, he is imaginary—

PETER: Of course I know he's—

ANNA: Believe me, I know how easy it is to get confused about that sometimes, but at a time like this, you have to keep it separate—

PETER: I have to!…That's what I'm trying to talk to you about! It's not my problem!

ANNA: Then why are you getting upset?

HENRI *(Offstage)*: I get to wear that shirt! That's not yours, Orphanne!

ORPHAN *(Offstage)*: N-now it is.

HENRI *(Offstage)*: You take it off!

ORPHAN *(Offstage)*: M-m-make m-me, Frog Boy.

PETER: It's very hard to talk around here sometimes.

HENRI *(Offstage)*: Don't call me Frog Boy!

*(Sounds of fighting.)*

ANNA: Look. I'm always ready to listen to your point of view, Peter...

PETER: Okay, then, I just want to explain why I think we should stop—

*(Sounds of Henri crying.)*

HENRI *(Offstage)*: I AM GOING TO KILL YOU, ORPHANNE!

ANNA: Ah, excuse me, Peter—

*(Anna gets up and crosses to the bedroom door. She stands there, with her back to us.)*

CECIL: Listen, you two. Will you please grow up? What is your problem?

*(Silence.)*

CECIL: Well, then, let Orphan wear that shirt today. Henri, you can wear my Fiorucci shirt with the fish—

HENRI *(Offstage; delighted)*: All right!

*(Anna returns to her seat. Beat.)*

ANNA: I'm sorry, Peter. You were saying?

PETER: Never mind.

ANNA: Oh, come on, Petey, don't be that way.

*(Peter drinks his coffee.)*

PETER: What way?

ANNA: Can I have a sip of your coffee? Oh, come on. Do you think the kid's going to come out with a mushroom head if I have some caffeine?

PETER: Okay. I think mushrooms are cute.

ANNA *(Swallowing)*: Oh my god—

PETER: Don't you have a doctor's appointment today?

ANNA: Tomorrow. At two.

*(Ruth enters, in a Fiorucci fish shirt.)*

RUTH: Good morning, Petey.

PETER: Morning.

RUTH: What did I do?

ANNA: I think Peter wants to talk to us, honey.

RUTH: Okay. Talk Peter.

*(Peter takes a breath for patience and strength.)*

PETER: It's about the kids—

RUTH: Oh. Okay, you guys. I've made a decision.

ANNA: We're going to stop?

RUTH: Well...not just like that.

PETER: I don't understand.

RUTH: Look, I want to get my last inch of fantasy out of them. I can't just stop doing them, just like that. I'll always be wondering: Will Cecil become a geophysicist? Will Henri go back to Paris? Will Orphan become fully socialized?

ANNA: So what are you proposing?

RUTH: We're going to tidy up the plots. No loose ends dangling. Starting tomorrow. We're going to kill them. One by one. First Orphan. Then Henri. Cecil will be the last to go.

*(Anna and Peter stare at Ruth. Ruth smiles.)*

## Scene Six

*Afternoon. Ruth is loosely bound in a chair with kitchen nylon cord rope. She has a gag in her mouth. Anna enters from front door, carrying shopping bag. As she turns, Anna sees Ruth.*

ANNA: Ruth!!

*(The shopping bag drops. Ruth casually removes the gag from her mouth with a free hand.)*

RUTH: Hi, honey. What'd the doctor have to say?
ANNA: What is all this!! Are you all right?—
RUTH: I'm sorry, I just wanted to surprise you—
ANNA: Surprise me!! Are you crazy?

*(Anna stops, pants.)*

RUTH: I'm sorry. Close the door. Are you all right?
ANNA: Christ. You almost made me break my water.

*(Anna sits.)*

RUTH: I'm sorry. It was stupid.
ANNA: What in the hell are you doing? Why are you bound and gagged?
RUTH: I'm not. Orphan is.

ANNA: Oh. I see.

RUTH: I'm afraid I have some bad news. About Orphan.

ANNA: You're pushing the envelope, Ruthie, you really are.

RUTH: Are you listening? He...he went into a convulsion shortly
after you left and I rushed him to St. Vincent's. Honey? You
know how all these months, Orphan's been, well, stuttering?
Biting? Having little fits?

ANNA (*Starting to giggle*): I don't believe this. Yes, yes, go on...

RUTH: And...and you know how hard it's been to get him to take
a bath? Well—it's serious. Brace yourself. All this time he's
had...rabies. And we didn't know.

ANNA: Rabies!!

RUTH: And now it's too late to do anything. He's in the last stages.

ANNA: I see.

RUTH: So the doctors let me bring him home.

ANNA: How much time does he have left?—Are we really going
through with this?

RUTH: Yes. We are. He...he doesn't have much time left. An hour
or two.

ANNA: And they let him out?

RUTH: There's...there's a shortage of beds.

ANNA: Uh-huh.

> (*Pause*)
> Rabies simplex or rabies complex?

RUTH: Come on, you have to play along with this! Do you want
to talk to Orphan?

ANNA: Is he lucid?

RUTH: Well, he goes in and out. Be careful. He might try to bite you.

ANNA: Okay.

*(Ruth replaces the gag and sits in the chair as Orphan. Anna
carefully takes off the gag, and Orphan almost bites her.)*

ANNA: Whew! That was a close one. Orphy? Baby? Can you hear
me?

ORPHAN: Grrr-grr-sah, sah, t-t-t—, the d-d-dogs, k-k-k-k—

*(Makes strange little popping noises)* Pop! Pop-pop-pop—

ANNA: Oh, God, Ruth, this is awful—

ORPHAN: M-m-m-milk.k.k.kkk; w-warmm, w-warm mmmilk... t-ttoo, t-too mmany others...have to k-kick them away. T-to ggett the m-m-milkkk...

*(Orphan makes suckling noises)*

ANNA: Oh, Jesus.

RUTH: He's coming round.

ORPHAN: Mmm-hmmm.

ANNA: Baby? Can you hear me?

ORPHAN *(Cooing agreement)*: Mmm-hmmm.

ANNA: Oh, sweetie. Are you in pain?

ORPHAN: Nah-noh. N-no pain.

ANNA *(Kneeling by Orphan and stroking his hair)*: Honey? How did this happen? Can you remember?

ORPHAN: Mmm-hmm.

ANNA: Did you get bitten?

ORPHAN: I, I was pp-playing by Port Authority and these b-b-boys were th-throwing s-stones at th-this d-d-dog. And th-that made me *mad*.

   *(Pops his eyes for a second)* So-so I, I called, "H-here, d-d-ddoggie." And it came to me.

ANNA: Was it walking funny?

ORPHAN *(Sweetly)*: Mmm-hmmm.

ANNA: How?

ORPHAN: L-l-like a c-crab.

ANNA: Oh, God.

ORPHAN *(Excited)*: A-and it had a b-b-beard. A wh-white b-b-beard. L-like Mmr. B-b-bbubble!

ANNA: Yes, honey. Like your bubble bath, Mr. Bubble. Then what happened?

ORPHAN: I-I petted the d-dog. B-because it reminded me...of...
   *(His voice goes strangely low)* Mother.

ANNA: Ruthie. I can't go through with this. This is just too awful.

RUTH: We've got to go through with this. It's almost over.

ANNA: Well, hurry up, then!

RUTH: Okay. He's going into his last grand mal. Look out. Stand back.

*(Orphan starts to make strange buzzing noises in his throat. When he erupts into speech, it should be reminiscent of the many voices of Mercedes McCambridge in* The Exorcist.*)*

ORPHAN: "Fuck Me, Jesus!" HEH HEH heh heh...*zzzzzz.* scratch. ZZZZZ.scratch. "A p-p-plague o-o-o' both your houses!!—z-z-zounds, a d-d-dog, a rrratt, a m-mouse, a k-k-k-kcat, to sccratch a m-man to death!!!!"..."W-washed, I said. Are they washed? Arggh, that unwashed gggggrrr-grape has transported her soul." K!!

K!! "Da-da-DAMIEN! W-w-why you d-do this to me?!" Pop!! Pop!! PoppoppoppopppPut out the l-light, and t-then p-put out the l-light! Mmm-hmmm..."Sahh, sa-hhhh-Sunn...Mother, g-give me th-the sahh-sun."

*(A small pause, then accelerated)* Poppoppoppoppopp-pp "Pardon me b-boys; is th-that the Chchchatten-chatenn-Ch—"GRRR!!!...Woof, woof, woof.

*(Bites the air three times)*

"Good night, ladies; good n-night, GooGooGooJoob!!—O, UNTIMELY DEATH?!"

*(Pause)*

Sit! Stay!!... "Out, d-damned Spot!!"

*(Suddenly, Orphan looks up, quiet, alert. Hums the theme song from "Lassie")*

*(Listens; then in a plaintive high voice)* "L-l-lassie c-come...hh-omme..."

*(Orphan suddenly slumps over in his chair. Orphan is still. A pause.)*

ANNA: Orphan? Orphan!!

*(Ruth sits upright and takes off the gag and rope.)*

RUTH *(Cheerfully)*: The End!!

## Scene Seven

*Cecil (Anna) and Henri (Ruth) hold a children's service for Orphan in the kitchen. They hold hands. Both are wearing black armbands. Cecil carries his bear, Sidney, who also wears an armband.*

HENRI *(Teary)*: So...so now what do we do, Cecil?

CECIL *(Pale and dry-eyed)*: Well, I, uh, think it might be appropriate to the, uh, occasion if we sing Orphan's favorite song.

HENRI: Okay.

*(The two sing in a sweet, high boy's soprano.)*

HENRI AND CECIL:

> Had a dog and his name was Blue
> Had a dog and his name was Blue
> Had a dog and his name was Blue
> Betcha five dollars, he was a good 'un, too.
> Here, Blue:
> You good dog, you.
>
> Old Blue died and he died so hard
> Old Blue died and he died so hard
> Old Blue died and he died so hard
> Dug little holes all over my yard.

Here, Blue:
You good dog, you.
Here, Blue:
I'm a comin' there too.

CECIL: Well, Orphan. I don't know if I think you're in heaven. I stopped believing in a Divine Presence when I was six, so there's really no way of knowing. But, uh, I do believe in the Laws of Physics. And that matter can't be destroyed, but only changed. So I know you're somewhere. And maybe you can hear me. And I just want to say, that, uh, I'll never forget you. You'll always be with me.

*(Gently turns to Henri)* Henri? Do you have something you want to say to Orphan?

HENRI *(Quavering)*: Well, Orphanne, I just want to say that...*(Starts to break)*...that when you wanted to eat my peanut butter and jelly sandwich, I'm sorry I didn't let you—

*(Gives vent to heart-rendering cries on Cecil's shoulder)* Oh, Cecilll...

CECIL *(Comforting Henri ardently)*: I know. I know, Henri. It's all right. We have each other.

*(Fiercely)* I won't let anything happen to you. I swear it!

## Prologue to Act Two

*When the house lights have dimmed, we hear light snoring, sweet and melodious, as only an eight year old's can be. The clown night-light is on.*

GHOST OF ORPHAN *(Ethereally)*: C-c-c-Ce-cillll...

CECIL: Hh-huhnh? *(Henri's soft snoring is the only response)* Henri? Did you say something? *(Henri whistles on)* Guess not.

GHOST OF ORPHAN: C-C-CECILLL!!

CECIL *(Wide awake)*: Who...who is that?!!

GHOST OF ORPHAN: O-o-Orphan...or a p-piece of him.

CECIL: O-o-Orphan? Oh, my God.

GHOST OF ORPHAN: L-list, l-list, O list! If thou didst ever thy d-dear brother l-love, Revenge his f-foul and m-most un-un-un-n-n—

CECIL: Unnatural—

GHOST OF ORPHAN: Mm-hmm!...M-murder.

CECIL: Murder? Murder?

GHOST OF ORPHAN: Mmm-hmm! M-murder m-most f-foul and m-most un-un-un-n-n—

CECIL: Unnatural—

GHOST OF ORPHAN: Adieu! Adieu! C-c-Cecil, remember me. Mmm-hmm!

CECIL: Wait!! Orphan?—Wait!
> *(Pause)*
> *(Then, urgent)* Henri! Henri!

HENRI: Zzzz—What? What is it, Cecil? Cecil? You're...you're shaking!

CECIL: It's just...Angst.— Henri, we've got to get out of here.

HENRI: What? But why?

CECIL: Do you think...what happened to Orphan...was strange?

HENRI *(Trembling)*: I...don't know.

CECIL: I don't think what happened to Orphan happened...by accident. I know it wasn't an accident.

HENRI *(Starting to cry)*: How...how do you know?

CECIL: I just know.

HENRI: Oh, Cecil—what are we going to do?

CECIL: We've got to get out of here.

HENRI: But where...where are we going to go?

CECIL: Listen. Henri, tomorrow I want you to act like nothing's different. I want you to pack a few things into the Channel Thirteen bag and hide it under the bed.

HENRI: Maybe we could sleep tonight with Uncle Peter!

CECIL: No. I don't think he can be trusted. I think Uncle Peter's one of them...We'll go to bed, and then when Anna and Ruth are sleeping, we'll slip on out of here.

HENRI *(Crying)*: I don't think Anna and Ruth would really, really harm—

CECIL: They're not themselves. Ever since that baby.

HENRI: Yeah. I hate that baby.

CECIL: We've got to run away.

HENRI: Okay.

CECIL: Try to get some sleep.

*(Henri cries softly; Cecil and Henri peer anxiously into the darkness as the lights fade up into Act Two.)*

## Scene Eight

*The next morning. Anna is making coffee. She wears a black armband. Peter sits at the table.*

PETER: So what exactly happened?

ANNA: Well, he frothed, went into a frenzy and badly misquoted Shakespeare. Then he died.

PETER: How are the other two taking it?

ANNA: They're devastated. Henri turned down ice cream last night.

PETER: Poor lad.

ANNA: That's easy for you to say.

*(Pause. Peter tries again.)*

PETER: So who's next? Henri or Cecil?

ANNA: Henri. It's my turn to bump him off. I want it to be painless. Orphan's demise was just too awful for me.

PETER: When's it gonna happen?

ANNA: Why? Want front-row seats?

PETER: I'm just asking, Anna. That's all.

ANNA *(Trying to control her irritability)*: I know. I'm sorry. I just don't know.

PETER: Tonight?

ANNA: I don't know. I don't know. Don't rush me.

PETER: Sorry.

(*Ruth enters, wearing a black armband and Peter's shirt.*)

RUTH: Morning, you guys. I gotta run.

ANNA: That's Peter's shirt.

PETER: Thought it looked familiar.

ANNA: Did you ask if you could wear it?

(*Ruth and Peter look at each other. There is a moment of uneasy silence.*)

RUTH (*Then, casually*): Um, Petey, would you mind terribly, old man, if I borrowed your shirt?

PETER: Not at—

ANNA (*Angry and starting to get loud*): That's not the point! Jesus, Ruthie, you can't just go around using other people's things without—

PETER: I really don't mind.

ANNA: But that's not the point!

RUTH: I asked him. Okay? I can't wear your things right now, they don't fit—

ANNA: There's gotta be some respect for other people's property around here.

RUTH: Sweetie, there's no reason to get—

ANNA: Don't fucking condescend to me! Like I'm the one who's crazy! It drives me nuts to hear the way you both talk to me, sometimes, like I'm a goddamn carton of eggs that has to be carried very carefully or—

PETER (*Very calmly*): We're not talking to you like that, Anna—

ANNA: Like hell you're not—

RUTH: What do you want from us?

ANNA: Just some respect! Some order in this household! Some quiet and some, some…You two just traipse in and out at all hours of the day while I sit here, bloated and tethered like some goddamn Good Year blimp on Super Bowl day. I'm supposed to give up coffee, smoking, drinking, fucking, spicy foods, and I'm expected to be understanding of what Ruth wants, what Peter needs.—Who the fuck am I, some kind of knocked-up Miss Manners? It's ninety degrees in August, and I can't get a seat on the subway! I fucking hate New York, and I just want to see my knees again! I WANT TO KILL, MAIM, MOON THE NEIGHBORS!

(Takes a breath; continues a bit more calmly) It would be nice, too, if Peter would pick his shoes up when he takes them off instead of leaving them in the middle of the floor for me to trip over, so I don't have to worry about dropping the goddamn baby in a burst of placental juice all over the—

RUTH: Maybe it would be a good idea if you went in and laid down. You're just having...

ANNA: I'm just what...What?

RUTH: You're having one...of...those—

ANNA: Don't say it!! Don't you dare fucking say it!

(Smashes her coffee cup. She crosses to the bedroom, stops, and says with great dignity) You can both suck my imaginary dick!

(She exits. There is a moment of silence. Ruth picks up a shard of the coffee cup.)

RUTH: I think we're having a fight.

ANNA (Offstage): AND DON'T YOU DARE TELL ME IT'S HORMONES!

(There is a crash offstage from the bedroom.)

PETER: Maybe I should...just pick up my shoes and leave the two of you alone for a while...

(Peter stands; Ruth rounds on him.)

RUTH: Don't start tippy-toeing out of here!

>  (*Beat*)

>  For once, when the shit starts to fly, just...just stay here, can't you?

(*Peter takes a breath.*)

PETER: Okay.

(*Ruth and Peter look around the room. Peter goes and picks up the various pairs of shoes and neatly arranges them under the table; Ruth, equally contrite, begins to pick up the shattered coffee mug and rinse the dishes. Peter straightens up magazines. Ruth picks up a few articles of clothing and takes them into the bathroom, while Peter waters the plants. They stop and look at the room, which is a bit more ordered. Then they sit at the table, tentatively smile at each other. Pause.*)

PETER: So...what are you going to do today?

RUTH (*Quietly and miserably*): Have a shitty day.

PETER: Sounds like fun. Can I join you?

RUTH: Listen, Peter—what are you doing this afternoon?

PETER: Nothing, I guess.

RUTH: There's something I want you to do for me.

PETER: Sure. What?

RUTH: Would you take Cecil and Henri to the zoo?

PETER: Me?

RUTH: It would cheer Ann—it would cheer them up. They're really upset. Would you?

PETER: Oh, Ruthie—do you really think we should be doing this outside the home?

RUTH: They won't be with us much longer. Please.

PETER: Well, they do need a strong male role model right now.

## Scene Nine

*Day Four. The same. Peter, Henri and Cecil at the zoo. All three are wearing black armbands. Peter holds Henri and Cecil by the hand.*

PETER: Look boys. The orangutans—they're always good for a laugh.

*(Cecil and Henri watch, glumly. Then, Henri, excited, begins to laugh.)*

HENRI: Uncle Peter! Look!! The monkey's pulling his pudding! In front of everybody!

*(Henri laughs again.)*

PETER: Oh, Henri, you always think the worst— *(He looks. Then, hurriedly)* —Ah, maybe we ought to go see the chimpanzees. Come on, Henri.
HENRI: But I want to watch the monkey pull—!
PETER: I said come on.

*(Peter drags Henri over to the next cage, a few feet away.)*

PETER: Look Cecil! The chimps!! They're your favorites, aren't they?
CECIL: Yes.

PETER: They're awfully cute.

CECIL: Yes.

PETER: God. They look just like humans.

CECIL *(Pensively begins to recite)*: "Never forget that every single organic being around us strives to increase in numbers; that each lives by a struggle at some period in its life; that heavy destruction inevitably falls either on the young or the old."

PETER: That's Darwin, isn't it? Come on, Ceepie, lighten up.

CECIL: "Thus, from war of nature, from famine and death, all organic beings advance by one general law—namely, Multiply, Vary, Let the Strongest Live, and the Weakest Die..."

*(Cecil suddenly grips Peter and buries his head into Peter's side, weeping softly.)*

HENRI: Uncle Peter?

PETER: Yes, Henri?

HENRI: What's angst?

PETER: It's a kind of...sadness. A German sadness.

HENRI: Is Cecil having angst?

PETER: Yes.

HENRI: Why?

PETER: Evolution. Come on, boys, let's go home.

## Scene Ten

*Late at night. Anna and Henri.*

HENRI: Is Uncle Peter in bed?

ANNA: Hello, baby. It's mighty late for you to be up, isn't it?

HENRI: I'm no longer a baby, Anniah. I have to talk to you—alone.

ANNA: Uh-huh. Is this about your allowance again?

HENRI: You would never, ever lie to me, would you?

*(Anna immediately becomes guilty.)*

ANNA: Of course not. Why?

HENRI: Cecil has some strange ideas. I told him he was wrong, but still—

ANNA: What strange ideas?

HENRI: Cecil thinks that...something terrible happened to Orphan. And that something terrible is going to happen to us.

*(Anna averts her eyes.)*

ANNA *(Trying to laugh)*: Where does Cecil get these ideas? I'll talk to him.

HENRI: No! Cecil must not know I have come to you. You would never let anything happen to me? Or to Cecil? Would you?

ANNA: Of course not! It's time for you to be in bed—

*(Anna does not look Henri in the eyes.)*

HENRI: Why do you not look at me?

ANNA *(Looks directly at Henri)*: I would never hurt you. You know that.

HENRI: I knew you would not. I knew Cecil was wrong. So we do not have to run away.

ANNA: Run away! You were going to run away?!—

HENRI: But now we do not have to. And I don't have to tell Uncle Peter.

ANNA: Tell *what* to Uncle Peter?

HENRI: Oh, nothing. Nothing you would want Uncle Peter to know. And as long as Cecil and I are safe, then I know nothing.

ANNA: What's that supposed to mean?

HENRI: Peter still thinks he is the father to your child. You have led him to think so.

ANNA: He most certainly is! I should know. Why are you—

HENRI: I have reason to think otherwise. We both have reason to think otherwise.

ANNA: I don't know what you are talking about—

HENRI: You will hear me out. I have learned a lot in your country. I know how to count up to nine. In English.

ANNA: What are you implying?

HENRI: That I am the father to your child.

ANNA: Whoa. Time out, Ruthie. We agreed never to—

HENRI: It was late in November. All the leaves had fallen. Ruse was out of town. We had seen that film which had made you so sad.

ANNA *(Starting to understand)*: Are we feeling a little bit jealous?

HENRI: I will always treasure that night. My "education sentimentale." And no one has to know.

ANNA *(Playing along now)*: Please, Henri, I thought we had agreed to forget all about it. It was late, you were crying, I was weak for a moment and—

HENRI: And little Emma was made?

ANNA: No!! That's impossible.

HENRI: But who will Peter believe if I tell him I am the father?

ANNA: Are you threatening me? Are you daring to—listen, I can send you home to Paris so fast it will make that little froggy head of yours swim—

HENRI: Fine. I go home to Paree, the culture capital of the world. I leave New York and its dirt behind. Au revoir. No regrets. Je ne regret rien. And you? Do you think Peter will leave the baby alone with you?

ANNA: Henri listen, honey—do you remember that night? When you cried against my shoulder and I brushed your hair? You were lonely, you missed Paris, you missed your friends the balloons—do you remember? And you begged me, and against my better judgment, I gave in. Do you remember what I said as I unbuttoned my blouse? "Years from now, when you speak of this—and you will—be kind."

(*Pause*)

Now I ask you. Is this kind?

HENRI (*Quiet, miserable*): No.

ANNA: Come here, baby. I'd ask you to sit on my lap, but it's a little difficult right now.

HENRI: I'm a big boy.

ANNA: That's right, you are.

(*With difficulty*) Listen—I can't undo what happened to Orphan. But I have never broken a promise to you, have I? Have I? And I promise you that nothing will...hurt you. Or...Cecil. You're my...treasure. And nothing ever will, nothing ever could, replace you. Okay?

(*Pause*)

What can I do to make it up to you? Is there anything I can do to make you feel better? To cheer you up? To make you stop this, this silly talk of *accidents* and patrimony? Hmm?

HENRI: Well...there is a tiny, little something...

ANNA: What can I do? Tell me...

HENRI: Do you remember last year, when you got some money? And at the time, you asked me what I wanted, and I told you—

ANNA: But Henri, baby—

HENRI: And with all that money, what did we get? A movie. Sneakers. Chicken McNuggets...

ANNA: But you like Chicken Mc—

HENRI: I told you what I wanted, and you laughed at me. You laughed at me!

ANNA: Henri! Where are we going to keep a pony in New York! Do you have any idea how much a pony costs? It's out of the question—

HENRI: I really, really want a pony.

ANNA: I'll think about it. I have to...talk to Ruth about this.

HENRI: And I'll never, ever ask for anything again in my whole life. You could buy it for me with the money for college—

ANNA: You're pushing your luck. I said I'll think about it. Now, I want your hands washed, your teeth brushed and the lights out.

HENRI *(Suddenly cheerful and obedient)*: All right. I love you, Anna. Good night.

ANNA: Good night.

*(Henri goes to the bedroom door and stops, suddenly overcome with doubt and fear.)*

HENRI: Anna?

ANNA: What is it now?

HENRI: Do you think maybe I could sleep with you and Ruth just for tonight?

*(Anna stares ahead in worry.)*

## Scene Eleven

*The next morning. Anna and Ruth sit at the kitchen table.*

ANNA: Okay. Here's how I want it to be. Henri's having a relapse, because of Orphan's death. He's seeing balloons again— every time he looks out the window, there they are, a flock of balloons. He's convinced that the balloons have come to take him home to Paris. Before we can stop him, Henri climbs onto the fire escape, and he...just disappears.

RUTH: Wait a moment—I thought—

ANNA: What did you think?

RUTH: I thought you...had a change of heart. Last night.

ANNA: I will not be blackmailed. Not by Henri, and not by— *(Stops herself)*
We've made a deal with Peter.

RUTH: I don't see why we can't change the...the narrative at this point.

ANNA: We can't stop now. Not in the middle of the story. Don't make this harder on me, Ruthie.

*(Ruth is almost to the point of tears.)*

RUTH *(Angry and sullen)*: Fine. Fine. Just don't make me be here when Cecil has to go.

ANNA: Okay, sweetie. I'm sorry. Let's get this over with.
*(Beat)*
Okay?

RUTH: Okay. How are we...what do you want Henri to do?

ANNA: He goes out on the fire escape, and before we can stop him—

RUTH: You mean he jumps?

ANNA: No! I don't want him hurt. The balloons come and take him away. He just...disappears. All right?

RUTH: All right.

*(Anna struggles for a quiet second with herself. Sighs.)*

ANNA: Henri? Henri, honey, would you come in here?

*(Ruth changes into Henri without a moment of hesitation. Henri is falsely cheerful.)*

HENRI: Hi, Anniah.

ANNA: What d'ya been up to, honey?

HENRI: Nothing. Just...thinking.

ANNA: Thinking about Orphan?
    *(Henri says nothing)*
    Henri, honey, you've had a major upset. We've all had a major upset. There's no rhyme or reason for these things. Death occurs by...chance. But it doesn't mean that anything will happen to you...necessarily.

HENRI: "Do not ask for whom the bell tolls."

*(Henri looks out the window.)*

ANNA: Listen, little man, it's late. Isn't it time you got dressed? I mean, how can we do things together with you still in your cowboy pajamas? Wouldn't you feel better if I got you a clean T-shirt? Hmm? And we'll all go out and do something together? We could go to the park—would you like that?

*(Henri furtively glances out the window.)*

HENRI: I...I do not want to go out.

ANNA: Why? Nothing will hurt you. You're with us.

(Henri looks out the window.)

HENRI: Grown-ups do not know everything.

ANNA: No, we don't.

HENRI: You could not help Orphanne, could you? Could you??!

ANNA: No.

(Pause)

Henri, why do you keep looking out the window?

HENRI: What?

ANNA: What do you see outside the window?

HENRI (Eyes downcast): I...I don't see nothing.

ANNA: The balloons are back, aren't they? You're seeing the balloons again.

HENRI: I...I don't see nothing.

(Pause; then) My balloons!!

ANNA: Where?

HENRI: They're waiting for me—outside the window—don't you see them?

ANNA: Henri, there's nothing there. Now I want you to listen to me. You're having a relapse. We're going to see Dr. Weinstein. You're going to get dressed, and then we're all going uptown to see her. Okay?

HENRI: You must believe me!

ANNA: Honey, I do believe that you see balloons. But I also know there's nothing there. Once, when you were a tiny little boy, you must have seen a movie—

HENRI: La Balloon Rouge—

ANNA: Yes, baby, that's the one. And it was a movie about a little boy in Paris who had a red balloon for a friend—

HENRI: It wasn't a movie!—

ANNA: Then one day, bullies came and popped the Red Balloon. And as it died, the little boy wept, and balloons from all over Paris came to him, lifted him up and carried him into the sky. And then the movie ended. It was a beautiful movie.

HENRI: It wasn't a movie!! It was my life!!

ANNA: Henri, you think it was your life. But with the help of Dr. Weinstein, the balloons went away. Isn't that right?

HENRI: My balloons left me...

ANNA: You got well.

HENRI (Excited): But now they've come back!

ANNA: Henri—

HENRI: They've come back for me!!

ANNA: You're going to get dressed. Ruth will help you. Then we're going uptown to see Dr. Wein—

HENRI: I have nothing to say to Dr. Weinstein! Nada! Rien!

ANNA: And then after we see her, we have a great deal to do. Don't we have a pony to pick out?

HENRI (Laughs sadly): A pony...

ANNA: Yes, that's right. A pony! It's got to be just the right pony for my Henri.

HENRI: I don't want a fucking pony.

ANNA: You'll feel differently when you see it, shy and pawing the ground in its own little stall. Yes?

HENRI: Anniah, look, forget what I said about the pony. I don't want it anymore. Let's forget about the whole thing, all right?

ANNA: But Henri, I thought you wanted—

HENRI (Frightened): I don't want a pony. I don't want nothing. I don't remember nothing. I just want to stay here with you. All right? Just to be your little boy...I know I've been a bad boy, but don't let anything happen to me, don't let them take me— (Henri is clutching Anna's neck)

ANNA: Henri, what are you talking about? Who's going to take you? You're shaking. Sshhh, calm down. Nothing's going to harm you.

HENRI: I've changed my mind. I don't want to go. I love you, Anna. Please, please let me stay—

ANNA: Wait a minute, Ruth—

HENRI: You could hide me. In the closet. I'll be good. Hide me from Ruth and Peter, they're trying to k—

ANNA: This is not what we agreed—!

HENRI: Ruth is going to kill me. You don't understand. She'll throw me off the fire escape—

ANNA: Ruth, that's not fair—

HENRI: Please, Anna, please, I don't want to die—

ANNA *(Crying out)*: Ruth! STOP IT! You're hurting him!!

*(There is silence.)*

ANNA: For God's sake, don't hurt him.

RUTH *(Quiet)*: I'm sorry.

ANNA *(Upset)*: Just take him out.

*(Ruth turns to go.)*

ANNA: —No, wait a minute.

*(Anna seizes Ruth's face, kisses it. Nods to Ruth. Ruth goes to the window, raises it and climbs out on the fire escape. There is silence. Anna sits, tense and upset. Ruth comes back in; closes the window. Ruth turns and goes to Anna.*
*Ruth holds out a deflated red balloon.)*

## Scene Twelve

*Peter stands in front of the window in the kitchen, searching the sky. Ruth sits, subdued, in a chair behind Peter. Anna holds her hand.*

PETER: What if he falls? What if he drops him?
ANNA: That won't happen. They'll hold onto him.

*(Ruth looks at Anna; Anna nods. Ruth quietly leaves the room.)*

PETER: All the way to Paris?
ANNA: He'll make it.

*(Pause.)*

PETER: Oh, my God, you guys—what are you going to tell Cecil?
CECIL: I hope you'll tell him the truth.

*(Peter turns and sees he is alone with Cecil.)*

PETER: No! I don't want to be here when—
CECIL: When what?
PETER: Cecil! You're home early!
CECIL: Yeah. Where's Henri?
PETER: Um, Cecil—

CECIL: Henri!! Henri, I'm home—

> *(Looks into the other room)*

> Henri? Hey, where is he? He's not in his room—is he in the bathroom?

PETER: Ahh, I think perhaps Ruth should be here—

CECIL: Ruth left. She said you wanted to speak to me. Alone.

*(Peter begins to sweat.)*

PETER: Cecil, I'm counting on you to take this like...a man.

CECIL: WHERE'S HENRI? What have you done to him?

PETER: Me? I've—the truth is, while he was with Anna and Ruth, he...disappeared.

CECIL: Disappeared?

PETER: He's gone. We don't know where. He...he was acting strange, talking about balloons, and then the next minute, he was gone.

CECIL: Gone?

> *(Laughs wildly)*

> Disappeared? Oh, that's rich—that's really good.

PETER: Umm—maybe I should leave you alone now and come back at a—

CECIL: Nobody leaves this room!

PETER: Cecil, I know what you must be feeling...

CECIL: I suppose he just "floated" into thin air.

PETER: Well, actually, there has been a sighting over the Atlantic by the Coast Guard—

CECIL: I should never have left him alone with the three of you.

PETER: Now wait a minute, Cecil, I have nothing to do with—

CECIL: Oh, yes. "For Brutus is an honourable man."

> *(Peter is silent)*

> It's good. It's really good. I have to hand it to the three of you. No bodies, no trace—

PETER: Look, I didn't want it to happen this way. I never meant to hurt anybody. I thought...that...that the kids should just go away, not be hurt.

*(Starts to laugh and splutter)* I mean, I'm not a…a mur-
derer, for God's sake, I'm just a…a—

CECIL: A father?

*(The laugh dies out. Beat.)*

CECIL: How will it happen to me, Uncle Peter? A pillow in the
night? Chinese food gone bad? An accidental case of toxic
shock?

PETER: Listen, Cecil, how about if we go inside and you lie down.
I'll bring you a glass of warm milk—

CECIL: Warm milk? Laced with what?

*(Beat)*

You know what I think, Uncle Peter? I think I knew
too much. That's why you have to do this. I know how you
got that scar on your temple when you were five. I know
what happened the night of your senior prom. How you
ran over the family cat in the driveway when you picked up
your date. How she sobbed, "Fluffy, Fluffy," and you
laughed. Or about the time on the Connecticut Turnpike
when you—

PETER: I told those things to Anna! In confidence.

CECIL: Yes. But grown-ups forget these things. Children remember. Children know a whole lot more than adults would like.
When Medea called her boys into the house, they knew.

PETER: Oh, God.

CECIL: Remember the night after your father walked out? You
went to your bedroom, and packed up all of your soldiers
and your airplanes and you marched down the street and
gave them away to the kids on the block.

PETER: I don't remember telling Anna that.

CECIL: First year in graduate school. After a party. You'd had too
much to drink. We have a lot in common, Uncle Peter; Anna
modeled me a little bit on you.

PETER: I didn't know that.

*(Beat)*

I guess I don't have to tell you that I've been freaking out a little bit.

CECIL: That's putting it mildly, Uncle Peter.

PETER: I've been trying to remember what my own house was like before my father left home. And all I can remember is how we would tiptoe around when Raymond came home, and he would solemnly put his neat tasseled shoes up on the hassock, while Mother brought him a dry martini.

*(Pause)*

Shoes with tassels!

CECIL: I don't think anyone drinks dry martinis anymore.

PETER: No. It's not a lot to go on, is it?

CECIL: I don't think Anna and Ruth would want Raymond to father their child.

PETER: I can't say I blame them.

CECIL: They chose you. Just...just make it up on your own, this father thing, okay, Uncle Peter?

PETER: Yes. Thank you, Cecil. I feel a lot better.

CECIL *(Sadly)*: I'm glad.

PETER: So...so now what do we do?

CECIL: The messenger always gets killed in the Greeks.

PETER: Look—do you think maybe we could...change the ending? Deus ex machina? I'd really like it if you could stick around.

CECIL: I don't think so. Not without Henri.

*(Tiny pause; a breath)*

It's been a good life. I'm ready to go.

PETER: I'm sorry...How do you want me to do this? I've never done this before...

CECIL: "Our Enemies have beat us to the Pit."

PETER: OK. Wait, wait...don't tell me...

CECIL: *Julius Caesar*, Act Five.

PETER: You want to die as the noblest Roman of them all!

CECIL: Yes, I think that would be appropriate to the occasion, don't you? "Hold then my sword, and turn away thy face."

PETER *(Now totally engaged)*: "Give me your hand first."

CECIL: Hold it steady.

*(Peter and Cecil arrange the "sword" a few times so that the angle misses Anna's belly.)*

CECIL: Good. Good man. By the way...I think you're going to make a wonderful father.
    *(He "runs" on the "sword")*
    *(Dying)* Promise...Me...

*(Peter holds Cecil tightly.)*

PETER: Anything.
CECIL: Don't...be afraid...to play with your child.

*(Cecil dies. Anna opens her eyes.)*

ANNA: Petey? Are you okay?

## Scene Thirteen

*The end of a very long day. Peter and Ruth.*

PETER: My hands are still shaking. I could barely get the keys out of the door. I feel like every pore in my body has been drained of sweat. My God. I never want to see blood again.

RUTH: Sit down. I'll pour us some vodka.

PETER: Did you ever imagine? Have you ever seen anything like that? It was nothing like that movie they showed us. Before tonight in that delivery room, I though *Aliens* was science fiction. Those things bursting out of people's bodies—it didn't look human? Did it?

Look at that!! Look at how my hands are still shaking—see? I don't know if I'm laughing or crying. Is this how you feel when you get your period?

RUTH: Drink this.

PETER: Have you ever seen that kind of pain? I don't know how women do it—

RUTH: It's all right now. It's over. Try not to think about it. They say you forget the pain.

PETER: I sure as hell won't. Natural childbirth! Natural! Like…like volcanoes, or tidal waves, or earthquakes—

RUTH: Drink up.

*(They sit and down the vodka. Pause.)*

PETER: The apartment is…so quiet. It's never been so quiet.

115

*(Pause. They listen to the apartment.)*

RUTH: He's got your face.

PETER: Do you really think so?

RUTH *(Quietly)*: He looks just like you.

*(Beat)*

I guess Anna and I really started talking about having a child after our first year together. You know how it is, that first year...you spend every moment in side glances at your lover, learning this new alphabet—her face, her walk, her gestures...the way she holds a pen, the way she chews the inside of her cheek in concentration; how her left nostril flares ever so slightly when she's amused—and you feel so ardent, you're in first grade all over again, in love with your teacher—so much in love that you wake early to study this alphabet while she's still asleep, memorizing her face on the pillow...

And I used to imagine that somewhere in the United States, there must be a pioneer geneticist, a woman in a lab coat we could go to, who would take some DNA from Anna and some DNA from me—and she'd combine us in a petri dish in a little honeymoon culture at just the right temperature—and then this growing synthesis would be transplanted in one of us, and when he or she would emerge, nine months later—the baby would have Anna's eyes winking beneath my eyebrows.

But finally I thought—well, I can always see my own face anytime I want to in the mirror. But I could see Anna's face at birth, Anna in diapers, a little Anna coming home from school. Or if the baby was born a boy—even better—I'd see his Adam's apple grow beneath her chin, or I'd experience that awkward moment right before puberty, before his voice changes, when I mistake his hello on the phone for hers—

Well. I guess I didn't think this all the way through.

PETER: Oh...Is my face such an awful face?

*(Ruth smiles at him.)*

RUTH: No. It's a very sweet face.
*(She strokes his face)*
I'm going to have to learn a new alphabet all over again.

## Scene Fourteen

*In the kitchen, right before supper. Anna is sitting in profile to the audience, nursing Nathan. Peter, with concentration, stands at the stove, stirring away at a large pot. Ruth is setting the table. Although all three are chipper on the surface, there is an underlying depression and sleep deprivation.*

ANNA *(To Nathan)*: Are you through, pumpkin?
    *(Pause)*
    *(Softly)* Nathan? Are you there? Nathan?...Out like a light.

RUTH: What d'ya put in the milk?

PETER: How would we like our pasta today? Al dente?

ANNA: I'm going to put him down.

RUTH: Anna? Did you get the wine?

ANNA: In the fridge.

PETER: We're just about ready.

*(Anna puts Nathan into a small bassinet near the table.)*

RUTH: The salad's on the table, already.

ANNA: Wish I could sleep like that.

*(The three assemble at the table; Peter bearing a large pot of pasta Raphael.)*

RUTH: Smells wonderful.

PETER: Pass the plates, please.

ANNA: Looks great. What are the green things?

PETER: Artichokes.

RUTH: Yum.

ANNA: So how was your day?

RUTH: Mine? Rushed.

ANNA: What's happening with the car?

RUTH: Well, I practically had to have sex with the mechanic to get him to even lift the hood. I think it's going to be expensive.

PETER: He's not giving a discount after the sex?

RUTH: I wasted two hours waiting to see if he could fix it, and barely made my eleven o'clock. I told him it's the carburetor.

ANNA: No—not the carburetor. The alternator. It's like going to a specialist—you have to come in with the diagnosis.

RUTH: We should have brought it in the beginning. The first time we noticed that burning egg smell.

*(They eat. Pause.)*

PETER: And what was your day like, Anna?

ANNA: Do you want wine, Peter?

PETER: No, thanks—I'll stick to water.

*(Peter raises his water glass to his lips; pauses. His hand shakes slightly. He does not drink.)*

ANNA: Well, I had a taxing day. The baby slept on and off; he's having some gas, I think.

RUTH: How do you know it's gas?

ANNA: He's smiling at me, all the time.

PETER: Maybe he's happy. Maybe he's dreaming about the womb.

ANNA: No. It's not normal for a baby to smile all the time. It's either gas or mental retardation...It's got to be gas. No more garlic in the food. Let me tell you, I can smell whatever I eat the next day when I change him.

*(Peter blanches slightly; clears his throat. He raises the glass of water to his lips, hesitates. Stares at his glass.)*

ANNA: The artichokes kind of remind me of—well, never mind. —He's still producing that postmeconium shade of green...

RUTH: Honey, maybe we should change the subject.

PETER: No, I don't mind. This is the life. Nathan dozing in his cradle; Anna talking about the intimate details—a quiet dinner, a new recipe. Just the four of us. The MacNeil-Lehrer report at 7:00. The dishes. The diapers. Most men dream of this.

*(The women look at each other. They say nothing. Pause.)*

ANNA: Well, that's all I have to report. It's heaven. I never want to go back to work. It's going to be a thrill the day he produces something solid. It's getting to be kind of monotonous right now—the same shade. My mother's living room used to be decorated in a similar avocado and beige—remember the sixties and earth tones?

*(Peter takes his glass and peers into it. Clears his throat again. He has a slight—a very slight—twitch. Ruth looks at him.)*

RUTH: Is there something in your glass?

PETER: What? Oh, no. It's only...w-w-water.

*(The women look at each other with raised eyebrows.)*

ANNA: So, Petey—how was the office?

PETER: Oh, you know, the same old shit.

RUTH: Did you get the annual report finished on time?

PETER: Yeah...no thanks to old Handjob.

ANNA: He should give you a raise. How's the new guy working out?

PETER: Fine. Dandy.

RUTH: I thought you said he was an asshole.

ANNA: An MBA from Wharton and he can't find his fly...

PETER: It's not very interesting to talk about at dinner.

RUTH: What did they think about your marketing idea?

*(Peter has raised his glass one more time to his lips.)*

PETER: Oh, you know...

*(This time, instead of drinking, Peter blows bubbles into his glass. The two women wait.)*

ANNA: Petey, we're trying to show an interest and you're not helping.

PETER: Sah-SAH!!-Sorry.

*(Peter begins to flinch. His leg twitches.)*

RUTH: Is there something you're trying to tell us?

PETER: What do you want to know? About the new Xerox machine? Our capital campaign? The percentage of earned income? The rate of overhead and indirect costs I calculated today for FY-94–95?

ANNA: What's come over you?

PETER: The projected contributions from the corporate sector for the next two years? Personnel benefits? I'm hot—now I'm cold—now I'm HOT! It itches! All the time! I can't swallow! My mouth's dry! But it foams! My head is burning! Aching! I'm drowning in saliva! SAH-SAH!!—

*(Peter falls from his chair and rolls on the floor.)*

PETER: Orphan! Revenge! Oorrrppphannnn...

RUTH: Orphan?!

ANNA: Orphan! What does he...

*(Peter shows the women his arm; whimpers.)*

RUTH: Orphan bit you! Am I right? Is that it?

*(Peter howls in the affirmative. The women are wide-eyed.)*

ANNA AND RUTH: Rabies!!

## Epilogue

*In the darkness, the clown light is on. We hear Henri and Orphan, giggling.*

HENRI: In his tushy! That's where.

ORPHAN: T-t-tushy!

CECIL: Cut it out, Henri! He does not!

ORPHAN: T-tushy! T-tushy!

*(Orphan and Henri giggle.)*

HENRI: There is no pretty way to say it. Derriere, heinie, behind—the doctor gives Uncle Peter shots in his tushy!

CECIL: He does not!

HENRI: He gets it in the same place little baby Nathan does—tushy shots!

CECIL: Shots are usually injected in the gluteus maximus because of the lack of nerve endings.

HENRI *(Gleeful)*: But it still hurts!

ORPHAN: Yeah!

CECIL: But in the case of hydrophobia—commonly known as rabies—treatment shots must be injected intramuscularly, in the stomach, which is a rather painful process.

HENRI: Tushy! Tushy!

*(Uncle Peter pops up from beneath the sheets.)*

PETER: All right, boys, what is it this time?!

CECIL: We were just...joking, Uncle Peter.

HENRI (*Solicitously and seductively*): How is your tushy, Uncle
Peter?

PETER: My behind is just fine. But yours may not be if you don't
settle down. Do you want to wake your brother Nathan up?

ANNA: I happen to know that Uncle Peter is very ticklish on his tushy.

PETER: No!

HENRI: Really?

PETER: No—don't start—

RUTH (*Interested*): On his tushy?

(*There is a tussling beneath the sheets; voices of all three
adults and three children mingle.*)

PETER (*With increasing panic*): No—Anna! Stop it! Ruth! Henri!
Ruth! No—NOOOOO!

(*At the sound of Peter's voice, Nathan wakes and cries.*)

ALL THREE: Oh, shit.

PETER: I'll take care of it. You just go to sleep like big boys, all
right?

ANNA: All right, Uncle Peter.

HENRI: Uncle Peter?

PETER: Yes, Henri?

HENRI: Would it make you feel better if I kiss your behind?

PETER: That's a sweet thought. But no. Sleep tight.

(*Peter crosses to the cradle and picks up Nathan and walks
into the living room.*

*Ruth walks over to the refrigerator and removes a bottle;
begins to heat it up.*)

HENRI: I think what baby Nathan wants is a peanut butter and
jelly sandwich.

PETER: Come with Daddy, Nathan.

*(Now Anna goes to the changing table.)*

CECIL: Actually, I think a diaper would be appropriate to the occasion.

PETER: Yes, yes, I know. It's a hard life, kid. Yes, it is.
*(Nathan quiets)*
That's a good boy. Daddy's boy! Are you Daddy's boy?

*(Nathan gurgles. Anna crosses to Peter. Ruth joins them.)*

ANNA: Look at that face! Who's face is that?

RUTH: He's our cutie.

ANNA: Yes, you are.

PETER: Do you know what we do with cuties? We eat them.

*(Nathan gurgles again. A spot begins to grow on them; as it grows, we become aware of New York outside of the apartment.*
*The walls become more transparent, and we become aware of the sounds in the street below: New York City at night.)*

PETER: That's right! Daddy's going to eat Nathan up!...

*(Peter makes gobbling noises. Nathan giggles.)*

PETER: I'm eating you up, yummyyummyyummyyummy-yummmm—Nathan's all gone!

*(We see Peter, Anna and Ruth cradling Nathan in their apartment—one apartment among hundreds of their neighbors. The lights stream from adjacent windows where other families in privacy keep their own nightly vigils.*
*The play ends as we hear Nathan's giggles and squeals.)*

END OF PLAY

# The Oldest Profession

## A Full-Length Play in Six Blackouts

The first reading of *The Oldest Profession* was produced February 1981 at the Hudson Guild in New York City. Gordon Edelstein directed the following cast:

| | |
|---|---|
| VERA | Alice Drummond |
| EDNA | Jenny Ventriss |
| LILLIAN | Virginia Downing |
| URSULA | Kate Wilkinson |
| MAE | Margot Stevenson |

The play was produced April 1988 by Theatre Network in Edmonton, Canada and 25th Street Theatre in Saskatoon, Canada. Tom Bentley-Fisher directed the following cast:

| | |
|---|---|
| VERA | Jane Roth-Casson |
| EDNA | Wendy Agnew |
| LILLIAN | Pamela Haig |
| URSULA | Barbara Reese |
| MAE | Mary Glenfield |

A reading of *The Oldest Profession* was presented  April 1990 at Brown University in Providence, Rhode Island. Paula Vogel directed the following cast:

| | |
|---|---|
| VERA | Rosmarie Waldrop |
| EDNA | Professor Coppelia Kahn |
| LILLIAN | Professor Anne Shaver |
| URSULA | Professor Susanne Woods |
| MAE | Dean Lydia English |

*The Oldest Profession* was produced October 1991 by Company One in Hartford, Connecticut. Juanita Rockwell directed, with sets by Carl Sprague, lights by Randy Glickman and costumes by Cassandra Hamilton. The cast was as follows:

| | |
|---|---|
| VERA | Cheryl Berger |
| EDNA | Susan Dreyfuss |
| LILLIAN | Alycia Evica |
| URSULA | Laurie Tyler |
| MAE | Gloria Pilot |

CHARACTERS

VERA: The youngest, 72. Loves the sun.

EDNA: Next in line, 74. A good time girl. Best friend of Vera. Loves her work.

LILLIAN: 75. Age has been gentle. Sure of herself, a woman of great style and great audacity. The Rose of Mae's stable.

URSULA: 79. Germanic, bossy, set and determined. Believes in rules, promotion, work ethic. Horsey and big boned, she slumps now. Can by very crabby. Can not stand the sound of Vera eating with loose dentures. Fond of adages with harsh, moralistic messages.

MAE: 83. A self-made woman, a leader who finds the management of men ridiculously easy, and has mastered the management of women as well. She looks after her girls.

TIME AND PLACE

A sunny day shortly after the election of Ronald Reagan in 1980.

*A sunny day shortly after the election of Ronald Reagan in 1980. A long bench on 72nd Street and Broadway, New York City. Five women sitting in the sun.*

VERA: ...and so last night I thought a bit of fish would be nice for supper—not too heavy, not too light—so I bought just the nicest bit of fish down the block at Joe's—fresh, pink—much nicer than the fish store up on 89th Street; their fish isn't fresh at all; it smells like a bad joke about ladies of the night— *(Whoops)* and it costs five cents more the pound—five cents! So I bought this fish from Joe; lemon sole it was, very good and tender. I do so love a nice bit of lemon sole. I melted some unsalted butter in the skillet, and chopped up, oh, about this much scallion, and then I just sautéed it on each side till it flaked with a fork and then just squeezed lemon and parsley over it—and I tell you, it melted in my mouth. Just melted.

URSULA: Last night was Friday.

VERA: Why, yes, it was.

URSULA: The Pope says you don't have to eat fish on Friday anymore. For the past ten years, you don't have to eat fish on Friday. And for the past ten years we've been hearing about your fish on Friday.

VERA: Well, Ursula, excuse me. I didn't mean to bore you.

URSULA: Well, then, try not to tell us in detail what you ate for dinner the night before. With or without your teeth in.

LILLIAN: Oh, really, Ursula, it doesn't matter. Just don't listen.

VERA *(Brightly)*: All right, then—let's discuss something else.

*(Sniffles)* We...we can talk about the weather. It's...it's a lovely day, isn't it?

LILLIAN: My God, Vera—you cry at the slightest little thing.

URSULA: Can't say "boo" to her—it sets her off.

MAE: Vera—stop that now.

URSULA: You can't take correction for your own good. Why do you always have to start sniffling? You are the tetchiest thing...

EDNA *(Nasty)*: Well, it can't be change of life.

MAE: All right, all of you—that's enough.

*(There is a silence. Vera sniffles softly. Edna looks through her handbag.)*

EDNA: Here—take my compact. Your nose is all shiny now.

*(Vera takes the compact, looks in the mirror, stops crying. Checks her makeup, smiles at herself. Pats on a little powder. Mollified, she hands the mirror back to Edna, who looks in the mirror, and spreads the powder on thick.)*

MAE: Edna, you put on entirely too much rouge. I don't like it. It makes you look like a grandmother tarting it up. Look at Lillian—she doesn't use any rouge at all.

EDNA: No—but she doesn't get any, either.

*(Edna and Ursula cackle.)*

LILLIAN *(Shrugs)*: Who wants it?

EDNA: I do.

*(There is a pause.)*

EDNA: Well, will you look at her—

URSULA: Where?

EDNA: Coming out of the Citibank...

LILLIAN: Oh? Which one?

URSULA: Oh, don't pretend, Lillian...you can't see your way to the john at night...

MAE: Those pants are so tight on her, she's practically parading her wazoo on Broadway.

URSULA: Think she's professional?

MAE *(Shrewd)*: No. I haven't seen her around before.

EDNA: I bet she gives it away for free.

VERA: Why—she's wearing a chain around her neck.

　　　*(Thrilled)* Edna—she's in chains!

URSULA: Amateur auto-erotic bondage...

MAE: It all went downhill after Guy Lombardo...

VERA: Why is she wearing chains?

LILLIAN: Who cares?

VERA: She looks like she's having fun.

MAE *(Stern)*: You need a little trip to Miami, Vera. Spend some time with normal folks down there.

*(For a moment, no one speaks.)*

URSULA: Yes, sir, the sixties was bad enough...what with long hair and miniskirts so short that young women were bein' rushed to St. Vincent's for frostbite on their female parts. But now—now there's Punk.

MAE: The Good Lord made safety pins for diapers, not for earlobes.

LILLIAN: I don't know. I side with Vera. They're just kids not doing anybody any harm...it's a free country.

URSULA: It's free for kids under twenty-one! But not for you and me! Not free for grandmothers to sit on park benches, what with the rapists and the muggers!

LILLIAN: Oh, Ursula, that's a load of horse manure and wishful thinking! Who'd rape you!

*(The two women have a stare down.)*

MAE: These kids don't know the meaning of work. They don't know about hunger; they don't know the pride that comes from giving a dollar's worth of work for a fifty-cent wage. Half the people we know in Jefferson Square don't even get birthday cards from their kids, let alone a Christmas visit.

EDNA: Thank Jesus we don't have any kids.

VERA: But we have each other; you always give me a nice card and a cake for my birthday. I love the cake you gave me last year from that Third Avenue bakery. I must have had two, three pieces of it, even though I kept saying "Now, Vera, you know you shouldn't eat it..."—But I did. It was made with Grand Marnier and had a sponge interior, iced with a butter frosting that was so light it just melted—

EDNA: Mr. Donovan's been asking for cigar money...and I said to him, "But Mr. Donovan, you've already got a cigar, and it smokes."

*(She cracks up. Alone.)*

So I finally asked him why he didn't call his big hot-shot son the banker on Wall Street for some extra cigar moola— and do you know what he said? "My son's secretary won't put my calls through—"

MAE: These kids are the Me Generation.

VERA: I like Donny and Marie.

*(The other women just look at her. Beat.)*

URSULA: All I can say is that it's a permissive generation; these kids are going to put us all out of business. Lord knows we're not getting any younger.

VERA: Well, Ursula, remember what they say: Youth is in the Mind. Take Mr. Jonathan: He was full of piss and vinegar to the last. When I went to visit him, all laid out in the Riverside Chapel, his face was still full of the devil...He was just so handsome in his gray flannel suit with the red tie that I just whisked up beside the casket, and when his family wasn't looking, I slipped my hand down the side and behind his coat tails and into his trousers, and then I tweaked the hell out of his marble behind for old times and I whispered: "Jonathan Rhodes, you old geezer—"

*(Vera whoops from the memory.)*

MAE *(Uneasy)*: Vera, now stop that morbid talk.

VERA: Why, it's not morbid to talk of the dead, Mae. Really it's not. We're all of us going to die.

LILLIAN: Not Ursula. "Waste not, want not." She's going to be preserved.

URSULA: Better that than a pauper's grave, paid for by Uncle Sam. Subsidized begging—Medicare. Social Security has no place in a free market.

LILLIAN: I wouldn't mind being eligible for a government subsidy each month in recognition of all my years of public service.

MAE: Any business woman with the slightest shred of pride doesn't need their handouts.

LILLIAN: You're wrong. It's a matter of principle, social security. It should be inviolate. If I could, I wouldn't be too proud to mooch off Uncle Sam.

URSULA: Oh, Lillian buys the whole Keynesian economy claptrap, which is just a fancy excuse for big government spending and borrowing! You'd have more than enough income to live on, much less die on, if you took what opportunities came along, instead of being so choosy!

LILLIAN: There's not much that comes along...

VERA: And besides, the cost of living's so high nowadays; what with prices and all—you know, Mr. Zabar's cheese is out of the question. It used to be that you could buy a nice hunk of...oh, Camembert or Brie, for maybe $1.50 and have change left over for their delicious bread—with the thick crusts so that the inside's all fluffy and light. But now, that same piece of Brie will cost you a good $2.75. Can't afford to go downstairs to Mr. Zabar's anymore—only the rich can buy down there. When I die I want to go to Mr. Zabar's and eat all I want with close-fitting plates—

URSULA: The reason living costs so much for you, Vera, is that you fritter your money away on luxuries. Fish. Cheese. Chocolates. I eat frugal, and I sock the money I save away, for sickness or old age. "A fool and his money are soon parted," so they say...I'm putting away every penny into sure investments; no use putting it into the bank so's the feds can profit. I learned that the hard way in '29. No one's going to have to take care of me—no charity case here. The rest of you can spend it all on sweet-tooth fancies. Or Lillian's lace panties that droop the second they're washed in hot water. But Ursula's a wiser bird than that. There'll be plenty of goodies left when I go, hidden, too. It's gonna take you a day just to find it all.

LILLIAN: You know, you really shouldn't store money in your rooms above Mr. Zabar's. It's just not safe.

URSULA: How many fool times do I have to tell you? It's not money—it's securities.

EDNA: I still don't know what "securities" mean.

URSULA: Something more solid than gold, more stable than oil, that's for sure. You'll have to wait for me to kick the bucket to find out what.

MAE: Why are you girls constantly harping on..."passing away" today?

URSULA: I'm not harping, Mae—I've got plenty of juice left in me. The rest of you will go before me.


*(Long pause. Vera stretches and smiles.)*


VERA: I just love the sun. Don't you?


*(No answer. The women bask in the sun.)*


MAE: Edna?

EDNA *(Drowsy)*: Yes?

MAE: Mind the time, now.

EDNA: The appointment's not till five. I'm watching the time—
I'm counting the minutes.

MAE: That's the spirit. Just mind the time.

*(Another pause.)*

VERA *(In tense aside to Edna)*: Uh-oh. Edna, look down the
street!

EDNA: What?

VERA: Trouble's coming. Edna, she's back again.

EDNA: Who?

VERA: That snippy chippy—

EDNA *(Looks)*: Oh, boy. We'd better tell Mae.
(*Urgently*) Mae! MAE! That cold piece of punk's back for
more...

*(The women, excited, sit up, alert. Mae stands.)*

MAE: I'll take care of this. *(Advances forward and yells to the
woman who is offstage)*
You! You!! Back for more? Asking for it? You've been
warned! Trespassing on my girls' territory. I'm gonna fix that
face the next time you even sniff the air downstream from
this park. Do you understand me? When I get through with
you, you'll only be good for night traffic when there's no
moon!! What?...What?...Old goods are we?
*(She listens to the woman offstage)*
Well, I'll tell you what—this has been our beat for over
forty-five years, and listen, baby, we still tick! We're built to
last! We give service we're proud of!! Unlike you, your plastic twat is gonna fall out in the road five years from now!
*(Gets winded)*

URSULA: That's right! Not like you, wham-bam-thank-you-ma'am
down the alley and overcharge twenty for it!

MAE: I said I'll take care of this, Ursula. I'm in charge.

*(Back to the woman offstage)* I MEAN IT! Scram and suck rats by the boat basin. This part of the West Side belongs to me!! WHAT did you call me! WHAT??!!

*(The women, backing their leader, stand as one, ready and mean for battle.)*

VERA *(Simultaneously)*: She can't get away with calling Mae that!
EDNA *(Simultaneously)*: Let's tear that tart to bits!
LILLIAN *(Simultaneously)*: Scratch that Snatch!
URSULA *(Simultaneously)*: Disrespectful Slut!!

*(Mae draws out a large, gleaming, wicked hat pin.)*

MAE: Cheap amateur whores don't know how to act like ladies; I'll teach you etiquette if I catch you...let me catch you around here again and you'll be laughing out the other side of your ASS!!

*(Mae, triumphant, gives the fleeing prostitute the finger. Mae makes her way back to the bench, exhausted, and sits. The others, worked up, sit one by one.)*

VERA: You were majestic, Mae.
EDNA: Scared the hell out of me, you did, Mae.
LILLIAN: Good show!
URSULA: She was outnumbered. Stupid little tart.
EDNA: Imagine her thinking she can just waltz in here and take over our clientele with her gaudy, swishy clothes and her gum chewing—
LILLIAN *(With real interest)*: What was she wearing? I...didn't get too good a look—
EDNA: She was wearing a tight cotton skirt slit up to Hackensack with a top so low you could see Hoboken.
VERA: That outfit was on sale in Bloomingdale's basement last month...

LILLIAN: That's nerve, coming to the West Side in reduced East Side castoffs.

URSULA: Oh, these upstart whores think all they have to do is buy a Bloomingdale's outfit and they can just open up shop for trade; but these young things will get their comeuppance: "A pretty pig makes an ugly sow."

VERA: I do so love bright colors.

EDNA: Well, we won't be seeing her again. You gave her what for, Mae.

MAE: When a woman can't defend her territory or her girls, it's time to get out of the Life. I tell you, it makes me sad. When I see the new generation of prostitutes working right on the street—gypsies, all of them—on their own with no group, no house to call their own, no amenities for customers, no tradition or...or finesse...where's the pride in the name of prostitute? It's all gone downhill since the government poked their nose in our business and booted decent self-respecting businesswomen out of Storeyville. Remember the House where we all first met? A spick-and-span establishment. The music from Professor Joe in the parlor; the men folk bathed, their hair combed back and dressed in their Sunday best, waiting downstairs happy and shy. We knew them all; knew their wives and kids, too. It was always Mr. Buddy or Mr. Luigi; never this anonymous "John" for any stranger with a Jackson in his billfold.

URSULA: And we were called Miss Ursula and Miss Lillian too...Men who treated their wives and mothers right treated their mistresses right, too.

MAE: There was honor in the trade...My father went to Storeyville often when I was a girl. Mother used to nod to Miss Sophie right in the street before Mass in the Quarter. Miss Sophie saved our lives, she did. The depression of '97—Papa lost work and there were seven of us to feed. So every morning before folks were up and about, Miss Sophie came and put groceries on the back step—Papa was a regular customer, she couldn't let us starve. And none of the neighbors knew a thing. Finally Papa got work again; the money came in for food on the table and Saturday nights at Miss Sophie's. And then my mother got pregnant again—I guess there was plenty of my father to go around. Mother had a boy. So Miss Sophie said she'd be real pleased if they named that boy after her gentleman protector. So they named my brother—

LILLIAN AND VERA *(In unison)*: Radcliffe.

VERA: I love that story. It's such a nice name, too. So refined.

URSULA *(Irritated)*: We've heard that old story before, Mae. The best thing that ever happened was the day the Navy closed Storeyville down because too many boys were jumping ship.

EDNA: You always say that, Ursula. I liked Storeyville when it was legal.

URSULA: Oh, sure. The working girls loved Storeyville.

MAE: We would have been Number One in the District if those military police hadn't of busted us. Hauled us to jail and slammed the Door shut. And then the bulldozers came in overnight.

URSULA *(Frustrated)*: I just can't get you to understand the Law of Supply and Demand. Anything Black Market fetches a higher price. Prohibition was the best thing for the liquor market—

LILLIAN: Uh-oh!! Ursula's off again about Prohibition! Check the bathtubs!

URSULA: That's not funny! I was making a pretty penny in 1927 until someone—one of you!—snitched on me. Butted their nose in my business. I'm still gonna find out who it was—

*(Ursula glares at Lillian; Lillian, Vera and Edna look blank.)*

MAE: Hold the line right here! Lillian, Ursula's arrest record is not a subject for levity. You hear me?

LILLIAN *(Mild)*: I can still hear you.

MAE: Second thing, for the record, I'm glad someone put a stop to your bathtub gin, Ursula. We were new here, and the last thing we could afford was to bring the law down on us. We're in the Life, not the distillery business.

URSULA: Well, we're not going to stay in the Life, Mae, unless you stop living in the past! It's a New Age: We've got to get off our fannies and sell!

MAE: Oh? Exactly what are you trying to tell me, Ursula?

URSULA: Smell the coffee! "Fair words butter no parsnips!" It takes different strategies to stay afloat in today's competitive market; that little chippy will be back.

MAE: If that little clapbox shows again, I'll—

URSULA: What? Beat her with your purse? Call her names? Have a stroke in the process?

MAE: Well, have you got any better ideas?

URSULA: I won't mince words, Mae. We've been working together too long for that. What's needed around here are new management ideas at the helm; someone who can make this business cost-effective.

VERA: Cost-effective?

MAE: And I suppose that person is you, Ursula.

URSULA: That's right. "He that is wise is he that is rich."

MAE: And what exactly would you do differently from me?

URSULA: Advertise.

LILLIAN: Advertise! Just lift your skirts, Ursula.

URSULA: Advertising's the soul of the modern marketplace. First thing to do is to place pithy personals in the *Village Voice*.

MAE: *Village Voice?* Who reads the *Village Voice?*

URSULA: A younger clientele. We've got to face the facts: Our gentlemen callers are a dying breed. Or they're in the hospital; or when you do get them in bed at home they can't get it up anymore.

MAE: Still, they do the honorable thing by us. They pay.

LILLIAN: You mean we'd have younger customers? We'd end up paying them.

URSULA: No, I don't think so. New York's a city of diversified tastes. I think we could specialize. You know, we could seek out a *Harold and Maude* situation. *(Grandly)* We could cater to the complexes of a small circle.

VERA: Edna, what is she talking about? Who the hell is Harold?

MAE *(To Ursula)*: I don't think we want to know any more ideas that are cost-effective. You're upsetting the girls.

LILLIAN: Not me. She's entertaining me.

URSULA: Wait. Let me have my say. We should up our fees. Change to a price list. Instead of seven dollars an hour, we could start with a seven-dollar minimum, and charge for the extras. We have to increase the rate of turnover, and make the girls more time-efficient. Lillian here stays in bed with Mr. Loman much too long...

LILLIAN: Well, I just can't jump into bed and jump out anymore, Ursula. It's not my fault, it's the arthritis—

URSULA: "It's a poor workman that blames his tools..."

MAE: Are you through?

URSULA: Then there's Entertainment Surcharge, Linen Tax, Mastercharge, Visa and—

EDNA: She's been reading the *Wall Street Journal* again.

LILLIAN: No, Dale Carnegie's *How to Win Friends and Influence People*. She's halfway through the course; she can influence people.

URSULA: Well. I'll keep my advice to myself in the future. "A bumblebee in a cow turd thinks himself a king."

MAE: I've listened to you, and now you're going to listen to me, Ursula Thaller. I've kept you girls together for over forty-five years. When we were closed down in Storeyville, I paid your bail; all of you got your train tickets North and a place to live. All of our gentlemen here are nice, and good to us, with a codicil in the will now and then. There's always been money for the doctor when any of you girls are sick, and food on your table. And you know I've never held back on anyone. If any of you girls want to leave this stable for greener pastures, you can go. No hard feelings. Well?

LILLIAN: I stick with Mae.

VERA: Oh, dear. I hate to see fighting on such a beautiful day. Let's forget the whole thing.

EDNA: Well, I think…I think…it's not time for a change. Not now.

MAE: Well. That's settled, then. You should be proud, Ursula, that you're apprentice to a Madam.

URSULA: I say whoopee-ding. For the past fifteen years—you call that merit promotion?

MAE: When I go, you'll get your chance. You're Second-in-Command. I think we're all agreed upon that. When you carry me out feet first, Ursula's in charge and you're all going to listen to her as if to me. It's important to me that we keep together. When I pass away, I'd like to think of you all carrying on.

LILLIAN: Nonsense, Mae. You're as strong as a horse.

VERA *(Trembling)*: Oh, Mae…

MAE *(Looking at Ursula)*: I don't intend to go anywhere, yet.

URSULA: I'm only trying to point out the facts of life. "Old Vessels Leak." You forgot to collect the money from this morning, Mae. You're losing your touch.

MAE *(Sniffs)*: I did NOT forget. I was…*(Clears her throat)*…I was just about to get around to that. You know, Ursula, you're a whore with the soul of a businesswoman. And I'm a businesswoman with the soul of a whore. And THAT is the difference between us.

   *(Briskly)* Ladies, please get out your purse and have your money ready.

*(The women rustle through their handbags.)*

MAE: All right, then: Vera, what do you have to report?

*(Vera stands and walks toward Mae; she hands over her money.)*

VERA: I have seven dollars plus a one-dollar tip.

MAE: Seven dollars plus a one-dollar tip. That's eight.

EDNA *(As Vera walks back)*: Well? Did he come today?

*(The other women laugh.)*

VERA: I don't think it's nice of you to make fun of Mr. Francis behind his back...he tries so hard.

LILLIAN: That answers your question, Edna.

URSULA: I don't understand why the fool tips if he doesn't get anything out of the deal...

VERA *(Tenderly)*: It's not just for the sex, Ursula. I...I hold him when he cries...He's a very nice man.

EDNA: Mr. Francis's idea of a lay is lying down.

MAE: He's a good and regular customer. Always pays up. Edna? What do you have?

*(Edna struts over with pride to Mae and hands her the money.)*

EDNA: Fourteen AND two dollars and fifty cents in tips.

LILLIAN: Good show.

MAE: Yes, that's good. Fourteen plus $2.50. That makes $16.50.

*(Edna walks back.)*

EDNA: And I had to work my ass for every penny. Mr. Andrew was a lamb, as always, but Mr. Benjamin! All around the room he was! I told him, "Mr. Benjamin, you'd make an eighteen year old scream!!" God, he's one cocky man...

URSULA *(Dour)*: It must be the medication he's on.

VERA: Whatever it is, I wish he could lend Mr. Francis some...

MAE: Mr. Benjamin's very fond of you, Edna. He's told me. So then, we're up to Lillian. Lillian?

   *(Lillian does not rise)*

   Well, Lillian, what about this morning?

LILLIAN *(Hesitating)*: I hope you won't be mad at me, Mae. But I didn't know what to do...

URSULA: Do about what?

MAE: Didn't you go up to Mr. Loman's room at 11:30?

LILLIAN: Yes, I went. But...

URSULA: But what?

MAE *(Warning)*: Ursula...

LILLIAN: I went at the appointed time; I kept my side of the bargain...but he's not very well.

MAE: Did he cancel?

LILLIAN: No, not exactly...he's all right in that department. I gave him the usual, but when it came time for payment...

MAE: Ah, I see. Short of cash, long on horn?

LILLIAN: No, he paid. He paid with these. *(Draws out of her purse long silk stockings circa 1945, with the seam running down the middle)* He insisted that I take these for payment. Said he's paid a lot of money for them while on the road in Boston; he...he said they were hard to get, what with the war going on and all. Mr. Loman thinks that stockings and chocolate are a better bet than our currency as long as...as long as the "Japanese are beating the pants off our boys in the Pacific Theatre." Those were his exact words.

MAE: Ah, I see.


*(There is a respectful silence as the women realize that Mr. Loman has lost his marbles.)*


MAE: Well, I think you did the right thing, Lillian.

URSULA: The right thing! Look at them! No one's wearing stockings with garter belts anymore! What good are they?

LILLIAN: I've been wearing a garter belt on Saturday morning for Mr. Loman; he's partial to 'em.

EDNA: I agree with Mr. Loman. They make women look sexy; it's definitely a "turn-on"...

URSULA: That's besides the point! This is worse than passing a bad check...

LILLIAN: Mae, what are we going to do? About Mr. Loman I mean?

MAE *(Slowly)*: I don't know. He's been left alone for too long.

LILLIAN: He looks forward to my visit once a week so much...

URSULA: Well, we can't have charity cases hanging on—we're not Meals on Wheels!

(*To herself*) Chocolates and stockings! What good are they? They're not even staples...

EDNA: Maybe we should say something to someone in charge at Jefferson Square...

MAE: That's the least we can do. Thing is, though, Jefferson Square's just apartments; the front desk doesn't look out for the tenants. They think they've done their responsibility just because they've installed handle bars by the toilet and the tub. If we tell them that Mr. Loman's...deteriorating, they'll say he should go to a home.

(*Pause.*)

LILLIAN: He was doing just fine...until this morning. Maybe it's temporary.

MAE: It's not a good sigh. Maybe he should go to a home. Jefferson Square's designed for folks with all their fixtures in working condition. Does he have any relations, Lillian?

LILLIAN: Two good-for-nothing sons who are only God-knows-where.

MAE (*Wearily*): Well. I'll drop by there tonight and have a chat with him.

(*Pause, as if a requiem for Mr. Loman. Then Mae, shaking her head, gets back to business.*)

MAE: All right now. We're up to you, Ursula. How did you make out?

(*Ursula stiffly hands over the money.*)

URSULA: Seven dollars.

MAE (*Frowning*): No tip?

URSULA: No tip.

LILLIAN: Mr. Ezra, last of the big time spenders!

URSULA: Well, he pays. I don't mind. At least he's not a gabber; he doesn't bend my ears with ramblings and soft words...

LILLIAN: I bet he doesn't.

URSULA: That suits me just fine. I like 'em silent. I come into his room and he's in bed, ready and undressed. No small talk. A man of business. I say, "Good morning, Mr. Ezra." He says, "Good Morning." And then he gets right to the point—

LILLIAN: Premature ejaculation?

*(Mae checks over the money and counts it again; she makes out a Citibank deposit slip.)*

URSULA: I get the same rate for five minutes that you all get for twenty. "The more fool he."

VERA: I like to cuddle with some of the gentlemen. Like Mr. Francis. He's got the softest gray hair on his chest. I could lie there for hours...

URSULA: That's what I mean by faster turnover. If they want to cuddle, give 'em their hot water bottle.

MAE: Well, we're a little short, today.

URSULA: It came to $31.50.

MAE: Thank you, Ursula, we can all count.

URSULA: That doesn't even pay the rent.

LILLIAN: Thank God Mr. Zabar's rooms are rent controlled. We're safe.

MAE: Edna, can you approach Mr. Benjamin on Thursday and ask him to consider three times a week? He can afford it.

URSULA: If spermatozoons were nickels, that man would be a millionaire by now.

EDNA: I don't know if I can take him three times a week. But I'm willing to die trying.

MAE: Good girl. Well, ladies, if you'll give me your undivided attention for a few minutes. Here's how matters stand: Earned income for each of us is forty-seven dollars and sixty cents per week. I pay each of you sixty dollars a week. Which means we are depleting our savings account to the tune of fifty dollars per month.

VERA: Oh, dear.

MAE: Some measures need to be taken. Lillian...

LILLIAN: Yes.

MAE: Next Tuesday you start with Mr. Sidney. As he's a new customer, we'll up the fee to ten dollars. We keep the fee the same for our regulars. Only new customers will be increased.

LILLIAN: Right.

MAE: Secondly...there will be no increase in your weekly allowance. It's adequate...

LILLIAN: Barely.

MAE: Well, we have no expenses right now. No carfare. We can walk down the seven blocks it takes...Remember, President Reagan has called on all Americans to reduce the deficit, and to balance the budget. We can start here. We can tighten our belts. No more two-hour lunches.

*(There is a united groan from the women.)*

VERA: I get gas when I don't digest properly, Mae. And there's nothing more embarrassing...

MAE: Well, then, moan or something. Cover it over. Mr. Francis doesn't hear too well, anyway.

To continue. All of our customers should be encouraged to increase the number of our visits. Mr. Benjamin. Mr. Franklin. Mr. Samuel. If it's not hazardous to their health. And Ursula. I want you to give a little extra to Mr. Ezra. If you give extra, he'll give extra. No more flat fees.

URSULA: It's squeezing water from a stone.

MAE: Then *squeeze*...All of you are hard workers; there's not a shirker in the bunch. We can't rely on legacies from our gentlemen. We have to pull our own weight. All of our gentlemen are very pleased; and I'm very proud when I stroll in the evening and meet our friends down the block—they all have lovely things to say. I'm very proud. But I'd appreciate it if you would all try especially hard in the next few weeks. Say nice things about how they look, and don't talk politics or money or about anything in the newspaper—it puts them off their feed. And it raises their blood pressure, too. Make them feel romantic and strong, and those tips will keep rolling in. Any questions, Edna?

EDNA: No.

MAE: Vera?

VERA: No, Mae.

MAE: We need to straighten up and fly right. We've got to be prepared.

URSULA: Just what are we preparing for?

MAE: Change. I think now would be a good time to tell them, Vera.

VERA: Oh, Mae, I don't know.

*(The women look at Vera with expectation.)*

MAE: I think we'd all like to share in your good news.

VERA: Well...Mr. Simon has asked for my hand in marriage.

*(There is a considerable stir on the bench.)*

EDNA: Mr. Simon!

*(Ursula begins to laugh. She laughs for a long time, which makes Edna and Vera laugh. Ursula tries to stop, but can't— the effort makes her cry. Pause.)*

URSULA: I don't know when I've had such a laugh.

LILLIAN: I don't know that it's that funny.

VERA: I don't mind, Lillian. It is funny, come to think of it.

URSULA: It's just that...Mr. Simon's going to make an honest woman of her.

*(Ursula starts laughing again.)*

EDNA: Isn't he Mr. Jonathan's former golf partner?

VERA: Yes. The three of us used to...have a good time together.

EDNA: Are you going to accept?

VERA: I haven't made up my mind yet. I don't know.

URSULA: If he's fool enough to ask, you should be fool enough to accept.

LILLIAN: I don't know, Vera.

MAE: And why not, Lillian?

LILLIAN: Hasn't he already had three wives?

MAE: Yes. So?

LILLIAN: Well, doesn't it make you wonder? Why they all died before him?

VERA: They didn't all die. Two of them left him first. Then they died.

EDNA: But we do know why they left. Boredom.

MAE: Mr. Simon has a pension. And money in the bank. It's security.

VERA: I don't know that I will.

MAE: Be sensible, Vera. He's much older than you are. He's eighty-six.

URSULA *(Bristling)*: That's not so old.

LILLIAN: I think he's a dull, stodgy old fart. Don't do it, Vera.

VERA: I haven't made up my mind yet.

URSULA: Well, Vera, I don't suppose you'll marry in white.


*(Ursula laughs.)*


MAE: Look, Ursula, this kind of thing happens all the time. Remember Jeannette? Pretty little girl. Left the Life, got married to an accountant.

URSULA: Of course he was an accountant. Knew a bargain when he saw one. Used goods go cheap.

MAE: Well, as far as we know, she made a good match.

URSULA: That was different.

EDNA: Why?

URSULA: Jeannette was all of eighteen. Vera's not just a Woman with a Past; she's a Woman with an Epic.

EDNA: Does Mr. Simon love you?

VERA: Well, I make him feel clever. He talks and I listen.

LILLIAN: Well, I wouldn't care if he was the King of Siam. I wouldn't do it.

MAE: There won't be many more offers down the pike. And when Mr. Simon's time is up, all of his benefits will go to Vera.

URSULA: Mr. Simon's better off marrying Vera than one of those grandmother floozies in Jefferson Square.

EDNA: Have you told Mr. Francis yet?

VERA (Desperate): I haven't made up my mind yet!

EDNA: He's going to be very upset.

VERA: Edna, if I do decide to marry Mr. Simon, you'd look after Mr. Francis, wouldn't you?

EDNA: Of course I would.

VERA: So I wouldn't have to worry.

EDNA: But even if you did marry Mr. Simon, couldn't you visit Mr. Francis now and then?

MAE: Vera will do nothing of the kind. Once a girl leaves the Life, she has to go straight all the way.

URSULA: That's right, Vera. It's "Till Death do you part."

EDNA: I don't know. I think Mr. Simon would look cute with horns.

LILLIAN: Oh, God. Marital sex is so dull.

URSULA: Wait a moment. What about Vera's customers?

VERA: Yes, that's right. I can't do this to you. I'll just thank Mr. Simon for the honor but—

MAE: We can figure it out. Make up new schedules.

URSULA: That's a lot of lost income, Mae, to just let whistle down the drain—

MAE: Vera should do what makes her happy.

URSULA: Of course, there will be less expenses this way, too.

VERA: Stop it! All of you! I'm not ready for this! I need to make up my own mind.

URSULA: If we're going to be so hard-pressed, Mae, why don't you take on some trade as well?

MAE: I'll pretend I didn't hear that suggestion, Ursula.

LILLIAN: What's wrong with you today, Ursula? You've been riding Mae all day…It's because of Mae in the first place that you even have one five-minute fuck—

URSULA: You're talking mighty big for someone who swaps for stockings…

LILLIAN: Listen, sister, I've just about had it with—

URSULA: You were just a scrawny virgin with big eyes in Storeyville while I was satisfying the troops—

LILLIAN: Seniority be damned…who cares if you were fucking at Gettysburg!

URSULA: Gettysburg!

MAE (*Overlapping*): Girls, girls! Enough! Now stop it—right on the street. I'm going to have to separate you just like you were in grammar school again. Edna, sit in between Lillian and Ursula. Lillian, move down next to Vera.

(*Edna gets up, sits in between, and smiles pacifically at Ursula.*)

LILLIAN: Suits me fine. Hi, Vera.

MAE: Edna—it's 4:30 now. Are you aware of the time?

EDNA: Yes.

MAE: Be especially nice to Mr. Lawrence today.

EDNA: I'll give him a good time.

VERA: 4:30 already, is it? That's why my stomach is growling…it's almost time for dinner. I have the strangest hankering for dinner tonight…I feel like going to the produce market up the street—the one on 76th is the best—and buying two pints of the first raspberries of the season. Did you notice that raspberries are back again? God only knows, I love those things…but they're so expensive. They're a very delicate fruit. What I'd like most is just a bowl of raspberries, washed ever so carefully, with cream on top. No sugar. Nothing else. My mother used to make babies in a blanket: raspberries wrapped in pastry and then sprinkled with confectionery sugar. I'd make myself ill eating those. But raspberries plain are the best.

## Blackout One

*There is a blackout. It should be of short duration. It is optional as to whether or not Vera's monologue runs through the brief darkness. When the lights come up, Vera, Edna, Ursula and Mae are still sitting as before. The women are clearly subdued.*

VERA: Those raspberries we had on Saturday were delicious. I offered some to Lillian, and she tried a little. She thought they were just right. Not too ripe and mushy; they were still tart. And I said to her, don't the seeds bother you, though? The way they get into the cracks of your plates and rub against the gums? And she said, "Vera, if it bothers you, just take your plates out. I won't mind." And she didn't mind. That's just the kind of person she was.

MAE: We all miss her very much.

*(Pause.)*

URSULA: Funny...

MAE: What is?

URSULA: Didn't think she'd be the one to go first.

MAE: Oh? Who did you think would be first?

URSULA: Just didn't think she'd be the one, that's all.

EDNA: She kept her looks to the end.

URSULA: She was blind as a bat, though.

VERA: Oh, Lillian always did have the loveliest skin. Beautiful eyes, too. I can remember begging to brush her hair when we all lived in the house...Do you remember how long her hair used to be?

EDNA: Miss Mae's Wild Irish Rose, the men used to call her.

MAE: She was the prettiest of us all.

*(Pause.)*

VERA: Well, I hope I'm next.

MAE: Vera!

VERA: Well, I can't help it, Mae, 'cause I do. I want to go like Lillian did—all of a sudden, with all of my faculties. Just talking one moment, and gone the next. It's been a good life. I'm ready to go.

MAE: I want all of that kind of talk stopped. Our gentlemen are bound to be upset as it is over Lillian; they need some calming down. No more talking of...passing away. They pay us to escape all of that, not to hear it analyzed in our arms. Do you hear, Vera.

VERA: Yes.

*(Pause.)*

URSULA: Well, I guess there's going to be a lot more work around here for everybody.

EDNA: Of a specialized sort...

MAE: Well, it's true that on account of Lillian's arthritis, I assigned her gentlemen with a special preference...a certain taste different from most of your clients.

URSULA: Oh, Mae, you don't have to be delicate with us! We know that Lillian was blowing half of Jefferson Square...

MAE: Ursula, what you'll never learn, after fifteen years of apprenticing, is that it takes style to run a stable right.

EDNA: Mae, what are we going to do about Lillian's friends?

MAE: Befriend them. Lillian only had three a week; that means one for each girl. I'll talk to Mr. Brett, Mr. Sidney and Mr. Adam this evening and make up a new schedule for all of you that won't be taxing.

URSULA: Vera likes to take her plates out; why don't you assign all three to her?

VERA: I do not take my plates out on the job!

*(Taking courage)* Now that Lillian's gone, Ursula, don't think you can start in on me in her place!

URSULA: My.

MAE: I think it would be dignified if we all banded together in Lillian's absence...

*(Pause.)*

EDNA: I hear Mr. Loman's gone to the Presbyterian Home...

VERA: Yes, that's right, there's to be a new tenant in 1116A.

URSULA: Oh? A new tenant?

VERA: A Miss McPherson.

URSULA: Oh. Well, I don't guess she'll need our friendship. Although, you never know...we could branch out in new directions.

MAE: I don't think that's funny. You're in a peculiar mood today, Ursula.

URSULA: I'm in a great mood today.

MAE: Well-well, I think that's scandalous.

URSULA: I don't brook hypocrisy. Let me tell you, when I saw Lillian laid to rest this morning, I felt just fine.

MAE: I don't want to hear it. You may have had your fights while she was alive, but she was still—

URSULA: Oh, you don't understand the first thing. It's not at all personal. I've been thinking all day: It's not me! It wasn't me! I'm still going strong!

MAE: Good. I'm glad to hear it, Ursula. You won't mind taking on Mr. Adam, then. He'll keep your mind to your business. We're all professionals; we need to put away the events of this day and get on with our responsibilities.

VERA: We're losing another client, too...Mr. Simon.

MAE: Oh...I forgot all about—so you've made up your mind.

VERA: Oh, no. I can't marry him. He's been kidnapped.

EDNA: How can a man his age be kidnapped?

VERA: By his kids. His kids have kidnapped him to New Jersey. I met them in the lobby, carrying poor Mr. Simon away. They've threatened to put him in a home if he doesn't behave himself at his age. I guess he won't be returning to Jefferson Square—he's going to live with them, now.

EDNA: Oh, no, Vera. I'm so sorry.

MAE: That's outrageous! That those kids could just waltz in and—

URSULA: Oh, they can and they did. All they have to do is contest his sanity in court. Got to hand it to them. Smart.

VERA: I don't want his money. I really didn't want to leave, even more so now that Lillian's gone. So that's that.

MAE: We're still short a hand...I've made a decision. When the going gets tough, the tough get going...I will pick up the trade again.

*(A decided stir on the bench.)*

VERA: There's really no need, Mae. Edna and I can take up the slack.

URSULA: Oh, Mae's just got the seventy-year itch.

MAE: Well, I've forgotten...how it feels. I want to remember. I don't want to die wondering. I think I'll take Mr. Samuel on.

EDNA: Oh, but Mae, Mr. Samuel is awfully rough trade to start with. Why don't you warm up gradually?

VERA: Mae? Do you think it's safe? After all these years, to just—

URSULA: Oh, if he dies, he dies...

EDNA *(To Vera)*: We can't let her start out with Mr. Samuel.
    *(To Mae)* What about Mr. Andrew? He's a lovely man. And very gentle.

VERA: Yes! He'll do. Mae? What about Mr. Andrew? Edna's 10:30 appointment on Tuesday?

MAE: All right, then—Mr. Andrew...I can't wait. I may be a little rusty...

URSULA: Not just rusty, more like lockjaw—

MAE: But it's like riding a bicycle, isn't it? What do you girls say to the client at the start of your appointment; how do you get them to relax?

URSULA: I usually say the management does not accept personal checks.

MAE: Do you think Mr. Andrew would like my blue dress or the peach chiffon?

(*Pause. Edna, Vera and Ursula look at each other; Edna and Vera are concerned about Mae's sudden amateur enthusiasm; Ursula is amused. Mae answers her own question*) The peach chiffon, I think.


## Blackout Two

*Another brief blackout. Lights come up to reveal Ursula, and Edna and Vera sitting closely together on the other end of the bench. Edna and Vera look intimidated.*

URSULA: I believe in punctuality. 1:30 is 1:30; not 1:45. Mae stood for frittering away time, but time is money. Now, if I may have your attention, I'd like to review some notes about the past week—

VERA: Oh, Ursula, please, we're on our lunch break. We only get an hour as it is now, and—

URSULA: You can sit there and digest while I'm talking. "Waste not, want not." Now then: I want to rearrange things and get them straight. I'm switching some of the customers around. Edna, I want you to take on Mr. Ezra—Vera's too much of a gadder for his likes. He couldn't concentrate last week. He's not pleased.

VERA: It's not my fault if he couldn't get it—

URSULA: The customer's always right. So, Vera, you're to replace Mr. Ezra's 10:30 slot with Mr. Adam. He's half deaf, so you can yak at him all you want. Second item: Since Mr. Francis is still in the hospital, and as Mr. Sidney will be leaving for Florida this week, I've scheduled in two new customers—

VERA: We're...we're taking on more customers?

URSULA: Well, I can't be expected to carry on the trade. I'm in charge now, and there are increased privileges that go along with the increased responsibilities. You two can manage perfectly well.

*(Edna grunts.)*

VERA: But…but Ursula, we're taking on all of Lillian's gentlemen too…

URSULA: As I've said before, a little more elbow grease…and less lolling about in bed. When your customer's through, firmly but politely get out of bed and say, "That will be ten dollars, please." He can count it out while you dress. So, we're increasing to two in the morning, two in the afternoon. Remember Edna—don't talk to Mr. Ezra. And Edna—I thought I made it plain last week about the new policy. Cancellations without a week's notice will be billed just the same as if services had been rendered. Mr. Benjamin owes ten dollars on his bill.

*(Edna is silent)*

Do you understand?

EDNA: Yes.

URSULA: What's wrong with you today? Cat caught your tongue?

EDNA: Bone tired.

URSULA: What?

*(Edna is silent)*

What did you say? Speak up; I didn't hear you.

VERA: She said she's tired. I'm tired, Ursula. It's just too much. If you must assign new customers, then give them to me. Let Edna alone. I'm younger than she is, I could take them on—

URSULA: Nonsense. We all have to pull our weight around here. We're getting spoiled; back in the old days we used to have men queued up outside the door, three an hour. Without coffee breaks and lunch breaks and piss breaks.

VERA: That was during the war. That was patriotism.

URSULA: "Charity begins at home." Times are changing; the overhead on this business is growing by leaps and bounds. The last management left the books a shambles…

VERA: Mae worked her ass off for us! And we still had time for a two-hour lunch…

URSULA: But what good was her working like a dray horse if she frittered all her capital away? That woman didn't even have enough put by to pay for the flowers, much less the priest...I'm the one who had to scrape up the extra...

VERA: That...was very good of you, Ursula. I'm sure Mae would have appreciated it; those flowers looked so real, didn't they, Edna?

EDNA: Yes.

*(Vera looks at Edna carefully.)*

URSULA: Well, Mae's not around to thank me for it, that's for sure. And she called herself a businesswoman. Dying in a customer's arms without a penny to her name! Let it be a lesson. When I go, you're gonna need two strong arms to carry away what's left.

*(Pause)*

Mae never understood the first thing about investments. That was her problem. Money makes money. She just let the money sit in the bank, wrote checks, and let the future go hang.

*(Pause)*

Yes, sir, other people made money off of our money. Just lying there in the account, bone idle. I suppose I should tell you...

*(Edna looks up sharply.)*

EDNA: Tell us what?

URSULA: I've made a decision. We simply can't go on depleting our capital, week after week. I thought at first I would invest the principal sum in my own commodities, but that would create a glut on the market. I'm keeping my little secret well guarded...

EDNA *(Sharp)*: What exactly are you trying to tell us, Ursula?

URSULA: I've set up two accounts. One account will be for our expenses, and if we live frugally, should be quite sufficient for our needs. You two have always lived high on the hog, in the past, and have to learn—

EDNA *(Overlapping)*: What Have You Done With The Money!?!

URSULA *(Overlapping)*: Don't leap to conclusions. There are savings and loans offering good rates these days; I've invested the principal sum in certificates of deposit at twelve-and-a-half percent annually—

EDNA *(Overlapping)*: A certificate of deposit!

VERA *(Overlapping)*: A certificate of...what's a—

URSULA *(Quickly)*: Where it will turn over a little profit. Any fool can see the merits of—

EDNA *(Overlapping)*: Oh, God.

VERA *(Overlapping)*: But Edna, what's a certificate of deposit? What's happening?

EDNA: She's just slammed away our money in an account where we can't touch it.

URSULA: That's not true. It's still our money. We only have to wait eighteen months.

EDNA *(In a dead voice)*: Eighteen months.

URSULA: You...you have to believe in the future.

VERA: We...we don't have any money left?

URSULA: Nonsense. We have a substantial sum to draw on in a regular checking account. My God, Edna, you're a pig-headed woman. Anyone else would say, "Thank you, Ursula," for my pains on your behalf.

VERA: But...but what if something should happen?

URSULA: Nothing will happen. Any business involves risk—

EDNA: Your business, our risk. You should have asked.

URSULA: "Too many cooks spoil the broth." Mae had carte blanche around here to do what ever fool thing she wanted, no questions asked. I come around and bring a little order, make things cost-effective, and what thanks do I get?

*(No one says anything. Edna shifts forward on the bench, pale. She quietly grips the edge of the bench.)*

URSULA: This is only the beginning. Eighteen months down the road, who knows? I'd like to get my fingers into a little real estate. Now there's money...and deregulation's just down the road. Yes, sir, trust in the future...alternative energies, junk bonds, cable TV, strip mining's going to come back in a big way, I can tell you—

*(Suddenly Edna lets out a small:)*

EDNA: Oh.

*(Edna stares intently in front of herself, gripping the bench.)*

VERA: Edna? Edna? What is it?

*(Pause.)*

EDNA: I...I have...a pain.

*(Vera jumps up and goes to Edna.)*

VERA: A what?
　　*(Rubbing Edna's back)* Where does it hurt? *(Edna does not respond. Edna closes her eyes)*
　　*(To Ursula)* This all comes from you—you and your money shopping around. Cost Efficiencies!
URSULA *(Alarmed)*: Cost-effective—
VERA: I don't give a cold crap what! Edna's sick! What good is all the money in the world if we drop dead in our tracks from exhaustion!
URSULA: Edna's just...a little under the weather. It's...the heat. Maybe she should take a little time off. Cancel her two o'clock.
VERA: Edna. Edna, do you want to go to the hospital?

*(Edna shakes her head no.)*

VERA: I'm taking her home, then. Right now. And in a taxi—and you're going to pay for it, Ursula.

URSULA: All right, all right. Here. *(Fishes in her purse and draws out two dollars)* Take this—just make sure you don't let him run the meter—

EDNA: Wait. Wait a minute...

*(Ursula and Vera stand still, tense, waiting. Edna lets out a belch. Then, she sighs, relieved. Edna even smiles.)*

EDNA: Thank God. Gas.

VERA: Gas?

*(Vera settles back down on the bench. The women relax. Pause.)*

URSULA: You've got to cut out the onions at your age, Edna.

EDNA: I've got to stop wolfing down my lunch in an hour.

URSULA: Well, according to my watch, it's almost two. Vera, Edna, you should go.

VERA: Ursula?

URSULA: What is it, Vera?

VERA: I'd like some time off this afternoon. Cancel my three o'clock.

URSULA: Why?

VERA: I...I told Mr. Francis I'd visit him this afternoon at Roosevelt.

URSULA: You just saw him two days ago.

VERA: Well, I know that, Ursula, but he's lonely. And...he's very sick.

   *(Sniffling)* He's lying in that semi-private room, looking so frail in bed. I never realized how tiny he is. And no one else visits him. He's...he's a great favorite with the nurses, though.

URSULA: I'm sure the nurses are taking very good care of him. Roosevelt's a good hospital. I'll bet he's paying through the nose for it, though. He's better off than we are.

VERA (*Smiling while sniffling*): You know...you know what he calls me? He introduced me to his roommate. He said, "This is my girlfriend." And he told all the nurses in the ward about me.

EDNA: He's very fond of you. Always has been.

VERA: The last visit, he just wouldn't let go of my hand. Kept holding my hand, and saying how cute his girlfriend was. Said I made him feel well again. I want to go to the hospital this afternoon, Ursula.

URSULA: What about Mr. David? Mr. Julius?

VERA: They won't mind.

URSULA: What about the twenty dollars? We're running a business, not a lonely-hearts club.

VERA: Oh, dock it from my allowance, then. I'm going to see Mr. Francis.

URSULA: I most certainly shall deduct it from your income. I find it shocking that you can just desert your duty—

EDNA: You're making me angry, Ursula Thaller. Vera hasn't taken sick a day since 1978. You're one to talk about duty and money, sneaking around making investments with our money.

(*To Vera*) Give my regards to Mr. Francis, will you? I do hope he's on the mend. Ursula had better not dare take a penny off your weekly pay.

URSULA: And who is the Madam here now? Things are deteriorating at a fast rate with your attitudes...

EDNA: Our attitudes? OURS?

VERA: Oh, I don't give a hang one way or the other about the money. It's not worth fighting about.

EDNA: She had better not touch one red cent. You had better not, Ursula.

URSULA: You're hardly in a position to be giving me ultimatums. I could break in and train any eighty-year-old grandmother with better results—

EDNA: Well, you just go and do that.

VERA: Please, now, Edna, don't get worked up; remember your gas—

URSULA: She only seems to have fits when she has to work—

EDNA: I've had it with you, Ursula Thaller. I quit.

URSULA: You can't quit. You're fired. Vera will take over your customers beginning at 10 A.M. sharp.

VERA (*Starting to cry*): Oh, no…Edna…Ursula…reconsider what you're saying…

URSULA: I have to take a firm hand. Once management gets weak, law and order goes right out the window.

EDNA: I don't want her to take me back. Not if she begged. I'll go over to the bench across the park and set up my own trade.

VERA: Be reasonable. The money in the bank belongs to you, too—

EDNA: I knew it would come to this. I warned Mae—

VERA: Edna, don't make things w—

EDNA: You should know, Ursula, that you're Madam by default. Years ago, we all voted for Lillian to come after Mae. But Lillian didn't want to. And Mae said you'd have more talent with the ledger book than with the customers. So we gave in.

URSULA (*Wounded*): I'm not running a popularity contest, I'm running a business.

EDNA: Not my business, you're not. I intend to take my regulars with me.

URSULA: When I get through with your reputation—

EDNA: Oh, you don't frighten me. I'm done with being scared.

(*Pause*)

The money thing has always gone to your head. The same thing happened when you were bootlegging liquor; you turned strange. I couldn't stand it. That's why I turned you in.

URSULA (*Struck; quiet*): It was—you? You turned me in? Not…Lillian?

EDNA: No. Lillian said it was your one chance out of the Life. She never said a word.

URSULA: So, it wasn't Lillian…

(*New tone*) Vera. I don't want you talking to that woman during hours. Sit over here by me; we have to arrange a new schedule.

VERA (*Wavering and making a decision*): Ursula, I stick with Edna. I can't scab on my own friend.

(*Vera sits back down on the bench by Edna; the two women scoot over nearer to the far end.*)

URSULA: You...you quit?

VERA: No—I'm not quitting. I'm...I'm striking. We're on strike.

EDNA: On strike? Oh, no—I don't know, Vera—I've never done a thing like that. I don't know if I could—

VERA: Of course you can, Edna. There's nothing wrong with striking. Everybody does it nowadays.

URSULA: Well, that's just lovely. After all these years, to find that I've been working alongside communists.

VERA: We're not communist. We're...labor.

(*Pause.*)

EDNA: Now what do we do?

VERA (*Thinking*): Why, I suppose we could sit in the sun in protest.

(*Edna and Vera smile at each other. They relax on the bench and throw their faces back toward the sun.*)

URSULA: Well, things are just going to the dogs. I never thought I'd live to see the day...when order would just crumble. No respect for authority.

EDNA: Oh, just cool it, Ursula. Enjoy the day. When you're ready to talk, we'll talk.

(*To Vera*) I suppose we should make a list of demands.

VERA: Why, yes.

EDNA: Longer lunch hours.

VERA: Shorter work weeks.

EDNA: Merit raises.

*(Pause.)*

VERA: I can't think of anything else.

*(Pause.)*

URSULA *(Shaken)*: Well, I'd better ring up the clientele and make cancellations. After fifty years. Left holding the bag. Mae would roll over in her grave.

*(Pause.)*

VERA: Ursula, are you all right?

URSULA: Oh, you needn't worry about me. Enjoy yourself.
    *(Sarcastic)* Just let it hang loose.

VERA: It already does hang loose.

EDNA: She'll be fine, Vera.

*(Pause. They sit in the sun. Ursula, stiff, pale, stares resolutely in front. Vera smiles. Edna watches the passersby.)*

VERA: So, now what do we do? Edna? What are we going to do the rest of the day?

EDNA: Why, I don't know. I could do anything. Let me see.
    *(Searches through her purse and counts the money in her wallet)* I think I have enough. Maybe I'll take in a movie. Gee, I haven't been to the movies since...*The Sound of Music.*

VERA: Oh, I loved that one. Julie Andrews was beautiful. Such a voice. I think I'll go to the hospital early. Give Mr. Francis a surprise. Maybe I'll give him a nice talcum back rub. Maybe I'll spend the whole day with him. We can watch the TV. And I can sit with him while he eats his dinner. He gets such pleasure from small things. It hurts whenever I have to leave— the way he holds on to me. And...and Edna—the look in his eyes. He knows, Edna. He knows.

## Blackout Three

*Another brief blackout. When the lights come up, Edna and Vera are sitting in the middle of the bench, looking relaxed. They smile, and lean back into the sun. Vera is clutching a small white bag of chocolates. Pause.*

EDNA: I thought she'd never die.

VERA: Edna!

EDNA: Well, it's true. Ursula was mean enough to live to a hundred.

VERA: I don't think she was that bad. She was cranky; but after forty-five years, you kind of get attached even to that.

EDNA: Maybe you got attached. I didn't.

*(Vera opens her small white bag and smiles.)*

VERA: Would you care for some chocolate, Edna?

EDNA: What kind are they?

VERA: Turtles. I felt like a little treat.

EDNA: Thank you.

*(Edna, with great deliberation, chooses one. Vera looks in the bag, takes one out and puts it in her mouth. The two women pause a moment, and let the chocolate melt.)*

EDNA: They're very good.

VERA *(Happy)*: Yes. They're sweet. *(Looks into her bag)*
   Still, who would have suspected that she was so batty?

*(Edna and Vera laugh.)*

EDNA: "You're going to need two strong arms to carry away what's left..." "More solid than gold, more stable than oil..."

*(Pause.)*

VERA: Edna, what are we going to do with all that sugar?

EDNA: Dump it.

VERA: All of that sugar? How much do you think she has?

EDNA: Well, the back room's piled ceiling to floor with five-pound bags. You can figure there's more than a thousand pounds—no wonder the floor's been sagging.

VERA: That explains why she insisted on having the large rooms at the back. And why she never invited us to her room.

EDNA: She must have been collecting those sugar bags before 1945…some of those bags are rotting through…and the roaches…*(Shudders)*

Mr. Zabar says it's up to us to clear out the room and exterminate. There may be more than roaches back there, too. I'll hire someone to do it first thing next week. I'm not stepping foot in there. As Ursula would say, "You can catch more roaches with sugar…"

VERA: Poor Ursula…Edna?

EDNA: Hmmm?

VERA: What happened to the certificate…certificate…

EDNA: Of deposit? Well, I got the money out. We had to pay a substantial penalty. So much for money making money.

*(Pause.)*

VERA: What are we going to do about the customers?

EDNA: Well, this is how I figure it, Vera. Let's just keep the ones we fancy.

VERA: Really? You mean it?

EDNA: There's no sense in us working ourselves to death.

VERA: Well, Edna, now that you're in charge…you know, you don't have to do any of the work at all…

*(Bravely)* I could arrange things and keep the books, if you want…the others did…

EDNA: No—I don't want to do that…I like my work. Besides, Mr. Benjamin would be furious if I left the Life. You know, I think that's what happened to Ursula…she quit working when she became Madam, and I think the...inactivity killed her.

*(Pause; then low)* Or maybe it was the strike. I don't feel good about that.

VERA: Why?

EDNA: I don't know—it just wasn't right. It upset...the way things are supposed to be. I feel bad about it.

VERA: Why, Edna, we meant no harm about it. It was fun. If Ursula had wanted to, she could have joined us—she could have gone on strike too.

EDNA: No, she couldn't—she was Management.

VERA: Oh. Well, I had a good time on strike. Edna, do you suppose we could go on strike again?

EDNA: You can if you like—I can't. I'm Management now.

VERA: Oh, yes, of course...

EDNA: You know, Vera, I don't much care if I'm in charge or not...you could take over the operations if you want...

VERA: Why, goodness, no, Edna, I couldn't take over the business. I have no head at all for numbers and dates... You're much better at that sort of thing. Besides, you're older.

EDNA: Yes, I guess you're right. It feels funny to be in charge. It doesn't feel right. I don't know...

VERA: You're doing a great job. Really. Besides, Mae would want it this way. Keeping to the order of things.

EDNA: Yes.

VERA: So, who are we going to ditch?

EDNA: First one to go: Mr. Ezra! No wonder he never talks—his breath could kill a horse at ten paces!

VERA: Mr. Adam?

EDNA: Mr. Warren!

VERA: Mr. Julius?

EDNA: Let's keep Mr. Sidney and Mr. Brett...

VERA: Oh, yes, Lillian's friends...and of course, Mr. David and Mr. Andrew.

EDNA: Mr. Samuel, Mr. Lawrence, Mr. Sheldon, and of course,

Mr. Benjamin. And Mr. Francis when he gets out. How is he doing?

VERA: Oh, he's much better this week. His appetite is back. They might let him come back any day now…

EDNA: Vera? Do you think maybe you could visit Mr. Francis tonight instead of this afternoon? Mr. Zabar's charging us for the fumigation; that's going to put us back at least forty dollars…

VERA: Well, I suppose so. I think if I took a cab, I could keep my appointment with Mr. Brett and still get to Roosevelt in time for dinner. I like to be there with Mr. Francis when he eats. It's so awful to eat dinner alone. Mr. Francis acts just like a child if I'm not there.

EDNA: Sometimes Mr. Benjamin acts just like a child when it's time to leave. He holds me around the waist and says he's not going to let me out of his sight. Then I have to slap his face, and say, "Mr. Benjamin, let go this instant. What makes you think any woman would have you?" And I rub the bristle on his face and say, "Shave this mug!" And then he rubs his beard on my face and I scream. And sometimes he says, "Edna, you've got to marry me! I can't afford to keep this up…" He doesn't really mean it, though. It's just one of our games…he's my good-time papa, that's what I call him. I like to sit on his knee and put my hands under his shirt; I like his smell—I know it after all these years. There was a time when he was still working on Wall Street that Mae would schedule me in regular for him at lunch time; I had the key to his apartment. He'd come through the door, three-piece suit and briefcase, and say "What's for lunch?" And I'd jump on him and wrap my legs around him…He's got a picture of himself in uniform on the night table, twenty-five years old and smiling. Gives me the willies to look at it. I don't like to think of Mr. Benjamin as a young man. It makes me sad. Don't you think young men are awfully sad?

## Blackout Four

> *Another brief blackout. Lights up on Edna and Vera, who
> have reversed their positions on the bench. Edna is slumped
> on the bench, pale and tired.*

VERA: Edna, you have to eat something.

EDNA: I'm not hungry.

VERA: Yes, but you have to try. And you're not sleeping. How can
you, adding numbers all night? I know it's upsetting that Mr.
Zabar's kicking us all out of the rooms upstairs, but we can
find another place in the neighborhood. We'll just have to
pay a little more. And just so he can make room to sell
espresso machines and cuisinarts!

> *(No answer)*

How about if I go and get something nice and light at the
corner deli—what about a BLT on toasted rye, the way you
like it?

EDNA *(In a trance)*: I don't know. Take that BLT. You look at it
and see a nice BLT, the way I used to.

But now it's all changed. I look at it and I see union struggles for lettuce workers in California...tomato harvests, pork-
er roundups, produce truckers, pigs to the slaughter...there's
a factory that's designed just to make the bacon package somewhere; machines that do nothing else but cut the cardboard.

And then there's the rye...someone is in a factory right
now who's sole job is taking care of those little seeds...thou-
sands of loaves on the conveyor belt, being sliced and
wrapped, loaded into big, greasy trucks...thousands and
thousands of hands just to make that one BLT.

And you know what? It's all automatic. They don't care.

VERA *(Alarmed)*: Edna!!

EDNA: I'm not hungry.

VERA: Look, I care. What if I made something from scratch...
nothing out of a can.

> *(Brightly, desperately)* What if I made you red beans and rice?

EDNA: That's a lot of trouble standing over a hot stove.

VERA: Oh, God, makes my mouth water just to think of it...red beans and rice...our mothers made it every Monday in the heat of summer, they didn't mind the heat...

EDNA: I haven't had red beans and rice in I don't know how long...Do you really think you could make some for me?

VERA: Well, my red beans never come out like Mama's. And I used to watch her make them, too. You'd ask her, "Mama, how much flour goes in the sauce?" And she'd respond... *(Cups her hand)* "Oh, about this much, and... *(Pinching her fingers together)*...and then a tad more." Her beans were heaven. She'd leave a bit pot simmering with the ham bone on the stove in ninety-degree heat, and then go out to the backyard and tackle the laundry. I could smell her beans a block away...the smell always makes me hungry. Thick, red sauce, over rice, with a bay leaf, and mopped off the plate with a thick crust of dilly bread...

　　*(Beat)*

　　I tried making them a while ago; I got some big ham hocks from the butcher's on 79th Street, and beans and tomatoes...but they turned out funny. I must have forgotten to put something in the sauce. I don't know what it is I forgot...

## Blackout Five

*There is a quick blackout. When the lights come back up, we see Vera, sitting alone in the middle of the bench. She just sits, plaintively quiet, at times watching the traffic. But she sits still, looking very frail, and a bit frightened. There is a slow fade-out to*

## Blackout Six

END  OF  PLAY

# Desdemona

*A Play About a Handkerchief*

*Desdemona* was given its first staged reading October 1977 at Cornell University in Ithaca, New York. Paula Vogel directed.

The play was co-produced by Circle Repertory Theatre under Tanya Berezin, Artistic Director and Bay Street Theatre Festival under Sybil Christopher and Emma Walton, Co-Artistic Directors; Tanya Berezin and Abigail Evans, Producers. It opened June 1993 at Bay Street Theatre Festival in Sag Harbor, New York, and subsequently in November 1993 at Circle Repertory Theatre, New York City. It was directed by Gloria Muzio, with sets by Derek McLane, lights by Michael Lincoln, costumes by Jess Goldstein and sound by Randy Freed. The cast was as follows:

| | |
|---|---|
| DESDEMONA | J. Smith-Cameron |
| EMILIA | Fran Brill |
| BIANCA | Cherry Jones |

## NOTE TO DIRECTORS

*Desdemona* was written in thirty cinematic "takes." The director is encouraged to create different pictures to simulate the process of filming: Change invisible camera angles, do jump cuts and repetitions, etc. There should be no blackouts between scenes.

*Desdemona* was written as a tribute (i.e., "rip-off") to the infamous play, *Shakespeare the Sadist* by Wolfgang Bauer.

# Prologue

*A spotlight in the dark, pinpointing a white handkerchief lying on the ground. A second spotlight comes up on Emilia, who sees the handkerchief. She pauses, and then cautiously looks about to see if she is observed. Then, quickly, Emilia goes to the handkerchief, picks it up, stuffs the linen in her ample bodice and exits. Blackout.*

# I.

*A mean, sparsely furnished back room with rough, white-washed walls. Upstage left there is a small, heavy, wooden back entrance. Another door, stage right, leads to the main rooms of the palace. There are a few benches lining the walls, littered with tools, baskets, leather bits, dirty laundry, etc. The walls bear dark wooden racks that neatly display farm and work equipment made of rough woods, leathers and chain.*

*In the center of the room, there is a crude work table with short benches. As the play begins, Desdemona is scattering items and clothing in the air, barely controlling a mounting hysteria. Emilia, dark, plump and plain, with a thick Irish brogue, watches, amused and disgusted at the mess her lady is making.*

DESDEMONA: Are you sure you didn't see it? The last time I remember holding it in my hand was last week in the arbor—you're sure you didn't see it?

EMILIA: Aye—

DESDEMONA: It looks like—

EMILIA: Like anybody's handkerchief, savin' it has those dainty little strawberries on it. I never could be after embroiderin' a piece of linen with fancy work to wipe up the nose—

DESDEMONA: It's got to be here somewhere—

EMILIA: After you blow your nose in it, an' it's all heavy and wet, who's going to open the damn thing and look at the pretty stitches?

DESDEMONA: Emilia—are you sure it didn't get "mixed up" somehow with your...your things?

EMILIA: And why should I be needin' your handkerchief when I'm wearing a plain, soft shift which works just as well? And failing that, the good Lord gave me sleeves...

DESDEMONA: It's got to be here!

*(Returns to her rampage of the room)* Oh—skunk water! *(A man's undergarment is tossed into the air behind Desdemona's shoulder)* Dog piddle!!

EMILIA: I'm after telling you m'lady—

DESDEMONA: Nonsense! It's got to be here!

*(There is a crash of overturned chair. Desdemona's shifts are thrown into the air)* Goddamn horse urine!!!

EMILIA: It was dear, once upon a time, when m'lady was toddling about the palace, and all of us servants would be follerin' after, stooping to pick up all the pretty toys you'd be scatterin'—

DESDEMONA: Emilia, please! I cannot bear a sermon.

EMILIA: There was the day the Senator, your father, gave you your first strand of pearls from the Indies—you were all of five—and your hand just plucked it from your neck. How you laughed to see us—Teresa, Maria and me—scrabbling on all fours like dogs after truffles, scooping up the rollin' pearls— *(There is a ripping noise)*

DESDEMONA: Oh, shit.

*(Two halves of a sheet are pitched into the air.)*

EMILIA: But you're a married lady now; and when m'lord Othello gives you a thing, and tells you to be mindin' it, it's no longer dear to drop it willy-nilly and expect me to be findin' it—

DESDEMONA: Oh, piss and vinegar!! Where is the crappy little snot rag!

*(She turns and sees Emilia sitting)* You're not even helping! You're not looking!!

EMILIA: Madam can be sure I've overturned the whole lot, two or three times…It's a sight easier hunting for it when the place is tidy; when all is topsy-turvy, you can't tell a mouse dropping from a cow pie!

*(Desdemona returns to the hunt; Emilia picks up the torn sheet)* Now see, this sheet here was washed this morning. Your husband, as you know, is fussy about his sheets; and while it was no problem to have them fresh each night in Venice—I could open the window and dunk them in the canal—here on Cyprus it takes two drooling orderlies to march six times down to the cistern and back again.

*(Regards the sheet carefully)* It's beyond repair. And now that your husband commands fresh sheets, my Iago has got it in his head to be the lord as well; he's got to have fresh sheets each night for his unwashed feet.

DESDEMONA: Emilia, please—I may puke.

*(Desdemona, in frustration, stamps on the clothes she's strewn from the basket.)*

DESDEMONA: It's got to be here, it's got to be here, it's got to be here—Emilia—Help me find it!

EMILIA: You're wasting your time, m'lady. I know it's not here.

DESDEMONA *(Straightening herself)*: Right. And you knew this morning that my husband wasn't mad at me. Just a passing whim, you said.

EMILIA: Ah, Miss Desdemona...not even a midwife can foretell the perfidiosity of men.

DESDEMONA: Give me strength. Perfidy.

EMILIA: That, too.

DESDEMONA: It can't have walked off on two feet!

EMILIA: Mayhap m'lady dropped it.

DESDEMONA: Oh, you're hopeless. No help at all. I'll find it by myself. Go back to your washing and put your hands to use.

EMILIA: Yes, m'lady.


## 2.


*Emilia and Desdemona. Emilia scrubs sheets.*


DESDEMONA: Will it come out?

EMILIA: I've scrubbed many a sheet, but this is the worst in my career...It's all that Bianca's fault. I paid her well for the blood, too. "And be sure," I says, "it's an old hen—one on its last gasp. Young chick blood's no good for bridal sheets, it's the devil to come out." "Madam's sheets," I says, "are the finest to be had in Venice, and we don't want them ruined and rotted from the stain." And Bianca swore, "I've an old hen on crutches that will wash out clear as a maidenhead or a baby's dropping."

Ah, but that chick wasn't a week old. And what with it bakin' in the sun for a month now—but if anyone can, Mealy will scrub it virgin white again.

DESDEMONA: Oh, hush about it. I can't stand to think on it...barbaric custom. And my best sheets. Nobody displays bridal sheets on Cyprus.

EMILIA: There aren't any virgins to be had on Cyprus.

DESDEMONA: Half the garrison came to see those sheets flapping in the breeze.

EMILIA: Why did the other half come?

DESDEMONA: To pay their last respects to the chicken!

*(They laugh.)*

**3.**

*We hear Emilia, in a good humor, humming "When Irish Eyes Are Smiling." Another clatter of heavy metal things being tossed onto the floor.*

DESDEMONA: JESUS! WHAT IS THIS?!

EMILIA *(In disbelief)*: You didn't find it!

*(Desdemona crosses to Emilia, holding a long, crooked bit of iron with a wicked point.)*

DESDEMONA: No—this!!

EMILIA: 'Tis a hoof-pick.

DESDEMONA: A hoof-pick? What is it used for?

EMILIA: After all your years of trotting m'lady's bum over field and farrow, and you've never laid your eyes on the like? When your mount picks up a stone in its foot, and it's deep, you take the pick and hold on tight to the hoof, and then you dig it in and down to the quick and pry it out—

DESDEMONA: You dig *this* in? Good lord—

EMILIA: Aye, takes a goodly amount of sweat and grease. It's work for a proper man, it is.

*(Desdemona, absorbed in fondling the hoof-pick, stretches out on the table.)*

DESDEMONA: Oh me, oh my—if I could find a man with just such a hoof-pick—he could pluck out my stone—eh, Emilia?

*(They laugh)*
Emilia, does your husband Iago have a hoof-pick to match?

*(Emilia turns and looks, then snorts.)*

EMILIA: What, Iago?

*(Desdemona puts her hand on the base and covers it.)*

DESDEMONA: Well, then—this much?
EMILIA: Please, mum! It's a matter o' faith between man and wife t—
DESDEMONA: Ahh—not that much, eh?
　　*(Covers more of the pick)* Like this?
EMILIA: Miss Desdemona!
DESDEMONA: Come now, Emilia, it's just us—
EMILIA: Some things are private!!
DESDEMONA: It's only fair—I'm sure you know every detail about my lord—
EMILIA *(Shrugging)*: When the Master Piddles, a Servant holds the Pot—
DESDEMONA *(Persisting)*: This much hoof?
EMILIA: Not near as much as that!
DESDEMONA: This much?

*(Pause.)*

EMILIA *(Sour)*: Nay.
DESDEMONA: Good God, Emilia, I'm running out of—
EMILIA: The wee-est pup of th' litter comes a'bornin' in the world with as much.
　　*(Desdemona laughs)*
　　There. Is m'lady satisfied?
DESDEMONA: Your secret's safe with me.

**4.**

*Emilia, scrubbing. Desdemona lies on her back on the table, feet propped up, absentmindedly fondling the pick, and staring into space.*

**5.**

*We hear the sound of Emilia, puffing and blowing. Lights up on Desdemona getting a pedicure.*

DESDEMONA: Where is she? It's getting late. He'll be back soon, and clamoring for me. He's been in a rotten mood lately... Headaches, handkerchiefs, accusations—and of all people to accuse—Michael Cassio!

EMILIA: The only one you haven't had—

DESDEMONA: And I don't want him, either. A prissy Florentine, that one is. Leave it to a cuckold to be jealous of a eunuch—

EMILIA *(Crowing)*: Bianca would die!

DESDEMONA: Then we won't tell her what I said, will we?
> *(Emilia becomes quiet)*
> What Bianca does in her spare time is her business.

*(Emilia's face clearly indicates that what Bianca does in her spare time is Emilia's business, too. Desdemona watches Emilia closely.)*

DESDEMONA: You don't much like Bianca, do you, Mealy?
> *(No response. Emilia blows on Desdemona's toes)*
> Come on, now, tell me frankly—why don't you like her?

EMILIA: It's not for me to say...

DESDEMONA: Emilia!

EMILIA: It's just that—no disrespect intented, m'lady—but you shouldn't go a'rubbin' elbows with one o' her class...Lie down with hussies, get up with crabs...

DESDEMONA: Her sheets are clean.

> *(Pause)*

> You've been simmering over Bianca for some time, Mealy, haven't you?

EMILIA *(Rancorously)*: I don't much like to see m'lady, in whose em-ploy I am, traipsing about in flopdens, doin' favors for common sloppots—Bianca! Ha! She's so loose, so low, that she's got to ad-ver-tise Wednesday Night Specials, half price for anything in uniform!

DESDEMONA: Well, purge it out of your blood; Bianca will soon be here—

EMILIA: Here! Why here? What if someone sees her sneaking up to the back door? What will the women in town say? A tart on a house call! How can I keep my head up hanging out the wash and feedin' the pigs when her sort comes sniffin' around—

DESDEMONA: She's coming to pay me for last Tuesday's customers who paid on credit. And to arrange for next Tuesday—

EMILIA *(Horrified)*: Not again! Once was enough—you're not going there again! I thought to myself, she's a young un-bridled colt, is Miss Desdemona—let her cool down her blood—but to make it a custom! I couldn't let you go back again—risking disease and putting us all in danger—

DESDEMONA: Oh, tush, Mealy—

EMILIA: You listen to me, Miss Desdemona: Othello will sooner or later find out that you're laying for Bianca, and his black skin is goin' to blister off with rage!! Holy Jesus Lord, why tempt a Venetian male by waving red capes? My Iago would beat me for lookin' at the wrong end of an ass!

> *(VERY WORKED UP)* Your husband will find out and when he does! When he does!! *(Makes the noise and gesture of throat cutting)* And then! And then!! AIAIaiaiaiahhh!! My lady!! What's to become of me! Your fateful handmaid! Where will I find another position in this pisshole harbor!

DESDEMONA: Stop it, Mealy! Don't be...silly, nothing will hap-pen to me. I'm the sort that will die in bed.

EMILIA *(Beseechingly)*: You won't leave your poor Mealy stranded?

DESDEMONA: You'll always have a position in this household…Of some sort. *(Mealy's face turns to stone)*

Oh, come now, Mealy, haven't I just promoted you?

EMILIA: Oh, m'lady, I haven't forgot; not only your scullery maid, but now your laundress as well! I am quite sensible of the honor and the increase in pay—of two pence a week…

*(Suddenly turns bright and cheery)* And whiles we are on the subject—

DESDEMONA: Oh, Christ, here it comes.

EMILIA: But m'lady, last time an opening came up, you promised to speak to your husband about it in Venice. I suppose poor old Iago just slipped your mind—

DESDEMONA: Look, I did forget. Anyway, I recommended Cassio for my husband's lieutenant. An unfortunate choice. But that subject is closed.

EMILIA: Yes, mum.

*(Emilia starts to return to her laundry. There is a knock at the door, and Desdemona brightens.)*

DESDEMONA: There she is! Emilia, let Bianca in—No, no wait— *(To Mealy's annoyance, Desdemona arranges herself in a casual tableau)*

*(The knock repeats. Desdemona signals Emilia to go answer the door. Emilia exits through the door to the palace, and then quickly returns.)*

EMILIA: M'lady, it's your husband. He's waiting for you outside.

DESDEMONA *(Frightened)*: Husband?…Shhhittt…

*(Desdemona pauses, arranges her face into an insipid, fluttering innocence, then girlishly runs to the door. She flings it open, and disappears through the door.)*

DESDEMONA *(Offstage; breathless)*: Othello!

*(And then, we hear the distinct sound of a very loud slap. A pause, and Desdemona returns, closes the door behind her, holding her cheek. She is on the brink of tears. She and Emilia look at each other, and then Emilia looks away.)*

## 6.

*Desdemona and Emilia. Desdemona frantically searches.*

DESDEMONA: It's got to be somewhere!!—Are you quite sure—

EMILIA: Madam can be sure I overlooked the whole lot several times.

DESDEMONA: Um, Emilia…should, should you have "accidentally" taken it—not that I'm suggesting theft in the slightest—but should it have by mistake slipped in with some of your things, your return of it will merit a reward, and all of my gratitude.

*(Tries to appear casual)* Not that the thing itself is worth anything—it's a pittance of musty linen—but still…

EMILIA *(With dignity)*: I've never taken a thing, acc-idently or not. I don't make no "acc-idents." Mum, I've looked everywhere. Everywhere.

*(Quietly)* Is m'lord clamoring about it much?

*(They eye each other. Pause.)*

DESDEMONA: Which position, Mealy?

EMILIA *(Puzzled)*: Which position?

DESDEMONA: For your husband.

EMILIA: Oh, Miss Desdemona! I won't forget all your—

DESDEMONA: Yes, yes, I'm sure. What opening?

EMILIA: It's ever so small a promotion, and so quite equal to his merits. He's ensign third-class, but the budget's ensign second-class.

DESDEMONA: Very well, the budget office. Can he write and account and do—whatever it is that they do with the budget?

EMILIA: Oh, yes—he's clever enough at that.

DESDEMONA: I really don't understand your mentality, Emilia. You're forever harping on how much you detest the man. Why do you beg for scraps of promotion for him? Don't you hate him?

EMILIA: I—I—

*(With relish)* I despise him.

DESDEMONA: Then?

EMILIA: You see, Miss, for us in the bottom ranks, when man and wife hate each other, what is left in a lifetime of marriage but to save and scrimp, plot and plan? The more I'd like to put some nasty rat-ridder in his stew, the more I think of money— and he thinks the same. One of us will drop first, and then, what's left, saved and earned, under the mattress for th' other one? I'd like to rise a bit in the world, and women can only do that through their mates—no matter what class buggers they all are. I says to him each night, "I long for the day you make me a lieutenant's widow!"

**7.**

*Emilia and Desdemona. We hear the sounds of scrubbing between the scenes.*

DESDEMONA: Please, my dear Emilia, I can count on you, can't I? As one closest to my confidence?

EMILIA: Oh, m'lady, I ask no greater joy than to be close to your ladyship—

DESDEMONA: Then tell me—have you heard anything about me? Why does Othello suspect Cassio?

EMILIA: Oh, no, m'lady, he surely no longer suspects Cassio. I instructed Iago to talk him out of that bit of fancy, which he did, risking my lord's anger at no little cost to his own career; but all for you, you know!

DESDEMONA: You haven't heard of anything else?

EMILIA: No Ma'am.

*(But as Desdemona is to Emilia's back, Emilia drops a secret smile into the wash bucket. Emilia raises her head again, though, with a sincere, servile face, and turns to Desdemona.)*

EMILIA: But if I did know anything, you can be sure that you're the first to see the parting of my lips about it—

DESDEMONA: Yes, I know. You've been an extremely faithful, hardworking servant to me, Emilia, if not a confidante. I've noticed your merits, and when we return to Venice...well— you may live to be my *fille de chambre* yet.

EMILIA *(Not quite sure what a* fille de chambre *is)*: I'm very grateful, I'm sure.

DESDEMONA: Yes, you deserve a little reward, I think. *(Emilia's face brightens in expectancy)*

I'll see if I can wheedle another tuppence out of my husband each week. *(Emilia droops)*

EMILIA *(Listlessly)*: Every little tiny bit under the mattress helps, I always says to myself.

*(A pause. Desdemona paces, comes to a decision.)*

DESDEMONA: Mealy—do you like the dressing gown you've been mending?

EMILIA: It's a lovely piece of work, that is, Miss. I've always admired your dresses...

DESDEMONA: Yesss...yes, but isn't it getting a bit dingy? Tattered around the hem?

EMILIA: Not that anyone would notice; it's a beautiful gown, m'lady...

DESDEMONA: Yes, you're right. I was going to give it to you, but maybe I'll hang on to it a bit longer...

*(Emilia, realizing her stupidity, casts an avaricious, yet mournful look at the gown that was almost hers.)*

EMILIA: Oh, m'lady...It's...it's certainly a lovely cloth, and there's a cut to it that would make one of them boy actors shapely...

DESDEMONA *(Peeved at the analogy)*: Hmmmm—though, come to think of it, it would fit Bianca much neater, I think...

EMILIA: Bianca! Bianca! She's got the thighs of a milch cow, m'lady!

DESDEMONA *(Amused)*: I've never noticed.

*(Emilia, sulking again, vigorously scrubs.)*

DESDEMONA *(In conciliation)*: No, come to think of it, I believe you are right—it's not really Bianca's fashion. It's all yours. After tonight.

EMILIA: Oh, Miss Desdemona!!

## 8.

*The same. In the darkness we hear Emilia singing a hymn: "La-la-la-la—Jesus; La-la-la-la—Sword; La-la-la-la—Crucifix; La-la-la-la—Word."*

*Lights come up on Desdemona, lying stretched out on the table, her throat and head arched over its edge, upside down. A pause.*

DESDEMONA: You really think his temper today was only some peeve?

EMILIA: I'm sure of it; men get itchy heat rash in th' crotch, now and then; they get all snappish, but once they beat us, it's all kisses and presents the next morning—well, for the first year or so.

DESDEMONA: My dear mate is much too miserly to give me anything but his manhood. The only gift he's given me was a meager handkerchief with piddling strawberries stitched on it, and look how he's carrying on because I've lost it! He guards his purse strings much dearer than his wife.

EMILIA: I'm sure my lord will be waitin' up for you to come to bed. Full o' passion, and embracin' and makin' a fool o' himself—You just see if your Mealy isn't right.

DESDEMONA: Yes, of course you're right. Good old Mealy, I don't know what I'd do without your good common sense. Oh, it's the curse of aristocratic blood—I feel full of whims and premonitions—

EMILIA: Perhaps it was something m'lady et?

DESDEMONA *(First she smiles; then she laughs)*: Yes—that must be it!

*(Desdemona laughs again. Mealy can't understand what is so funny.)*

## 9.

*Emilia and Desdemona.*

EMILIA: Ambassador Ludovico gave me a message and is wantin' a response.

DESDEMONA: What does my cousin want?

*(Emilia digs into her bodice.)*

EMILIA: It's somewhere in here...wait... *(Searches)*

DESDEMONA: Oh, good Lord, Mealy, you could lose it in there!

*(Desdemona runs to Emilia, peers in her bosom and starts to tickle her.)*

EMILIA: Miss Desde—! Wait, now—no, STOP!! Here it is now—

*(Emilia finds a folded paper. She hands it to Desdemona, and then peers over Desdemona's shoulder.)*

DESDEMONA *(Sighing)*: Oh, Ludovico, Ludovico. "Deeply desiring the favor…" etceteras. "…Impatient until I can at last see you in private, throwing off the Robes of State to appear as your humble friend." He's just too tiresome.

EMILIA: What response are you wanting me to give?

DESDEMONA: Oh, I don't know. Let the old lecher wait. I told him it was entirely past between us, and then he bribes his way into being appointed Ambassador!

*(Desdemona in a loquacious mood. Emilia gives her a rub-down.)*

DESDEMONA: Ah, Emilia, I should have married Ludovico after all. There's a man who's always known the worth of ladies of good blood! A pearl for a pinch, a broach for a breast, and for a maiden-head…

*(Breaks into laughter)*

Ah, that was a lover!

EMILIA: I don't know how those sainted sisters could let such is-sagnations go on in their convent—

DESDEMONA: Assignations. Really, Emilia, you're quite hopeless. However can I, the daughter of a Senator, live with a washerwoman as *fille de chambre*? All fashionable Venice will howl. You must shrink your vowels and enlarge your vocabulary.

EMILIA: Yes, mum. As-signations, as it were.

*(Muttering)* If it were one o' my class, I could call it by some names I could pronounce. I've put many a copper in their poor box, in times past, thinkin' them sisters of charity in a godly house. Not no more. They won't get the parings of my potatoes from me, runnin' a society house of ass-ignations!

DESDEMONA: Oh, those poor, dear sisters. I really don't think they knew anything about the informal education their convent girls receive. For one thing, I believe myopia is a prerequisite for Holy Orders. Have you ever noticed how nuns squint?

*(Beat)*

Each Sunday in convent we were allowed to take visitors to chapel. Under their pious gaze Ludovico and I would kneel, and there I could devote myself to doing him *à la main (Gestures)* right in the pew! They never noticed! Sister Theresa did once remark that he was a man excessively fond of prayer.

## 10.

*Emilia's credo.*

EMILIA: It's not right of you, Miss Desdemona, to be forever cutting up on the matter of my beliefs. I believe in the Blessed Virgin, I do, and the Holy Fathers and the Sacraments of the Church, and I'm not one to be ashamed of admittin' it. It goes against my marrow, it does, to hear of you, a comely lass from a decent home, giving hand jobs in the pew; but I says to myself, Emilia, I says, you just pay it no mind, and I go about my business. And if I take a break on the Sabbath each week, to light a candle and say a bead or two for my em-ployers, who have given me and my husband so much, and who need the Virgin's love and protection, then where's the harm, say I?

*(Breath. Gets carried away)* Our Lady has seen me through four and ten years of matreemony, with my bugger o' a mate, and that's no mean feat. Four and ten years, she's heard poor Mealy's cries, and stopped me from rising from my bed with my pillow in my hand to end his ugly snores 'til Gabriel— *(Stops and composes herself)*

Ah, Miss Desdemona, if you only knew the peace and love Our Lady brings! She'd help you, mum, if you only kneeled real nice and said to her...and said...

*(Emilia can't find the words that such a sinner as Desdemona should say as polite salutation to Our Lady. Desdemona erupts into laughter.)*

**11.**

*Emilia eats her lunch. Desdemona plays in a desultory fashion with a toy.*

DESDEMONA: *(Frightened)*: Emilia, have you ever deceived your husband Iago?

EMILIA *(With a derisive snort)*: That's a good one. Of course not, Miss—I'm an honest woman.

DESDEMONA: What does honesty have to do with adultery? Every honest man I know is an adulterer...

   *(Pause)*

Have you ever thought about it?

EMILIA: What is there to be thinkin' about? It's enough trouble once each Saturday night, than to be lookin' for it. I'd never cheat—never—not for all the world I wouldn't.

DESDEMONA: The world's a huge thing for so small a vice.

EMILIA: Not my world, thank you. Mine's tidy and neat and I aim to keep it that way.

DESDEMONA: Oh, the world! Our world's narrow and small, I'll grant you; but there are other worlds—worlds that we married women never get to see.

EMILIA: Amen—and don't need to see, I should add.

DESDEMONA: If you've never seen the world, how would you know? Women are clad in purdah, we decent, respectable matrons, from the cradle to the altar to the shroud...bridled with linen, blinded with lace...These very walls are purdah.

EMILIA: I don't know what this thing called "purr-dah" means, but if it stands for dressing up nice, I'm all for it...

DESDEMONA: I remember the first time I saw my husband and I caught a glimpse of his skin, and, oh, how I thrilled. I thought—aha!—a man of a different color. From another world and planet. I thought, if I marry this strange dark man, I can leave this narrow little Venice with its whispering piazzas behind—I can escape and see other worlds.

(Pause)

But under that exotic façade was a porcelain white Venetian.

EMILIA: There's nothing wrong with Venice; I don't understand why madam's all fired up to catch Cyprus Syph and exotic claps.

DESDEMONA: Of course you don't understand. But I think Bianca does. She's a free woman—a new woman—who can make her own living in the world, who scorns marriage for the lie that it is.

EMILIA: I don't know where madam's getting this new woman hogwash, but no matter how you dress up a cow, she's still got udders.

Bianca's the eldest one of six girls, with teeth so horsey she could clean 'em with a hoof-pick, and so simple she has to ply the trade she does! That's what your Miss Bianca is!

DESDEMONA: Bianca is nothing of the sort. She and I share something common in our blood—that desire to know the world. I lie in the blackness of the room at her establishment...on sheets that are stained and torn by countless nights. And the men come into that pitch-black room—men of different sizes and smells and shapes, with smooth skin, with rough skin, with scarred skin. And they spill their seed into me, Emilia— seed from a thousand lands, passed down through generations of ancestors, with genealogies that cover the surface of the globe. And I simply lie still there in the darkness, taking them all into me. I close my eyes and in the dark of my mind—oh, how I travel!

## 12.

*Emilia and Desdemona. Desdemona is recklessly excited.*

EMILIA: You're leaving?!! Your husband?!!

DESDEMONA: It's a possibility!

EMILIA: Miss Desdemona, you've been taking terrible chances before, but now—if my lord catches you giving him th' back wind, he'll be after murdering both of us for sure—

DESDEMONA: Where's my cousin Ludovico? Is he in his room?

EMILIA: He said he was turnin' in early to get some rest before th' morning—

DESDEMONA: Yes, he'll catch the first tide back. Well, there's no harm in trying.

EMILIA: Trying what!

DESDEMONA: Trying on the robes of the penitent daughter. Ludovico can surely see how detestable this island, this marriage, this life is for me.

*(Has worked herself to the point of tears. Then she smiles)*
Perhaps a few tears would move him to intercede with my father on my behalf. If the disgrace of eloping with a moor is too great for Venetian society, a small annual allowance from Papa, and I promise never to show my face in town; and then...who knows...Paris! Yes, I'll go write Ludovico a note right away, asking to see him tonight.—Mealy, just in case, could you pack a few things for me?

EMILIA: And what if your husband discovers—

DESDEMONA: I'll leave first thing in the morning.

EMILIA: If I may make so bold to suggest—

DESDEMONA: What, what—

EMILIA: That you by all means sleep with your husband tonight. So's he won't suspect anything. While you and he lie together, and if your cousin agrees, Mealy could pack up your things quiet-like in your chamber.

DESDEMONA: Yes, that's good. My life rests on your absolute discretion, Emilia.

EMILIA: No one will hear a peep out o' me. But, my lady—

DESDEMONA: Now what is it?

EMILIA: What becomes of me?

DESDEMONA: Oh, good heavens, Mealy—I can't think of trivia at a time like this.

> *(Smoothly)* I tell you what. Be a good girl, pack my things, and, of course, should I leave tomorrow, I can't very well smuggle you on board, too; but I will send for you within the week. And your services will be remembered in Venice; with freer purse strings—who knows? Eh, my *fille de chambre*?

*(At this sop to her feelings, Emilia becomes fierce.)*

EMILIA: That won't do, m'lady. If you leave me behind, I'll not see you again, as your laundress, much less as your "*fee der schomer.*"

*(Desdemona, realizing the power that Emilia now has, kneels beside her.)*

DESDEMONA: All right. I'll intercede with my cousin on your behalf. I'll plead with him to take you, too. But I can't promise anything. Are you sure it's what you want? *(Emilia nods)*

> You'd leave your husband behind? *(Emilia nods vigorously)* Then—not a word. *(Rises)*
>
> *(In turning to go)* Oh, Emilia, since you're just dawdling over that laundry, why not stop and peel some potatoes for Cook. When my husband comes in, he'll want his usual snack of chips before he turns in—just the way he likes them... *(Shudders)* Greasy.

EMILIA: But, Miss, it's not my place no more to peel potatoes! I'm promoted now! I'm no mere *(With disgust)* SCULLERY MAID!

DESDEMONA: Now, Mealy, just this once—

EMILIA: You said I wouldn't have to do potatoes anymore!

DESDEMONA *(Harshly)*: I can leave you rotting on Cyprus all together, you know. Do as you're told. Peel the potatoes, and then look sharp and have that wash on the line by the time I return. Do I make myself clear?

EMILIA: Yes, m'lady.

DESDEMONA *(Sweetly)*: And Emilia, dear, if Bianca comes when I'm gone, let me know immediately—I'll be in my chamber.

EMILIA: Very good, Miss Desdemona.

*(Desdemona exits. Emilia grudgingly gets up, and finds the barrel of potatoes. On the bench there is a paring knife. Emilia brings everything back to the table, sits, and begins paring potatoes—venting her resentment by gouging out eyes, and stripping the skin from a potato as if flaying a certain mistress alive.)*

EMILIA *(Snorts out in contempt)*: "Fee der shomber!"

*(Then she pauses again, and wonders if Desdemona might not be for real in her offer. She questions the empty room)* "Feeyah der schomber?"

*(Before Emilia's eyes, she visualizes splendid dresses, the command of a household of subservient maids, a husbandless existence—all the trappings that go with the title.*

*Emilia begins energetically, resolutely and obediently to slice the potatoes.)*

**13.**

*Emilia is hanging up the wash. Bianca knocks several times; then enters.*

BIANCA: Gaw Blimey!

EMILIA: And where is't you've lost your manners? Lettin' the door ajar and leavin' in drafts and the pigs—

BIANCA: Aw'm sorry, Aw'm sure...

*(Bianca closes the door. She hesitates, and then with friendly strides, goes toward the clothesline.)*

BIANCA: 'Ow do, Emilia!

EMILIA: I'd be doin' a lot better if ye'd stop your gaddin' and lend a hand with these things.

BIANCA: Oh. Right you are, then.

*(Bianca goes briskly to the clothesline, and works. Silence as the women empty the basket. Emilia leaves Bianca to finish and starts in on her sewing. Pause.)*

BIANCA: Well, it's—it ain't 'arf swank 'ere, eh? *(Indicates the room)*

EMILIA *(Snorts)*: Swank? What, this? This is only the *back* room. The palace is through those doors—

BIANCA: Oh. Well, it's swank for a back room wotever it 'tis. Aw niver got to see it much; the Guv'nor in the owld days didn't let me near, said Au made the men tomdoodle on their shifts; like as they'd be dis-tracted by me atomy. Aw think it's sweet o' him to gi' me such credit; me atomy ain't that bleedin' jammy—but then, the owld Guv was the first to gi' me the sheep's eye 'imself. Very sweet on me, 'e was. So you see, Aw'd niver got close to the place before. Aw fink it's swank!

EMILIA *(Icily)*: I'm sure you do.

BIANCA: Yes, it's quite—wot do ye call it—lux-i-o-rious.

EMILIA: Lux-i-o-ri-us!! If I was you, I'd large my voc-abulary, an' shrink me vowels.

BIANCA *(Offended)*: 'Ere now! Wot bus'ness is me vowels to you?! Leave me vowels alone—

EMILIA: I'm after talking about your voc-abulary—your patter— not your reg-ularity.

BIANCA: Oh.

(*Keeping up a friendly front with difficulty*) Right. Well, then, is Desdemona 'ere?

EMILIA (*Sharply*): Who?

BIANCA: Uh...Des-de-mona—

EMILIA: Is it m'lady you're referrin' to as if she were your mess mate?

BIANCA: Look 'ere, Aw'm only doin' as Aw was towld. She tells me to call her Desdemona, and she says Aw was to call and settle up accounts for last Tuesday night for those johns who paid on tick—oh, you know, who paid on credit, as yew la-de-da Venetians would say.

EMILIA (*Softly hissing*): You listen to me, lassie: You're riding for a fall the likes of which you never got paid for by your fancy men. The mistress of this house is not at home, nor will be to the likes of you. What m'lady does in the gutter is her own business, same as yours, but what happens here is the common buzz of all.

BIANCA (*Stunned*): Wot! Miss Desdemona herself is callin' us mates—Aw niver—

EMILIA: Then she's gullin' you, as sure as 'tis she's gullin' that ass of a husband who's so taken with her; but let me tell you, you'll go the way like all the other fancies she's had in Venice...*I* should know. We all of us servants in her father's house talked on end about Miss Desdemona.—For a time, she wanted to be a saint, yes! A nun with the sisters of mercy. At age twelve, she was washin' the courtyard stones for penance, with us wiping up behind her. Then she was taken with horses, thank Jesus, and left sainthood behind. And then in turn again, she thought she was dyin'—stopped eating, and moped, and talked all dreamy and a little balmy-like—until her father finally saw sense and sent her to the convent to be bred out of her boredom. You're nothin' but the latest whim, a small town floozy with small town slang, and if she's lucky, she'll tire of you before the master finds out. (*Significantly*) If she's lucky.

BIANCA *(Somewhat subdued)*: So wot am Aw t'do, Emilia? Aw arsks you—

EMILIA: Then ask me by "Miss Emilia" to you—

*(With great dignity)* I'll have you know, I've hereby been promoted to *"fee der shimber"* and if I was you, I'd keep on my right side.

BIANCA *(Impressed, scared)*: Oh—*"fee dar shimber"*—Aw niver met one o' those before—Aw arsks yer pardon, Miss Emilia, Aw'm sure.

EMILIA: That's a bit of all right. You just listen to me: I know what side of me bread is buttered; behind this whimsy-cal missus is a power of a master—so you mind yourself; the smell of your sin's goin' to catch m'lord's whiffin' about, and he's as jealous as he's black. If m'lord Othello had a mind to it, he could have that little lollin' tongue of yours cut clean out of your head, with none of the citizens of Cyprus to say him nay. And then what would you do for your customers! If he catched you degineratin' his wife—

BIANCA *(Starting to cry with fear)*: Aw swear, Miss Emilia, Aw'm not degineratin' m'lady; we was just mates, that's wot. If Missus Desdemona wants to lark and gull her smug of a husband, that's her business, then, ain't it? Aw done as she towld me, an' that's all. She's a good lady, an' all, and Aw've just been friendly-like to her—

EMILIA: Don't be a little fool hussy. There's no such creature, two-, three- or four-legged, as "friend" betwixt ladies of leisure and ladies of the night. And as long as there be men with one member but two minds, there's no such thin' as friendship between women. An' that's that. So turn yourself around, go out and close the door behind you, and take all traces of the flophouse with you, includin' your tall tales about your "friendships" with ladies—

BIANCA *(Anger finally conquering fear)*: You can call me wot you like, but Aw'm no liar! Aw'm as 'onest a woman as yerself! And wot's more, mebbe you can wipe yer trotters on women who have to crack their crusts by rolling blokes in Venice, but 'ere it's differnt.—Aw have a place 'ere and Aw'm not ashamed t'own it. Aw'm nice to the wives in town, and the wives in town are rather nice to me. Aw'm doin' them favors by puttin' up wif their screwy owld men, and Aw like me job! The only ponk Aw has to clean up is me own.

(Starts to leave, but) And wot's more, Aw likes yer lady, whefer you think so or not. She can see me as Aw am, and not arsk for bowin' and scrapin'. She don't have to be nobby, 'cause she's got breedin', and she don't mind liking me for me own self—wifout th' nobby airs of yer Venetian washer-women! Aw'm at home 'ere in my place—you, you Venetian washerdonna, you're the one out o' yer element!

(Bianca stalks to the door, but before she can reach it, Desde-mona enters.)

DESDEMONA: Emilia.


## 14.

The same. Desdemona, Emilia and Bianca.

DESDEMONA: Emilia. I thought I told you to tell me the instant Miss Bianca arrived. Well?

EMILIA: I didn't want to be botherin' m'lady with the Ambassador—

DESDEMONA: I want none of your excuses for your rudeness to our guest. My dear Bianca! I've been waiting impatiently— I could have just died of boredom.
(Bestows a warm hug on Bianca)
May I kiss you?

(Desdemona "kisses" Bianca by pressing both sides of their cheeks together.)

BIANCA *(Stammering)*: Aw'm not worthy of it, m'lady—

DESDEMONA: Oh, Bianca, so stiff and formal!—What have I done that you should be so angry with me?

BIANCA *(Quickly)*: Nofing! Your lady's been all kindness to me... but mayhap...Aw'm not the sort o' mate for one o' your company!

DESDEMONA: Nonsense! I'll decide my own friendships...

*(Desdemona looks meaningfully at Emilia.)*

DESDEMONA *(To Bianca)*: You must excuse my entertaining you in such a crude barn of a room; my room's much cozier, but I don't know when my...my..."smug"—is that right? *(Bianca nods)* —When he'll return. *(Laughs)*

Right now Othello's out in the night somewhere playing Roman Orator to his troops.

*(Desdemona guides Bianca to the table; they sit side by side)* Emilia...Ask Miss Bianca if she'd like some wine. *(To Bianca)* It's really quite good, my dear.

*(Emilia glumly approaches Bianca.)*

EMILIA: Well, are you wantin' any?

DESDEMONA: Emilia! "Would you care for some wine, Miss Bianca?"

EMILIA *(Deep breath; red)*: "Would you care for some wine, Miss Bianca?"

BIANCA: Why thank you—D-Desdemona, Aw could do w' a sneaker—

DESDEMONA *(Laughs)*: How I love the way you talk!...Emilia, fetch the wine and two goblets. That will be all.

EMILIA: Yes, mum.

*(Emilia exits and Bianca relaxes.)*

DESDEMONA: My poor Bianca; has Emilia been berating you?

BIANCA: Well, Aw don't know about that, but she's been takin' me down a bit. Aw don't thinks she likes me very much.

DESDEMONA: Oh, what does that matter! Why should you want her friendship? You don't have to care what anyone thinks about you—you're a totally free woman, able to snap your fingers in anyone's face!

BIANCA: Yea, that's wot all right—but still, Aw likes people to like me.

DESDEMONA: Oh, well, you mustn't mind Emilia. She's got a rotten temper because her husband—her "smug"—is such a rotter. Oh, Iago! *(Shudders)* Do you know him?

BIANCA *(Smiling, looking away)*: Aw know 'im by sight—

DESDEMONA: You know the one, then—the greasy little man. He's been spilling his vinegar into her for fourteen years of marriage, until he's corroded her womb from the inside out. And every day she becomes more and more hallowed out, just—just a vessel of vinegar herself.

BIANCA *(Disturbed)*: Wot a funny way of lookin' at it—

*(Bianca is bewildered.)*


## 15.

*Bianca and Desdemona.*

BIANCA: So you don't fancy Iago, then, do you?

DESDEMONA: Detest him. But of course, I don't have anything to do with him—I only need suffer his wife's company. Poor old Mealy—

BIANCA: "Mealy?"

*(Bianca laughs, her fear of Emilia diminishing.)*

DESDEMONA: Yes, I've nicknamed her that, because I suspect it annoys her. Still, it fits.

*(Desdemona and Bianca giggle.)*

DESDEMONA: Alas, when Othello and I eloped it was on such short notice, and my husband's so stingy with salary that the only maid I could bring was my father's scullery maid.

BIANCA: Yer scullery maid! Not...not yer—wot-de-ye-call-it— "*Fee dah—Feyah der—*"

DESDEMONA: "*Fille de chambre!*" Heavens, no! I keep her in line with the prospect of eventual advancement, but she's much too unsuitable for that—why she doesn't speak a word of French, and she's crabby to boot. Still, she's devoted and that makes up for all the rest.

BIANCA: Wot makes you fink she's devoted?

DESDEMONA: Ah, a good mistress knows the secret thoughts of her maids. She's devoted.

BIANCA: Well, it's a cooshy enough way to crack a crust...

DESDEMONA: Crack a crust?

BIANCA: Oh, beg yer pardon; Aw mean t'earn a livin'—

DESDEMONA *(Enthralled)*: "Crack a crust!" How clever you are, Bianca!

## 16.

*Desdemona, Bianca and Emilia. Emilia stands before Desdemona, bearing a pitcher and two mugs on a tray.*

EMILIA: Wine, m'lady...

DESDEMONA: Ah, excellent.

*(Emilia serves Desdemona first with all the grace she can muster; then she negligently pushes the wine in the direction of Bianca.)*

BIANCA: Thank you, Mealy.

DESDEMONA *(Toasting Bianca)*: Now, then: To our friendship!
BIANCA: T' yer 'ealth—

*(Desdemona delicately sips her wine, as Bianca belts it down so that the wine trickles from the corner of her mouth. Emilia is aghast. As Bianca wipes her mouth with her hand, she notices Emilia's shock.)*

BIANCA *(Blurts)*: 'Scuse me guttlin' it down me gob—
DESDEMONA: Oh, tush, Bianca. Mealy, haven't you mending to carry on with?

*(Emilia silently seats herself apart and picks up the drawers.)*

DESDEMONA: I tell you, Bianca, it's a disgrace. My husband refuses to buy new linen for his drawers, so Emilia must constantly mend the old.
   *(Confidentially)* He's constantly tearing his crotch hole somehow.
BIANCA *(Amused)*: And how does that happen?
DESDEMONA *(Demurely)*: I have no idea.—More wine, dear?


**17.**

*The same. Bianca and Desdemona, drinking. Emilia sews.*

DESDEMONA: How about another...round?
BIANCA: All right, then.
   *(Desdemona pours generously)* But not so much! Aw could get lushy easy.

*(Bianca sips her wine; Desdemona knocks it back, and wipes her mouth with her hand. They laugh.)*

## 18.

*Desdemona and Bianca, drinking. They are giggling help-lessly, spluttering. Emilia sews. Desdemona starts to choke on her wine from laughing.*

## 19.

*The same. Desdemona and Bianca try to control themselves. Then Desdemona holds up the hoof-pick, and Bianca and Desdemona explode in raucous laughter. Emilia is furious.*

## 20.

*The same.*

BIANCA: Listen, luvs, where's yer five-minute lodging?

DESDEMONA: My…what?

BIANCA: Yer Drury Lane? Yer—where's yer bleedin' crapper! Yew know—where do yew make water?

EMILIA: M'lady makes her water in a hand-painted Limoges pot, a holy sight with angels havin' a grand time—it's not for the like of you!

DESDEMONA: There's an outhouse in the back by the shed…care-ful of the muck and the pigs.

BIANCA: Ta. Be back in a few…Aw've got t' go see a bloke about a horse.

*(Bianca exits.)*

EMILIA: And you're after havin' yourself a proper time.

DESDEMONA: Oh, Mealy, I'm sorry—we were just having fun—

EMILIA: At my husband's expense. You finagled that out o' me, and then you went and told it to My Lady of the Public Square…

DESDEMONA: It…It just…slipped out.

> *(Goes into another gale of laughter; then)* Mealy, I'm going to ask her about Cassio!

EMILIA: Why must you be knowin' every man's size?!

*(Desdemona laughs again.)*

DESDEMONA: No, I mean I'm going to tell her that Othello suspects him.

EMILIA: Are you daft from the wine?

DESDEMONA: Why not? Maybe we can get to the bottom of this…

EMILIA: Why is it mattering? Tomorrow morning we're leaving with the Ambassador—

DESDEMONA: Yes, yes, but I can find out why—

EMILIA: I don't understand why m'lady is in such a rush to havin' her throat slashed our last night on Cyprus—

DESDEMONA: Look, I'll just tell her that my husband is under some false impression, and ask her for—

EMILIA: And why should she be believin' you?

DESDEMONA: She'll believe me! She'll believe me because…I'll give her…I'll give her…my word of honor.

EMILIA: And just how much goat cheese does that buy at market?—I know the world! I've seen flesh buckets fightin' for their fancy men in the streets in Venice, and a pretty sight it was!

DESDEMONA: Oh, Mealy—

EMILIA: You'll be bleedin' on the wrong time of the month! Those trullies, all of them, carry slashers down in their boots—

*(Bianca throws open the door and sticks her head in; Emilia and Desdemona are startled.)*

BIANCA: Did-jew miss me?

## 21.

*Bianca, Desdemona and Emilia.*

BIANCA: 'Ere now—let me settle w' you fer Tuesday night. Let's see... *(Rummages in a pocket of her dress)* It were six pence a john, at ten johns makes fer...five bob, an' tuppence fer tips.

*(Emilia gasps.)*

DESDEMONA: I can hear what you're thinking Mealy—Holy Mother, I made more in twenty minutes than you do in a week of washing!

EMILIA: Five bob...

DESDEMONA: How large now the world for so small a vice, eh, Mealy?

EMILIA: I'm...I'm not to be tempted, Miss Desdemona.

DESDEMONA: Brave girl!

BIANCA: 'Ere's the brass ready. Tuppence for tips is bleedin' well for a Tuesday.

DESDEMONA: Really?

BIANCA: It so be as how Wednesday is payday 'ere; Tuesday nights are the cooshiest layin', but the stingiest payin'—

EMILIA: Aye, "Men earns their money like Horses and spends it like Asses..."

DESDEMONA: Never mind Mealy, Bianca; she's over there calculating what price fidelity. Now about next week—

EMILIA: You two can cackle with laughter at me if you like, but it's a duty for me to stop your ladyship from gettin' into danger—

BIANCA *(Offended)*: Danger! Wot danger! She helped me out on me Adam an' Eve Night—there's no danger. Aw gave her me lambs; the feisty, firkin' lads come on th' other nights, not on Tuesday. It don't take no elbow grease; Tuesday's just lying back and Adam an' Evein' it—

EMILIA: I don't understand your "Adam and Eve" and I don't think I want to...

DESDEMONA: Oh yes you do, Mealy; "Adam and Eve" is what you and Iago did on your wedding night...

BIANCA: She just might fink it means fallin' asleep—

*(Emilia vigorously stitches the linen.)*

DESDEMONA: She's right, though, Bianca, she's only trying to protect me.—How about if we leave next Tuesday night open. If I can sneak away into the darkness of your boudoir, then I'll send word by Emilia—

BIANCA: Right, then, but you understand me, Miss Desdemona, there'll be no firsky johns when you comes clan-decently; just the meek ones who are low on pocket-brass, or the stingy-mingy-gits who don't want to pay for nothin' wild. An' there'll be a fresh bed, an' the room so dark that your own husband wouldn't know you—

DESDEMONA: Oh, Bianca—what a thought—do you think he'd come? I'd die for sure— *(Laughs)*

And wouldn't he be mad if he'd paid for what he got for free at home!!

BIANCA: Well, the room's bleedin' black—blacker than he is.

*(Bianca and Emilia laugh together; Desdemona is affronted.)*

DESDEMONA: I beg your pardon?

BIANCA: No, no, all my Tuesday johns are reg'lars—Aw know 'em all. So if you want, let me know—it'll be treacle next to wot Aw had today—

DESDEMONA: Do tell, Bianca—

EMILIA: Hasn't m'lady had enough—

DESDEMONA: Oh, hush, Mealy—just mend your crotches, and don't listen.

BIANCA: All right, then. Aw have this one john who comes once a week for an L 'n' B—

DESDEMONA: "L and B?"

BIANCA: In th' Life, it's known as a lam an' brim—first they lam
you, an' mayhap you lam them, then you brim 'em...

(Desdemona looks blank) You know—first they beat you,
an' then you beat them, and then you give 'em wotever—an
Adam an' Eve, or a Sunny-Side Over—

DESDEMONA (Dawning): You mean men actually pay to beat
you? And to be beaten?

BIANCA: Oh, well, it costs 'em a pretty penny, Aw can tell you;
there's nothin' doin' for less than two bob.

DESDEMONA (Eyes wide): My. Well, carry on.

BIANCA: Well, there's this one john, an owld mate, who's been on
tick for some weeks, an' 'e's got quite a bill. But Aw feels
sorry for 'im, 'is wife really lams 'im at 'ome, an' Aw figure
'e needs t' get it off 'is chest. So 'e comes in, an' Aw says,
"Tom, you owe me over two quid, now; when's it comin'?"

"Gaw, Bianca," 'e says, "Aw just been out o' collar, an'—"

DESDEMONA: "Out of collar?"

BIANCA: Wot yew call un-deployed...

"Bianca," 'e says, "Gawd luv yew, me owld woman an'
Aw've had a row, an' Aw'm all done in. Aw'll pay th' soddin' bill, some'ow; but fer now, fer owld times..." 'e says.

Well, Gawd's Wounds, wot was Aw t'do? "Right, then,
Tom," Aw said. An' Aw lays down on the bed—'cause 'e
liked me to go first—an' 'e puts the straps on me.

"Tom," Aw says, "listen, luv, th' straps are bleedin'
tight!" An' before Aw knew wot, 'e was lammin' me fer
real!! 'E did me fer a jacketin' such as Aw thought would be
me last L 'n' B!!

Aw bite me teeth not to scream, 'cause the bobbies won't
put up with no row, no matter how many quid Aw pay 'em...
Well, Tom finally gets it over wif, an' it's *my* turn.

"Aw'm sorry, Bianca," 'e says, "if Aw got a bit rough."

"Oh, it's nofin', Tom," Aw says—'cause Aw'm determined t' get me own back...So, Aw tie 'im down on th' bed—
'e's a big strapper o' a bloke—an' then Aw lam th' *pudding*

out o' 'im!! An' 'e's 'ollerin' like it's th' Second Coming.
Then after Aw gi' 'im a royal pasting, Aw go through 'is togs,
an' in the back pocket Aw find a soddin' crown!

"You been 'olding out on me, Tom! Aw've had it wi' yer
dodges an' flams—wot kind o' a soup kitchen do yew fink
me?" An' Aw let into 'im again!!

"Bianca—let me go, an' Aw'll niver flam to ye again!"

"BLEEDIN' RIGHT!" Aw says. So Aw copped 'is brass,
takes up the belt, an' let 'im loose—straight into the street 'e
runs, naked as a blue jay. Aw had to throw 'is togs after 'im.

"Yew Owld Stringer!" Aw yelled. "'Ere's yer togs, an' fer
yer change, Take This!" *(Raises her fist and slaps her elbow.
Excited, she catches her breath)*

DESDEMONA: Jesus. Weren't you scared?

BIANCA: Aw'd be lyin' if Aw said nay. Aw thought it was me last
trick. You can't be too careful, there's a lot of maggot-
brained doodles in me bus'ness. But Aw can take care o'
meself.

DESDEMONA: Doesn't...doesn't it hurt?

BIANCA: Naw, not usual. It's stingy-like, but it's all fakement.

*(Looking into Desdemona's eyes, gets an idea)* Aw c'n
show you if you likes...C'mon, it won't hurt you none—

DESDEMONA: Well...yes, all right, Bianca, show me.


## 22.


*The beating scene. Emilia, Bianca and Desdemona.*


EMILIA: Are you out o' your mind? Lettin' a strumpet strap you
in your own house like a monk in Holy Week?

DESDEMONA: Turn around, Emilia, and mind your own business.
Go on, turn around, and say your beads. Pay no attention.
*(To Bianca)* Sorry—please continue.

*(Emilia says her beads through the following.)*

EMILIA: Hail Mary Full of Grace the Lord is with Thee...

BIANCA: Get up on the table wi' yer tale end up—

EMILIA: Holy Mary, Mother of— *(Turns and sees Desdemona spread-eagled)* —GOD!!!

BIANCA: Right now. Aw'll just take a strap 'ere, an' Aw'll just brush you wi' it—but when Aw let's go, you move yer tail up. All right?

DESDEMONA: I...I think so; it's rather like rising to the trot on a horse—

BIANCA: Right then. One—up. Two—down. All right, now. One. *(Desdemona moves up)* Two. *(Lightly straps Desdemona as she moves down)* One. *(Desdemona moves up)* An' Two. *(Desdemona moves down; a strap)* Does it hurt?

DESDEMONA: No...no, it doesn't, really.

BIANCA: Right then. Let's have some sound e-ffecks. One. Two. *(Desdemona screams, Emilia clutches her rosary)* NO!!— Not that loud! The bobbies would be in on yew so fast yew wouldn't get yer panties up—just a moan enow to get 'im excited...Right, then? Now: One—Two; One—Two; One— Two; One—Two; One—Two; One—Two!!

*(Desdemona perfects her synchronized moans, building to a crescendo, at which point she breaks into peals of laughter.)*

DESDEMONA: It's smashing!—Mealy— you really must try it!

## 23.

*As before.*

BIANCA: Aw want you t'take this in th' right way now—but if you weren't born a lady, you'd a been a bleedin' good blow-zabella. One o' the best. An'—well, no matter what fate holds, there's always room fer you in me shop.

*(Bashful)* Aw means it, too—

EMILIA: Holy Mother, if anyone had so much as whispered in Venice that you'd be makin' a bonnie whore, there'd be a blood duel to settle in the streets!

BIANCA: Aw'm payin' yer lady me respecks as one pro-fessional t'anofer. You...you got as much notion of me craft as a donkey has of Sunday.

EMILIA: Why, thank you—at least someone has noted me merit.

DESDEMONA *(Gently)*: I'm very complimented, Bianca...and I really did enjoy Tuesday night—but I don't think I'd better risk covering for you again—

BIANCA: You're...you're not brimmin' fer me anymore?

DESDEMONA: No—I don't think I'd better.

EMILIA *(To herself)*: Heigh-ho! On to the next—

BIANCA *(Trembling)*: But...but we c'n still be mates, wot?

DESDEMONA: Of course we can! I want that very much. I never tire of hearing your stories. They're so lively, so very funny. What else have I got for amusement's sake.

*(Bianca is disturbed. Emilia smiles)*

But you haven't told me yet about your evening off with Cassio last Tuesday...did you enjoy yourself?

BIANCA: You don't want to 'ear about it none, it's not anyfing amusing—

DESDEMONA: Now, just tell me all about it, Bianca; you can tell me your secrets, too. Woman to woman. What did you two do?

BIANCA *(Shyly)*: We just talked.

EMILIA *(Snorting)*: *All* night?

BIANCA: Yes! 'E's differnt, you know. 'E's a gen'l'man, 'e is. An' 'e makes the rest o' the blokes round 'ere look like the ninny-hammers they are—

EMILIA: Oh, he's diff'rent, all right. You'd think after all week of tomfoolin' with the like of hicks, you'd have more sense than to go prancin' about with some *Nancy* town stallion.

BIANCA: Wot! Nancy! Nancy, is it? Who're you callin' "Nancy"?

DESDEMONA: Now, Mealy, don't tease her—

EMILIA: The way I see it, it's no acc-i-dent for himself to be an army man—

BIANCA: Aw tell you wot, m'lord Cassio 'twill make a smug more obligin' in bed than the one you've got—

DESDEMONA *(Warningly)*: Ladies, ladies—

EMILIA: Well, you'll never find out what it is to be havin' the like of a proper husband in the bed.

BIANCA: Mayhap Aw will, too. Aw'm ready to let my way of life go fer wash the second 'e arsks me.

DESDEMONA: What!

BIANCA: Aw'm giving 'alfe me brass each week to the priest, Father Donahue, so's 'e c'n pray fer me sins an' t' gi' me apsolution. Aw'm ready t' say yes whenever 'e arsks me an'—an' Aw c'n go to th' altar as unstained as you were on yer weddin' night.

EMILIA *(Seeing Bianca in a new light)*: So, you're after goin' to the priest reg-ular?
      *(Impressed)* That's a lot of money.

BIANCA: Bleedin' right.

DESDEMONA: *(Crestfallen)*: Oh, Bianca—oh, surely you're...you're not the type that wants to get married?

*(Depressed, Desdemona goes and pours herself another mug of wine.)*

BIANCA: Wot's wrong wif that? Aw'm still young, an' Aw've got a tidy sum all saved up fer a dowry. An' m'lord Cassio's only got t' arsk fer a transfer to th' garrison 'ere. We'd make a bleedin' jolly life of it, Aw c'n tell you. Aw'd get us a cottage by th' sea, wif winder boxes an' all them kinds of fings, an' 'e could go to th' tipple'ouse as much as 'e likes, wifout me sayin' nay. An' then...then Aw'd be bearin' 'im sons so's to make 'im proud—

EMILIA *(Triumphantly)*: There! There's your new woman, m'lady! Free! Does for herself!

BIANCA: Why, that "new woman" kind o' fing's all hogwash!
      *(Emilia nods her head in agreement)*
      All women want t'get a smug, it's wot we're made for,

ain't it? We may pretend differnt, but inside ev'ry born one o' us want smugs an' babies, smugs wot are man enow t' keep us in our place.

DESDEMONA *(Quietly into her wine)*: I don't think I can stand it...

BIANCA: 'Scusin' my cheek, but you're a lucky lady, an' you don't even know it. Your 'ubby might be wot you call a bit doo-lolly-tap-tap up 'ere *(Taps her head)* but th' maritle knot's tied good 'n' strong. Every time Aw 'ear, *(Dreamily)* "'Til deaf do us part," Aw starts t' snurfle. Aw can't 'elp it. If only Cassio would say them words an' make me th' 'appiest o'—

EMILIA: And what makes you think m'lord Cassio—who's Venetian born, an' wears silk next to his skin, not none of your Cyprus scum—is goin' to be marryin' a tried-on strumpet?

BIANCA: 'Coz a gen'l'man don't lie to a bird—Aw should soddin' well know where ofs Aw speak. Besides, m'lord Cassio gi' me a token o' 'is es-teem—

EMILIA: Hmmpf! And I'm after supposin' you gave him the same, as you've given tokens of esteem to all your customers—a scurvy clap—that's your token.

*(Desdemona becomes curious.)*

DESDEMONA: Hush, Mealy.

*(To Bianca)* Never mind her, Bianca—I believe you. What type of token did Cassio give?

BIANCA *(As enthused as a teenage girl)*: It's a real flashy bit o' goods. It's a muckenger so swank Aw don't dare blow me beak in it.

*(Confidentially)* So Aw carry it down in me knockers an' next to me 'eart.

DESDEMONA *(Lost)*: A swank...muck...

BIANCA: Wot Aw mean is, it ain't yer typic sneezer.

*(Gropes into her bodice, and tenderly takes out an embroidered handkerchief; proudly)* 'Ere it is, now.

DESDEMONA *(Starting)*: Why... *(Looks carefully; then in relief)* Oh, thank God, Bianca, you've found it. I'm saved.

*(Stops)* But what—whatever are you doing with my handkerchief?

EMILIA *(To herself)*: Oh, Jesus, he gave it to Cassio!

BIANCA *(Blank)*: *Your* handkerchief? *Yours?!*

*(Dangerously)* What's Cassio doin' wi' your hand-ker-chief?

DESDEMONA: That's precisely what I want to find out—Emilia!

BIANCA *(Fierce)*: Aw bet. So—you was goin' t' 'elp me out once a week fer Cassio?

*(Advancing)* You cheatin' hussy—Aw'll pop yer peepers out—

*(Bianca lunges for Desdemona; Emilia runs.)*

EMILIA: She's Got a KNIFE!—

DESDEMONA: Listen, Bianca—

BIANCA: When Aw'm gulled by a woman, she don't live to do it twice—

DESDEMONA: Bianca, I swear!—

*(Bianca sees the hoof-pick and picks it up, slowly advancing on a clutching Desdemona, who backs away toward the clothesline.)*

BIANCA: Aw'll carve you up into cag-meat an' feed you to the pigs. Aw'll gag yer puddings out yer gob, you'll choke so hard—

DESDEMONA: I never!—

*(Bianca swipes at Desdemona with the pick; the two clench each other. Breaking away, Desdemona falls, and picks up a wine bottle in defense.)*

BIANCA: Yer gonna snuff it, m'lady—so say yer prayers, yew goggle-eyed scab o' a WHORE!

*(Desdemona ducks behind the hanging clothes, with Bianca
following. We hear a scuffle, grunts and screams.*
  *Emilia runs for the palace door, calling:)*

EMILIA: GUARD! GUARD!!—

*(Emilia flings the door open. Then she realizes she can't call
the guard, and quickly closes the door behind her, turning to
face the room with grim desperation.)*

EMILIA *(Softly)*: Jesus.
BIANCA *(Offstage)*: BLOODY!—
DESDEMONA *(Offstage)*: MEALY!!

*(Emilia runs away from the door, taking out her crucifix.)*

EMILIA: Oh, Jesus. Oh, Jesus.

*(And then, we hear a scream, a splash and the sound of a
bottle breaking. Slowly a dark, wet stain spreads on a cloth
drying on the clothesline. For a moment, there is silence.*
  *Bianca, looking grim and fierce, strides out from behind
the clothes, holding the hoof-pick. She looks at Emilia, who
backs away. There is a pause.*
  *Then, Desdemona steps from behind the hanging clothes,
holding a broken wine bottle. The torso of her gown is
splashed with dark, indelible burgundy.)*

EMILIA *(Softly)*: Oh, thank Jesus—
DESDEMONA: Bianca!...Bianca, I never did.
BIANCA: Leave me alone...Aw've lost me chance of a smug!
     *(Erupts into weeping, starts to wipe her nose with the
     handkerchief)* There! Take yer filthy linen! Aw wouldn't
     blow me nose in it—
DESDEMONA: Bianca—I never did. I never did.
BIANCA: Aw loved 'im—

DESDEMONA: Bianca—

BIANCA: An' Aw lost 'im—

DESDEMONA: Bianca—

BIANCA: An' oh, oh, the cottage by the sea...

DESDEMONA: If it makes a difference, I didn't.

BIANCA: You gulled yer 'usband an' you gulled me! An' Aw thought we was mates!

*(Bianca starts to leave; Emilia calls after her.)*

EMILIA: I told you there's no such thing as friendship with ladies—

BIANCA: You!! Washerdonna!! Shut Yer Potato-Trap! Don't you be so 'igh an' mighty smart!!

　　*(Reaching the door, she opens it, and turns)* And just where was your Iago last Tuesday night!

*(Triumphantly, Bianca slams the door behind her.
A very long pause. Then, Desdemona tries to sound casual.)*

DESDEMONA: Um, Emilia, dear, just...just where was Iago last Tuesday night?

EMILIA *(Distressed)*: He...he said...he said he was on guard duty...

*(Emilia begins to cry. Desdemona sits beside her, and tentatively puts her arms about Emilia. Then, Desdemona rocks her maid.)*

## 24.

*Lights up on Desdemona and Emilia, seated at the table, drinking wine, saying nothing.*

## 25.

*Desdemona and Emilia, at table, staring ahead into air. Desdemona wearily looks into her cup, and pours herself and Emilia another cup of wine. They look at each other, nod to each other, and drink together.*

## 26.

*Desdemona is drinking. Emilia grasps her mug.*

EMILIA *(In a low voice)*: Do you know which one he was?
DESDEMONA: No...I don't think so. There were so many that night.
EMILIA: Aye, you were having a proper time at it. Travelin' around the world!!

*(Pause.)*

DESDEMONA: There was one man...
        *(Hesitating)* It might have been him.
EMILIA *(Laughs harshly)*: My husband's a lover of garlic. Was that the man you're remembering?
DESDEMONA: No, it's not that—although...
EMILIA: Well, what is it you remember!
DESDEMONA: There was one man who...didn't last very long.
EMILIA: Aye. That's the one.

## 27.

*The same.*

EMILIA: When I was married in the church, the knot tied beneath the Virgin's nose, I looked forward to the bed with as much joy as any girl after a hard day. And then Iago—well, he was still a lad, with the softness of a boy, and who could tell he'd turn into the man?

*(Pauses to drink)*

But all that girl nonsense was knocked out of me by the nights. Night followin' night, as sure as the day's work came after. I'd stretch myself out on the bed, you see, waitin' for my good man to come to me and be my mate—as the priest said he could—but then...But then I saw it didn't matter what had gone on between us—the fights, my crying, a good meal or a cold one. Days could pass without a word between us, and he'd take his fill of me the same. I could have been the bed itself. And so, you see, I vowed not to be there for him. As he'd be lying on me in the dark, I'd picture up my Rosary, so real I could kiss the silver. And I'd start at the Blessed Cross itself, while he was somewhere doin' his business above, and I'd say the first wooden bead, and then I'd finger the next bead in my mind, and then onto the next— *(Stops)* But I never did make it to the medallion. He'd be all through with me by the time of the third "Hail Mary."

*(Pause)*

Does my lady know what I'm saying?

DESDEMONA: I'm not sure. I...I don't think it's...happened to me like that.

EMILIA: Ah, well, men are making fools of themselves over you. The Ambassador is traipsing from the mainland just to hold onto your skirt; and your husband— *(Stops herself)* Well, maybe it's all different for the likes of you.

*(Desdemona says nothing)*

And then, maybe not. It's hard to be seeing, when you're young and men watch you when you pass them by, and the talkin' stops between them. But, all in all, in time you'll know. Women just don't figure in their heads—not the one who hangs the wash—not Bianca—and not even you, m'lady. That's the hard truth. Men only see each other in their eyes. Only each other.

*(Beat)*

And that's why I'm ready to leave the whole pack of them behind and go with you and the Ambassador. Oh, to see my husband's face tomorrow morning! When he finds out that I can get along by myself, with no thanks to his plotting and hatching! But it's leave him now or be countin' my beads through the years, waitin' for his last breath!

DESDEMONA *(Quietly)*: Emilia, I'll be honest with you, even if it puts me in risk to do so...You're to stay behind tomorrow. I've asked my cousin for my own safe passage. I wish to go alone with Ludovico.

*(Emilia stands very still)*

I am in your hands. You can run and tell my husband all—but I don't want to trifle with your feelings and desert you with the first tide. This way, you see, I'm only temporarily leaving you behind. But I promise I'll need your service in Venice as much as tonight. So, you're to follow me when all household matters are in hand, taking with you whatever my husband permits. As a token of my esteem—here— *(Takes off a ring, and gazes at it wistfully)* I want you to have this. It's a memento given me by Ludovico for...well, never you mind what for. Little did he think it would wind up 'round the finger of an honest woman. *(Desdemona gives the ring to Emilia)*

EMILIA: This ring is for me? but it's of value, m'lady...

*(Emilia tries to return it; Desdemona insists. Emilia makes a decision.)*

EMILIA: Listen, Miss, you've gone and leveled with me, and I'm after doing the same with you!

*(Blurts)* M'lady, don't go to your husband's bed tonight. Lie apart—stay in my chamber.

DESDEMONA: Why? Whatever for? It would raise suspicion.

EMILIA: I'll say you're ill—with woman sickness.

DESDEMONA: But why?

EMILIA: Because...because...oh, m'lady, you know how easy it is to be seduced by a husband's soft word, when it's the like of angry words he pours down upon your head—

DESDEMONA *(Very still)*: Emilia—what have you done?

EMILIA: I took the handkerchief.

DESDEMONA: You took the handkerchief...I thought you did.

EMILIA: It was to be a joke, you see; my husband put me up to it, as a lark, he said, just to see—

DESDEMONA *(Very softly)*: Iago—Oh, my sweet Jesus—

EMILIA: And he was laughing about it, ye see, and he was as gay as a boy; he said he'd just...hide it for a while, all in jest—

DESDEMONA: Oh, no—he...he must have...planted it on Cassio— that's why...

EMILIA: It was just for a lark!

DESDEMONA: Emilia, what has your husband been thinking!

EMILIA: I don't know what he thinks.

*(Desdemona twists the handkerchief.)*

DESDEMONA: What use is this to me now! If I return it, my husband will say that my lover gave it back to me!!

EMILIA: Miss Desdemona—oh my lady, I'm sure your husband loves you!

DESDEMONA: How do you know that my husband—!

EMILIA: More than the world! He won't harm you none, m'lady— I've often seen him—

DESDEMONA: What have you seen?!

EMILIA: I've seen him, sometimes when you walk in the garden, slip behind the arbor just to watch you, unawares...and at night...in the corridor...outside your room—sometimes he just stands there, Miss, when you're asleep...he just stands there—

DESDEMONA *(Frightened)*: Oh, Jesus—

EMILIA: And once...I saw...I came upon him unbeknowin', and he didn't see me—I'm sure—he was in your chamber room and he gathered up the sheets from your bed, like a body, and...and he held it to his face, like, like a bouquet, all breathin' it in—

*(The two women pause: They both realize Othello's been smelling the sheets for traces of a lover.)*

DESDEMONA: That isn't love. It isn't love.
    *(Beat)*
    Why didn't you tell me this before?
EMILIA *(Carefully)*: I always thought it was not my place.

*(The two women do not speak for a moment. Emilia looks toward the palace door.)*

EMILIA: Well, what are we to be doin' now?
DESDEMONA: We have to make it to the morning. You'd better come with me—it's not safe for you, either.
    *(Emilia says nothing)*
    We'll have to leave all behind. It's not safe to pack.

*(Desdemona thinks.)*

DESDEMONA *(Carefully)*: Now listen, carefully, Emilia. I'll go to my own chamber tonight. You're to wait up for my husband's return—tell him I'm ill and I've taken to my own bed. He's not to disturb me, I'm not well. I'll turn in before he comes, and I'll...pretend to sleep if he should come to me.
    *(Pause)*
    Surely he'll not...harm a sleeping woman.
EMILIA: I'll do it.
DESDEMONA: Good. I'd better go to bed.

*(Desdemona starts toward the palace door and stops.)*

EMILIA: Would you like me to brush your hair tonight? A hundred strokes?

DESDEMONA: Oh, yes, please, Emilia...

## 28.

*Emilia brushes Desdemona's hair. Desdemona leans back, tense, listening to the offstage palace.*

EMILIA: Now, then—
    *(Starts)* One, two, three, four, five, six...

## 29.

*The same.*

EMILIA: Forty-five, forty-six, forty-seven...

## 30.

*Desdemona and Emilia. Emilia reaches the hundredth stroke.*

EMILIA: Ninety-seven...ninety-eight...ninety-nine...

*(They freeze. Blackout.)*

END OF PLAY

# Hot 'N' Throbbing

A workshop of *Hot 'N' Throbbing* was directed by Anne Bogart at Circle Repertory Theatre in October 1993 with the following cast:

| | |
|---|---|
| GIRL | Kristina Lear |
| BOY | Allan Heinberg |
| WOMAN | Leslie Lyles |
| MAN | Jeffrey LeBeau |
| VOICE-OVER | Zoey Zimmerman |
| THE VOICE | Robert Watson |

*Hot 'N' Throbbing* opened April 16, 1994 at the Hasty Pudding Theater in Cambridge, Massachusetts. The play was produced by American Repertory Theatre under Robert Brustein, Artistic Director, with a grant from the Fund for New American Plays, a project of the John F. Kennedy Center for the Performing Arts with support from the American Express Company, in cooperation with the President's Committee on the Arts and Humanities. It was directed by Anne Bogart, with sets by Christine Jones, lights by John Ambrosone, sound and music by Christopher Walker and costumes by Jenny Fulton. The cast was as follows:

| | |
|---|---|
| GIRL | Amy Louise Lammert |
| BOY | Randall Jaynes |
| WOMAN | Diane D'Aquila |
| MAN | Jack Willis |
| VOICE-OVER | Alexandra Loria |
| THE VOICE | Royal Miller |

SOME PLAYS ONLY
DAUGHTERS CAN WRITE.

*Hot 'N' Throbbing* was written on a National Endowment for the Arts fellowship—because obscenity begins at home.

I began work on this play in 1985. While I was driving the streets of Providence late at night, suddenly the vision of the play's ending came upon me with a terrible clarity. I knew that I would have to face this play in my future, and that certainty fueled a fear that kept me driving the deserted downtown streets in circles.

It was not until 1990, after my brother's illness and *Baltimore Waltz*, that I sat down with a reading list to begin research on the play. Again, late at night, as I began reading about domestic violence, I thought I heard a woman's cry—it was past midnight, and the street outside my house was abandoned. I would turn a page of my book, hear a faint cry, stop and listen. Was it an intimate response somewhere in the night to a couple's love-making or something more dangerous? I concentrated on the sound until I could pinpoint the source. Taking my house keys with me, I ventured out on the street. There I saw, half a block down, a car idling in the middle of the street. When I heard a man's voice say: "Shut up, bitch," and thought I saw a drawn knife inside the car, my worst fears were confirmed. I ran back to the house, started my own car and drove behind the car at a fast pace until I could flag down a police car to pursue the chase. Finally, the car was stopped by police; a shaking woman emerged, bleeding from a cut to her face.

She declined to press charges.

As I continued to work on the play, I kept a file filled with clippings from the *Providence Journal* on incidents of domestic violence. Providence is a relatively small city, of approximately

190,000 residents. Within less than a year, the file was crammed two inches thick. Domestic violence was all around us as I wrote.

Incentive to finish the play came from Senator Jesse Helms and Congress; the obscenity pledge now had to be signed by all recipients of the National Endowment for the Arts fellowships, in which fellows would pledge not to write or create art that caused offense to the community. I applied for an NEA grant, received one and wrote *Hot 'N' Throbbing* to see just what would be perceived as pornographic, eager to test the censorship of the NEA pledge.

Ironically, now, five years later, I realize that Jesse Helms and the fundamentalist Right are not the greatest threats to the arts community. Rather, it is our own cooperation with the Right within the arts community. For some time now, many theatres have been choosing their seasons from fear rather than conviction. We have quietly, silently, drifted to the Right in our seasonal offerings of benign and often vacuous theatre: boulevard theatre (now termed "classic") of the 1930s to 1950s; new comedies in the '90s written within the mode of *Harvey*; and an occasional political drama imported from South America, South Africa or England to expiate our own lack of moral courage. And of course, we have trumpeted *Angels in America* (rightly, in terms of its dramatic and political importance) with an almost hysterical relief: So many of us are now "off the hook." For the rest of the decade, we can relax. We can point to *Angels in America*, rather than produce a continuing dialogue with Tony Kushner's ground-breaking work.

Peter Franklin, my agent, a man of both literary discrimination and marketing savvy, read the first draft of *Hot 'N' Throbbing*. His remark: "I think we may get two productions of this play—one here and one abroad."

To date, only two artistic directors of professional companies—Robert Brustein of the American Repertory Theatre and Andrew Manley of the Harrogate Theatre in England—have produced this play. The premiere of *Hot 'N' Throbbing* occurred two months before the murder of Nicole Simpson.

To return to the play: I was interested to learn that "obscene" came from the Greek, for "offstage." Violence in the Greek theatre was kept "offstage": Platforms on wheels brought the bodies onstage to show the outcome, rather than the act. We have abdicated our responsibility for showing the results of violence to film, which all too often fetishizes the act rather than its impact. At a time when the Simpson trial became a media frenzy, my play itself has been kept "offstage"—many artistic directors have told me that it is too disturbing; audiences won't want to "see that onstage" (the same audiences that pack *Pulp Fiction*); or that the play is anti-pornography; or that the play is pro-pornography.

Domestic violence respects neither gender, race nor class. No politically correct approach can encompass all aspects of this problem. I worry that there is no longer a place for audiences to come to a civic space—the theatre—to confront the disturbing questions of our time. I remain scared of the dark—scared of our darkness—and I seek a communal light in the darkness of our theatres.

Censorship is alive and well in 1995: a benign censorship, a censorship within. If we cannot confront domestic violence on our stages, we will not be able to eliminate it from our living rooms.

*Paula Vogel*
December 28, 1995

CHARACTERS

GIRL: About fifteen.

BOY: About fourteen.

WOMAN: Almost thirty-four. Wears Lina Wertmuller glasses. On-again, off-again member of Weight Watchers.

MAN: Over thirty-four. Holes in dungarees. Almost a beer belly. (Note to actor: You've got to go gangbusters on this role. The bigger the asshole you are, the more we'll love you. Trust me on this.)

VOICE-OVER: Hard to tell her age under the **blue lights**. Voice-Over (V.O.) narrates the script that The Woman is writing, her inner voice. She is a sex worker: at times bored with her job; at times emphatically overacting, trying to land a role in a legitimate film. Voice-Over watches the stage action from her glass booth, where she dances. Her voice is amplified through a microphone. Her voice is sensual and husky.

THE VOICE: He is a presence, more than a person. At times he acts as a bouncer/owner in the erotic dance hall. His voice is also amplified through a microphone, and it is always theatrical, rich, baritone and commanding. The Voice breathes a lot through the mike. The Voice's dialect varies from German, French, Victorian British and Brooklynese. It often sounds just like The Man. The Voice also acts like a live DJ, spinning the score of the piece, always impassive to the onstage action. The Voice may wear headsets and sunglasses.

Note on Krafft-Ebing for The Voice. Krafft-Ebing has three sides in this piece: his lectures on sexuality to first-year medical students, his condescending talk to a ladies' club luncheon and his impassive dictation during an autopsy for police.

S E T

There are two play worlds in this piece. The **stage lights** and the **blue lights**—reality, constructed as we know it; and the erotic dance hall, as we fantasize about it.

First, the **blue light**: The interior of the nude dance hall, The Foxy Lady. On either side of the stage, there are glass enclosures. Stage left is the glass encasement of The Voice-Over, like the cheap porno acts, live, for a buck. Stage right is the sound booth where The Voice reigns with his equipment, microphone and tinted glass. Both booths are very high-tech in appearance.

In the midst of the dance-hall interior there is a platformed construction of a living room, almost like an island floating in the deep **blue light**. It should look like the living room of a town-house that cost $79,900 five years ago, on a 9½% mortgage, no deposit down. Although we never see the upstairs, we know there are two bedrooms, one bath; downstairs there is a half-bath. These preconstructed developments are called "empty-nesters."

Both The Foxy Lady and the living room have this in common: They are stages for performance, for the acting out of erotic fantasies, for viewing.

A few pieces. A sofa that folds out, in a tweed. A matching armchair. A coffee table. Television set, which may or may not be running erotica—if there is erotica, no one in the family notices.

The door to the half-bath. A front door. On the lower stage left, a large, white office-desk complex, with a secretary, holding a computer and printer. Along the wall behind this office-island, where the dining room was supposed to be, is the ubiquitous sliding patio doors, looking out onto the parking lot in a suburb. Premade, cream curtains that sort of match the tweed. And, oh yes—wall-to-wall shag.

On the other side of the sliding patio doors, a red ramp curves its way out into the audience in the shape of an engorged tongue—a runway/dance area for stripping.

MUSIC NOTES

I wrote this piece to several soundtracks: Janet Jackson's *Control* (particularly "Nasty"), and Kaoma's *World Beat*. After The Girl's last appearance, with the mention of horror movies, I wrote to the tape of Michael Jackson's *Thriller*, and the soundtrack to *Silence of the Lambs*. Sound tapes from horror movies, and A.M.G. and other rap might be played under the action (Frank Sinatra is also a nice possibility). The main thing is that the music changes from erotic to terrorific.

Two more props. **Blue light** where indicated and music. Music always helps to get it up.

*In a growing **blue light**, we see The Girl dressed in very tight pants and a halter top, making suggestive stripper or vogue-ing movements. At end of Voice-Over, we see an older woman sitting at a computer screen, typing. Living room.*

V.O.
"CUT TO: INTERIOR. NIGHT. VOICE-OVER:

She was hot. She was throbbing. But she was in control. Control of her body. Control of her thoughts. Control of…him.

He was hot. He was throbbing. And out of control. He needed to be restrained. Tied Down. And taught a Lesson.

But not hurt. Not too much. Just enough. Enough to make the burning hotter, the throbbing hotter. Just…enough. She would make his flesh red all over. She would raise the blood with her loving discipline. And she would make him wait. Make him beg. Make them both wait…until she was ready."

WOMAN AND VOICE-OVER: And she would make him wait. Make him beg.

WOMAN *(Types)*: Sounds too male-bashing—"Make him ask?" Oh, fuck it. "Make him beg…Make them both beg…"

*(Suddenly the bathroom door slams open in **stage light**. The Girl stands in front of the sink dressed as before.)*

GIRL *(Screams)*: MAAHM! WHERE'S YOUR EYELINER?
WOMAN: ON THE TOP SHELF! BY THE BEN GAY!

*(Back to flat, narrative tone at computer.)*

WOMAN: "Until she was ready. Ready to release them both at the end of a long, hard night. Ready to heave herself to the other side of her love throes, ready to give it up—"

GIRL: MAAHM! CAN I USE YOUR MASCARA!!

WOMAN: Sounds like upchucking. "Ready to pant, ready to scream, ready to die in each other's arms…"

    *(Stops; calls out)* Leslie Ann! What are you doing?

GIRL: Puttin' on some pancake.

WOMAN: Why are you putting on makeup.

GIRL: I already told you.

WOMAN: No you did not tell me.

GIRL: I Did. So.

WOMAN: Why are you wearing makeup.

GIRL: I'm Going. Out.

WOMAN: Where?

GIRL: Out. To Lisa's. To Spend The Night.

WOMAN: This is the first time I've heard about it.

GIRL: I Told You!

WOMAN: I don't want you going to Lisa's.

GIRL: But Why?!

WOMAN: Because I. said. so.

GIRL: I'm goin'.

WOMAN: Her parents do not supervise that young lady. You are not going to Lisa's.

GIRL: But all the girls will be there!

WOMAN: You are not all the girls.

*(The Girl slams bathroom door. We hear the water running.)*

GIRL *(Offstage)*: I'MM GOING!

*(The Woman sighs; types.*
    ***Blue Light.*** *The Boy enters. The Girl emerges from bathroom in tight pants.*

*Exaggerated movements of Boy humping Girl from behind with clothes on.)*

### V.O.

"VOICE-OVER CONTINUED:

He wanted to enter her. Penetrate her secrets with his will. He wanted to gently pry open that sweet channel that leads to joy, and fill her with his passion until the dull pain faded into pleasure, until her hips locked into a rhythm to match his. Together they would rock each other, clinging to each other as the tempo got faster, faster, faster and faster, faster and faster and faster, faster..."

*(The Boy stops as **lights** go back to **normal**, and slumps on sofa. The Girl stands facing The Woman.)*

GIRL: You just don't care. You want me to stay in this boring house until I rot like you and four-eyes on the sofa over there.

WOMAN: Leslie Ann. I am behind my schedule. I've got to get out forty pages by the first mail tomorrow morning, and I'm on page twenty-six.

GIRL: Layla. I am not answering to a dumb-shit name like Leslie Ann.

BOY *(Singing riff, and then)*: "LAY-LA!! YOU'VE GOT ME ON MY KNEES."

GIRL: MAH-HM.

WOMAN: I'm sorry, sweetie. Layla.

BOY: "LAY-LA! I'M BEGGING DARLIN', PLEASE."

GIRL: Shut up, creep!

BOY: Are you going out in those tight pants?

GIRL: What business is it of yours?

BOY: Those pants are so tight you can see your P.L.s.

GIRL: Shut up.

*(The Woman looks up from typing with interest.)*

WOMAN: What are P.L.s?

*(No Answer.)*

GIRL: Nothin'.

BOY: Hey, as long as I don't have to walk you up the aisle for some shotgun wedding, you trouncing around with your P.L.s hanging out...

WOMAN: P.L.s?

GIRL: Why don't you just go beat-off in your room, you little pervo...

WOMAN: Those pants are too tight. Did you spray-paint them on?

GIRL: Betcha wish you had my thighs, huh, Ma?

WOMAN: We are not discussing the subject of my thighs. You are not leaving this house dressed like that.

GIRL: Huh. That's funny. Coming from you.

WOMAN: What's that supposed to mean?

GIRL: Nothin'.

WOMAN: I could kill your father for telling you kids a thing like that. I do not write *pornography*. There's a mile of difference between that and...*adult entertainment*. He wouldn't know the difference.

BOY: I think it's cool, Mom.

GIRL: Shut up, toady.

WOMAN: This is not about me. You will not fling...the *way* I make.a.living into my face every time I give. you. a. directive. The way I put food on the plate, and Reeboks on the feet. You are not leaving this house, period, young lady. I want you to go upstairs to your room and do some homework for a change. Your grades last quarter were a disgrace.

GIRL: Calvin gets to go out.

WOMAN: Calvin has a 3.5. Calvin can go out all he wants on a Friday night. You are staying home and opening up a book. You'll like it. *Silas Marner*. I loved that book.

BOY: Her book report's due Monday.

WOMAN: You children can read quietly in your room. I've got to get this section done. Go on upstairs and open up your books.

BOY: The only thing Leslie Ann wants to open is her P.L.s.

WOMAN: Calvin! Quit picking on your sister!

GIRL: Get your little tattletale nose out of my P.L.s., creep!

WOMAN: I'VE HAD IT! What are you talking about? Leslie Ann?

GIRL: Ask Calvin. Go ahead, little brother, tell Mom what you've been calling me.

WOMAN: Calvin?

> (No response)

I asked you a question.

BOY: P.L.s are a name for a girl's...you know.

GIRL: It's not very nice. You know, for an honor-roll creep, you sure use some nice language.

WOMAN: When I was growing up, I didn't have a room of my own. And so I was determined that my children would each have their own privacy. Your mother sleeps on a convertible sofa that has to be made up each morning so you can have your own space. I want you both to go upstairs to your rooms, if you can't be quiet and act normal down here.

GIRL: Some privacy. The walls are paper-thin. How can I concentrate when all I can hear is four-eyes beating-off?

BOY: I do not! You have the mouth of a slut, Leslie Ann!

GIRL: You beat-off! In the catcher's mitt Daddy gave you for Christmas! I can feel the walls shaking!—

WOMAN (Suddenly interested, making notes): Catcher's mitt. Open Window. Show Clipboard. Notes: Leather catcher's mitt—

BOY: Mind Your Own Business!

GIRL: That's not what Dad meant when he said practice. Catching pop-up flies—

BOY: Shut up!—

GIRL: That's why you wear glasses, Calvin. Nobody else in this family does, little brother. 'Cause you violate yourself.

BOY: Mom wears glasses!

*(Startled, the two teenagers suddenly look at their mother with a horrified new idea; The Woman, oblivious, stares into her computer screen, typing with a vengeance. The siblings stop and erupt in laughter.)*

GIRL: Shut up, pervo!—
BOY: Musta learned it from you, P.L.—
GIRL: Quit calling me that, and I might just learn you something interesting—
BOY: Yeah?

*(They both look at their mother, deep into her typing.)*

GIRL: Yeah. So you won't haveta hang in the bushes outside the house. You do, don'tcha?

*(The Boy is suddenly quiet, beet red.)*

GIRL: Yeah. I thought that was you. Watching me undressing. In the bushes. Straight-A student. Yeah. I just might let you learn—

*(**Light** change. **Blue light**: The Girl dances closer to The Boy. Another Voice, a dark, rich, European baritone, whispers:)*

THE VOICE: "Lolita, light of my life, fire of my loins. My sin, my soul. Lo-lee-ta: the tip of the tongue taking a trip of three steps down the palate to tap, on the teeth. Lo. Lee. Ta."[1]

*(There is the sound of an automobile horn. Loud.)*

THE VOICE: "Lo. Lee. Ta."

*(The horn imitates The Voice. Three times. **Lights** change back abruptly.)*

[1]Note: References for cited material are listed at the end of the play.

GIRL: That's my ride! Mom! I've got to go.

WOMAN: You are not leaving this house. Young lady.

GIRL: You said I could!

WOMAN: When! When did I say that?

*(Voice-Over lights up a cigarette, bored, waiting. She puffs.)*

GIRL: Last night. I asked you. And you said you didn't care what I did. So I told Lisa yes.

WOMAN: Is that Lisa outside? I don't like you riding with her. Go out and tell her I said no.

GIRL: You said you need peace and quiet. I'm going to give you some. It's an overnight. A slumber party. I'll be back tomorrow.

WOMAN: You march upstairs. Right. this. minute. You are not leaving this house—

*(Once more, the car horn trumpets: Lo-lee-ta.)*

GIRL: I'll see you!

*(The Girl rushes to the door, exits and slams it behind her. There is a pause. The Boy watches The Woman. She returns to her computer.)*

WOMAN: Oh, Jesus. I could use a cigarette.

BOY: You quit smoking.

WOMAN: I know. I miss it at times like this. Jesus Christ. Page... twenty-six.

BOY: Fourteen to go.

WOMAN: What's on your agenda for tonight?

BOY: I'm staying here with you, Mom.

WOMAN: You're not worried, are you, Cal?

BOY: Nope. Not me.

WOMAN: Because I can take care of myself. Nothing's going to happen.

BOY: I know.

WOMAN: Because if you want to go out, you should just go ahead—

BOY: I don't wantto. I'm just going to sit here, quietly, and read, all right?

WOMAN: All right.

*(The Woman stares at the computer screen. The Boy stares at her. She looks up and sees him staring.)*

V.O.

"What are you looking at?"

THE VOICE: What are you—

V.O.

"looking—"

THE VOICE: —looking at?

*(The Boy looks down at his book, quickly. The Woman goes back to the screen. The Boy stares at her again. The Woman tentatively starts to type. Stops. Starts again. Stops.)*

V.O.

"What are you looking at?"

THE VOICE: What are you—

V.O.

"looking—"

THE VOICE: —looking at?

BOY: Writer's block, Mom?

WOMAN: I'm running out of words.

BOY: How about...

THE VOICE *(Whispered)*: —Throbbing—

BOY: —Throbbing?

WOMAN: Don't make fun of me, son. My writing puts food in your mouth.

BOY: I wasn't making fun! I was just trying to help!

WOMAN: I know. I'm sorry. Maybe after you go to college, you'll be able to be a real writer. I'd like that.

BOY: I'm not going to college.

WOMAN: We'll see.

BOY: To Allegheny Community? With all the geeks?

WOMAN: That's where I went, remember. But I meant maybe somewhere away from home. It would be good for you to get away.

BOY: Leslie Ann's the one who wants to go away.

WOMAN: I worry sometimes that she'll get as far as the backseat of a car.

BOY: I don't think so. I bet she's scared to death...

*(Pause. The Voice breathes heavily twice.)*

WOMAN: Why?

BOY: No reason.

*(Pause.)*

WOMAN: Okay.

*(The Voice stops breathing.)*

WOMAN: Page twenty-six...I need some words that pack a punch...

BOY: So how about throbbing?

WOMAN: I've got throbbing all over the page. There are only so many ways to say throbbing...

V.O.

—"Pulsating—"

THE VOICE: —"Beating—"

V.O.

—"Heaving—"

THE VOICE: —"Battering—"

V.O.

—"Pulsing—"

WOMAN: Wait a moment!—that's it, Charlene—when in doubt, cut to...cut to...

*(Light change to blue. The Boy stands, like a somnambulist, with his catcher mitt, looking up, staring.)*

V.O.

"CUT TO: EXTERIOR. In the bushes outside the house. Nighttime. We see a YOUNG BOY, not yet old enough to shave. He is peering up through the bushes at:

CUT TO: BOY'S POINT OF VIEW. We see an attractive older WOMAN, full-hipped, through her bedroom window, looking at herself in the mirror. THE WOMAN removes her glasses, and gazes at her image."

*(The Woman removes her glasses at the computer. The Boy stares at her.)*

V.O.

"CUT TO: THE YOUNG BOY. Standing now. He watches as she strokes her face. We see him raise his hand, which holds a baseball mitt. He strokes the leather with his free hand, softly feeling the texture."

*(The Boy follows the instructions of Voice-Over.)*

V.O.

"CLOSE-UP: On the mitt. THE BOY fists it several times, then raises the glove to his face, breathing in the leather.

CUT TO: THE WOMAN, who begins to feel her own body.

CUT TO: YOUNG BOY, who begins to run the glove across his chest.

CUT TO: THE WOMAN, who closes her eyes and runs her fingers over her rounded hips, and down into her waistline.

CUT TO: CLOSE-UP on leather mitt, rubbing up and down THE BOY's blue-jeaned thighs—

CUT TO:—"

*(Suddenly, an overlapping voice, deeper, darker, cuts in: The Boy stands frozen; The Woman halts at the computer. It is the voice of Krafft-Ebing, nineteenth-century sexologist.)*

THE VOICE *(À la Krafft-Ebing)*: "The pale complexion, the glassy gaze indicate the lunatic victim to this vice. Loss of memory, apathy and...impulsiveness of action are characteristic of chronic dementia resulting from—"

V.O.
*(Simultaneously with The Voice)*
—"masturbation in young men."

THE VOICE *(Simultaneously with Voice-Over)*: —"masturbation in young men."[2]

*(**Lights** change back. The Boy sits on the sofa, fondling his catcher's mitt.)*

WOMAN: What was that?! Shoot. Lost it. "Cut to—Cut to...cut to..." Fudge. Fiddlesticks.
BOY: Something wrong, Mom?

WOMAN: I don't know. I'm distracted, I guess. Other voices are coming in over the airwaves.

                        V.O.
                     *(Smoking)*
          "Cigarette. Lo-lee-ta. Cigarette."

WOMAN: Concentrate, Charlene. "Cut to—"

                        V.O.
          "Do the dishes. Dishes. Dishes."

WOMAN: Oh, God. Time for a break. Power down. First—save; exit; close; quit. Ah.
    *(Pause)*
    Calvin?
BOY: Yeah, Mom?
WOMAN: Where does your sister go on weekends?
BOY: Ya know. Out.
WOMAN: Out where? Where does she go with Lisa?

*(**Blue Light** strikes the area outside of the sliding doors. The Girl does a slow, expert teasing dance for an imaginary male clientele; The Boy parallels her movements.)*

BOY: Well…see, first they hitch into town with some suburban father-type in his Volvo station wagon. They then hop the crosstown bus, the M2, to the corner of Pike and 7th. They get off by the bus station, and walk two blocks east. They check to make sure they're not being followed. Then they duck into this joint, it's all red brick on the front, with the windows blacked out, except for the Budweiser sign. The door is solid metal. They nod to the bouncer, who always pats Leslie Ann on the fanny. They trot behind the curtains in back of the bar, quick, see, so the clientele won't see them in their street clothes. And backstage, Al, who's the owner, yells at 'em for being late.

And they slip into this toilet of a dressing room, where they strip off their jeans and sweats in such a hurry, they're inside out, thrown in the corner. And they help each other into the scanty sequins and the two inch heels. And they slink out together in the blue light as the warm-up act, and wrap their legs around the poles. And Al keeps an eye out on the guys, who haven't got a buzz on yet, so they're pretty docile, 'cause the girls are jailbait. And Leslie Ann and her best friend Lisa shake it up for only one set. And before you know it, the twenty minutes are up, just a few halfhearted grabs, and they're doing full splits to scoop up the dollar bills that will pay for the midnight double feature at the Mall and the burgers afterwards at Big Bob's.

*(**Blue Light** out on The Girl. The Woman, who has been mesmerized, breaks out of the reverie.)*

WOMAN: Calvin!

BOY: Jesus, mom. Take a joke, will ya? She probably hangs out at Lisa's being dumb.

*(Pause.)*

WOMAN: Don't you have a nice girl you can take to the movies tonight?

BOY: I don't know any nice girls.

WOMAN: Well, how about calling up some of your friends and doing something with them?

BOY: All the boys at school are creeps.

WOMAN: I know. But it's Friday night!

BOY: So.

WOMAN: Calvin, sweetie, it's not right for you to spend every weekend in the house.

BOY: Am I bothering you?

WOMAN: That's not the point. You're never going to meet someone slumped on the sofa.

BOY: I'm not slumping.

WOMAN: You are. Sit up straight; you're wearing the springs down that way—When I was your age—

BOY *(Agonized)*: *What. Do You* Want *From me?*

WOMAN: I just want you to have some *Fun.*

BOY: I'm going.

WOMAN: Where?

BOY: What does it matter? I'm going Out. I can't even sit in the privacy of my own home—

WOMAN: Now wait, sweetie, I don't want you to take it like that—

BOY: Jesus. I'm gone.

*(The Boy stalks to the door, opens it and slams out.)*

WOMAN *(Guiltily)*: Have a nice time! Don't stay out. Too late...

*(The Woman pauses, then turns the computer back on.)*

WOMAN: Boot up. Drive A.

*(The Woman waits. Pauses. The Woman stealthily turns, opens up a desk drawer, takes out a pack of cigarettes. Waits. Carefully selects one. Fishes out matches from the drawer.)*

WOMAN AND VOICE-OVER: Our little secret, Charlene.

*(The Woman lights up. Starts to type.)*

V.O.

"CUT TO: CLOSE-UP:

She tentatively licked the tip, a gentle flick of the tongue, before perching it on her lips. Her head instinctively reared back, before its acid taste. She gently sucked, letting it linger in her mouth—she gently sucked—"

*(The Woman pauses, reads what she wrote, inhales and exhales. The voice of Krafft-Ebing begins. Charlene, struck, listens.)*

THE VOICE: "The married female—"

V.O.
"She...sucked...the tip...she..."

THE VOICE: "If the married female conceives every second year, during the nine months that follow conception she experiences no great sexual excitement."[3]

WOMAN: Where is that coming from?

*(The Woman begins to type.)*

THE VOICE: "While women are suckling there is usually such a call on the vital force made by the organs secreting milk that sexual desire is almost annihilated...The best mothers, wives and managers of households are not very much troubled with sexual feeling of any kind. Love of home, children and domestic duties, are the only passions they feel."[4]

WOMAN: Jesus. I can't use that crap. Erase. "Cut to—"

V.O.
"CUT TO: EXTERIOR. THE BOY, in the bushes, watches THE WOMAN smoke. His tongue gently flicks his own lips in response."

*(We see The Man at the picture window, easing himself against the sliding glass window, watching The Woman.)*

V.O.
"CUT TO: INTERIOR. THE WOMAN, in front of the mirror, oblivious to being watched. She arches her throat and releases a jet of smoke."

*(The Man at the window disappears.)*

### V.O.

"CUT TO: EXTERIOR. Now we see THE BOY begin to manipulate himself with the gloved hand, through the denim, his excitement growing. He closes his eyes, and begins to sway.

CUT TO: INTERIOR. THE WOMAN hears a noise, and turns to the window. She gazes below and sees THE BOY who—

CUT TO: THE BOY begins to grow urgent in his need, and begins to strike his limbs, softly at first, and then he begins pounding the cupped glove—"

*(There is a pounding at the door; The Woman is puzzled.)*

### V.O.

"Pounding, pounding the cupped glove—"

*(The pounding at the door grows louder.)*

WOMAN *(With some fear)*: Who is that?

MAN *(Offstage)*: Special Delivery! I got a *package* for you, Charlene—

WOMAN: CLYDE?!! Goddamn you—I'm calling the police—

*(The Woman races to her trimline on the desk; she dials 911 but we hear nothing but clicks.)*

WOMAN: Shit! What did you do to the phone?

MAN *(Offstage)*: You don't need the *phone,* baby. I'm here to reach out and *touch* someone—

WOMAN: Goddamn! You're drunk again, aren't you?! Get away from here, Clyde! I told that stupid-ass judge a restraining order wouldn't work—

MAN *(Pounding; offstage)*: Open the fuckin' door. Now. I wanta talk to you.

WOMAN: I'm working.

MAN: I asked! Nicely!

*(We hear the door being violently kicked. The Woman, with a grim calm, reaches into the desk drawer and pulls something out. We hear a click—possibly amplified. She sits back down at her computer, and waits. Starts to type.)*

### V.O.
*(Urgently)*

"CUT TO: EXTERIOR. THE BOY thrusts himself against the front door. His hands hold onto the frame of the door.

CUT TO: INTERIOR. THE WOMAN, on the other side of the door, presses against it, moving her body gently against the wood—"

MAN *(Offstage)*: I'm Coming! I'm Coming In—

*(With another savage kick, the door flies open.)*

MAN: Shit!!

*(The Man flies in, disheveled, drunk. The Man grins, sings:)*

MAN: "I hear You KNOCKIN' But You Can't Come In!"

WOMAN: Get out of here, Clyde. Your last chance.

*(The Woman pretends to type.)*

MAN: I'm here to audition. To Give You. New Material. The E-Rot-icly UnEmployed. To get your undivided attention. Write this up, Baby.

Oh my god! Is that a doorknob in my pocket or am I just happy to see you?

Baby? Stop looking at that goddamn screen. Look. At. Me.

*(Before The Woman can stop him, The Man pulls the computer plug from the outlet.)*

MAN: Ta-DA!!

And Now! The Burlesque Theatre of Allegheny! Presentin'! SEX—ON—WELFARE!

*(The Man begins to strip and grind, taking off his T-shirt, and unzipping his dungarees, while singing the trumpet "stripper theme.")*

MAN: "BWAH-BWAH-BWAH!!! BWAH-BWAH-BWAH-BWAHHH!!! BWAH-BWAH-BWAH!! BWAH-BWAH-BWAH-BWAH—bwah—**BWAHH!!**—bum-bum **BWAHH!!**—bum-bum **BWAHH**—bum-bum **BWAHH**—bum-bum…"

*(At this point, he has turned his back on The Woman, and has lowered his pants and underwear, mooning her. The Woman stands, calmly, with a gun in her hand.)*

WOMAN: I want. you. to stand. Very Still. Don't move, Clyde. Don't. Move.

*(The Man, seeing the gun, stops, still bent over, exposed.)*

WOMAN: I don't want to kill you. By accident. I'm just going to shoot you just enough to send you to the hospital.

*(The Man, panicked, begins to rush for the door.)*

MAN: Jesus Christ—Char-LENE!!

*(**Blue Lights On.** There is the sound of an amplified gun shot. Very slowly, in stylized motion, The Man grabs his behind, and writhes, a slow, sexual grind in agony. A male porn star voice dictates:)*

THE VOICE: He was Hot. He was throbbing. He was Hot He was Throbbing. He was Hot He was throbbing He was hot and throbbing He was hot He was throbbing He was hot and throbbing He was hot He was throbbingHe was hot and throbbing He was hot He was throbbing—

*(When the **regular lights** come up, The Man is lying on his stomach on the sofa. The Woman, holding towels, stands over him. The Man is crying.)*

MAN: Jesus H. Jesus H. Christ. I can't believe it. My own wife. I can't believe—

WOMAN: Hold still. Calm down and quit wiggling like that. I can't see anything with you moving around—

MAN: Am I gonna haveta be in a wheelchair? For Life?

WOMAN: I said. hold. still. I don't want any blood on the carpeting.

*(The Woman regards the wound. The Woman regards The Man's butt.)*

WOMAN: Yup. I gotcha, all right. How does it feel?

MAN: How does it feel? How does it *feel*?! Like someone rammed a poker in my flesh! That's how it feels!

WOMAN: Don't move.

V.O.

—"Don't—"

THE VOICE: —"Don't Move."—

V.O.

*(Seductive whisper)*

CUT TO: FLASHBACK—FIVE YEARS AGO.

*(**Blue Light** comes on. The Man turns on his back, and The Woman straddles him. They start to make out.)*

THE VOICE *(As Krafft-Ebing; through following, Voice-Over breathes heavily)*: "**Case 103.** Mr. C., aged thirty-six; an unemployed steel worker of hereditary taint, asymmetry of the skull and other signs of degeneration. Mr. C. evidenced constant alteration of exaltation and depression. The subject, as a schoolboy, faced disciplinary action due to hyperesthesia sexualis—Masturbatio Coram Discipulis in Schola." *(Voice-Over giggles)* "Subject, as an adolescent, showed enormous development of the zygomae and inferior maxilla."[5]

*(Voice-Over is impressed.)*

V.O.
*(Erotically)*

"Ooooh."
*(Back to her screenplay/dominatrix voice)*
"CUT TO:—"

*(Abrupt lighting change: Back to bright **stage lights**. The Woman stands over The Man, now on his stomach again, with bandages, tape and antiseptic.)*

WOMAN: I said Lie There! You're gonna mess up my sofa! Thank God for Scotch-guard…There. That's better. You might not need stitches.

THE VOICE *(In a thick Scottish dialect)*: "Tha's got such a nice tail on thee. Tha's got the nicest arse of anybody."[6]

WOMAN: I'm going to put some antiseptic on it now; it's gonna be cold.

*(The Woman pours on liquid from the bottle; The Man roars.)*

MAN: AAHHH!!

WOMAN: It's not supposed to sting like that—

MAN: Don't You Tell Me How It Feels! You Ain't My Butt!!

WOMAN: Compliments will get you nowhere. I can't do anything with you when you get in moods like this.

*(The Woman efficiently bandages him; tears the tape with her teeth. She whiffs the air.)*

WOMAN: Hooey! God, Clyde. You can't afford ta buy yourself bvd's, but you can throw it away on alcohol.

MAN: It's my money.

WOMAN: I'm getting you some coffee before we go to the hospital. Sit up slowly. And sit on the towel.

*(Like a man missing a limb, The Man tentatively feels his behind. Slowly, he pulls up his underwear. He tries to pull up his jeans, winces, and leaves himself undone. He sits up penitently, like a little boy, on the towel, favoring his good cheek.)*

WOMAN *(Offstage)*: There's no milk in the house! So you haveta drink it black!

*(**Blue Light**. While The Voice narrates, The Man slowly reaches into the back of his pants, wetting his hand with the blood. Hypnotically, he stares at the red on his hand, either getting faint or aroused. The Man closes his eyes, bringing his hand closer to his face. He breathes in the scent of the blood, and then almost tastes his hand.)*

THE VOICE: "**Case 103** continued. Although subject continued self-abuse through his adolescence, authorities noticed nothing unusual at the time. C. married early, a woman of his own age from the same village. At first, he fulfilled his marital duties in a typical if somewhat energetic manner, not yet exhibiting the traits of hysteria virilis that led to the breakdown of said marriage."

*(In a change of voice from Krafft-Ebing to porno film director; the lights change back to **stage lights**.)*

THE VOICE: Jump Cut!

*(The Woman hands coffee to The Man.)*

WOMAN: Jesus! How did you get blood all over?
MAN: I guess I sprayed a bit when…the shot…hit me.
WOMAN: Drink this. Slowly. Then we'll go.
MAN: Okay.

*(The Man and Woman sit at opposite ends of the sofa, sipping their coffee.)*

MAN: Good coffee.

*(The Woman looks suspiciously at him.)*

MAN: You're looking good. Filling out a little bit?
WOMAN: I've quit smoking. Or I'm trying to—
MAN: It looks good on you…really…So—this is like old times, huh? Us sitting up, drinking coffee—
WOMAN: Forget it, Clyde. Whatever you're thinking, forget it.
THE VOICE: CUT! Take two.
MAN: So this is like old times, huh. Us sitting up, drinking coffee—
WOMAN: Forget it, Clyde. Whatever you're thinking, forget it.
　　*(Pause)*
　　How does it feel?
MAN: The more coffee I drink, the more it throbs.
THE VOICE: I want you to—
WOMAN: "I want you to *feel* it. Maybe then you'll—"
THE VOICE: —*listen.*

*(The Woman just hears what she has said.)*

WOMAN: Jesus. That sounds like something you would say.

*(Pause.)*

MAN: Say, uh, what happened to the—?

WOMAN: Don't worry about the gun. I know what I'm doing. Just behave yourself, and it won't go off.

MAN: Call me old-fashioned, but I prefer the days when havin' protection in the house meant your supply of birth control.

WOMAN: You're a laugh riot tonight.

MAN: Seriously, Charlene, I don't like thinking about you havin' that kind of shit in the house—

WOMAN: It's my house.

*(The Man stands with some pain.)*

WOMAN: Where are you going?

MAN: I can't talk to you when you're like this.

THE VOICE: CUT! Take three.

MAN: I came to talk and you shut me out.

WOMAN: You're about ten years too late.

THE VOICE: Jump Cut!

MAN: So. How's work?

WOMAN: I was on page twenty-nine when you arrived. I'm behind deadline. The shoot's scheduled on location for Monday morning. I guess I can always fax it.

MAN: How are...the "gals?" At work?

WOMAN: The women?

MAN: Right. Are you starting to turn a profit at—? I don't remember the name of your production company.

*(The Boy goes to the booth upstage where Voice-Over is caged, and begins to funnel quarters in. Voice-Over moves, obligatorily erotic, for ten seconds each time The Boy feeds the slot, abruptly stopping.*

*Again, Voice-Over moves, almost mockingly, and then stops. The Boy searches his pockets for change and, frustrated, starts to shake and kick the booth, in silent mime. Voice-Over laughs at him.)*

WOMAN: Gyno Productions.

MAN: Right. I knew it rhymed with wino. I never can remember it.

WOMAN: It's the root for "woman." In Greek.

MAN: I can see that's important. But it's still hard to remember.

WOMAN: Yeah. It is. But we just designed a new logo, for our stationery and business cards—want to see it?

MAN: Sure.

*(The Woman goes to her desk, opens the middle drawer and takes out a business card—she gives it to The Man.)*

MAN: Wow. Charlene Dwyer. Story Editor, Gyno Productions. They promoted you. That's really nice, Charlene.

WOMAN: No, not that—what do you think of our new mascot?

MAN: Well, I'm not sure—what is that thing on here? What is it doin'—it's dancing?

WOMAN: It's a Rhinoceros—"Rosie the Rhino." She's dancing.

MAN: Uh-huh. That's...cute. But, don't you.think. Those pink... pasties...are goin' a bit far?

*(Looks closer)* And the G-String? A Rhino in a G-String does not inspire me. I mean, as well you know, I like my women with flesh on their bones, but this mascot looks a little like you—*before* Weight Watchers. But what do I know? Maybe I'm not your average guy on the street.

WOMAN: I like the G-String. It was my idea. And it's supposed to be...funny. For women.

MAN: I don't know. It looks like a stripper in a lesbo bar to me who's just taken off her flannel shirt.

WOMAN: Oh, forget it. Are you done with your coffee?

MAN: Look, do you want to talk? Talking involves disagreement. Or do you just want me to nod my head, yes, sure, that's great, Charlene—if I don't tell you what I'm thinking, even if it's ignorant, how can I learn anything about what you're doing when you say you're working.

WOMAN: Yeah? Like what do you want to know?

MAN: Well—do you ever think you're gonna run out of words when you're writing like that?

V.O.
She thinks about it all the time.

*(The Woman stares at The Man.)*

WOMAN: I think about it all the time.

*(By this point, The Voice becomes a bouncer, crosses the stage and stops The Boy from beating up Voice-Over's booth.)*

WOMAN: Forty, fifty pages a day, seven days a week—it's a lot like the Victorian theory about masturbation and young boys.
THE VOICE *(To The Boy)*: Ya gotta have money to be a player.
WOMAN: They believed that men only had so much semen; over the years, men could spend all the pennies they had in the bank.

*(The Boy reluctantly digs in his pants for change. The Voice gives him quarters; The Voice and Voice-Over try not to laugh. The Voice leaves. The Boy slowly slips in another two bits.)*

MAN: Huh. That's funny.
WOMAN: Yes, it is.

*(They giggle; The Woman a lot more than The Man, who looks a bit worried.)*

MAN: But it's not true.
    *(Quickly)* Is it?
WOMAN: No, of course not.
    *(Pause)*
    Can I have my business card back, please?

MAN: I'd like to keep it, if I may. As a...memento. I know it has...your work number on it—but I won't use it. Okay?

WOMAN: Right.

V.O.

Shit, that was dumb, Charlene.

*(The Woman sits tensely.)*

MAN: Just relax, will ya? So where do all these words come from?

WOMAN: I don't know. When I really get going, it's like a trance— it's not me writing at all. It's as if I just listen to voices and I'm taking dictation.

THE VOICE: "**Case 103** continued. Subject, however, experienced constant excitation, due to what the subject described as inner 'voices' usually urging him to erotic acts."

MAN: Doesn't that spook you? I mean, whose voices are these? Who's in control?

V.O.

But she was in control.

WOMAN: Well, they're the characters speaking, or the script itself. I mean, I know it's me, but I have to get into it. At first it spooked me a little. But now I know when I hear them, it's a good sign. And I am in control.

MAN: I used to think that porno flicks were all pictures and no words—

WOMAN: Look, Clyde, I don't write *porno*. I didn't appreciate you telling Leslie Ann that.

*(The Boy, out of pocket change now, starts to rattle the booth again. A silent fight erupts with Voice-Over.)*

MAN: Well, what do you call it? What was the title of your last opus? *Moonfuck?!* So what is that—Bergman?

WOMAN: It was a critique and satire of *Moonstruck.*

MAN: Uh-huh.

WOMAN: Gyno Productions is a feminist film company dedicated to producing women's erotica.

MAN: Erotica is just a Swedish word for *porn*, Charlene. Just face what you're doing. Take pride in it.

WOMAN: What's the use? Are you through with your coffee?

*(By this point, The Voice becomes a bouncer, crosses the stage and seizes The Boy. The Voice roughs up The Boy and throws him out.)*

MAN: Look, this is what happens every time I challenge you. You just.shut.down. As if I'm bullying you. And it's just my way. Of showing interest. A burning interest, as it happens. It's the way men learn to argue through contact sports. As if words were body grease, so you gotta grab hard to pin your opponent. And I'm stuck here, feeling stupid and cut off, because you won't explain things in plain English. You speak in a code. A code designed for signals between members of the female sex. Well, pardon me, but I did. not. go. to college.

WOMAN: In plain English: I am not a pornographer. I write erotic entertainment designed for women.

MAN: Yeah. So to return to what I was askin': What's the big difference?

*(The Voice and Voice-Over begin to make orgiastic noises when The Woman says "aroused.")*

WOMAN: For one thing, desire in female spectators is aroused by cinema in a much different way. Narrativity—that is, plot— is emphasized.

MAN *(Stares at her)*: Yeah. There are lots more words. So what else?

WOMAN: The "meat shots" and "money shots" of the trade flicks are not the be-all and end-all of Gyno Productions.—Why are you laughing?

MAN: I seen one of your movies—and it had tits and ass just like *DEEP THROAT*.

WOMAN: Physical expression is the culmination of relationships between characters. Most importantly, we try to create women as protagonists in their own dramas, rather than objects. And we try to appreciate the male body as an object of desire.

MAN: Now you're talking!

*(In his enthusiasm, The Man moves too much and flinches.)*

MAN: Oh, suffering Jesus on the cross!

WOMAN: Is it bad?

MAN: Yeah.

WOMAN: Come on, let's go—

MAN: No, wait a minute, wait a second. I'm a…little woozy. Do you have anything in the house. For the pain?

WOMAN: Whatd'ya mean, for the pain?

MAN: I could use a shot of something.

WOMAN: You want me to give you a drink, Clyde? Are you insane?

MAN: One drink is not gonna hurt. In fact, it will dull the throbbing in my butt. And since it was your bullet that's in my butt, I think you owe me. One.

WOMAN: You get mean when you drink. I don't want to participate in enabling behavior.

MAN: Goddamn Oprah Winfrey! Just get me something, will ya, Charlene? My Butt is bitchin'…

WOMAN: One shot. That's all. I'll get some for me.

*(The Woman exits. While she is out of the room, The Man quickly searches under the sofa pillows and cushions for the gun. She returns with a bottle and two shot glasses. The Woman pours them drinks and hands The Man his glass.)*

MAN: Wow. That's nice.

WOMAN: It's Remy.

MAN: It's been a while…since I had Remy. Well—let's toast. To love and success and a long film career—to you.

WOMAN: To…to you. To you, Clyde.

*(They sip. Pause.)*

THE VOICE: Jump Cut!

WOMAN: You've got to let go now.

MAN: I…kinda lost my head when I got that restraining order today, Charlene. Some things will never be *over*. Like everything you taught me.

WOMAN: What did I teach you?

MAN: You taught me all about desire. That's not over. I think about you all the time. I have since high school.

WOMAN: You're not thinking about me—you're obsessing. On me. It could have been anything, just as long as it kept your mind off of your job. And now that you've lost your job, you're obsessing about me to keep your mind off the fact that you don't have a job.

MAN: No—I think differently than you do. That's all…And because you can never understand what's going on inside a man's head, you imagine the worst.

THE VOICE *(Krafft-Ebing)*: "**Case 103** continued. However, in time the constant excitation of hysteria virilis leads in turn to paresthesia sexualis. The subject became convinced in his mind that only violence done to his fetishized obsession could restore him to his former virility."

THE VOICE: Jump Cut!

MAN: I'm gonna put myself together—get retrained in something. Maybe go back to school like you did. It really changed you, Charlene, when you went back to school.

WOMAN: I think that would be wonderful.

MAN: I have to work out my "karma." Because I really fucked it up in this lifetime. And I have to pay for that by trying.

WOMAN: I don't believe in "karma."

MAN: I do. I believe in it. There's no other way to explain stuff like high school proms...

*(The Woman laughs. The Man smiles.)*

WOMAN: I forget sometimes how unique you are. When you're not drinking.

THE VOICE *(Brooklynese)*: "She will embrace me warmly, as if we had never embraced before. We will have only a couple of hours together and then she will leave—to go to the dance hall where she still works as a taxi girl. I will be sound asleep when she returns at three or four in the morning...I love her, heart and soul. She is everything to me."[7]

MAN: You're everything to me.

THE VOICE: Jump Cut!

WOMAN: I...think about you. I try to figure it out. All the time. Why I stayed with it so long. And then one day, I realized that every dish in the house had been replaced with plastic ones. Part of me got off, living on the edge like that. But I was losing control.

THE VOICE: Jump Cut!

MAN: I never stop thinking about it. It's this tape loop. It's torturing me. I'm standing outside my body, watching this actor doing that to you. A stunt man who's got my face.

THE VOICE *(Krafft-Ebing; as lyrical as a German sexologist can get)*: "Woman is a harp who only yields her secrets of melody to the master who knows how to handle her...the husband must study the harp and the art of music..."[8]

WOMAN: Try to make the next woman in your life lucky. It will be better, the next time.

## V.O.

She can...smell...his sweat. So warm, she can smell—

THE VOICE: "So close, she can almost taste—"

V.O.

Smell. His.—

THE VOICE: "Sweat."

*(A **blue light** fills the stage again. There is a rustling at the sliding glass window. We see The Boy against the glass, watching. He stretches his arms against the frame.)*

MAN: It will never be as good as it is with you.

THE VOICE: "CUT TO: INTERIOR. THE WOMAN closes her eyes."

*(The Woman closes her eyes.)*

THE VOICE: "CLOSE-UP on her lips as she kisses THE MAN, hard, on the mouth."

*(The Woman sits by The Man and gently kisses him. They look at each other. Then they kiss again—a long, hard kiss, breathing each other in.)*

V.O.

"VOICE-OVER: What are you doing, Charlene?"

THE VOICE: "THE MAN and THE WOMAN look at each other for a long time."

V.O.

"VOICE-OVER CONTINUED: This is not a movie, Charlene."

THE VOICE: "THE MAN and THE WOMAN move toward each other, lips parted."

V.O.
*(Urgent)*
"CUT TO: EXTERIOR. We see the door of the house burst open and—"

THE VOICE *(Cutting in)*: "THE WOMAN begins to breathe, quicker; THE MAN moves closer and presses against her, urgent now—"

V.O.
*(Trying harder)*
"CUT TO—CUT TO: EXTERIOR! We see THE WOMAN run from the house—"

THE VOICE: "THE WOMAN sighs; THE MAN reaches out and strokes her hair—"

V.O.
*(Insistent)*
"Get out of the house!"

THE VOICE: "LONG SHOT. EXTERIOR. THE BOY watches through the window."

*(There is a freeze: The Man and Woman on the sofa; The Boy, stretched on the window. The **blue light** changes to the **normal lights**, and then dims. The Man starts unbuttoning The Woman's top.)*

WOMAN: What about your—? —No, Wait—
MAN: Shh! Don't talk. Not now.

*(The Man and Woman resume. Just then the door flies open violently; The Boy flies into the room.)*

BOY: I AM. GONNA. *KILL* YOU!!

MAN: What the fuck—?

*(In a fury, The Boy throws himself on top of the couple. The Man and Boy roll onto the floor. The Man screams.)*

MAN: SHIT! AAAAH!

WOMAN: CALVIN! NO! STOP! Watch out for his butt!

*(The Man and Boy wrestle. They stand. The Boy, from behind, gets The Man in a lock, one hand pinned and twisted; The Boy's arm is locked around The Man's throat, choking him.)*

MAN *(In a squeezed voice)*: It's getting harder to...be a...family man...these days.

BOY: You leave her alone. Understand?

WOMAN: Calvin. It's not. As it looks.

BOY: *You* don't live here anymore. Get it?

MAN *(Appreciatively, in the same squeezed voice)*: You're getting...mighty big, son.

*(And just as quickly, The Man slips around and out of The Boy's grip, quickly kneeing him in the groin. The Boy gasps and falls into a fetal position on the rug.)*

WOMAN: Jesus Christ, Clyde!

MAN: He's playing with the big boys now.

*(The Boy says nothing. His face, beet red, presses into the rug.)*

WOMAN: Calvin—

MAN: Don't touch him. He'll be all right.
    *(Pause)*
    Son? You all right?

*(The Man offers his hand to The Boy, who refuses it, and slowly gets up.)*

MAN: I'm sorry. Reflex action. No man likes to injure the family jewels.

WOMAN: Calvin—

BOY: What's he doin' here?

WOMAN: Your father...just...

MAN: Dropped in. For a little adult conversation.

BOY: That's not what it looked like to me.

WOMAN: Honey, I can appreciate your concern, but he's still your father—

BOY: What's he doin' here?—

MAN: Look, maybe I should just call it a night.

WOMAN: No, wait a minute, Clyde. No matter what's happened between you and me, you and Calvin have to learn how to talk to one another. I will not be used as an excuse for getting in the middle of the two of you. Do you both hear me? I want you to both act civilized to each other in my living room for at least sixty seconds.

   *(Beat)*

   I'm putting on a fresh pot of coffee.

*(The Woman exits.)*

MAN: Whatta night, huh?

*(As The Man hobbles past The Boy to sit on the sofa:)*

BOY: Hey, what happened to your butt?

MAN: Your poor, defenseless mother shot me.

BOY: Mom? Mom? She shot you?

*(The Boy starts to laugh.)*

MAN: I don't see anything particularly amusing about it. Men might hit you by the balls, but they do it to your face. Women—they shoot you in the butt.

BOY: You musta deserved it.

MAN: This is something private between your mother and me.
(*Pause*)
So—how's school?
BOY: Okay.
MAN: And life? In general.
BOY: Okay.

*(ANOTHER PAUSE.)*

MAN: Aren't you going to ask me how I'm doin'?
BOY: How are you, Dad?
MAN AND BOY *(Together)*: I'm warmer than shit and tighter than mud.

*(ANOTHER PAUSE.)*

MAN: So—how's your sister?
BOY: Okay, I guess.
MAN: You guess? You don't know? You gotta keep an eye on her, son. She's at...that age. Know what I mean?

*(Man punches Boy in arm.)*

BOY: Yeah, sure I do.
MAN: That's right. You're the man of the house, now. Best thing to do is just lock her up for a couple a years. She's gonna cause a lot of men heartbreak. You gotta watch her, son.
BOY: I do. I watch her all the time.
MAN: I mean, it's not her fault, right? But that body of her...you know what I mean?
BOY: Yeah.
MAN: That body of hers...your sister should be *licensed*.

*(**Blue light** stage left of glass door. The Girl begins to work to the music. The Man and Boy stare appreciatively.)*

MAN: Where is...your sister?

BOY: She said she was goin' to some sleepover.

MAN: And your mother believes that crap? We don't believe that crap, do we?

*(The two share a laugh, settle back and watch with glazed attention.)*

THE VOICE: "One of the things that made Cleo's dance fascinating was the little pompon she wore in the center...it served to keep your eyes riveted to the spot. She could rotate it like a pinwheel or make it jump and quiver with little electric spasms. Sometimes it would subside with little gasps, like a swan coming to rest...It seemed to be part of her. Possibly she had acquired it in an Algerian whorehouse, from a French sailor. It was tantalizing, especially to the sixteen year old who had still to know what it feels like to make a grab for a woman's bush."[9]

*(**Blue Light** out on The Girl. The Woman enters with a tray; a coffee pot, two mugs, a plate of cookies. And a tall glass of milk. The Woman pauses, watches them. She sets the tray down on the coffee table.)*

WOMAN: You two are just...chattering away like magpies.

MAN: We've been talking. Right?

BOY: Yup.

MAN: Man talk.

BOY: You just caught us during the pause.

WOMAN: I've fixed us a late-night snack. A last cup of coffee before I drive your father to the hospital.

MAN: I don't think that's...necessary, Charlene.

WOMAN: This is nothing to fool around with, Clyde. Let me see how it's doing. Turn over.

MAN: Not in front of the boy, goddamn it.

WOMAN: For Christ's sake, he's your own flesh and blood. Turn over.

*(The Man turns his wounded cheek toward her. She carefully lowers his pants and examines the wound critically; The Boy peeks.)*

BOY: Wow.

WOMAN: It's still bleeding. Not as bad as before, though. It needs stitches and a fresh bandage.

*(Pause.)*

BOY: Mom? Didja really shoot Dad?

WOMAN: Yes.

BOY: Cool. Mom?

WOMAN: Calvin, we're not going to discuss it.

MAN: Why don't you just drink up your milk and go to bed...

*(The Boy stares with disbelief and disgust at the glass of milk.)*

BOY: You have got to be shittin' me...

MAN: Lucky for you this is your mother's house. I'd turn the strap on ya for language like that...

BOY: Mom! Milk?!! MILK!?

WOMAN: Well, sweetie, it's too late for you to be drinking coffee, and I saved the last glass of milk to go with your cookies.

BOY: I'm not drinking that shit.

MAN: Growing boys need their milk? Right?

WOMAN: Let's just drop it, Clyde.

MAN: Only wusses are scared of milk. A real man can drink milk.

BOY: You drink it.

MAN: Okay, son—I'll show you how it's done. How a real man drinks milk—

WOMAN: Stop it. Stop it. I hate this.

*(The Man abruptly grabs the milk, and guzzles half the glass. It dribbles down his chin and shirt.)*

MAN: Num, num. A man who can't drink milk can't love women. Is that a problem for you, son? Are you that kind of man?
WOMAN: Why does everything turn into a nightmare around here?
MAN: Show your old man. Drink the milk.

*(The Man presses the glass into The Boy's face. They freeze.)*

THE VOICE *(Irish)*: "There's the mark of his teeth still where he tried to bite the nipple I had to scream out aren't they fearful trying to hurt you—"[10]

*(End freeze.)*

MAN: Drink the milk.
BOY: No. Shit! Get out of my face.
MAN: It's just Milk. What are you scared of? Milk can't hurt you—

*(The two tussle with the milk; it splashes them both.)*

BOY: You're. An. Asshole!

*(The Woman and The Boy instinctively flinch. A moment's pause.)*

MAN *(Quietly)*: What.did.you.call.me?
WOMAN: —Enough!

*(The Boy goes to The Woman, scared.)*

BOY: You don't scare me. This is not your house. You keep away from us. Stop thrusting yourself on Mom, You.Hear.Me?
MAN: I wasn't thrusting myself on your mother. Quite the opposite. Did I thrust myself on you on the sofa, Charlene? Did I?

WOMAN: I'm taking you to the hospital.now.

MAN: Your mother kissed me. First.

WOMAN (Together with Boy): —This is getting ridiculous—

BOY (With Woman): —That's a lie! Isn't it, Mom?

WOMAN: We're ending this conversation. Now.

MAN: Tell him. You kissed me.

BOY: Don't be scared of him, Mom. I'm here.

MAN: I know it's hard to believe, Calvin. She's amazing when she kisses—

BOY: Did.You.Kiss.Him? Mom? After all he's done?

THE VOICE: "...and his heart was going like mad and yes I said yes I—"[11]

WOMAN: Calvin—honey, it's hard to explain, at your age—it was just...for old time's sake!

BOY: I DON'T BELIEVE YOU!

MAN: Don't raise your voice like that to your mother—

WOMAN: For God's sake, Calvin, I'm a human being, too—I have needs—

BOY: I'm Getting Out.Of.Here—

MAN: When your mother kisses a man, it's like your heart gets squeezed. Too bad she's your mother and you'll never know—

BOY: ARGHH!!

(Holding his head, The Boy rushes for the door, opens it and runs out into the night, screaming:)

BOY: I AM SO FUCKED UP! (Door slam)

THE VOICE: "She kissed me. I was kissed. All yielding she tossed my hair.

Kissed, she kissed me.

Me. And me now."[12]

(The Man and Woman sit, weary and tense.)

WOMAN: Why do you always do that?

MAN: Do what?

WOMAN: Oh, you know. You know very well.

MAN *(Getting angry)*: Christ!

*(Man and Woman look at each other. **Blue Light**.)*

### V.O.
### FLASHBACK—THREE YEARS AGO.

*(The Man strikes The Woman hard on the face; in slow motion, it almost looks like a caress. The Woman falls on the sofa. The Man drags on cigarette and then moves it toward Woman's face.)*

THE VOICE: "**Case 103** continued. Subject increasingly resorted to violence against wife as an erotic stimulus for erec—"

### V.O.

CUT TO:—

*(Abrupt lighting change: Back to bright **stage lights**. The Woman stands, scared.)*

WOMAN *(Trying to be composed)*: Calm down.

MAN: Calm down—I don't have a job, I've got no fuckin' family, no wife—I've got shit for a life!

WOMAN: Maybe you should go now.

THE VOICE: "We will have only a couple of hours together and then she will leave—to go to the dance hall where she still works as a taxi girl."[13]

MAN: Christ, Charlene. I just wish—shit, I just wish we could go back, ya know? Before college, before I got fired, before everything started busting apart. I wish I could just close my eyes and you'd be coming home through the door in your uniform, after your night shift.

WOMAN: Oh, God. I hated that fucking uniform. It made my backside enormous. Made me into a tired, washed-out Cow in White.

MAN: You'd come in, tired but sweet. I'm under the covers. First you flip on the coffee in the kitchen, and the aroma comes up to me before you reach the bed. And then I feel your hands on my stubble, stroking it, and then I hear the sound of your shoes hitting the floor, one by one. And the zippers. The sound of the uniform sliding down your slip. And then the next thing I know, there's your warmth in bed. And your voice urging me up to work. Already slipping into sleep.

And every morning, I went to work with a hard-on. It was great.

WOMAN: Great.


*(The Woman stares into nothing as she slowly pours the coffee as a trickle into a cup.)*


V.O.

And every night, she would stand in the middle of the ward and think, 'I can't do this any longer.' Holding another bed pan, swimming with someone's fluids. Urine, excreta, blood, infection, vomit, mucus. Bodies and mess.

Mess and food. Cleaning up messes. Cleaning up messes. This is where a high school diploma gets you, Charlene. Other people's messes.


MAN: You're going to spill that coffee.


*(The Woman speaks, far away, holding the coffee.)*


WOMAN: I hated that fucking job. I hated how I had to see human flesh.

MAN: But then you came home. To me and the children.

*(The Woman laughs, but decides not to say what she's thinking. Pause.)*

WOMAN: This writing is...saving my sanity. I'll never go back.

*(Pause.)*

MAN: So where's Leslie Ann at tonight?

WOMAN: She's spending the night with a friend.

MAN: A friend, huh.

WOMAN: Yes. A girlfriend. She asked my permission.

MAN: It's your house.

WOMAN: Don't you dare start implying—

MAN: What? Who? Who's implying—

WOMAN: I work very hard at being a good mother.

MAN: You're a great mother.

WOMAN: I try, that's all.

MAN: Leslie Ann's just at...that age, is all. You know.

WOMAN: No, I don't know. What age is that?

MAN: You can't be too careful. Look, I'm hardly the one to give
    you advice...seeing a how my backseat activities got me into
    messes.

WOMAN: I know exactly where my children are. I know exactly
    where Leslie Ann is, right now.

### V.O.

"CUT TO: INTERIOR. In the rec room of Lisa's
house. Night."

*(On the ramp, The Girl, now in an oversized T-shirt, hud-
dles in her sleeping bag, addressing her best friend Lisa. The
Girl and Voice-Over speak to each other.)*

GIRL: You're my best friend, Lisa. You.*know*.that. Since Seventh
    Grade. And you're gonna be my best friend long after I get
    married and have kids. If it wasn't for the fact.that.I get to

see you for homeroom and lunch, I woulda stopped goin' to that stupid school a long time ago.

V.O.

Uh.huh. Is your sleeping bag warm enough?

GIRL: I feel like there's nothin' you couldn't tell me. You know? I would die before one'a your secrets would roll out.of.my. mouth.

V.O.

Me too. You could tell me—anything.

GIRL: That's good. Are the other girls...asleep?...Do you— do.you—

V.O.

What? Come on, you can tell me anything—

GIRL: And you won't tell?

V.O.

I swear. I swear! Com.mon, what is it?

GIRL: I've never said this to anyone else before. I'll kill you if you—

V.O.

—You can tell me. Anything.

GIRL: Well. Do you...do you...think of boys a lot?

V.O.
(Giggling)
All the time.

GIRL: I mean at night, when you turn the lights out?

V.O.

Especially at night. When the lights are out.

GIRL: But I mean do you think about...think about...

V.O.

What? What? About...doing it?

GIRL: Yeah, but not just that—

(*In a rush*) I mean, I think of that, too, but sometimes...do you think of them, like, "hurting" you? Well, I don't mean like hurting you, but like, you're tied down and you can't stop them and they do things to you that hurt you, that make you scream but you can't and you wouldn't really want it to happen in real life, you would really get hurt, but when you close your eyes, you see it and it makes you get hot only it's 'cause it's not for real?

(*Pause*)

Lisa? Lisa? Are you asleep?

(*Film slate clap.* **Lights** *back up on living room.*)

WOMAN: Leslie Ann is still a child. And I want her to have every second of childhood that she can get.

MAN: A child, huh? Have you looked at your daughter lately?

WOMAN: I had a body like that when I was her age. Remember?—

MAN: —Now we're talkin' ancient history—

WOMAN: There's too much pressure on her, already. Lectures on safe sex, birth control, condoms. The boys in the hall at school hitting on her, accusing her of being frigid. The married men on their way to work who leer and wink at her and her friends. I want her *left.alone.*

MAN: Okay, okay. You're her mother. But have you walked out of your front door lately? Seen the world?

(*Pause. Through the next beats, the tension escalates.*)

WOMAN: It's not the world outside I'm worried about her seeing.
MAN: What's that supposed to mean?

*(Pause.)*

WOMAN: I think we should go now. I'll drive you.
MAN: I can drive myself.
WOMAN: Let's go, then.
MAN: I'm not ready.
THE VOICE: Cut! Take two.
WOMAN: It's late. I want you out of here.
MAN: I just got here. I'm not ready to go.
WOMAN: Don't.
MAN: What am I doing? Having a cup of coffee?
WOMAN: You can't stay, Clyde. I need you out of here.
THE VOICE: Cut! Take three.
WOMAN: I want you out of here.
MAN: I'll leave when I'm ready. Or are you going to make me?
WOMAN: If I have to.
MAN: Oooh. I'm scared.
WOMAN: Don't mock me, goddamn you—

*(There is the sound of door keys, loud heavy metal music and door slam. The Girl enters. They all blink at each other.)*

MAN: Hi, baby girl.
GIRL: Daddy!
      *(To Woman)* You didn't tell me he was gonna be here.
WOMAN: What are you doing here?
GIRL: I came back for somethin'—Lisa's waiting outside—
WOMAN: Why don't you just go back out to the car and Lisa—
GIRL: —Why didn't you tell me my father was coming tonight?
WOMAN: Did you notice the knob is off the door?
MAN: Don't I get a kiss anymore?

*(The Girl runs to her father and hugs him.)*

MAN: That's more like it.

GIRL: It's good to see you, Daddy.

MAN: My God, you're getting big. What are you doing tonight, princess?

GIRL: I'm doin' a sleepover at Lisa's—she's my friend in the car. Do you want to meet her?

MAN: No—that's okay. What do you girls do together?

GIRL: We're watching movies, mostly. *Friday the 13th, Halloween*—

V.O.

*(À la horror movie)*

"Get out of the house! Get out of the—"

WOMAN: I don't know how you can watch those.

GIRL: They're just movies, mom.

(To The Man) Are you coming back home?

WOMAN: No! He was just leaving—we were on our way out—

GIRL: I just got here!

WOMAN: Leslie Ann, your father and I are in the middle of something—

GIRL: —Lay-la. Where's Calvin?

MAN: He left after a little chat.

GIRL: Are you gonna be here when I get back?

WOMAN: No.

GIRL: You just came over for a visit, Daddy?

MAN: I wanted to try to talk to your mother, that's all.

*(The Man hands Girl five dollars.)*

GIRL: Good luck. She's hard to talk to.

WOMAN: Okay. That's enough. Go on with Lisa—

GIRL: Why don't you two just try to talk it out? Daddy, you've got to give up drinking, that's all. And get another job. It's no big deal. I don't see why you two can't work it out.

MAN: Well, I'd like that, Layla.

WOMAN: It's more complicated than that, honey.

GIRL: I don't want to be just another kid in a one-parent home. I don't see why I can't have two parents, like you're supposed to have. I hate being a latchkey kid, if anyone wants to ask about my feelings.

WOMAN: You're not a latchkey kid. I'm always home, working.

GIRL: Oh, great! I'm in a one-parent home, with a working mother, who types porno all day long on her butt in the living room! You can't even work a nine to five—

WOMAN: Listen, young lady. My nerves are just about. shot. Don't push me. Not you, too—

GIRL: I'm gonna tell Lisa to go on without me.

WOMAN: No. You are going. With Lisa. And have a nice time.

GIRL: Everybody gets to talk to him but me!

*(There is the sound of a car horn. Three times…"Lo-lit-ta.")*

THE VOICE: Daddy's girl…

*(The Girl goes to the door and yells:)*

GIRL: Go on without me, okay?!

*(There is the sound of a car horn again, with The Voice echoing:)*

THE VOICE: Daddy's girl…

GIRL: I wanna stay here and talk.

WOMAN: Not tonight. I mean it.

GIRL: I can't even talk to my own father!! Why can't we be like other families?

Don't I even get a chance? Where's my fucking 4-H club! When did we ever say grace at the dinner table! I'm a fucking statistic from a broken home! A goddamn teenage statistic without enough money for a fucking double-feature who has to lie that my mother's a secretary and that my father's a secret agent so no one finds out I've got a pervo for a mother, a drunk for a father and a four-eyed geek for a brother who beats-off in his catcher mitt! FUCK!

*(The Girl slams out of the house.)*

WOMAN: I'm not a mean woman. But I'm really going to enjoy watching her when she has children of her own.

MAN: I don't remember talking to my mother like that.

WOMAN: The only reason Leslie Ann thinks the sun shits out of your ass is 'cause I've lied to her all these many years. She thinks I'm just…clumsy.

MAN: Yeah, well you are.

WOMAN: I wasn't "clumsy" until after we got married.

MAN: Okay, Charlene. I've ruined your life. Okay? I'm fucked-up as a husband and a father, and I've ruined whatever fucking chance at happiness you and my children have in this lifetime.

WOMAN: I'm not asking you for that, Clyde.

MAN: What do you want from me?

WOMAN: Why'd you come over?

MAN: I…wanted to see you.

WOMAN: Why? What is it you want?

MAN: I want…I want…what's the use.

*(The Man gets up to go.)*

WOMAN: Just tell me the truth. Okay? I'm listening.

MAN: You…you'll hate me if you know…

WOMAN: I can't hate you more than I have for the past ten years.

MAN: Well. Okay, this is hard for me, all right? It's…it's a fuckin' Friday night. Right?

And so what do we do, Friday night? Go out, drink some beer, and…ya know…cruise the strip. I mean, if you're a guy who's alone, that's what there is to do in this town on a Friday.

WOMAN: I'm with you so far.

MAN: Right. So I…take a shower, you know, spruce up a little bit. And I count out the change I have left. And it's not much. And that gets me a little depressed, but I think, okay, shit, I'll economize, I'll buy a six-pack for the truck, and I won't drink out, you know? So I go downtown, and hit the streets…and

I go in to a few...places...but mostly there are minimums. So I think, fuck, I can't even watch the live action.

WOMAN: You gotta have money to be a player.

MAN: So...so...so I go into a corner bookstore, and it's packed. And I change a five into quarters, and slip into the booth... and I—

WOMAN: —You watch—

MAN: Right. And all it does is get me even more agitated. I'm thinking, this is not what I want, on A Friday Night, the feeling of my own fist in a booth—I'm like numb to that by now— and so I get back into my own truck, and I drink a few beers, to get my nerve up—and I empty out my pockets...I check the dash and under the seats, and I count—and I come up with a lousy eighteen dollars and thirty-seven cents.

WOMAN: Well, that's better than nothing.

MAN: Are you being...funny?

WOMAN: No. I'm not. I'm not making judgments. Go on.

MAN: Well, I think, you know, times are hard, maybe some working girl will consider it—you know? Maybe I'll get lucky, or I'll hit someone green on the street—so I crank up the engine, and start to drive it slow, down the side streets. And I see them, it's warm out tonight, and they're there, in groups— laughing, wearing next to nothing, and they're so close, they're laughing at me, calling out to me—

WOMAN: —So why didn't you ask someone?—

MAN: —I don't know. They were all together. I couldn't get one off by herself; I thought they'd laugh—I couldn't just call out, you know, "How about $18.37?!" I just...just lost my nerve, I was so...down by then...then...and then I just kept driving and the truck kind of drove here by itself.

WOMAN (*Quietly*): So you're telling me that you drove to your ex-wife's house because you couldn't afford a prostitute.

MAN: Jesus, Charlene, don't make it sound like that!

WOMAN: I'm not taking offense, Clyde. I'm telling it like it is. It's the truth. I'm a grown woman. I can take the truth. In fact, I prefer it.

MAN: I mean, the truth is...the truth is...that lately nothing really seems to do it for me. I don't know what...what's happening to me...but all the usual...uh...escapes...turn me on but they don't work anymore—I just get more and more depressed and anxious—like what if it just won't work at all, I mean, it happens, sometimes to men, and something's happening in...in my head—well, frankly, it scares the shit out of me. And it's building up into a big problem now.

WOMAN: I don't understand.

*(The Man starts to shake, ever so slightly, trying not to cry.)*

MAN: I mean like magazines, or girls in the booth, you know? I'll try to watch them, to use them, but...something's changed... I start thinking, she's young enough to be my daughter, or...I'll bet she's married, or she's someone's mother...the words I read in the books I buy, I start to wonder if some woman's writing them, the way you do, to pay the rent for her kids...and...I think I'm really, really fucked-up. I'm sorry...I don't mean to do this to you, I know you've got problems of your own, but I just think I need to talk to a woman, you know...

*(The Man is crying, quietly.)*

WOMAN: Sit down. Just...sit down. Okay? *(The Man does so)* It's okay. It happens. I think you should find someone to talk to about this, okay, Clyde? I mean a professional. It's not anything...insoluble...Just take a second, now.

*(Pause. They sit quietly beside each other on the sofa. The Woman makes a decision.)*

WOMAN: How are you feeling? Does it still hurt?
MAN: Huh? Oh, that—no, I barely feel it. I think it's stopped bleeding.

WOMAN: Okay—listen. I'm just a woman on a Friday night, okay? I've come down on my price for you—just one—just tonight—for $18.37. You've hit the jackpot, mister. I am not your wife—or anyone's mother right now. Just this once—Clyde—we've got to be quick, before the kids come back. Put the chain on the door, and make the sofa bed up, okay? The sheets are already on it, you've just got to take the cushions off and pull it out. I'm going…to change into something.

*(The Man has a hard time talking.)*

MAN: You don't have to…

WOMAN: I know I don't.

MAN: I'm not sure if I can…if I—

WOMAN: Then we'll just hold each other. All Right? Quick, now, before I change my mind. I'll be right back.

*(The Woman exits into the bathroom. The Man, unable to believe his luck, sits for a few moments on the sofa. Then slowly, he gets up, in pain. He draws the blinds closed. He begins to take the cushions off the sofa. When he turns his back to the audience, we can see that his jeans are soaked in blood. He sees that he has drenched the cushion, and quickly turns the bloody side to the wall. He stops and calls out:)*

MAN: Charlene! Uh—Charlene—

WOMAN *(Offstage)*: What!

MAN: I don't have…anything on me…you know? In case—

WOMAN *(Offstage)*: That's okay. I've got some protection in the house. *(Laughs)* The other kind. A girl scout is always prepared…

*(The Man stops, scowls. **Blue light** blends with **stage lights**, slowly.)*

THE VOICE: She's got protection in the house.

V.O.

A girl scout is always...prepared...

THE VOICE: She's got plenty of protection. She's prepared.

V.O.

Always prepared.

THE VOICE: "**Case 103** continued. In June of this past year, authorities were notified by subject's wife and promptly charged Mr. C. with a restraining order. However, Mr. C. ignored said order, and managed to isolate his ex-wife in her home, where, unable to arouse himself by normal stimuli, he was overcome with a desire for what I term 'lust-murder.' Only after he had satisfied himself with violence on ex-wife's body was subject apprehended."

*(Steadily angry, The Man begins to pull out the bed. He reaches his hand into the sofa frame, and stops again. He feels something. The Man slowly pulls out a gun. He stands there, thinking, holding the gun. He checks the ammunition. Then he tucks it into his waistband, and finishes making up the bed. Then he sits, brooding. The screenplay goes on while he waits:)*

V.O.

*(Breathy)*

"She was hot. She was throbbing. But she was in control. Control of her body. Control of her thought. Control of...him.

He was hot. He was throbbing. And out of control. He needed to be restrained. Tied Down. And taught a lesson...

Okay. Now we separate the men from the little boys—"

THE VOICE: —Cut! Listen, there's been a change in the script—

V.O.

What change?

THE VOICE: Al says he wants the bondage in reverse. Okay?

V.O.

That's not what we rehearsed...

THE VOICE: Since when are movies made by screenwriters? Directors make the movies. Not some broad sitting on her ass. Improvise, can't you? Your dialogue has gotta be as good as the dumb ass writer...

V.O.

But I thought—

THE VOICE: Do we pay you to think? You're a professional, aren't you? Do you want the role or don't you—we're wasting overtime—

V.O.

Okay. The show...must go on.—Hey, guys, wait, these restraints are on awfully tight—

THE VOICE: Come on! Let's finish this take...Ready, camera, action—

V.O.
(Bad acting)

"Please don't hurt me..."

THE VOICE: I'm not gonna hurt you, baby...I'm just gonna teach you a little lesson...a lesson you'll remember...

*(There is the sound of a large switch.)*

V.O.
*(Pain)*

Shit! Wait a minute, guys—that really hurt. Larry—
stop the camera—Larry? Where's Larry?

THE VOICE: We told Larry to take a walk.

V.O.
*(Scared)*

I don't know any of you guys...are you guys with
Gyno Productions?

THE VOICE: This is not your screenplay.

V.O.

I don't understand...

THE VOICE: Ever hear of snuff films?

*(Just then, the bathroom door opens, and The Woman, in a
peignoir, reenters the room. With a well-developed animal
instinct, she stands stock-still, smelling the change in the
atmosphere. The Boy and Girl have appeared as well,
pressed against the window glass. The Boy, watching the
action, cries, but The Girl watches as if filming.)*

THE VOICE: What are you—
MAN: What are you looking at?
WOMAN *(Scared)*: Nothing. Maybe this was a stupid idea.
THE VOICE: You look great.
MAN: You look...great.
THE VOICE: Really great
MAN: Really great.
WOMAN: Really? Worth $18.37, huh?

THE VOICE: Ya gotta have money to be a player.

MAN: Let me...hold you. Come here.

THE VOICE: Lights, camera, action!

*(The Woman goes to The Man; they embrace.)*

WOMAN: This feels good.

MAN: You smell good.

V.O.

Get out of the house!

MAN: I've been thinking—ya know, trying to figure out women. What turns them on. And I think tonight I've found the answer.

WOMAN: Let's not talk.

MAN: Is it our smell? Our torso? Our butts?

WOMAN: Let's not bring that subject up.

*(The Woman gently strokes his wounded half and stops at the wetness.)*

WOMAN: Hey—wait a moment—

MAN: I think women really get turned on to men in pain. That's what they like—

*(The Woman breaks away; in fear she examines her hand, now bloodied.)*

WOMAN: Oh my god—Clyde, you're—

MAN: Blood! Blood?! Does it excite you, baby? Get you hot?

*(The Man reaches in to the back of his pants, and rubs her face with the blood.)*

WOMAN: Oh my god—

*(The Woman starts to dash for the door, but he gets there first. The Man carefully draws out the gun.)*

MAN: You left your "protection" under the sofa.

WOMAN: Clyde—listen—

MAN: Shut. up, god. damn. you! *(The Man savagely hits The Woman)*

*(As soon as Clyde strikes Charlene, in the next section, The Man and Woman lip-sync the voices which are provided by The Voice and Voice-Over. The lip-sync should be very crude; we watch their mouths move like puppets, mechanically and exaggerated.)*

| MAN | THE VOICE |
|---|---|
| *(Lip-sync)* | *(Live)* |
| "Do you remember the last time?" | Do you remember the last time? |

*(The Woman starts to cry in elaborate pantomime; Voice-Over sobs into mike.)*

| MAN | THE VOICE |
|---|---|
| *(Lip-sync)* | *(Live)* |
| "I asked you a question. Do. you. remember. the last time." | I asked you a question. Do. you. remember. the last time. |

| WOMAN | V.O. |
|---|---|
| *(Lip-sync)* | *(Live)* |
| "When...we...made love?" | When...we...made love? |

| MAN | THE VOICE |
|---|---|
| *(Lip-sync)* | *(Live)* |
| "No. When I beat you to within an inch of your life. You didn't learn did you?" | No. When I beat you to within an inch of your life. You didn't learn did you? |

| WOMAN | V.O. |
|---|---|
| *(Lip-sync)* | *(Live)* |
| "No." | No. |

| MAN | THE VOICE |
|---|---|
| *(Lip-sync)* | *(Live)* |
| "I. can't. hear. you." | I. can't. hear. you. |

| WOMAN | V.O. |
|---|---|
| *(Lip-sync)* | *(Live)* |
| "No." | No. |

| MAN | THE VOICE |
|---|---|
| *(Lip-sync)* | *(Live)* |
| "I'm going to have to teach you all over again." | I'm going to have to teach you all over again. |

*(The Voice starts to play rap music.)*

| WOMAN | V.O. |
|---|---|
| *(She is having difficulty breathing and only shakes her head)* | *(Live)* |
| | Please—stop— |

| MAN | THE VOICE |
|---|---|
| *(Lip-sync with difficulty)* | *(Live)* |
| "Shut.Up...Now—get on the bed like a good wife." | Shut.Up...Now—get on the bed like a good wife. |

| WOMAN | V.O. |
|---|---|
| *(Live, simultaneous)* | *(Live, simultaneous)* |
| Please— | Please— |

*(The Man strikes her again.)*

| MAN | THE VOICE |
|---|---|
| *(Lip-sync)* | *(Live)* |
| "Stop crying or—" | Stop crying or I'll give you something to cry about. |

THE VOICE
*(Recorded sound from before)*
"The woman is a harp."

MAN
*(Lip-sync)*
"On. the. bed!"

THE VOICE
*(Live)*
On. the. bed!

*(The Man backhands The Woman and she falls on the bed.)*

THE VOICE
*(Whispered under)*
Now. don't. move.

WOMAN
*(Together with Voice-Over)*
Don't.

V.O.
*(With Woman)*
Don't.

MAN
*(With The Voice, live)*
Don't Move.

THE VOICE
*(With Man)*
Don't Move.

*(Voice-Over starts to plead quietly—"please" and "don't"— until The Voice plays James Joyce.)*

THE VOICE *(Taking over)*: I'm beating you to teach you a lesson Understand? And I'll stop when I feel like it. Bitch. What makes you think, with your big fat butt and your cow thighs, that you're worth eighteen bucks? Huh? What man would pay for that?

*(The Man unbuckles his belt, draws it from the loops, as The Woman continues to cry. A cry erupts from The Man's throat at the same instant that The Woman, The Voice and Voice-Over cry, becoming one voice with four breaths, a strange keening.)*

MAN (*Crying*): You're the one making me do this, Charlene. You
shouldof never—never gotten that restraining order—kicked
me out of my own home! Jesus Christ, Charlene—why did
you do that? Why?

WOMAN: Don't cry—don't—

(*The Woman embraces The Man.*)

MAN: A man's home is his Castle. His. fucking. Castle. What we
do in here is our business. It's our fucking sacred business...
Not the goddamn judge's!

(*The Man punches The Woman in the stomach and loops his
belt around her neck and begins to strangle her.*)

THE VOICE (*Whispered under/simultaneous with Voice-Over*):
"...when I put the rose in my hair like the Andalusian girls
used or shall I swear a red yes and how he kissed me under
the Moorish wall and I thought well we well him as another and then I asked him with my eyes to ask again yes and
then he asked me would I yes to say yes my mountain flower
and first I put my arms around his yes—"[14]

V.O.
(*Simultaneous with The Voice above*)
Get to the door Charlene can you shit keep calm no
you can get out of this one no keep fighting try to
try to get under the strap no ask him with your eyes
to no please ask him would he no theres no air left
no for the kids stay calm you can make it stars put
your arms around him squeeze don' stop stay calm
keep eyes open ask oh god would I no to say no my
god my god and no no air I can't no—

(*The Woman breaks free for a second.*)

WOMAN: —Why?!!

*(The Man strangles The Woman with his bare hands. He leaves. The Voice and Voice-Over follow him and The Boy and Girl disappear from view. But a tape recording of The Voice begins and then slows down, warped.)*

THE VOICE: "…and drew him down to me so he could feel my breasts all perfume yes and his heart was going like mad and yes I said yes I will Yes."

*(There is a flash of light, and a blackout. When the lights come back on, the stage is empty, except for the body of The Woman, strewn across the bed. The door opens, and The Girl walks in.*

*The Girl should see the body of The Woman. She stands still for a beat. The Girl walks quietly and quickly to the bed, and touches the body.*

*Then, The Girl steps into a spotlight, as the light dims on the body. The "stripper theme" music plays. She does not bump or grind.*

*If this play were a film script, we would see The Girl age before our eyes, transformed over the years from what she has just seen. The Girl dresses to the music. She puts on kneesocks, and a long-sleeve shirt. Then thick jeans and, finally, running shoes. She arranges her hair, tied back. Her body becomes a bit more worn, more protected from our gaze, her bones less light, her face more determined. She picks up the glasses The Woman wore and dons them. She walks over to the computer, turns it on, and as the theme music fades, she begins to type.)*

GIRL: "Setting: At the beginning of the play we see a living room in a suburban townhouse. Downstage left, we see a large, white office desk, holding a computer. At the top of Act One, the mother is typing a screenplay."

"CUT TO: INTERIOR. NIGHT.—"

*(The Girl hears something; abruptly looks over her shoulder—is there someone outside the window? Beat.*

*The Girl sits still. Beat.*

*The Girl quietly stands and looks toward the window. She makes a decision.*

*The Girl crosses to the window. Beat. Then, tensing, The Girl violently pulls the blinds up. There is nothing there. Beat.*

*The Girl relaxes, and quietly draws the blinds close.*

*Beat. The Girl turns, now facing the room. The Girl crosses to every light in the room, one by one, and turns them on until the room is blazing.*

*She returns to the computer. Sits. Takes a deep breath.*

*Then she turns back to the computer.)*

GIRL: "VOICE-OVER: She was hot. She was throbbing. But she was in control. Control of her body. Control of her thoughts."

*(Blackout to:)*

END   OF   PLAY

## CITATIONS

1  Vladimir Nabokov, *Lolita*, Vintage International Books,
   New York, 1989.

2  These words were actually written by William Acton, nineteenth-
   century sexologist, *The Functions and Disorders of the Reproductive
   Organs in Childhood, Youth, Adult Age and Advanced Life
   Considered in Their Physiological, Social and Moral Relations*, 3rd
   American ed., Philadelphia, 1871. But in this play they should be
   delivered as if written by Krafft-Ebing.

3  Ibid.

4  Ibid.

5  I fabricated Case 103 quotes in the style of Krafft-Ebing's
   *Psychopathia Sexualis*.

6  D. H. Lawrence, *Lady Chatterly's Lover*, Grove Press,
   New York, 1959.

7  Henry Miller, *Plexus*, Grove Press, New York, 1965.

8  T. H. Van de Velde, *Ideal Marriage: Its Physiology and Technique*,
   Covici Friede, New York, 1930.

9  *Plexus*.

10 James Joyce, *Ulysses*, Garland Publishing, Inc., New York, 1984.

11 Ibid.

12 Ibid.

13 *Plexus*.

14 *Ulysses*.

PAULA VOGEL won a 1992 Obie Award for Best New American Play for *The Baltimore Waltz*. Her plays have been produced at American Repertory Theatre, Circle Repertory Theatre, Center Stage and Yale Repertory Theatre, as well as throughout the United States and abroad. A member of New Dramatists, she has received grants and awards from the Pew Charitable Trust, the Guggenheim Foundation, the Rockefeller Foundation, the McKnight Foundation, the Fund for New American Plays, the AT&T OnStage award and the National Endowment for the Arts. For the past ten years, she has directed the MFA playwriting program at Brown University. Her screenplay adaptation of *The Oldest Profession* is currently in development, and she is working on new plays, *The Mineola Twins* and *How I Learned to Drive*.